Edwin A. Abbott

St. Thomas of Canterbury

Vol. II

Edwin A. Abbott

St. Thomas of Canterbury
Vol. II

ISBN/EAN: 9783337200824

Printed in Europe, USA, Canada, Australia, Japan

Cover: Foto ©Raphael Reischuk / pixelio.de

More available books at **www.hansebooks.com**

St. Thomas of Canterbury

HIS DEATH AND MIRACLES

BY

EDWIN A. ABBOTT, M.A., D.D.

FORMERLY FELLOW OF ST. JOHN'S COLLEGE, CAMBRIDGE
AND HULSEAN LECTURER
AUTHOR OF 'PHILOCHRISTUS,' 'ONESIMUS'

IN TWO VOLUMES

VOL. II

LONDON
ADAM AND CHARLES BLACK
1898

CONTENTS

SECTION IV

WILLIAM'S ACCOUNT OF THE MIRACLES

CHAPTER I

HIS FIRST AND SECOND BOOKS

§ 1. His object. § 2. Visions. § 3. The folly of impatience and of trusting in physicians; the injustice of the Irish war. § 4. Vows to St. Thomas must be paid; physicians must be despised. § 5. Emma of Halberton and Gode-lief of Laleham. § 6. Revivification. § 7. Leprosy. § 8. Chapels are to be built to St. Thomas   .   .   .   .   .   .   Page 3

CHAPTER II

HIS THIRD, FOURTH, AND FIFTH BOOKS; OR THE DEGENERATION OF THE MIRACLES

§ 1. Degenerate miracles. § 2. Miracles for the King's sake. § 3. Chance; losing and finding. § 4. St. Denis and St. Thomas; "the divine gift of dumbness." § 5. A man of many miracles. § 6. The evils of business; St. Thomas's object in receiving money. § 7. St. Thomas will not interfere with the Archbishop of York. § 8. Credulity and incredulity. § 9. The Water of Canterbury is changed to milk. § 10. Revivification of a sucking-pig; of a gander. § 11. A babe sings "Kyrie Eleison"; a dead pilgrim, thrown overboard, comes back for his berth. § 12. St. Thomas orders prayers for Fitzurse. § 13. St. Thomas supports a man on the gallows. § 14. Bird-miracles. § 15. "Fatuous antiquity"; a story in Virgilian prose. § 16. A man of blood, a devotee of St. Thomas. § 17. Restoration of one struck by lightning   24

CHAPTER III

HIS LAST BOOK AND APPENDIX

§ 1. St. Thomas's eggs. § 2. Mad Gerard of Liège. § 3. Crossing Marlow bridge. § 4. Richard of Reading is cured of fits. § 5. Restoration of mutilated members. § 6. A pilgrim is brought to life to die in peace. § 7. A Templar's dream ; cure of the Earl of Warrenne. § 8. An unattested wonder. § 9. Weighty evidence from John of Salisbury. § 10. "Festive" miracles. § 11. St. Thomas forgives a reproachful pilgrim. § 12. Responsibilities of "a saint in vogue." § 13. Distant cures unknown ; revivifications. § 14. A historical digression. § 15. William degenerates still more. § 16. Evidence of date. § 17. The consequences of finding an ancient mortuary vessel. § 18. Miracles from Sefrid the ecstatic. § 19. William oscillates between credulity and incredulity. § 20. William decides to accept the statements of rich people. § 21. William becomes slightly cynical. § 22. A married priest. § 23. Wiscard, the King's falcon. § 24. A starling invokes St. Thomas ; miracles worked for a hospital at Shooter's Hill. § 25. St. Thomas at Devizes. § 26. St. Thomas among friends. § 27. The Saracen of Palermo. § 28. St. Thomas kills a cow. § 29. St. Thomas revivifies a cow. § 30. Miscellanea. § 31. A story cut short. § 32. Comic verses   Page 45

SECTION V

THE PARALLEL MIRACLES [1]

§ 1. Sir Thomas of Etton is miraculously visited with quinsy and miraculously cured. § 2. (i.) Eilward of Westoning in Bedfordshire, mutilated for theft, is miraculously restored ; (ii.) a similar miracle recorded by William alone ; (iii.) a similar miracle recorded by Benedict alone; (iv.) suggestion of partial explanation. § 3. The ship that came back by herself. § 4. How St. Thomas pushed a ship off a shoal. § 5. Recovery of anchors. § 6. How the son of Yngelrann of Golton was visited with paralysis by the Martyr and then healed. § 7. Jordan, son of Eisulf. § 8. Cecily, daughter of Jordan of Plumstead, is restored, when supposed to have died of cancer. § 9. The son of Hugh Scot is restored after drowning. § 10. Elias, a monk of Reading, after [pretending to] resort to Bath for the cure of leprosy, is cured by St. Thomas. § 11. Queen Eleanor's foundling. § 12. Geoffrey, a monk of Reading, is restored, when in extremity. § 13. Deliverance from the fall of a wall. § 14. Miracles wrought on James, son of the Earl of Clare. § 15. The cure of Hugh of Ebblinghem, a leper ; William adds another. § 16.

[1] With Latin renderings.

William of Gloucester is saved from a fall of earth. § 17. Salerna of Ifield, having thrown herself into a well, is preserved from death. § 18. John of Roxburgh is saved from the Tweed . . . Page 76

SECTION VI

LEGENDARY ACCOUNTS OF MIRACLES

CHAPTER I

LEGENDS RECORDED BY AUTHORITATIVE WRITERS

§ 1. St. Thomas's fish. § 2. The Vision at Pontigny, (i.) the statements. § 3. The Vision at Pontigny, (ii.) the silence of Anon. I., commonly called " Roger of Pontigny." § 4. The vision at Pontigny, (iii.) all evidence from Pontigny to be regarded with suspicion. § 5. The Vision at Pontigny, (iv.) the probable facts. § 6. The Vision at Pontigny, (v.) the growth of legend . 274

CHAPTER II

LEGENDS RECORDED BY NON-AUTHORITATIVE WRITERS

§ 1. Giraldus Cambrensis and Grandison. § 2. Pseudo-Grim. § 3. Poetic legends. § 4. Poetry and Romance. § 5. Oral Tradition the source of early legend. § 6. Prevalence of legend inevitable unless contradicted by history . 285

SECTION VII

INFERENCES FROM THE MIRACLES

CHAPTER I

THE GOOD AND EVIL OF THE MIRACLES

§ 1. The evil. § 2. The good. § 3. Did the miracles result from the man or from the circumstances? § 4. St. Thomas a true Saint, though militant . 296

CHAPTER II

THE MARTYR AND THE SAVIOUR

§ 1. The parallel between them. § 2. The parallel in facts. § 3. The parallel in documents. § 4. Its bearing on New Testament criticism . 305

INDEX

VOL. II

ST. THOMAS'S MIRACLES

(continued)

CHAPTER I

THE FIRST AND SECOND BOOKS

§ 1. *His object*

[589] ON the strength of the many miracles mentioned in William's book as reported from Ireland, and also because of his vehement condemnation of Henry's Irish war, Mr. Magnusson has conjectured that William himself was a native of Ireland. He certainly has a Celtic faculty of fluent and versatile speech, and is master of methods of variety. But in part this may arise from a long study of classical literature. It has been noted above that, after seventeen months of reporting, Benedict was found inadequate by the Canterbury Chapter, and William was called in to aid him. Under such circumstances, the latter would be on his mettle to show what he could do in the way of style.

[590] It may be assumed as almost certain that William himself in his own recondite Latin is writing his own apology —though it appears in the Prologue nominally indited by the monks—when he says, " We ask the whole body of our readers, sympathizing with the brother's diligence—for it is not his fault that he does not discharge in full the stewardship entrusted to him—not to ' arch their eyebrows ' above

measure at the want of arrangement of his words, and the poorness of his thoughts.[1] He confesses indeed that he has deserved a flout, but he hopes for a milder censure. . . . He pledges you in·a draught from a vessel of potter's clay, but drawn from a spring of living waters. Let the delicate liquor excuse the uncouth cup-bearer." There is more to the same effect, more than enough to shew that the writer is not deeply in earnest, not in the same mood in which Benedict took up the pen, seventeen months before, to dispel the cloud that obscured the light of the Canterbury Martyr. The difference is natural. Then the King, and the lords, and almost all the bishops were hostile. Now they were friendly, quite persuaded, and ready to be interested, some indeed desiring to be amused. It seems to have been, in large measure, to meet this new demand, that William supplied his Book of Miracles.

[591] We shall look in vain here for those graphic descriptions of cures at the tomb, some of them incomplete, some followed by relapses, which Benedict gives us so frequently, thereby establishing his character at once for veracity, candour, and (so far as observable facts go, distinguished from inferences) for careful observation. And as William's book professedly ignores chronological order, it throws no light at all on any developments, changes, or deteriorations, that may have taken place in the manifestations at the tomb or elsewhere. However, it does contain a good many important letters attesting distant miracles. Some of these are found also in Benedict's book, and will be considered in the comparison, given further on, between the two versions of the Parallel Miracles : but others, even though written to Benedict himself, are not included in Benedict's book, perhaps because they were transferred by him, when he was

---

[1] i. 139 "in hac incompositione verborum, in hac tenuitate sententiarum, *modice narem corrugare*" (Hor. *Epist.* i. 5. 23). I have expressed it by a phrase from Pope, *P. S.* 96. For the meaning of "i. 139," see 1*a*.

busy as Prior, to the monk in charge of the tomb. In any case, we shall approach the Parallel Miracles in a better condition for discriminating between what is true and what is William's addition to the truth, or colouring of the truth, if we first review his work so as to elicit the characteristics of the narratives that he alone records.

§ 2. *Visions*

[592] Before miracles, William places visions. And here we see at once the foreign element, which was almost entirely absent from Benedict's work, placed prominently at the very outset. A clerk at Orleans foresees the Archbishop's death, which is predicted in a quotation from Lucan " mors est ignota Catonis."· Two more visions of the Orleans clerk are followed by another—which surely must have gratified, even though it surprised, King Henry.

A Canterbury Doctor, Fermin by name, saw (as early as Whitsuntide in 1170) a procession passing by the bell-tower of the Cathedral. The King and the Archbishop were there, cheerfully riding together. A cross was borne before them, and a voice from heaven said, " Whosoever can touch this cross, and place on it pure gold and precious stones—their names shall be written in the Book of Life." Then the Archbishop " placed gold in great quantity and precious stones on the crown " that was above the cross. " Likewise also the King, although long afterwards, was seen [1] to have done the same."

This Fermin, who is described as " a man of respectability," [2] was doubtless present at the public penitence of King Henry in July 1174 when he promised a large sum of money to the Abbey ; and it is quite possible that that event may have recalled to his mind—perhaps with some material modifications—a previous dream about a reconcilia-

---

[1] i. 143 " visus est."   [2] " vir honestae conversationis."

tion between the King and the Archbishop. There is irony, perhaps unconscious, in the subtle distinction between the Archbishop, who *gave*, and the King, who "*was seen*, or *seemed*, to have given." We have seen above [3] that Benedict had great difficulty in persuading Henry to fulfil his promises. If Henry read as far as this in the book which the monks presented to him, he may have been stimulated to keep his word. In a second vision, the same Fermin saw the crypt, "where the Martyr's body rested *for several years*," [4] frequented by multitudes of queens, and a golden cross with a man crucified on it. Neither of these visions is attested. But the last is remarkable as indicating a late date. For the body "rested" in the crypt till 1220. It would appear that William's book has been re-edited here.

[593] More interesting—and, from internal evidence, much earlier—is a vision that must have occurred before the canonization of St. Thomas in February 1173. Reginald, priest of Wretham near Norwich, dreamed that he went into a chapel to hear divine service, and found monks in white standing before the choir and engaged in a commemoration of the Saints. "When this was finished, the one on the south [side of the altar] signed with his hand to the one on the north to make a memorial to the Martyr Thomas." As the other did not understand, the first said aloud that an antiphon was to be sung to the holy Martyr. The second replied that it was not "authentic": [5] for Thomas had not yet been placed by papal authority in the list of martyrs. To which the former patriotically answered, " Then at least let it be sung in English." After this had been done, the former thus addressed Reginald : " Brother, you have heard our antiphon. Go tell it to the brother that is over the weak brethren of the Church of Christ in Canterbury." " Sir," replied the priest, " I do not yet know the antiphon."

---

[3] (541).   [4] i. 144.   [5] i. 150 "non authenticam."

" I am going to say it to you," said he, and he repeated it thrice.

[594] William then quotes the antiphon thus :—

" Hali Thomas of hevenriche (*heaven-kingdom*)
Alle postles (*apostles*) eve[n]liche (*even*, or *equal*),
Dhe martyres dhe understande
Deyhuamliche (*daily*) on here (*their*) hande.
Selcuth (*seld-zouth*,[6] i.e. *seldom-known*) dede ure Drichtin (*Lord*)
Dhat he dhi wetter wente (*changed*) to wyn.
Dhu ert help in Engelande,
Ure stefne (*voices*) understande.
Thu hert[7] froure (Ed. *frofer*, *comfort*) imang mankynne,
Help us nu of ure senne."

This, says William, may be expressed in Latin as follows—

" Holy Thomas, citizen of heaven,
To all Apostles equal,
The Martyrs thee receive
Daily in their hands.
A rare thing did our Lord
That He thy water changed to wine.
Thou art a help in England.
Our cries do thou receive.
Thou art comfort among mankind,
Turn us from our sins.
Evo vae."[8]

[595] From some such poetic tradition as this (" He thy water changed to wine ") may have sprung the prose legend related by Arnold of Lubeck, who flourished less than forty years after the Martyrdom, that the Saint, while

---

[6] Comp. "un-couth," which originally meant "un-known."

[7] The spelling "thu" for "dhu," when combined with "hert" for "ert," suggests that the last two lines may be a moral appendix of later date than the first part.   There are instances of old May-day songs having new appendices of a Puritan or moralising kind.

[8] "*Evo vae* (properly *Euouae*) is an abbreviation of 'Seculorum Amen,' using only the vowels," *Mat.* iii. Introd. xxix.

at table with the Pope, repeatedly changed water into wine.[9] But William's story is also of interest as a proof that St. Thomas was pre-eminently the Englishmen's saint, canonized in the hearts of the common people before the Church had ratified their decision. From visions William passes to two cases [10] in which blasphemy against the Martyr was miraculously punished. In a third, punishment falls on an oppressor who refuses to make restitution to a widow asking for mercy in the name of St. Thomas.[11]

§ 3. *The folly of impatience and of trusting in physicians ; the injustice of the Irish war*

[596] Coming now to the miracles of healing, he places first of all a letter from burgesses of Bedford attesting the far-famed restoration of eyesight (or rather of eyes) to Ailward of Westoning. After the letter come the facts. These will be considered later in the Parallel Miracles. Here we may merely note that the position of this miracle, which does not come till the beginning of the Fourth Book of Benedict's work, shews that William does not attempt to cover the ground occupied by Benedict, any more than to follow the chronological order adopted by the latter.

[597] In the next miracle, Levive, a dropsical patient, is a neighbour of the above-mentioned Ailward, and perhaps owes her position here to this fact. She is made for the readers an example of the folly of impatience. Having waited at the tomb for three days, she returned, not with a cure, but with cares multiplied,[1] and was bold enough to blame the Saint. Beginning with statements about "the foolish woman," and "the fleshly mind," William passes into something like a sermon, "Ye worms and food of worms,

---

[9] ii. 291, where the Editor adds, "The miracle of the change of water into wine is somewhat differently related by Roger of Hoveden, ii. 11, ed. Stubbs" (813).   [10] i. 151-3.   [11] i. 154.
[1] i. 158 "quia non curata, curiosa."

lift not your voice against heaven." After half a page of this, he breaks off with "But enough of this," to tell us that the Saint, appearing to the woman in a vision, instructed her how to compound a medicine. She drank it and was completely cured.

[598] Another narrative begins with a description of three kinds of epilepsy (or "epilensy").[2] After mentioning Petronilla, a nun of Polesworth, as suffering from this disease, it praises her for not resorting to "hirelings and those who are not [true] physicians," but to the true Shepherd and true Physician, Thomas of Canterbury, from whom she departed without knowing that her prayer was granted. But from that day she suffered no more. Thus the good Physician made good his name to her, as also to one of the Canterbury monks, whom he healed of a chronic cough, sitting by his bedside in a vision, after the monk had prayed at the tomb for three or four days.[3] Then follow three cures of falling sickness, of no particular interest.[4] Presently we read that Robert, Priest of Lincoln, recovering from illness, was bidden by St. Thomas to pay his vow. But he had not made one, and he told the Saint so. The answer came back, "You did not vow: but others vowed for you; and on you falls the payment."[5] Miracle is piled on miracle for Richard of Coventry, who is healed of fever, has a bone caused to vanish in his throat, is cured of toothache, and freed from a tumour. His wife and son are also made the subject of miracles.[6]

[599] The introduction of the story of Simon, Canon of Beverley, sounds like the beginning of a clerical discourse. "Hearing the name of Canon Symon, brethren, let our mind be turned to obedience. Let it be turned also to our Rule, that on the one hand we (lit. "our mind") may be zealous

---

[2] i. 162-3.   [3] i. 164-5.   [4] i. 165-7.   [5] i. 169-70.
[6] i. 171-3. The preceding narrative may be noted as mentioning a relapse, followed by final cure: "As for the reason, I only know that the Lord knows."

to prefer the will of the orthodox to our own, and on the other hand we may learn habitually to restrain ourselves within the bounds of the discipline of the Rule. By the one practice we avoid the sin of idolatry," etc., etc.[7] The gibes against physicians are far more frequent in William than in Benedict. Radulf of (?) Chingford,[8] a man of letters, was thus addressed by his doctor: " I return to you the money you have given me. I depart. Provide for your soul." But the sick man replied, " You have not seen yet. Wait till you know and see ": and he began to amend on the day (for he had counted the days) when his votive candle was lighted at St. Thomas's tomb.[9] William, a clerk of Lincoln, cured by the Martyr, had gained nothing from doctors except expense, and except despair.[10] When the King's own physicians examined Ralph de la Saussaie they said his soul would be out of his body in a week : but now was verified the truth of the words " I will destroy the wisdom of the wise and the prudence of the prudent will I bring to naught," for, " fixing all his hope on Him who is Day of Day, he saw that day which his physicians despaired of his seeing,· and following days, too, by favour of that Physician, slain [of men], to whom he devoted himself as a pilgrim." [11]

[600] Ralph was engaged in the Irish war when this happened to him ; and the narrative, which says that " when the high and mighty King of England invaded Ireland, many of. those about his person were attacked with divers plagues and pestilence," indirectly suggests that the war was not a just one. This is more distinctly stated in the case of a " young man from the place called Marcha-

---

[7] i. 175.   [8] i. 176 "in pago barbari nominis Chenefare."
[9] i. 176-7.   [10] i. 179.
[11] i. 181. The next story mentions the cure of a young man " de villa Dyena," wounded in tilting, and cured by washing with the Water. A bone 3½ inches long was extracted and gratefully deposited on the Martyr's tomb.

neus."[12] Finding himself disabled by the reopening of an old wound, the patient soliloquizes at considerable length : " If I rightly understand the gift of divine grace, the Martyr Thomas leads me from war to turn me to goodness. I go from camp to camp—from the camp of (?) sedition [13] and seduction [14] to the camp of charity and peace. No more of this barbarity for me ! I desert to the tents of spiritual warfare. But I must go to the sacred spot of martyrdom and present the Martyr himself with a gift. . . ." What follows is brevity itself: " He spoke, and with a flow of matter squeezed from the wound he recovered."

§ 4. *Vows to St. Thomas must be paid ; physicians must be despised*

[601] Thomas of Beverley was not so wise as the knight Adam of Ritherfeld near Winchester. The latter, after promising a yearly pilgrimage, set out at once, and was cured on the way ; the former, putting it off for four days, was smitten with a swelling in the neck and jaw. However, he took warning, and, as soon as he had crossed the Humber, found himself daily better. These two brief stories,[1] each little more than a sentence, seem inserted for no other reason except to impress on the reader the value of a speedy pilgrimage. This point is emphasized far more by William than by Benedict. Earlier,[2] Robert, son of Guy of Winchester, after being healed in consequence of a vow to St. Thomas which he neglects to pay, is thus accosted by St. Martin in a dream, " Ho (Heus) ! Robert, you are un-wise to be so careless about paying your vow. Unless you quickly cut short your perilous delay, you will find that the

---

12 i. 181. The Editor suggests " Marcham, Berks."
13 MSS. read " sedititionis."
14 " Seductionis," (?) " revolt from righteousness."
1 i. 182.   2 i. 173.

debt will be strictly exacted."[3] And now,[4] the story of
Paul of Rouen, a vine-dresser, teaches the same lesson.
Being weather-bound at Winchelsea, he invokes St. Thomas
and obtains a fair voyage to Sandwich. (Here William
quotes Deut. xxxii. 21 about provoking God, and refers to
the journey to Emmaus.) Deferring his pilgrimage, he is
wonderfully driven back, while two companion ships proceed
prosperously. Then comes the moral : "Hence it is clear
that the Martyr would have his earthly remains visited and
reverence paid to him as Primate and Legate of the Roman
See, to the intent that he who was once forbidden to pass
through the villages and towns of England, and to visit his
diocese when alive,[5] may be visited by all England now that
he is dead."

[602] At this point William introduces, in a new aspect,
his old theme of the uselessness of physicians. A certain
Roger of Middleton[6] had gained no relief from dropsy after
trying for almost a year the remedies of many (doctors).
After preparing for death and receiving the sacrament, he
travelled with great difficulty to Canterbury and began his
journey back in improved health. But the fatigues and
hardships of his return brought him home with his disease
increased. He was now awaiting death, when, in a vision, a
youth appeared, and guided him to two physicians. These
he found to be St. Thomas and St. Edmund, whom he besought to help him : "St. Thomas replied, 'You have loaded
your system with potions and medicaments.' St. Edmund
the Martyr added, 'Even more than was needful.' Then
said St. Thomas the Martyr, 'If you had tasted one medicine

---

[3] i. 174. "Exigendum," the gerundive, often used by William for the future
infinite passive.   [4] i. 183-4.
[5] This refers to the royal prohibition in 1170, restricting the Archbishop to
Canterbury.
[6] i. 184-6, the Editor adds "of Suffolk," presumably because of the subsequent
mention of St. Edmund, which might be taken to indicate that Roger was familiar
with the shrine at Bury St. Edmunds.

more, you would not have tasted any other.' " The sick
man apologised on the ground of his desperate condition.
But St. Thomas closed the dialogue by saying that he must
give up human medicines and resort to prayer alone: " Pray
unto the Lord, and we will pray with you." The man
obeyed. Three days afterwards, having nothing digestible
to eat, he *deliberately and against the advice of his household
ate what he knew would not agree with him* "that his disease
and his despair might be simultaneously ended" : William
then proceeds to minute and unpleasing details of the cure
that rapidly followed.

[603] One might have anticipated that a physician
patronized by the Archdeacon of Canterbury would be
treated somewhat leniently by a monk of Canterbury : and
accordingly this physician is recognized as being, at all
events, able to perceive that the dropsy of Robert, a knight
of Bromton,[7] "required exact care." But he is also described as "vainly distinguishing four species of dropsy,"
and as handing the knight over to the care of some other
doctor, on the ground that he himself was too much occupied
with public business. While Robert was on a journey, he
was warned in a dream to leave other physicians and keep
to the physic of St. Thomas. He accordingly travelled, but
not on foot, some distance in the direction of Canterbury.
A second dream warned him that he must not ride, but
walk. He begged, on the plea of weakness, to be allowed
to come part of the way on the Thames and the rest on
foot.[8] Thus he came, and was wrapped in the garment[9]
in which the Saint fulfilled his martyrdom. On his return,
being shaken by his carriage, he turned aside to Newington.[10]
There, after sleeping soundly, he awoke, and "found

---

[7] i. 187.   [8] " Petens quod vel a fluvio sibi permitteretur hoc facere."
[9] " Pellicia."
[10] See above (533). It was a place where the Archbishop had stood while
holding a confirmation ; and many miracles occurred there.

himself restored to health, except that his feet still shewed traces of the disease." In William's opinion, the reason for these was that he had not obeyed the Saint in coming all the way on foot, so that he had not deserved to be altogether cured.[11]

§ 5. *Emma of Halberton and Godelief of Laleham*

[604] These specimens will shew that we have not much to learn from William that Benedict has not already taught us, so far as concerns the manner and means of cures effected in the name of St. Thomas.

As to means, the main difference between Benedict and William seems to be that the latter lays less stress on passionate faith and more on the necessity of a journey to Canterbury. Probably the monks were right—whatever their reasons or motives may have been—in magnifying the importance of a pilgrimage. The hardships of a pilgrim were sometimes severe, but the compensations were many. Immediate change of scene and air, abstinence from physic and medical remedies, regular exercise, the excitement of a journey—often diversified by novel experiences and almost always by interchange of discourse with other pilgrims from different parts of England—all these influences, combined with a hopeful faith in the Martyr to whom they were journeying and who often seemed to be bestowing on them already a foretaste of restoration increasing with every mile of the journey, might very well suffice to explain in a natural way the cure of diseases that had puzzled the

---

[11] i. 188. He is somewhat obscure, and appears to use "omnino non" (*i.e.* "absolutely not") for "non omnino" (*i.e.* "not completely"). He seems to put first a materialistic explanation, which he rejects, and then a moral one, which he accepts. The first is, "vel quia pedes ierat (either because he had come [*part of the way*] on foot." The second is, "vel secundum nostram opinionem, quia monenti medico in somnis non paruit, et, quia jussam viam pedes omnino non fecit, forsan omnino curari ad tempus non meruit." To this he adds, "For with what measure ye mete, it shall be measured again to you."

physicians of the twelfth century and would baffle many of the nineteenth.

[605] But we also learn from William many new and interesting facts illustrating the abuses that rapidly attached themselves to the cultus of St. Thomas. Emma of Halberton [1] ventured to stitch on a hook and eye that had come off her little sister's cloak—and this on the Wednesday in Whitsuntide! Her fingers were immediately contracted. With tears and prayers she resorted to the relics of St. Thomas in the village church, and in the presence of the priest and dame Caecilia, the respected wife of a neighbouring knight, the casket containing the sacred treasures was applied to the girl's hand. Virtue came forth, her fingers were restored, the church bells were set ringing, and they blessed God.

[606] Next day, however, the girl fell into so heavy a slumber that she was thought dead. When her friends succeeded at last in rousing her, she blamed them bitterly. She had had a vision of St. Thomas, she said: he had assured her that her chastening was not on her own account but for the cure of the sins of others. " Thy hand," said the Martyr, "is my hand. Whomsoever thou shalt bless with this hand [of thine] shall be healed from his infirmity"; and he was on the point of uttering the mystic word that would have imparted the divine power, when she was awakened and deprived of the celestial benefit. However, she had other dreams and visions, one, for example, warning her mother to continue her customary *eleemosyna* — three masses a week for her deceased husband, and a candle as well—as long as she had a farthing. [2]

A more doubtful revelation was that her mother was to dismiss her maid-servant. But this did not seem to have been acted on. "We know not," says William, "the cause

---

[1] i. 193-5.
[2] i. 195 "donec ei vel una supererit nummata (?) substantiae."

of this precept: but it happened that some little time afterwards the maid voluntarily gave notice."[3] Perhaps Emma
had made her life uncomfortable, though Osanna (the mother)
had not discharged her. Lastly, Emma revealed to William
at Canterbury that she "had seen punishments prepared for
a young kinsman of hers, a fellow-pilgrim, because he had
sinned with a certain maid, and had not duly brought forth
fruits of repentance." On being cross-examined by William,
the young man replied that "she (*i.e.* Emma) knew nothing
at all about his offence till it was [divinely] revealed to her":
but how this negative was proved, William does not explain.
In any case, Emma does not seem quite a satisfactory
character, or the sort of person to whom the real St. Thomas
would say, "Whomsoever thou shalt bless shall be delivered
from his infirmity."

   [607] To Godelief, a woman of Laleham,[4] St. Thomas
appeared standing over against the altar barefoot. This
was to suggest penitence. "Many," he said, "who attend
your church are excommunicated. Your priest himself has
committed a sin and has not repented. Prompt him, in my
name, to offer works of satisfaction." After giving parti-
culars of the sin, the Martyr added, "His diocesan [5] Heinulph
is guilty of the same sin"—and he made known [6] his offence
—"I warn him to confess and return to a right mind. Else
let him know he will be cut off this year. He is a pilgrim
of mine. I am loth that he should perish. You have also
among you the woman Johet, doing works of mercy indeed,
but failing to gain merit because she seeks praise and vain-
glory." Then follows censure of Adelicia, which William
thinks may be obscure "because perhaps it would not be
profitable to express it clearly." This vision was not perhaps too hard on Henry the priest of Laleham, for William

---

[3] "peteret missionem."
[4] i. 198, text "Lalham." Ed. suggests Laleham.   [5] "diocesanus."
[6] "Innotuit," regularly used transitively both by Benedict and by William.

adds that "from the day when he received this heaven-sent admonition, he has given more heed both to himself and to his flock." Possibly, too, Adelicia's conscience, interpreting the obscure revelation that concerned her, may have admitted its truth. But if not, she may have thought it severe. And in any case, a person who had such visions might manifestly be tempted to shape them according to prejudice, and do a great deal of harm in a country village.[7]

§ 6. *Revivification*

[608] Two cases of revivification having been reported above,[1] it is remarkable that William should introduce a third, as though it were an unheard-of wonder :[2] "Let your affection, brethren, give me its best attention. For we are about to relate something wonderful to tell, raising (so to speak) the dead [before your eyes.]"[3]   He proceeds to make a little sermon about the need of new miracles to strengthen faith in old miracles. There is nothing specially remarkable in the story itself except that the parents had tried rings and charms,[4] hung round their child's neck, before they resorted to the Martyr's Water : and the case itself affords but one of many proofs that apparent death often sets in before actual death. But the introduction is important as suggesting that this miracle was *the first of the kind recorded by William himself,* and that the two others (which both belong to the Parallel Miracles) were later in time, though placed by William earlier. Another case is accompanied by some lines of rhyming Latin which shew

---

[7] Godelief is said to have received from St. Thomas "a silver ring with a precious stone in it," which he placed on her finger saying, "If any one doubts that I have spoken with you, produce this as a proof of our conversation together."

[1] i. 160, 190.   [2] i. 199.

[3] "suscitantes" agreeing with "nos."   [4] "brevia."

that the practice of dropping the Water into the lips must
have been long established.[5]

[609] The revival of the child of the Earl of Clare,
described by Benedict as well as William,[6] will be found
below among the Parallel Miracles. It has a preface on the
participation of the powerful and rich, as well as the lowly
and poor, in the mercies of God. But another story, which
immediately follows, and which Benedict omits, is in some
respects more pathetic. The funeral mass had been said,
and the father, Adam of Aldham (or Hadham) had left the
room in despair, after sitting by the bedside of the child
(a little boy of three years old) up to the last : " The eyelids
had been closed, the hands laid across the breast,[7] the feet
arranged, all the exequies duly performed, and about as
much time had elapsed as would take a good walker to go
a mile.[8] But while some still remained in the room, the
body was sprinkled with the sacred Water, and it began at
once to stir. Some conjectured this to be a sign of the
Divine compassion ; others that it was the effect of wind
pent up in the body. A few moments afterwards, the child
shifted one arm, gave a great cry, and called for its mother."
The account says that the revivification was accompanied
with an exudation of matter and perspiration—a detail not,
I believe, mentioned in other cases ; and the chronicler
vividly describes the " bounding joy "[9] of the father, and the

---

[5] i. 210. That the rhymes were not composed specially for the case described, appears from the introduction—" Yet their single hope was fixed on
Thomas, because he oftentimes wrought like [wonders] :

> ' Cujus nomen dum vocatur,
> Spes vocantum non frustratur.
> Nam cum liquor instillatur,
> Qui cruore rubricatur,
> Collum marcens integratur,
> Vita redit, vox laxatur.' "

[6] (758).   [7] i. 230 " cancellatae."
[8] i. 231. This phrase, resembling one assigned by Euripides to a messenger,
but very unusual (if it occurs at all) in these treatises, may have come from Adam
himself. See 529.   [9] " tripudium."

immediate vow that the little one, if spared, should go to Canterbury. The child gained strength, but could, at first, only eat "strawberries and mulberries." However, as soon as the pilgrimage was commenced, he got his appetite again, "for it was but fit that considering the little one's age and devotion, his victual should be restored to him, lest, if his viaticum failed, he, too, should fail on the way."

§ 7. *Leprosy*

[610] Perhaps in relating cases of leprosy so called— liable as they seem to have been to frequent relapses, and often not cured till after long waiting—William felt that there was special need of variety and rhetorical style. The following is, at all events, a startling introduction :—" Why, woman Agnes, did you not return to St. Thomas your healer?[1] You came here once contaminated with leprosy : you ought to have returned at least once to your healer when cleansed, in order that what was done for your healing might be repeated for [his] praise. It will be well to unfold what we saw and what we heard in your case. Your nose was not a little swelled, and your chin too ; your eyes were running," etc. etc. This had been going on "from the Paschal days until the length of days diminished and Phoebus revolved in a shorter circumference." When the time came for her to be banished from her town (which is called "castrum Zignien "), her brother Solomon compassion-ately brought her in June to Canterbury, where she remained four days.

All this William tells Agnes herself, and then continues : "You applied no external remedy at all, except that you bathed your rough, swelled face with the healthful Water of the new Martyr. And the pimples began to diminish, your hairless eyebrows began to feel the influence of the super-

---

[1] i. 216 "curatorem."

infused dew. . . . And I can conjecture from what we saw
in you, that, unless you had remedied your fleshly disease
with a spiritual fomentation, you would have incurred an
incurable one." He proceeds to inform the woman that
she left too soon, owing to her brother's pressing business,
before she had been fully cured, and concludes by bidding
her, at all events, give her thoughts to her benefactor if she
cannot give him her presence as a pilgrim.

[611] Peter, a monk of Poitiers, a leper also, is next
made the subject of a most pedantical discourse,[2] which
relates how he came to Canterbury and "experienced the
salutary streams of Jordan—not that old one which waters
Palestine, but the new Jordan, which, emerging from the
head of the new Martyr, flows toward the west, glides
toward the north, and does not omit the east and the
south."[3]   But the next leper, brother Daniel from Dublin,
is addressed, like Agnes above, in the second person:[4]
" Brother Daniel, you shewed yourself to the priests of the
Canterbury church on the last day of August, testifying that,
from four years ago, leprosy had been creeping over you.
In your ignorance of the Scriptures, you did not give heed
to the ceremonies of the old Law, but, with the simplicity
of a layman, you asked to be made clean at the arbitrament
of the priests."   Then, after Daniel has been told over
again all that he told the monks about his previous life, he
is addressed as follows : " These facts you habitually and
frequently asserted near the Martyr's tomb.   But if you
had produced suitable witnesses of this statement — else
you could not have been believed owing to the [need of
guarding against] false and deceiving brethren—you would
have been clearly pronounced to be clean among the clean

---

[2] i. 217-19.
[3] [611a] "derivatur in *disim*, allabitur *arton, anathole mesembriamque* non
praeterit." William is shewing off his knowledge of misspelt Greek.
[4] i. 219.

by the common judgment of all. . . . And the appearance
of your face spoke for itself, hardly needing the interpreting
tongue.   Nevertheless, we could not glorify the Lord in you
as we should have done if we had had perfect knowledge of
the facts."

[612] It is characteristic of William that in briefly
mentioning [5] six or seven more cases of leprosy, he omits
details and sometimes even the name and place—on the
ground that the Gospel describes the cure of ten lepers at
once and omits the names of all—yet finds room to tell us
the precise Irish words heard by one leper to whom St.
Thomas said in a dream (while striking him with his pastoral
staff), " Heri aere nech flantu," which " is, being interpreted,
says William, ' Arise, Irishman, thou art healed.' " [6]   This
might be alleged by some as favouring Mr. Magnusson's
theory that William was himself Irish.   Perhaps, however,
it is merely an indication that William had a smattering of
Irish, as he had a smattering of Greek.   He seems to be
fond of quoting technical words that are out of the way.
Above, when describing the voyage of Paul of Rouen,[7] he
spoke of the " saphon," the " anguinae," and of that " quod
nautae lovum vocant."   He is afflicted with that perverse
confusion, or love of disproportion, which makes so many
witnesses assume that, when accumulating and exaggerating
details, they are setting forth the essential truth.   However,
we may feel sure that he is really giving us the Irishman's
words ; and indeed there is something different from the
commonplace English visions in his sight of the Martyr,
" going up to heaven again, following three candles, which
were held out to do him worship."

[5] i. 221-2.
[6] i. 221, note: "The Editor has been kindly informed that this ought to be
Eirigh, Eirionach, slânta."   Above (594), William has preserved the exact English
words of an antiphon imparted in a vision.
[7] i. 183.

§ 8. *Chapels are to be built to St. Thomas*

[613] A blind young woman of Pevensey, Seivia by name, travelling to Canterbury under her aunt's guidance, was deserted by the latter when she could go no further through fatigue. But the Saint appeared to her, saying, " In this village dwells a worthy man, Robert the son of Elgar. He will be the first person you will see. He will come to you. Tell him, as a command from St. Thomas, to build a cross on this spot." Robert seems to have raised no objection.[1] Not so, in a similar instance, the Earl of Albemarle, who was much more bound to be grateful. For he had been cured of more than one disease, and delivered from excruciating tortures. Yet he did not come to the tomb till some time afterwards, " when the miracles became numerous and the disturbers of the church became few."[2] And further, when the Martyr appeared to one Brother Robert, saying that the Earl had not paid his vow and that he must build him a chapel in Hedon (in Holdernesse), the Earl seems to have refused compliance unless the brother would swear on the sacraments that he had not given this message out of desire of gain. So natural was it, when miracles and visions came into fashion, for noblemen to suspect monks of inventing them. However, the chapel was built.

[614] The rest of the miracles of this, the Second Book of William's treatise, for the most part merely repeat the characteristics mentioned above. It is fair, however, to mention the exceptional case of a blind woman of Eynesford,[3] who, being very poor, and being unable to induce her relations to take her to Canterbury, heard a voice by night saying, " I see thou art sad because thou hast not wherewith to visit the Martyr's tomb. Thy sorrow shall be turned into joy. To-morrow go to the shrine of St. Laurence, rub thine eyes with the altar-cloth, and thou shalt see." And so it was.

---

[1] i. 240.   [2] i. 224.   [3] i. 241.

[615] Towards the end of this book, William seems to group together a number of miracles, not because they are of the same nature, but because they are attested by priests, chaplains, archdeacons, or bishops. The last but one [4] describes the Archbishop of Rouen consecrating an altar to St. Thomas at Barfleur for Prince Henry, who found it possible to sail next day, after being weather-bound fifteen days : and it adds that, in a short time, many blind and lame were here healed. Finally, as the climax of the Second Book, comes the cure of Foliot, Bishop of London, effected by the promise of a pilgrimage made in his name by the Bishop of Salisbury at his bedside. Here William naturally becomes rhetorical against the Martyr's former enemy : [5] " What was he to do, confronted by Reflection as a prosecutor, and by Conscience as a witness ? What was he to allege at the bar where allegations are carefully examined by Wisdom as judge ? Was he to deny his fault ? Truth would have cried out against him. . . . Was he to colour his discourse with tricks of rhetoric . . .? Was he to lie . . .?" and much more of the same sort.

[616] He concludes by calling attention to the wonderful and unprecedented novelty of a Saint who feeds and heals his enemies with his own blood. The Lord Himself, he says, " condemns those who drink of His blood, unless they be worthy. . . . But the Martyr Thomas in accordance with his Master's promise,[6] ' doing greater works,' and in a gentler mood, offers his blood not only to friends but also to enemies. . . . Wherefore let all without fear drink of that blood who desire to obtain salvation of body or soul." [7]

---

4 i. 250.   5 i. 251.
6 John xiv. 12 " *Greater works* than these shall he *do*."
7 Comp. Garnier ll. 5806-10, quoted above (442).

CHAPTER II

WILLIAM'S THIRD, FOURTH, AND FIFTH BOOKS, OR THE DEGENERATION OF THE MIRACLES

§ 1. *Degenerate miracles*

[617] In William's later books there appears a rapid increase of the tendency to collect amusing stories and to desist from the task of collecting attestations. Occasionally, indeed, he gives us the latter, and, among these, some very remarkable letters written to the Prior of Canterbury. But these more weighty narratives are mixed with childish stories about the healing of hawks, the preservation of the flesh of dead pigs, and other drolleries interspersed for pleasure (" jucunditas "). On more than one occasion, the author confesses that he throws in these letters, written by the hands of others, to give himself leisure for accumulating stories of a more attractive kind.

§ 2. *Miracles for the King's sake*

A good many of these lighter tales refer to gentlemen and noblemen, and some few to the King himself. Nothing but the interest attaching to royalty can explain the insertion of one that comes early in the Third Book.[1]

[618] Alfred of Gloucester was bound to sell fish to none but the Gloucester monks. But a pressing customer came, saying that he was once the late Archbishop's porter. To him, for the sake of the Martyr, the fisherman sold two fish " for a moderate price." Next night the Martyr appeared,

---

[1] i. 275 (1a). It is entitled, "Concerning a vision pertaining to the King."

riding on a white horse above the waters of the Severn, surrounded by four suns : " Yesterday," he said, "you sent me two fish. Now you must do something more." Alfred is then bidden to go to Canterbury, and to tell his lord the Abbot of Gloucester to do the same. " Your King," the Martyr proceeds to say, "flees from my face. Never will he prosper till he visits my tomb and there obtains God's mercy. . . . Go : I send you to take him word that he is to come to my Memorial." Fifteen days afterwards, the King came from Normandy to England on his way to the reduction of Ireland. The Martyr appeared the second time. "Ha !" he cried, "you have not done my errand. Execute your orders. The King will pass this way, close to your house." It happened just as the Martyr said, and Alfred went so far as to take hold of the King's bridle,[2] intending to give him his message. " But, seeing his Majesty distracted with manifold thoughts and fearing that he might speak to his own harm, he allowed his servile terror to check the words that were on the tip of his tongue." Many days afterwards, when Henry came back from Ireland by that same way, the Martyr deigned to give the fisherman a third warning : and Alfred once more went out to meet the King. But again he was abashed. So nothing came of it all. The three neglected visions of the Saint did not even result in a punishment.

[619] More came from the next vision.[3] Guy, on a charge of manslaughter, was imprisoned and fettered in Stafford. It was Whitsuntide, and a pilgrim happened to bring round the Canterbury Water. Guy drank some : " Strange to tell ! The iron felt the force of the draught, and the bolt leapt apart, and set the prisoner free in the act of drinking." His keepers "locked it again with all their force " ; but soon afterwards, while the choir of the clergy

---

2 '' fraenum regis apprehenderet.''   3 i. 276-7.

was passing by, the chains were again unlocked. They were again bolted. But "when, for the third time, the bar let into the chains leapt out in front of the altar"— apparently the prisoner and his captors must have been in church together—"the priest, full of gratitude,[4] hung up the chains in the church, and wished to keep the prisoner. This the guards would not suffer. So Guy was led out, placed in charge of a gaoler, and chained to a beam by a fetter round his waist. For they imputed to witchcraft and charms what was really the work of divine power."

Their efforts were all vain. Thrice did a voice in the night come to the sleeping prisoner bidding him "Awake, call on Thomas." He did so, and his chain fell off.[5] When the gaoler entered, Guy related that he had been visited from heaven, and pointed to his chain as a proof of it. Word was now taken to the King that the gaol could not keep Guy safe, and he was summoned to the royal presence. "It is your hell-craft,"[6] said the King, "that loosens our chains and breaks our bars." "Hell-craft, my lord," replied the prisoner, "there is none of mine, but the heaven-craft[7] of St. Thomas is great." To which the King answered, "If Thomas has freed him, for the rest let none trouble him. Let him go in peace."

Now comes the reason why the miraculous release was not at first completed by opening the prison door as well as the fetters : "The Martyr was able, as we believe, to bring the prisoner out of the gaol unseen by all ; but it was meet to soften the King's mind at the mention of his name by a more profitable[8] miracle."

---

[4] "gratiosus."

[5] At this point, we might have expected the prison door also to fly open, but William presently explains why it did not.

[6] "maleficia."   [7] "beneficia."   [8] "salubriori."

§ 3. Chance ; losing and finding

[620] Sir Guy,[1] returning from tilting, loses a horse laden with two breastplates near the forest of Ponthieu. He prays to St. Thomas, and scarcely has he reached the exit from the forest when the horse comes to him. " Some one," says William, "will say that this is to be imputed to chance, not to the Martyr. I ask what he means by chance." Going into the question, he proves that nothing happens by chance, for there is a cause for each thing, and a First Cause for all things, " the Cause of causes, whereof there is no cause, by the direction of which [First Cause] there was brought about that miracle which we relate." He does not, however, enter into the question how, after admitting the First Cause, men are to distinguish between the claims of a number of antecedents claiming to be secondary causes.

[621] Miracles of finding, some suggesting obvious explanations, some wildly and grotesquely impossible, are here grouped together. Robert,[2] a retainer of the Earl of Chester, loses a ring containing relics of St. Thomas. After long search, alarmed lest he should have incurred the Saint's displeasure by his carelessness, he resolves to go on a pilgrimage, and puts into a casket six silver pieces to offer at the tomb. When he took them out at the shrine, there was the ring ! " Yet he constantly asserted that he had merely put in the empty casket six silver pieces, and that he was not conscious[3] that he had put in anything else."

Ralph,[4] a priest, returning from Canterbury to a place on the north of the Thames, recovers, on the northern side, a spur that he had lost, twenty-six miles away, on the southern side of the river ! One of his companions, seeing the priest pick up something on the road, cried "Halves !"

---

[1] i. 282-3.   [2] i. 284.
[3] " nec fuisse in conscientia ejus."   [4] i. 285.

But Ralph replied that there was no "halving" where a man found his own lost property. Apparently William seems quite confident that Ralph was right, and that if the companion thought it was an ordinary "find," the companion was wrong. It is difficult to see any grounds for William's view except the fact that, at the time of the loss, the loser had "deposited a slight and friendly remonstrance in the Martyr's ears."

A pilgrim from the neighbourhood of Bury St. Edmund's lost an obol at Sudbury, where it slipped out of his hands and vanished as he was putting it into his purse.[5] He happened to say jestingly, "A pilgrim of St. Thomas has lost his obol." Three days afterwards, he puts his hand into his purse at Rochester,[6] and finds that same coin.

[622] On the other hand, as a mark of reprobation,[7] St. Thomas returns to a man and a woman, who are living together in sin, the two obols that they have severally offered. The one the woman finds before her threshold, the other in a pitcher.

§ 4. *St. Denis and St. Thomas ; "the divine gift of dumbness"*

[623] Among several cases of madness, or possession, one is caused by the Martyr as a punishment for dissuading a pilgrimage. The man was healed on making a vow to St. Thomas.[1] The next case is that of a Frenchman, and it is stated that the French Martyr St. Denis deliberately transferred the healing of this man to the new Martyr St. Thomas, in order that the latter, "as being new and not yet known,"[2] might be glorified.

[624] Just before the healing of a case of dumbness—an infirmity comparatively seldom mentioned—comes a miracle incidentally revealing that the monks drove a trade in wax

---

[5] i. 286 "clausuram ligaminis et visum possessoris evasit."
[6] "Rovecestriam," called just before (i. 285) "urbem Rofam."
[7] i. 288-9.   [1] 303-4.   [2] i. 304.

near the Martyr's tomb. Cecilia had bought a pound from
them : " From this she prepared seven candles, two for herself and her husband, the rest for her (?) sick animals,[3] one
for each. They were all about the same size and shape:
and she said to her husband, 'Were there but one more,
there would be enough, and there would be one for each,' at
the same time putting them down on the bed. Coming
back, she found an eighth."

[625] Now comes a discourse on dumbness : " What we
have just related, happened within Canterbury walls ; what
we now relate, in Canterbury Minster. The maid Melota
was three years past the marriageable age, but hopeless of
marriage since from her birth she had not uttered a word.
And thereby she was free from much occasion of sin, had
she but understood the Divine gift." After a digression
about such " gifts," explaining that God " condemns many to
silence lest they should perish through speech," William
adds, " But we, not abiding by the Divine judgment, but
prone to our own ruin, importune heaven, not for what is
needful but for what is fleshly and pleasurable. Hence it is
that, leaving Market Weighton, the above-mentioned maid
came with fellow-townsmen to the Martyr's tomb. But
when her companions departed, having fulfilled the object of
their journey, she sat there still alone, awaiting the Martyr's
compassion. So, because her acquaintance forsook her, the
Lord took her up,[4] and opened her mouth for utterance.
So, abiding some months by the Martyr's shrine, she learned
the Lord's prayer, and made progress in speaking day by
day." Thus ends William's Third Book, with something
really approaching to what is commonly called a miracle,
giving two vague sentences to the actual cure, and more
than twice as many to his descant on the providential

---

[3] i. 311 "animalibus suis morbosis."

[4] Ps. xxvii. 10, quoted above more fully (i. 240) in the case of the young
woman of Pevensey.

advantages of being dumb.   The supposition that the dumbness was an imposture is made unlikely by the presence of
Melota's fellow-townsmen.

§ 5. *A man of many miracles*

[626] Book IV. opens with a disquisition on demons
and their designs on female purity.   After a number of
miscellaneous miracles, comes one [1] (dated by the Editor
1173 A.D.) describing the adventures of William, a clerk of
Monkton in Thanet, sent by the monks of Canterbury to
Rome.   Marvels follow him everywhere.   A phial of the
Water is miraculously emptied, and then miraculously found
full.   A sick person is restored by it.   William's money-
box, deposited with his host at Piacenza, and broken open
by a thievish maidservant, is washed from the roof and
brought empty to the mistress.   The host, journeying to
Pavia to catch the thief, is led on by a miraculous guide
whom the attendant groom cannot see, though he can hear
his voice.   Brought back to Piacenza and refusing to give up
her thievish habits, the woman is punished with fits, but is
restored at the clerk's intercession ; and finally—passing
safely through perilous regions " where, in accordance with
the Emperor's edict, those who bore the seal of the living
God and of the blessed apostles St. Paul and St. Peter were
liable to loss of hands and eyes "—the clerk of Monkton
" gladdened the brethren of Canterbury by his return and
his success."

§ 6. *The evils of business ; St. Thomas's object in receiving money*

[627] George, sailing from his home in Sandwich [1] for
purposes of commerce, and driven back by storms, affords

---

[1] i. 321.   The style shews signs of different hands.   "Guillelmus" occurs
on p. 321, yet "Willelmus" on p. 322.   Another miracle (i. 324) has Gwillelmus.
[1] i. 325.

William an opportunity for enlarging on the evils of business: "For few engage in business who are not enriched by the losses of others." Perhaps it is this sentiment that leads the author, in the next miracle but one, to set forth a theory to explain [2] "why the Martyr gives heed to vows and promises as though he were pleased with men's gifts." After stating that, when men make vows, St. Thomas hears them, not for his own sake but for theirs, that they may obtain fruits of well-doing, he adds, and seemingly does not reprobate, another view: "But some say that the Martyr, while in the flesh, during his voluntary exile, had borrowed large sums to expend on his companions and attendants. And, because his sudden decease prevented him from discharging these debts in the course of his life, he wished after death to provide for indemnity to his creditors,[3] lest by remaining under a perpetual obligation he should make himself a laughing-stock and leave room for complaint: and hence it is, they say, that Kings and Archbishops . . . have flocked as it were to pay their debts to him, binding themselves to pilgrimages and various payments." [4]

§ 7. *St. Thomas will not interfere with the Archbishop of York*

[628] A long and pedantical account of the healing of a leper—Simon, a mason of Derby,[1] who took the disease while in the employ of Roger Archbishop of York—gives William an opportunity for enlarging on the Martyr's magnanimity in not curing Simon at once, but, as it were, referring him back to his patron, the rival Archbishop, so as to give the latter a chance of seeing what he could do.

---

[2] i. 327.

[3] "de indemnitate creditoribus suis providere." Does this mean that the Archbishop had borrowed from funds belonging to the Monks of Canterbury?

[4] "peregrinationibus, pensionibus, et capitationibus." For the early mention of "kings" honouring St. Thomas, see 441.   [1] i. 334-6.

However, as Roger did nothing, the poor leper had to beg
for money to enter a leper-house. While doing this, he
received an internal admonition that he was to try Canterbury again. Fastening a coin round his neck as his intended
offering, he set out, and was cured.

[629] A letter[2] attesting another leper-healing comes
to Prior Odo from Prior Humbald of Wenlock. Incidentally
mentioning that brother Osbert (who had been in the habit
of seeing the patient and taking her an allowance) had
"written more fully about it," it gives us a glimpse into
one very natural explanation of some of the Parallel Miracles
presently to be considered. The Canterbury Chapter may
sometimes have received *two* letters. Of these William
may have followed one, Benedict the other.

§ 8. *Credulity and incredulity*

[630] At the head of a number of revivifications comes
that of a pet lamb,[1] which fell from a bench and was mercifully killed by the owner (who plunged a knife of a palm's
length into its throat, and afterwards gave it a second wound).
"For the sake of piety and the Martyr," he gave the carcass
to his godson, and it was taken into a poor woman's cottage.
Next day, word was brought that it had come back to life.
The man went to see it, and took the trouble to shear off
the wool, to look at the scars, but there were no traces of
them to be seen! "Behold!" says William, "The great
Wonder-worker called back to life a brute beast! What
sacred mystery, brethren, are we to suppose herein? . . .
We read that St. Silvester called back a bull to life. But
that was required by the infidelity of the Jews. . . . Was
the brute revived bodily that brute irrational men might be
revived spiritually? Or were we thereby to be called to
higher beliefs, to the intent that, being assured concerning the

---

² i. 338-9.   ¹ i. 343.

restoration of this present life for those [animals] for which God careth not,[2] we may feel no doubt about the future resurrection of those who were created in His image ? "

[631] This is in remarkable contrast with the sober incredulity displayed in the case (coming soon afterwards) of the child of a woman of Lichfield.[3] She said it had been restored to life after death under a mill-wheel. But she could not satisfy the brethren in their demand for witnesses. They were obliged to "suspect the malice of the times, because of false brethren privily brought in, who strive to darken truth by mixture of falsehood, lying in wait for the Saint and provoking the Victor even after his victory."[4]

§ 9. *The Water of Canterbury is changed to milk*

[632] Many cases have been mentioned where the Martyr's Water was changed into blood, but now[1] Turbert, a native of Canterbury, and priest of a place about a mile away, finds the contents of his phial changed into milk, which heals a sick person miraculously. Coming to Canterbury and conversing on the metamorphosis with some nobles of the King's court, he was asked by some of them to give them a portion of the milk : "And when he had poured it into several vessels, there was found in one—whereof we were eye-witnesses—pure water." There follows a short sermon on the mystical meaning of the Martyr in this " transmutation."

---

[2] An allusion to 1 Cor. x. 9.   [3] i. 347.

[4] Among the revivifications that follow comes an interesting fact, that one Durand, a Norman (i. 348), "brought his son over to England in order to teach his language to a knight's son." Apparently, it was already difficult for knights in England to ensure that their children should speak good French. Comp. Garnier (l. 5820) " My language is good, for *in France was I born.*"

[1] i. 354-7.

§ 10. *Revivification of a sucking-pig ; of a gander*

[633] A sucking-pig drowned in a stream was brought into the house of one Walter, once a dean, well known in the diocese of Norwich.[1] The mother of the family stirred it with her foot and bade them fling it out of doors since it was dead. Finding her orders neglected, she tested the pig again, and, as there was no life in it, repeated them. " No," said the daughter of the house, " it shall not be cast away, but set aside for St. Thomas." So saying, she took up a pair of scissors and snipped the creature's ears. Straightway it stood up, shook itself, disgorged the water it had taken in, and resumed its original size. When it grew up, in condition to become a full-grown boar, a further miracle followed ; for when his brothers were castrated, he contrived to hide himself. Walter, perceiving that the pig's hiding himself was a benefit bestowed on him by the Martyr, conceived a confidence that, as long as that boar lived, his herd would multiply and prosper.

[634] " Something of the same kind," continues William, " happened near Canterbury." A gander had died, and the children had amused themselves by twisting its neck and pulling out its feathers. When their mother bade them throw it out of doors, " We won't do that," said one of them, " we'll dedicate it to St. Thomas, for we have heard that he bestows his grace even on brute creatures." So they finished their sport with it and then threw it under a bench.

What follows is described in a quaint mixture of Horace, the Vulgate, and William's own : " ' Who will believe our report ? '[2] If not ' the Jew Apella,'[3] if not a Gentile deceived by sleight of error, yet at least let one to whom ' the arm

---

[1] i. 358 "agit in bonis dies suos vir clericalis professionis, quamvis saecu-lariter, ex rebus tamen ecclesiasticis vivens." The " saeculariter " seems intended to prepare the reader for a " materfamilias " in Walter's house.

[2] i. 359. Is. liii. 1, quoted in Rom. x. 16.   [3] Hor. *Sat.* i. 5. 100.

of the Lord hath been revealed'[4] believe it in faith. For herein hath been wrought a most miraculous miracle,[5] to the intent that 'out of the mouth of babes should be perfected praise.'[6] For when, as often happens, other geese entered the house and raised a cackle all about it, he that had been (so to speak) carried out to his funeral began to raise a counter-cackle, and, as though aroused by the noise of his brethren—or perhaps we should preferably say by the voice of the Father [*i.e.* St. Thomas] to whom he was dedicated—he leapt up in a flash, and, amid a great clapping of wings, once more joined himself in companionship with his own flock. Witness of this is the respectable man from whom the gander was reared from the egg! Witness is the Martyr's tomb to which that gander was brought! Witnesses are my respectable brethren by whom that gander was welcomed and eaten!"

§ 11. *A babe sings " Kyrie Eleison"; A dead pilgrim, thrown overboard, comes back for his berth*

[635] The next sentence is [1] "We must now discuss the resurrection of certain rational beings," and the writer shews (in a page and a half) that brutes are revivified merely to prove the resurrection of men. As a specimen of human revivification, he mentions an infant Thomas, restored to life on the day of its birth and death, who laughs when it returns to existence. Eight months afterwards this baby is taken to the Martyr; and, when its parents "saluted Canterbury, seven miles away," the little Thomas, "in a quite wonderful fashion, burst out into praises and began to sing *Kyrie eleison*, though he had never heard the words nor come to the age of speaking!"

[636] A story that may contain some elements of truth

---

[4] Is. liii. 1, quoted by John xii. 38.   [5] "signum insigne."

[6] Ps. viii. 3, quoted by Matth. xxi. 16.   [1] i. 360.

relates how a German, a former Canterbury pilgrim, voyaging in the Mediterranean on a pilgrimage to Jerusalem, died, and was stripped, and thrown overboard. This was just before sunset. When the night was far gone, the steersman was horrified at seeing the dead man approaching him alive : " St. Thomas," he said, " has restored me to life and to your ship : and you must restore me the berth I paid for, and my clothes, too, for I am chilled with cold." A clerk of Canterbury heard this from the steersman himself, and told the monks of it ; " and a certain man of (?) Brindisi,[2] fellow-townsman of the steersman, told us the same thing and in the same terms."

§ 12. *St. Thomas orders prayers for Fitzurse*

[637] The Fourth Book concludes with two or three miscellaneous miracles. Some pilgrims to Jerusalem are rescued from dangers after compliance with the Martyr's command, given in a vision, to pray for Fitzurse[1]—an interesting story as supporting the tradition that Fitzurse, and not Tracy, was the chief murderer. Recording the restoration of Theobald, a knight who died from disease in the Irish War, William once more inveighs against those who[2] "causelessly harassed their helpless neighbours, a nation barbarous indeed and uncultivated, but obedient to the faith and observant of the Christian religion." Then follow two ordinary revivifications. One is after drowning. In this case, says William,[3] "there are three things that cause me wonder :—the restoration, the vanishing of a boy [who brought word that the child had fallen into the pool], and the water swallowed, which returned to nothing." The other revivification is after fever : but in that case William himself doubts whether life had departed.[4] The Fourth Book ends

---

[2] i. 362 " Brandaciensis." But the Editor suggests " Brundusiensis."
[1] i. 363.   [2] i. 364.   [3] i. 366.   [4] i. 367.

with the story of a young knight set on by four men on horseback. He escapes with his life by invoking St. Thomas. The robbers, however, carried away his horse. So he again invoked St. Thomas. Three days afterwards, through the Bishop of Perigueux, his horse was restored to him.[5]

§ 13. *St. Thomas supports a man on the gallows*

[638] The Fifth Book begins with a well-attested case, not indeed of revivification, but of the prolongation of life from noon till about 8 P.M. in a man suspended on a gallows. Girald, a weaver of La Tour Blanche, near Perigueux, had committed a malicious theft, and was handed over to the judges by his lord, the Prior. Before trial, he was bound and cast into a cellar. The hole at the top was covered by a stone that three men could scarcely move. He called on St. Thomas, and " a dove with human voice " bade him quit the cellar. " By divine aid," says the writer, " the stone was rolled away, and he rushed out ":—only, however, to fall into the hands of servants, who " knocked him on the head and thrust him back again, while all the time he kept praising the Saint who had caused his exit." [1] Presently he was brought before the judges. " Girald," said they, " know the truth, and the truth shall make you free." [2] This Scriptural quotation seems to have been taken literally by the accused, as his crafty judges desired : " The simple fellow believed that his freedom depended on revealing the truth : so he confessed the reasons and motives for which he had committed the theft. They said, ' With your own mouth you have condemned yourself.' He replied, ' I said I would say the fact : let the truth make me free. I commend

---

[5] i. 367-8.
[1] i. 370. So far, it is easy to understand that the servants may have rolled the stone away, and hidden themselves, to play a trick on their prisoner.
[2] A quotation from John viii. 32.

myself to the Martyr St. Thomas, Confessor and Archbishop :
I beseech them [8] to free me.'"   When all was ready for the
execution, the thief in vain asked for the sacrament. " The
eucharist," said the chaplain, " must not be given to thieves."
But my advice to you is to forgive your judges—who are
bound by oath to carry out the law—as you would have the
Lord forgive you.   And let earth or grass be your sacrament."
" He said this," adds William, " because it is the vulgar
belief that the sacrament of the Lord's body and blood can
be thus taken."

[639] Girald was now hanged, and kept hanging, till, as
the day went on, he was believed to have breathed his last :
" There were also some who shook his legs to see whether he
still had any breath in him."   When they all departed, the
Martyr's voice was heard by him: "Fear not. As I brought thee
forth from the cellar, so will I support thee on the gallows."
In perfect calm he awaited the result, borne up by a heavenly
hand, till his wife, at sunset, by a divine inspiration, came
to cut him down, having obtained permission to bury him.
Hearing her lamentations, he called to her for help, which
she hastened to give.   As soon as he fell to the ground, he
cried out to know where his supporter had vanished.   Then,
" jumping up, he rushed like lightning into the chapel of
Saint Eparchius, where the condemned take sanctuary."

[640] There was no need of this precaution.   The whole
town " turned out to praise " [4]—presumably God.   " The
judges themselves kissed the limbs they had doomed to
death, and besought pardon.   After the lapse of some four

---

[3] "ipsos."   The Editor suggests "ipsum (him)."   If "ipsos" is right, the
thief must make two persons out of " Martyri Thomae, Confessorique et Archiepiscopo."   Now he presently takes refuge in the chapel of a St. Eparchius : and
a letter of the Bishop of Poitiers, attesting this miracle, describes St. Thomas as
(i. 373) "calling *into partnership with himself* St. Eparchius, the special patron
of the neighbourhood."   Perhaps there is some confusion.

[4] " ad laudes cucurrerunt " : does this mean "ran to Lauds" in chapel, or
"ran together to praise God"?

months, Girald gratefully presented himself at Canterbury
with a part of his halter.   The Abbot of Angoulême kept
part : for 'virtue went out of it and healed many.'[5]   The
cords that fastened his hands were carefully sought, but have
not been found to this day."

[641] After stating that the monks of Canterbury had
heard this in detail from Girald himself, William adds, " we
have decided to confirm it by a brief letter of attestation."
This is from the Bishop of Poitiers to their Prior, Odo.
There is not much of interest in it, except so far as it distinctly claims a share of the credit for St. Eparchius : " As
is clearly proved by the assertion of the thief himself, our
glorious Martyr—who, as he was once urbane in matters
of this world, so now is found pleasantly humorous in his
miracles—calling into partnership St. Eparchius, the special
patron of the district, preserved life intact in the above-
mentioned [man], after he had been on the gallows for several
hours."   The letter recognizes that other marvels of a
decidedly miraculous nature occurred to Girald in his prison,
which the writer has ascertained to be true.   Finally, a
request is made that the monks of Canterbury will allow the
messengers from Poitiers admission to "those more inward
holy things[6] to which entrance is not granted except to
those who bring letters of commendation " ; and that they will
be so liberal as to impart a scrap, however small, of the
blessed Martyr's vesture, or somewhat else that may increase
devotion : " for they have it in their desires to erect an altar
to the holy Martyr in their land."[7]

---

[5] Luke vi. 19.   [6] i. 373 "ulteriora sanctuaria."

[7] A similar but still more remarkable miracle is given later on by William
(i. 515), attested by the Castellan of St. Omer.   There one man is hanged and
dies, while another, his companion at the foot of the gallows, is hanged and
saved.   It is said that the latter had a log attached to his feet.   But the impression given by both stories is that hanging in France was not expected to
produce death very quickly.

§ 14. *Bird-miracles*

[642] The mention of a hawk cured of a broken leg, and of another recovered,[1] leads William to explain that these concessions of small gifts are intended to make men ask for greater gifts. This prepares the way for a number of bird-stories, culminating in one about a clerk's concubine. Wanting a woodcock for the sick man, she receives one that is chased by a hawk into her bosom.[2] Another bird-miracle had previously happened in favour of a hawk belonging to this same clerk:[3] and now William relates a second miracle (making three altogether) performed by the man's concubine. This is a beast-miracle. She revives an ox that was seemingly dead. Offerings are of avail in some of these cases. In one, a hawk revives just when the oblation, sent to Canterbury in its behalf, had reached the Martyr's tomb.[4]

§ 15. *"Fatuous antiquity"; a story in Virgilian prose*

[643] A miracle performed on a lady of Lisieux gives William an occasion for exulting in it as[1] "proving the emptiness of that error of fatuous antiquity that 'Nothing can be reduced to nothing,' which proposition, says Boetius, none of his contemporaries dared to dispute." Reflections such as these are really his object, not the narration of facts. Moral maxims, and devices of style, are always in his mind. He ought before this, he says,[2] to have related the wonderful recovery of Guy, Count de Nevers ; but, since that task demanded "a higher style and more elaborate compliance,"[3] he had put off the reader for a time with "such fare as he had at hand."

[644] In the same spirit, now,[4] having to relate the cures of Margaret of Hullavington (Wilts?) and Sygerid

---

[1] i. 388.   [2] i. 391.   [3] i. 390.   [4] i. 389.
[1] i. 394.   [3] i. 385.   [3] "paratius obsequium."   [4] i. 395-6.

of Yorkshire, he makes a little drama of them.　First comes
" brother William " [*i.e.* himself], " returning to the shrine
to hear what new thing the people brought."　Then follow
two long orations, in florid Latinity, from the father and
the husband of the two women.　The stories themselves
are not of interest, except that the first gives a glimpse
into the life of school-girls in the twelfth century.[5]

[645] In the next story,[6] William, a clerk of York,
narrates, in tags of Virgilian verse, how he kept back a
piece of money destined by his dying mother for the
Martyr, who clearly manifested that he would insist on
his rights in accordance with "that saying of Justinian,
' Legacies go straight to the legatee.' "　First a fever, and
then a vision, brought the defaulter to a better mind :
" ' Why,' said St. Thomas, raising his staff as though to
dash my eyes out, ' why have you all this time kept back my
money ?　You shall not do it for nothing.' "[7]　The sinner
awoke shrieking, and hastened to Canterbury with an
offering of his own in addition to his mother's.

§ 16. *A man of blood, a devotee of St. Thomas*

[646] Among a number of miracles wrought for French-
men of noble birth comes the revivification of Hugh de

---

[5] Margaret speaks in the first person through her father : "My parents had
delivered me at the age of five to the study of letters, that, according to the
word of the Wise Man, I might become wiser, and, when arriving at the age
of understanding, might possess self-control (gubernacula)."　Playing with her
school-fellows, she fell on a knife.　The "patronus" of the church where this
happened came in with his "vicarius," and sewed up the wound, which was
big enough to allow of the insertion of three fingers.　Next day it had vanished.
The girl had invoked St. Thomas.

[6] i. 397.

[7] From Virgil, "Non impune feres."　The original—condensed above—has
also "si forte tuas pervenit ad aures" (mentioning the clerk's father).　The
narrative begins, "You ask, brother William, who I am, why and whence I
am come.　I am called by your name, born of a father of your name, who, ' if
by some chance that name hath reach'd your ears,' is clerk and syndic of the
church of York."

Perac, of Meyssac (?), of the county of Turenne.[1] Hugh
was a cruel and unscrupulous soldier, from the time when
he became a belted knight.   From that same year (which
happened to be the year of the Martyrdom), "in all that
he did, good or bad, he made mention of his last end (at
least superficially)[2] and, even in the moment of perpetrating
some sin, would beseech the Martyr Thomas that the sin
he was perpetrating might not bring him damnation."   A
severe wound, received in an assault on some castle, sowed
the seeds of a disease that brought him to the threshold
of death.   Now, looking forward, he had no hope.   To
take the cross seemed his only chance.   But his friends
would not let him do this ; he, on his side, would not let
his physician examine him.   Forced at last to realize that
"men of blood and guile do not live out half their days,"
he silently commended himself to St. Thomas.   After that,
he knew nothing of what went on around him.   He was
laid out as a corpse upon ashes, and so remained from
five o'clock in the evening till cock-crow at dawn.   With
the daylight came light also to him.   " The angel of the
English" stood near him clothed in white, and touched him
thrice, thrice saying, "the Lord hath risen," and marking
him with the sign of the cross.   The sick man sprang up
to clasp the Saint ; but he had vanished.

[647] The household rejoiced, and the church-bells were
set ringing.   After mass, the priest suggested in his sermon
that the people should build a chapel to St. Thomas.
Eagerly agreeing, they at once, according to their several
power, began to specify what they could give, to measure
out a site, and to bring the stones for the building.   That
very night, a paralysed woman was cured on the ground
destined for the Martyr.[3]   Three hundred women spent
the night with her in prayer on the spot to which she

---

[1] So Editor's marginal note, i. 397-8.
[2] "novissima sua specietenus memorabat."   [3] i. 401.

had been carried by others and from which she returned on her own feet.

[648] This moved the people to hold a vigil on the same spot next night. But the candles were extinguished by the wind: "Then a youth, moved by the spirit, seized his own candle, and bearing it lighted through the street, cried out to the rest, 'If St. Thomas has chosen this spot, and desires that we should pay him honour herein, then, in despite of air and wind, he will not suffer the light to be put out.' So saying, he set down his light. The towns-folk, seeing this, lighted their candles too. And for all they were so many, not one, during all that night—though the place was open and unsheltered—was extinguished by the wind."

§ 17. *Restoration of one struck by lightning*

[649] A novel case is that of Geoffrey, a carter, in Hoole (?),[1] two miles from Chester. Geoffrey (with a companion) was overtaken by a thunderstorm while carting turf. He hastened homeward, but it was too late. A black hairy dog, gliding down in a whirlwind, with big staring eyes and projecting tongue, slipped between his two oxen. Forthwith, one of them was struck by lightning and burned to a cinder, the other had its yoke split and went mad. Geoffrey himself[2] was burned from the waist upwards and fell down lifeless. When his master[3] wished to have him buried with full rites, the priest replied that he could not do it without consulting the Archdeacon. The latter decided that, as the man had died by the will of

---

[1] i. 404. "Hoole" is suggested by the Editor. The text is "villa quae dicitur Cohel."

[2] A reason is apparently suggested: "Se signo crucis et fidei palma parum munierat." Yet he attended the Sacrament on the previous Sunday.

[3] "cujusdam Pagani, civis Cestrensis." In ii. 175, "Paganus" is applied to a priest. Here it seems to mean a village farmer who had the rights of a citizen in Chester.

God, whose judgments are hidden, and as he had on the previous Sunday partaken of the Sacrament, and had been sprinkled with holy[4] water, it would be inhuman to exclude him from the sepulture that is the common right of catholics. Meanwhile, the man had been sprinkled with St. Thomas's Water.

[650] It was about three o'clock in the afternoon when he was struck. The night was more than half gone[5] when he came to life—the interval being allowed, as the chronicler suggests, for the purpose of shewing that the man had really died and was really restored to life. But the battle was not yet won. Satan, the author of death, seeing himself baffled, sought revenge by driving into madness the victim he had lost, so that the poor man, not knowing his friends, tried to bite and wound them. "But," continues William, "let my loving hearers but note how weak is the power of the evil [? spirits]. More powerful is a small piece of a fringe of the Martyr's vesture than the resistance of reprobate spirits." And so it proved. Geoffrey's master caused him to drink some water in which he had dipped this "fringe"; and "the element, nay rather, the sacrament"[6] had its effect. The evil one was cast out, and Geoffrey returned to his senses.

---

[4] "exorcizata."
[5] "ex maxima parte perfluxerat."
[6] "elementum, immo jam sacramentum." In the next sentence, "malignus," used for "the evil one," shews that, above, "the evil (malignorum)" means "the evil spirits."

CHAPTER III

§ 1. *St. Thomas's eggs*

[651] William's Sixth Book begins with a brief prologue, of which the first sentence is this : " Certain miracles,
meanwhile, inscribed by the hands of others, it seems good
to insert here, that our steed, wearied with his burden, may
take breath and get his wind again, and complete the more
speedily the spacious course he has commenced: for 'that
which knows not to rest knows not to last.' "[1]   He proceeds
to quote a number of letters attesting miracles.

[652] The first of these letters[2] comes from the clergy
of the Cathedral of Exeter to Odo Prior of Canterbury.[3]
Their Bishop had been on the point of death, with fever
and pleurisy : the last rites for the dying had been ad-
ministered, and the monks were arranging for the trans-
ference of his earthly remains to their last resting-place.
A large part of the household, too, was suffering terribly
from "the influenza (catarrhus), which has devastated the
realm and carried off many." In this crisis St. Thomas
appeared to brother William, a young man of spotless life
and character (nephew of that Archbishop Theobald who
had once been Becket's patron). Having instantly delivered
the youth from the epidemic, the Saint charged him with

---

[1] ' Quod caret alterna requie durabile non est ' is a hexameter, and perhaps
a quotation.

[2] i. 407-9 : for the meaning of reference numbers, see 1*a*.

[3] This proves the letter to have been written before the end of 1175, in
which year Odo ceased to be Prior.

a message to the rest. All were to recover, including the
Bishop. The apparition was not in a dream—so the young
man insisted—but in a waking vision. The monks, after
cutting their " roasted eggs " into quarters in the usual way,
were to inscribe them with the Martyr's name. Eaten
thus, they would be a remedy. And so they were. Moreover the Bishop recovered on the 14th day after taking
the Water.

§ 2. Mad Gerard of Liège

[653] Gerard, a clerk of Liège, had been driven mad
(by a stepmother's poison, he said), and, having visited the
little house of charity at Mizy (?) near Provins[1] (presided
over by Reginald of Estampes, formerly Prior of Bermondsey),
had made himself so intolerable there that they were forced
to turn him out. When he intruded again, Reginald asked
him whether he would drink the Water of St. Thomas. He
assented and was almost immediately cured. Up to that
time, Gerard, though knowing both French and German,
was not able[2] to talk anything but Latin. But now the
same venerable lady, who in a nightly vision appeared to
Gerard promising him health, also exhorted him to speak
what Gerard calls " Romance language."[3] Consequently,
says Reginald, " henceforth he began to talk French and
to behave with such discretion that we all wondered, and

---

[1] i. 410 " Ad nos divertens, qui penes Pruvinum castrum Mesi habitamus."
[2] " Non poterat." Reginald seems to mean that Gerard's madness, or the
devil, *obliged* him to talk Latin—*to the great inconvenience of some of the unlearned
members of the house.* It will be remembered that, above (404 n.), Benedict addressed the Martyr in French, but the Martyr replied in Latin. It would be very
interesting to know what prompted Benedict to dream this. Did Becket set himself against French ? And was this the result of a purely ecclesiastical feeling that
Latin was the language for Churchmen ? Or did he prefer Latin as the language
of the learned ? Or was there a touch of another feeling that in English houses
of religion, English monks (such as Grim) ought not to find French the prevalent
language ?
[3] " ut Romanum jam loquerer."

congratulated, and could scarcely believe our eyes." After waiting till the moon had waned, for fear of a relapse, the patient was sent to Canterbury; and, as Reginald had no seal of his own, he forwards attestations sealed by the Abbot of Jouy and the Prior of Rueil in the diocese of Meaux.

§ 3. *Crossing Marlow bridge*

[654] In a group of miracles reported from Reading, the first place is given to a private letter from brother Anselm of Reading to brother Jeremy of Canterbury.[1] Returning to Reading from Wycombe (where he had been sent by his Abbot on business) Anselm was crossing the Thames on a rickety bridge at Marlow.[2] Fortunately he let his horse go first and followed on foot. The horse fell partly through a hole in the bridge, and his hind-quarters stuck fast. The neighbours came up and did their best : but in vain. Their final advice was to widen the hole and let the animal drop into the river. But Anselm demurred, forbidden by "the shortness of the day, the strict charge of the father [Abbot], the quick approach of night, and the length of the journey." So they bade him good night and left him. Then, says Anselm, in bitterness of soul, being left quite alone on the bridge, "drawing sighs from my very marrow, I began to invoke the blessed Martyr Thomas, whose sacred gifts I was wearing round my neck. Wonderful to relate ! Forthwith, in some way past telling, without human support, at my invocation of the blessed Martyr, the Lord set the horse on his feet, and directed my steps, and placed in my mouth a new song, even a thanksgiving to our God who is over all things, blessed for ever."

---

[1] i. 415.   [2] "apud villam Merelave."

§ 4. *Richard of Reading is cured of fits*

[655] There follows a cure of leprosy described below in the Parallel Miracles, and then the cure of a brother Richard [1] of Reading, who had fallen down in a fit in the choir. When placed in the infirmary, Richard had been at one time motionless, and seemingly lifeless ; at another, so violent that five men could not keep him in bed. The brethren, flocking round him in sorrow, obtained the Abbot's assent (this seems a proof that the miracle is an early one) to devote the patient to St. Thomas. Then, by degrees, he began to amend. Presently the Martyr appears to him in a vision with messages to Joseph, the Abbot, and Edward, the Prior. He adds, " I have a long journey before me ; this night must I cure a hundred and thirteen sick folk." Richard prays him to restore his health. But St. Thomas, for the present merely concedes such use of his senses as will enable him to confess and to communicate. So much he accordingly at once receives. But he spent many weary days in the infirmary, feeling that he was a drone among the bees, and a burden to the brethren, and importuning the Martyr for a further blessing. At last he received a new command : " Go into the chapel. Take a phial that you will find with a fracture just at the top. Sprinkle your side and you will be healed." It seems superfluous, adds the letter-writer (for unquestionably this is a letter, and not William's production), to ask whether he obeyed.

§ 5. *Restoration of mutilated members*

[656] Next comes a very important letter from Hugh de Puiset, Bishop of Durham, attesting the restoration of the mutilated parts to a man punished for theft,[1] followed by a narrative describing how the judge who had condemned the

---

1 i. 417-9.   1 i. 419-22.

man, happening to be himself in Canterbury Cathedral when the latter came on a pilgrimage of gratitude, confirmed the truth of the man's story. But this will be best considered with the similar miracle on Ailward (above mentioned),[2] attested by the burgesses of Bedford, and related below among the Parallel Miracles.[3] With this is grouped another case[4] (also from the diocese of Durham) where a boy in the house of one Roger de Burnebi loses his middle finger, which comes off as the result of a disease of the bone—and receives another in its place, though not so large as the original. Then comes the case of a clerk, mutilated by a jealous husband, attested by a letter from Richard Becke, Bishop of Coventry, addressed to Richard, Becket's successor as Archbishop of Canterbury. The physiological question, and possibilities of self-deception or fraud, are best considered by experts, in connection with Ailward's miracle, and the similar one just now mentioned. It is introduced, in abominable taste, with a pun borrowed from Plautus,[5] and accompanied by some still more distasteful punning verses.

§ 6. *A pilgrim brought to life to die in peace*

[657] After some narratives of visions, and one of relighted candles, comes a story about a pilgrim who dies on his return from Canterbury at St. Maurice unhouselled, in consequence of the scruples of the Abbot to give him the sacrament after he (the Abbot) had taken "carnal food."[1] Soothing the man's anxiety, the Abbot had actually ventured to promise him that his life would last till next morning..

---

[2] 543, 596.   [3] 710.   [4] i. 423-4.

[5] i. 427-8. The Bishop of Coventry is called by William "The Bishop of Chester (Cestrensis) of venerable memory," which would imply that he was dead at the time of William's writing. In the following narratives, one (i. 431) bears on the question, above touched on (589), whether William was an Irishman or understood Irish. A kinsman of Roderick, king of Connaught, brings with him "a monk as interpreter." No suggestion is made that the Irishman could have been understood by William without an interpreter.   [1] i. 439.

But he died about midnight, and the Abbot was now in an
agony of remorse.   While he was tearing his hair and rending
his cheeks by the pilgrim's bed-side, the dead man sat up.
" Do not flee," he said to the terrified monks.   " By the merits
of St. Thomas, and this man's prayers, I am restored to life
that I may not be deprived of the viaticum."   The Abbot,
with all alacrity of devotion, at once celebrated the sacred
mysteries for the man who had come to life for this purpose,
and who, "having been helped by the viaticum toward that
which is life indeed, delivered up his spirit, and rested in the
Lord."

§ 7. A Templar's dream; cure of the Earl of Warrenne

[658] A very wild dream of a Templar, who lived at
(?) Lillieshalle,[1] in the diocese of Chester, recounts how he had
visions of the blessed Mary, St. Edmund, and St. Leonard,
scraping his disease away from his bowels.   But St. Thomas,
he continues, "seeing that they had not quite removed the
mischief, as though in anger, plunged both his feet into my
intestines, and ejected the remnant of my disease."   He was
in a terrible condition afterwards, but recovered, because of
his invocations to St. Thomas, after lying apparently dead
for a whole night.   The story is remarkable for its introduction : "Let my loving brethren hear what the English
King, when a pilgrim at the Martyr's tomb, heard from
brother Robert, minister of the Temple at Jerusalem."   This
was in July 1174.

[659] Another miracle that might have interested King
Henry was that of Hameline, Earl of Warrenne, his bastard
brother.   In old days,[2] Hameline had called Becket a traitor,
and Becket had called him a scoundrel and a bastard.   This
might appear to make things even between them.   William,
however, recounting the Earl's semi-blindness, and its cure by

---

[1] i. 440.   Text "villa Beleshale."   [2] i. 39.

a relic of the Martyr, puts the case rather unevenly, thus:
" For as the justice of God required that the sinner should be
punished, so the compassion of heaven required that he
should experience the power after death, of him whom he had
called traitor while he was alive." [3]

§ 8. *An unattested wonder*

[660] It is surprising that William makes no attempt to
attest, or apology for inserting without attestation, a miracle
of revivification after seven days of apparent death.   Yet he
justly comments on the wonder as unique in his experience :
" Bethany has seen a four days' corpse revived ; England
(like other countries) has often seen a two days' or three
days' case: but the Lamp of England enlightens the land of
Touraine still more brightly."   And then he relates how the
father of two sons, one of whom had thrown the other down
from a tower, refused to bury the child, though his neck was
broken.   Trusting in St. Thomas, he persisted for seven
days, after which time the boy opened his mouth and asked
for something to drink.   No vow is mentioned, no pilgrimage, no letter of attestation, no attempt to attest.[1]

§ 9. *Weighty evidence from John of Salisbury*

[661] In contrast with this, comes a weighty letter from
John of Salisbury.   At an assembly at Bourges, he says,
consisting of bishops and nobles convened by the King of
France, the Bishop of Clermont publicly related miracles
wrought by St. Thomas.   Being asked whether he had seen
one of these miracles with his own eyes, he answered that
there was in Clermont a knight named John the Scot, " who
had as large rents in the city as the Bishop," and who, having
been seized with leprosy, had been cut off, in the ordinary
way, by the decision of the clergy and laity, from public

---

³ i. 452.   1 i. 444.

intercourse, being abandoned also by his wife. This leper, having gone to Canterbury, after the long delay of almost six months,[1] had been cured, and had returned in health. The Bishop had begged him to come to the council in order to manifest the glory of the Martyr : but he had replied that it was bad enough that any one knew he had been a leper. On hearing this, the King and the rest gave thanks to God. But Count Theobald added that, by reason of his ingratitude, the aforesaid John would be a leper [again]. The letter however, proceeding to relate other cures, does not mention any retribution on John the Scot.

Appending a confirmatory letter from the Bishop of Clermont, John of Salisbury urges that miracles such as these must be published abroad in order to diffuse the " cultus " of the Martyr, "which, I take it, consists especially in this, that the cause esteemed by him more precious than his own life—I mean the integrity of Divine law and the liberty of the inviolable Church—be justified and preserved intact for ever." [2]

§ 10. " Festive " miracles

[662] Such a cure as that of John the Scot would have been apparently left undescribed and unattested by William if it had not come round to him from John of Salisbury. Yet it was better worth describing than several that William now gives us of his own narration. Possibly he deliberately introduces these as a relief to the excessive seriousness of

---

[1] i. 458. The delay probably means "waiting at Canterbury." But the ambiguity of the English represents that of the Latin.

[2] [661a] i. 460. This letter is addressed (i. 458) to "Odo Prior and William Sub-Prior," and in i. 482 a miracle is said to be related and an offering made to "our Sub-Prior." Although William was an extremely common name, these two passages indicate that *our* William was by this time Sub-Prior under Odo. And he is called Sub-Prior by the *Quadrilogus* (*Mat.* iv. Introd. p. xix.). If so, Benedict would be under him at this time, but above him, as Prior, before the end of 1175.

medical miracles. For example, at Arthington[1] in Yorkshire, Turgis, a working man, had received a pig from
Godfrey, a monk of Pontefract, as wages for work on a
chapel in honour of St. Thomas. Losing the pig in crossing the Wharfe, he expostulated with the Martyr, and told
Godfrey; but he would not take a second pig. "I must
not," he said, "be paid twice over." Pleased with the man's
honesty, St. Thomas preserved the dead pig for forty days,
and washed it on to the bank in such excellent condition
that, when it was recovered, Turgis and his household were
able to enjoy it.

[663] The next miracles are various, but similarly
trifling. Austen,[2] a London metal-caster, fusing a number
of Canterbury phials for some work of a sacred nature, finds
one that obstinately remains unmelted, and cannot explain
it, till he ascertains that it once held relics of the Saint.

A pilgrim, returning from foreign parts, brings in his
wallet a bezant which he destines for St. Thomas: a pirate
seizes it and cannot stir till he has cast the wallet away.[3]

[664] Norway at last sends two pilgrims to Canterbury.
One of them gives thanks for the recovery of a lost falcon,
chased back to him by two eagles.[4]

[665] A Dorsetshire woman, recovering the whole of a
stolen web (placed before her threshold one morning) sends
a part of it to Canterbury in accordance with her vow.[5]

[666] Galiena, vaguely described as a woman of
England,[6] was guilty of sewing to her shoes ornaments of
various colours, as well as gold. "Tumour of body," says
William, set in to punish "tumour of mind"; and her limbs
became as many-coloured as her shoes. But she repented

---

[1] i. 464 "Hardintona."   [2] i. 464-5.   [3] i. 466.   [4] i. 466-7.

[5] i. 469. The vow might really have had something to do with the recovery,
especially if accompanied by an appeal to St. Thomas to punish the thief.
Knowing what the Martyr could do, the culprit might prudently repent.

[6] i. 469 "Anglicana."

and—presumably by the aid of St. Thomas, though he is not mentioned in the whole story—was restored to health.

§ 11. *St. Thomas forgives a reproachful pilgrim*

[667] Early in the treatise, Gerard of Flanders had been mentioned as cured of fistula.[1]   Now he appears to have gone on a second pilgrimage.   But, on his journey back, he had a renewal of his disease.   In his agony he blasphemed Thomas, calling him "a fellow of naught and an old madman, no martyr, but a gallows-bird."[2]   He even ventured to repeat such words to pilgrims on their way to the shrine, and, as though in magnanimous contempt, forwarded through them an offering to the Saint who was treating him so ill.   His hearers were surprised that the Martyr tolerated such a blasphemer.   But William says that those who knew the Saint's patience while he was alive could easily understand it now that he had become the kindly Physician, who takes no heed of the patient's or lunatic's passion.   So in this case—especially as the man blasphemed "in word but not in heart"—St. Thomas was kind, and speedily delivered him from his pain.

§ 12. *Responsibilities of a Saint in vogue*

[668] In a group of nautical miracles, it is not only asserted that St. Thomas frequently aids mariners belonging to the ports round Canterbury, but also that he sometimes sends those lights at the mast-head, which are more commonly attributed to St. Elmo, and which, by the Greeks and Romans, were assigned to Castor and Pollux.   The fact is worth noting as an instance of the rule that a Saint in fashion may be made responsible for almost all contemporaneous inexplicable phenomena—coincidences, marvels and so-called

---

[1] i. 280.   [2] i. 471 "strangulatus."

miracles. He is the power most commonly invoked : and, if the invocation succeeds, to him is the glory. For example, two priests bring thanks to St. Thomas for averting or extinguishing fire.[1] In the latter case the instrument is a phial of St. Thomas, which is not melted. At Waterford, in Ireland, the houses of those who had built a chapel to St. Thomas are alone preserved in a general conflagration.[2]

§ 13. *Distant cures unknown ; revivifications*

[669] That many cures, partially effected at the tomb, and completed afterwards at a distance, never reached the ears of the Canterbury monks, may be inferred from many circumstances mentioned by William, and, among others, from a letter written by the Bishop of Bayeux to all the clergy in his diocese describing the cure of a leper, William of Rouen, following on a pilgrimage to the Martyr. It is inserted by William without preface or comment.[1]

[670] The revivifications of two children are placed at the conclusion of a distinct section of the Sixth Book. They present interesting contrasts. In the former, the father (a nobleman named Bernard FitzReginald) acquiescing in the death of his little one, turns away from the bed-side with a pious utterance of resignation to the Martyr's will, and it is left for the nurse to appeal: "In the name of the Lord and the blessed Mary and the holy Martyr, I bid thee, my son, desert me not till I hear one word from thee"—upon which the child awakes to life.[2] In the other, the father, a townsman of Oxford, determined that the child, who had apparently died in convulsions, should either be restored alive to him, or taken dead to Canterbury.[3] The same night, the child was restored.

[671] To this the writer adds, "Several accounts of

---

[1] i. 477.   [2] Ib.   [1] i. 479-80.   [2] i. 483.
[3] i. 484 "aut hic mihi vivus reddetur, aut Cantuariam mortuus efferetur."

persons revivified remain to be written. But if they desire
to live after death and to be remembered to posterity, they
must wait for another pen than ours, though their cases are
roughly noted down[4] in our tablets. Nor can we complete
other accounts of healing bestowed by the kindness of the
Martyr. For by reason of impediment from the evil times,[5]
we have neither the necessaries nor the leisure for writing."
Possibly, he is referring to the great fire which, in Sept. 1174
(just after King Henry's pilgrimage), destroyed a large part
of the Cathedral and may very well have interfered with the
leisure and convenience of the Sub-Prior.

§ 14. A historical digression

[672] Taking up the pen, after an apparent interval,
William remarks that "by these and such like miracles,
within four years[1] from his passion," the Martyr was not
only fanning the fires of faith in the Church but also arousing
the affection of the King, under whom Thomas had once
served as a soldier, when in the flesh. This leads him to
describe the simultaneous hostility of Prince Henry, the
French, the Earl of Leicester, and the King of Scotland, to
meet which the King threw himself on the Martyr's compassion, doing penance at his tomb.

[673] The King desired[2] the people of Canterbury to
remove their property beyond the Medway for fear of
depredations from the south. But while the men of Thanet
were watching the coast, three men[3] and two women had
visions from St. Thomas promising deliverance.[4]

---

[4] i. 484. "Praenotentur" seems to mean a first rough draft.
[5] "malitia temporis impediti."
[1] i. 485 "infra quartum annum."   [2] i. 489.
[3] One of these is called "Walvord." "Thanet" is here called "Tenedos."
[4] [673a] i. 489. This is not remarkable. But it is most extraordinary that
a similar promise should have been given to a native of Kingstone (near Canterbury), *not from St. Thomas, but from St. John.* The explanation probably is,

The very day of the King's penitence saw the capture of
the King of Scotland : and all Henry's other enemies were
almost simultaneously brought to naught.   Then follows an
account of a vision of St. Thomas to Henry by which the
latter is induced to take Benedict, the new Prior, into his
favour, and to expedite the fulfilments of his promises to the
monks.[5]   The section ends with a Charter confirming the
liberties of the Cathedral.

§ 15. *William degenerates still more*

[674] Here we might expect William's treatise to end.
But he introduces an Appendix of miracles, of a miscellaneous
character, some few attested by letters sent to the Prior,
but others unattested, frequently foreign, and almost always
frivolous.   The style becomes now more detestable than
ever.   One marvel is introduced with the Virgilian question
" What say you, reader ? Shall I speak out or be silent ? "[1]
The writer repeatedly recurs to the device of accosting the
patients and telling them what they have told him—on one
occasion, with a proviso, " If, Walter, I remember aright
what you related about yourself."[2]   Once he converses with

---

that the Kingstone man was, as he is described, " old and full of days," too old
and too conservative to take to his heart the new Martyr and Saint of England.

[5] i. 493-4.

[1] i. 504. " Eloquar an sileam ? " Virgil, *Aen.* iii. 39. Following this,
amid a mass of uninteresting matter, there is a too brief account (i. 506) of the
cure of a deaf and dumb man, who came from Provins, and was enabled to speak
on the way. But " with the *possibility* of speech, he had not received the *act*
(actum)," so that he had to learn " like a child of two or three years old."
Another dumb man, in Normandy, by recovering speech, recovered his feudal
possessions, of which he had been deprived by his lord.

[2] i. 508. It concludes, " In relating this, you deserved that your relation
should be believed, since you were both a priest and a dean." This will, in part,
explain the disproportionate space given to the cures of the clergy. It is not
merely that they were more susceptible to the Martyr's influence ; it is also
because their single testimony sufficed, in William's judgment, to attest their
stories. Many of the miracles wrought on the laity might be discredited and not
recorded : and probably a great number from one and the same neighbourhood

his own hand: "Hand, write as follows. 'No,' says my hand!"[3]

§ 16. *Evidence of date*

[675] The first of these miracles[1] must have happened at a time when the day of St. Thomas of Canterbury had come to be regularly observed. A Norman thresher, threshing on St. Thomas the Martyr's day (kept for the first time on 29th Dec. 1173), was punished by finding his flail stick to his fingers, but was delivered by a vow made by his master.

[676] The cure of an epileptic Canon of Oseney[2] is worth mentioning because it has a definite date, the Whitsuntide of 1171; and the question arises why (if for any reason beyond William's neglect of chronology) it comes so late in order. Possibly the reason is that the poor Canon was anxious not to exult too soon till he knew the disease would not return. It had attacked him in 1151, at intervals gradually diminishing from 2½ years, and 1½ years, down to 6 months, and at last 4 months. He now resorted to Canterbury. But his case is unique in this point, that he did not go straight to St. Thomas but to a namesake of the Martyr among the monks of Canterbury known as Thomas of Maidstone, a man given to visions, of whom St. Thomas had said in the flesh "I have found a man after my own heart." Through his intercession he was restored, and, as the monks of Oseney say in a letter unfortunately not dated, "from then *till now* he has not felt a touch of his infirmity." Not improbably

---

were, when recorded, accompanied by a letter of attestation from the priest of the district, which has not been inserted.

The next miracle is wrought on the son of "one Stephen, parson of Chesterfield (*gerens personatum* ecclesiae villae Cestrefeld)." He is not called "priest."

[3] i. 524.   [1] i. 496.

[2] i. 509. "Willelmus de Stokingeberi" (Ed. suggests "Stockbery"). He had been a rich man, but "ex divite canonicum induerat"; and his brother monks of Oseney honoured him for that, as well as for his goodness.

they would wait till at least the longest of the intervals above
mentioned (2½ years) had passed away, *i.e.* till 1173, and
possibly till 1174.

§ 17. *The consequences of finding an ancient mortuary vessel*

[677] Among several letters of attestation that here
follow, is one from the Abbot of La Sie en Brignon (Bring-
nonnensis)[1] describing how a labourer unwittingly broke
with his mattock a glass vessel of most wonderful beauty,
and then irreverently handled the contents ("black earth
and small bones"). Almost at once he lost his sight—
perhaps (though the Abbot does not suggest this) owing to
some dust or vapour from the mortuary urn. Resorting to
the church, and mass, and prayers, and a vow to St. Thomas,
he saw in a dream the martyred Archbishop saying to him
that he would receive his sight on the following Monday at
the same time at which he lost it : "And so it came to pass.
. . . This miracle is testified unto you in the sight of God and
His angels by our monks and certain of the laity who had
seen [the matter], and had carefully noted the hour in which
he lost his sight and also the hour in which he received it."

§ 18. *Miracles from Sefrid the ecstatic*

[678] The next six miracles, or rather groups of
miracles, appear to have been reported to Benedict from

---

[1] i. 516. This, and two that precede, and several that follow, are addressed
to Benedict as Prior.

One (i. 512-4), from Pontigny—where St. Thomas had once been an exile and
now had an altar—describes how the Abbot, after administering extreme unction
to a dying monk and seeing to the arrangements for his burial, was startled by his
presenting himself among the brethren that were waiting for the holy water :
"fateor, stupefactus expavi." Concerning the suspicious character of evidence
from Pontigny, see **801**. But this seems credible.

This is followed (i. 515) by a letter from the Castellan of St. Omer, mentioned
above (**641** n.), concerning a man on the gallows preserved alive for several hours
by St. Thomas.

France together with a letter of attestation from the Abbots
of Trois Fontaines and Haute-Fontaine (in Champagne), who
had received them from the Abbot of a place called Claustrum.   They seem all to depend on the evidence of a monk
of Claustrum called Sefrid.   A chapel had been built there
by a devout knight who had returned from Canterbury with
relics of St. Thomas ; and the place at once began to teem
with miracles and with Sefrid's reports of miracles.[1]

[679] A man paralysed from the waist downwards
spent the night in the chapel.   His votive candle, "as it is
said," lasted seven times as long as it ought naturally to
have done.   He arose from prayer, healed, and went towards
the knight's house.   Meanwhile the knight had heard a voice
saying that there was "that going on in the chapel which
would rouse a thousand men."   He arose with his wife, and
met the paralytic, whom the lady, beholding, "saw clothed in
splendour and as if adorned in vesture of angels."   Taking
him into the house and seeing him in rags, she asked what
had become of his fine clothes.   He said he had never had
any: "she, on the contrary, affirmed that she had seen them
on him, whence it may be perpended [2] that she had received
a vision from God, to the manifestation of the Martyr's
power and the increase of the lady's devotion."

[680] Sefrid proceeds to pile on miracles.   Six are
recorded in a page.   One is the case of a woman possessed
for eight years, "by whose tongue the demon was wont to
talk in Latin, German, and various ways."[3]   One woman
had been delivered from dumbness during mass ; another
had been struck dumb for blaspheming the miracles.

[681] A knight, who had promised to walk barefoot in
a knights' procession in honour of the Martyr, came to the
door, when his comrades set out in the morning, and said
he was too tired and sleepy.   So he went back to bed.

---

[1] i. 518-20.   [2] "perpendi."   [3] "modis."

Suddenly he was pierced through the foot with a knife. Getting the knife out as well as he could, he limped after his companions and was healed when he reached the chapel.

[682] Probably Sefrid was wildly ecstatic, or slightly mad. He had mutilated himself, as Origen did, and for the same reason, to preserve his chastity. But then, lamenting that he was barred, by his own act, from priestly ordination, he appealed to St. Thomas, who restored him. Concerning this and other miracles the two Abbots write, "The miracles we have transmitted to you we possess [in writing] certified (certa) and confirmed by the seal of the Abbot of Claustrum.[4] Moreover from the mouth of brother Sefrid, whose mutilation has been healed, as we have said, by St. Thomas, we have ascertained the truth of the written statements. For he has testified that he has seen some of these miracles himself, and that he knows for certain the truth of others though he has not seen them."

[683] The words "as we have said" shew that what precedes was written by the Abbots, not by William; but the latter has taken so little pains in arranging the preceding matter that he has not only put the letter of attestation *before* the miracles but has *entitled* it "The Confirmation of six *afore-mentioned* miracles." These facts are important because they shew that many of the miracles in William's book, and possibly in Benedict's, may have been written out by others and transcribed with little or no alteration by the Canterbury chroniclers. And this sometimes may have been done without acknowledgment.[5]

---

[4] "Certa habemus" might mean "we regard as certain." But that does not so well suit with "et . . . confirmata," which can hardly mean "we regard as confirmed by the Abbot's seal." Perhaps it means "we regard them as certain, and [they have been] confirmed."

[5] For an instance in which Benedict does this, see Parallel Miracles (752).

§ 19. *William oscillates between credulity and incredulity*

[684] As soon as we pass from these letter-attested miracles we are in a different atmosphere. Not indeed that Sefrid's was not an atmosphere of portent. But that was plain, unadorned ecstasy, plainly and simply recorded. William—whose " tired steed " above-mentioned may be supposed to have "taken breath "—now that he resumes the pen, tells us frankly that, if people seem to him respectable, he does not see his way to doubting their miracles. And it is by a preface to this effect that he introduces the last section of his book.[1]

[685] "When pilgrims," he says, "ascribe a thing to a miracle, and become pilgrims on account of it, I do not like to reckon it non-miraculous, or to contradict them concerning those whom they have actually seen die. For, if one is satisfied about the good fame and life of the narrators, one ought also to be satisfied about their veracity. Speak, therefore, Elfwin, living about eight furlongs the other side of the Thames, and give glory to God." Then Elfwin speaks, describing the rescue and reanimation of his drowned daughter, and concludes, "If you incredulously deny that which you have not seen, we can make contrary affirmation, proving what we have seen from her compressed lips, which could not be opened owing to the *rigor mortis*, and from the interval between death and life." And here Elfwin ends, without even telling us what the "interval" was. Instead of asking him for it, William, under the same title, despatches another miracle. "Deliver you, too, Robert of Flanders, your testimony to Christ [and][2] the Martyr. ' I found,' he replied, ' my son in a cave, drowned ; and I rejoice

---

[1] i. 522.

[2] The Editor supplies "et." Herbert of Bosham often calls Becket "the Lord's Christ," *i.e.* anointed, in describing the Martyrdom. But that meaning is improbable here.

that he was restored to me through invocation of the
Martyr.'" That is all.

[686] In the next case, William actually told Henry of
Minster in Devon that he could not take his unsupported
word as proving that his child had died. But the man
seems to have appealed to the testimony of the whole
village (perhaps to be ascertained by letters to the priest).
He also appeals to Truth, and to the fact that for three days
afterwards the little one's life was manifested by nothing but
breathing.[3]

[687] To this, William makes no reply, but passes to
the next case : " You say, Eadwin, that your son, for whose
sake you give thanks, dying humanly speaking, received
breath again through the Water of the Martyr, after his eyes
had been closed and his exequies performed. You tell me
his name, age, and birth-place. But beware lest, while you
are [for] extolling the Martyr's name, you utter a fable or jest,
and, in accordance with your name, make yourself a jest."[4]
To this the man replies, "I should deserve to be thought
Eadwin, according to the abuse of the word by your French
folk[5] (who say that Edwin[6] and a fool are the same), if I
assigned to the Martyr what the Martyr had not done. For
a man may not know letters, and yet know by nature that
falsehood does not please the Truth."

§ 20. *William decides to accept the statements of rich people*

[688] Next comes Lucy, wife of a knight of Mont-paon.[1]
Some of her friends thought her dead because she could not
move ; others thought her not dead : " The Martyr settled

---

[3] i. 523.
[4] i. 523. It seems to have been a French joke that "Edwin" meant a
"fool." "Fieri fabula" means "make oneself ridiculous."
[5] "vestratum."
[6] So MSS., having "Edwin" here, but "Eadwin" above.
[1] Ed. suggests "in Rouergue or Provence ?"

the dispute, for, when she was devoted to him, her spirit (or breath) was called back and he roused her limbs to motion." [2]

William does not tell us whether this "settled" that she had been dead, or that she had been motionless. He passes rapidly to Mabilia's son: "Write, O hand, that Mabilia, a noble English lady, placed her first-born son dead, on the [funeral] ashes,[3] but received him alive, upon [4] [the use of] the Martyr's Water." "No," quoth my hand, "I must not write anything that is not known for certain." "The lady," answered the scribe, "has been heard by us, and examined by us, so far as her noble birth made it seemly, and we can presume the truth of her relation from her pilgrimage and devotion. For, although faith is rare, because many people speak many [lies],[5] yet, just as it is natural to conjecture a beggar to be a liar, so it is by no means natural to make such a conjecture about the nobility, who propitiate and conciliate heaven by pilgrimages."

[689] A lamentable but common-sense confession! It was not worth the lady Mabilia's while to come all that way to Canterbury, perhaps part of the way on bare feet, and to keep vigils, and make prayers and offer gifts, and all for a lie: but it might well be worth Edwin's or Eadwin's while to beg his way to the Martyr and back, along with a conveniently revivified son, returning with a pocket full of *denarii* and with the reputation of one favoured by St. Thomas.

§ 21. *William becomes slightly cynical*

[690] Hence, perhaps, we may account for the rapid increase in William's neglect of facts, and sometimes cynical

---

[2] i. 523-4.

[3] i. 524 "in cinere." It was customary to lay the dying on ashes, that they might not die on a bed ("in plumis" it is once called).   [4] "super."

[5] "multi *multa* loquuntur." Probably William is referring to such passages as Prov. x. 19 "in the multitude of words there wanteth not sin," so that "multa" implies "lies."

manner in recording such facts as he does record. The miracles
were by this time both too many and too much for their
reporters.   It is creditable to him that he sometimes avows
a feeling of doubt when he inserts some stories.   But he
might surely have left some out—such, for example, as this :
" Some man told me that his wife had hanged herself, and
shewed me the halter.   But as he kept it hidden from his
neighbours, lest they should be put to shame[1] by the
Martyr's visitation, I do not wish to reveal her disgrace.
What [kind of act] she did, I leave undefined.[2]   What
things she did,[3] saving modesty, I leave hidden.   The reason
why she did it, I take to be diabolical suggestion.   Where
she did it—to avoid saying nothing—[it was] in the world.
When she did it—I heard but do not remember.   She was
delivered from the halter by her husband, from death by the
Martyr : by the former with a knife, by the latter through
a vow."   This outburst of frankness is continued in the
following narrative, in which he expresses his opinion that a
scribe, as well as a judge, ought to pronounce his censure
when a matter passes the bounds of truth, and then describes
the alleged revivification of Elizabeth of Lisieux "who, in
consequence of sickness, completely *surceased* (I say not
deceased, though she says she *deceased*[4]) so that she lost all
bodily feeling and seemed to have departed [this life]."

§ 22. A married priest

[691] Perhaps "the little Nicolas," son of a priest in
Necton (of the diocese of Norwich), is introduced in the last
of these stories of revivification[1] in order to point a moral.

---

[1] i. 524. "Confundantur."   Apparently "they" means "he and his wife."
[2] "Quod fecit, in genere propono."
[3] "Quae fecit."   Could this mean "what [things] she did [to lead her to the
act]"?
[4] i. 525 "penitus defecit (non dico *decessit*, quamvis se decessisse perhibuerit)."
[1] i. 526.

The father, being a priest, ought not to have had any children after he was a priest ; but the epithet applied to Nicolas implies that his father had probably thus transgressed. "Little Nicolas" died within a year of his birth. How long he remained lifeless, William does not tell us. The father, whom he charitably leaves unnamed, "although a priest, although learned in the doctrine of the gospels, thinking prayers useless in the presence of the proofs of death, had no hope that life could be recalled : but the mother, full of faith, by a vow of pilgrimage obtained [such an answer to her prayers] that the child opened one of his eyes and then by degrees revived." But the result was bitter. Perhaps the married priest was ashamed to face the monks of Canterbury. In any case, the parents neglected to pay the vow. As a first punishment, two sons were taken from them. After that, a daughter fell into the fire and severely burned herself. Even then, it needed a vision seen by the woman, before this married priest could be induced to discharge the debt incurred by the mother of his child.

§ 23. *Wiscard, the King's falcon*

[692] After two ship-stories, in the latter of which a man who had fallen overboard is found by his rescuers "sitting on the waves,"[1] William passes to one[2] that might have amused King Henry if he had glanced at the end of the book dedicated to him. The King's falconer, Radulph, had under his charge, beside the other and inferior birds, one falcon of special excellence, hence called Wiscard. Some one whom he desired to oblige asked him to bring down a crane, and Wiscard was the bird to do it. But Radulph had misgivings, for the weather was unfavourable, and, says William, the King did not allow Radulph to trifle with Wiscard as with the other hawks. However, he risked it,

---

[1] i. 528.   [2] i. 528-9.

with the unfortunate result that the noble bird, after bringing down one crane, was run through the eye by the bill of another. Radulph, fearing to face the King, made off to Tours, with Wiscard in a drooping and dying condition. By the advice of a priest there, he tried a vow to St. Thomas, and it proved effectual. The Martyr—partly because he felt for the falconer, partly because he wished to bestow a new obligation on his ancient lord, the King—told him (in a dream) to look for twelve pimples in the bird and open them. Next morning, finding three or four, he called his friends and said that, if he could find the whole twelve, it would be no fancy but a real vision. He found them and carried out the Saint's orders: "the bird opened its eyes and called for its food. When the King was told the story, he thanked the Martyr for saving the favourite companion of his sporting hours."

§ 24. *A starling invokes St. Thomas; miracles worked for a hospital at Shooter's Hill*

[693] The climax of the miraculous is reached in the next story, which William introduces with this preface,[1] " I relate what is commonly related in Brittany and is known to have happened there." A starling had been taught by its mistress to repeat, among other phrases, an incantation to St. Thomas. Seized by a kite, it invoked him. The kite, releasing its prey, dropped down dead."

[694] After this, other things are bathos. Yet at least there is variety. One Fretus, building a hospital, apparently on Shooter's Hill,[2] in honour of St. Thomas, and finding no water, was on the point of giving up the site in despair, when he was told by the Martyr in a vision to dig under a bramble bush where he would find eels. He sensibly inferred that

---

[1] i. 529.
[2] i. 530. So the Editor suggests. The text is "septimo milliario ab urbe Lundoniarum . . . quo vitae viantium latrones insidiari consueverant."

eels imply water. So he dug, and found it so. Another
dream, again from the Martyr, tells him to bid a certain
Londoner named Jocius give up a book, which Jocius could
not use himself, for the chapel of the hospital. Jocius gives
it : and "from the cheerfulness of him that gave may be
conjectured the power of the will of him that sent the message
to give."

§ 25. St. Thomas at Devizes

[695] The next story tells about poor people who seem
to have been in earnest. Near Devizes,[1] a deaf man was
told by the Apostle Thomas and the Martyr Thomas to go
to Priest Alured and bid him build a chapel in the market-
place to the latter. The deaf man pleads inability ; but the
two Saints carry him on his bed to the site and mark it out ;
" And when the Apostle had measured a distance of twelve
feet with his right foot, and the Martyr thirteen with his right
and left, after the manner of his nation,[2] they brought him
back again." The deaf man is not said to have delivered
the message. But he began to come regularly to this spot
to pray, and to tell people his vision. However, for some
days, he only got laughed at.

But time went on. The two Saints appeared to a blind
man of the same place, and told him to go with the deaf
man to one Ralph, the head of the town,[3] and bid him cut
down a tree—which would be found marked in three places yet
not with an axe—and set up a cross from the wood thereof.
The blind man obeyed : "When the commands of the
two Saints had been fulfilled in each point, the Lord in that
spot began—nay rather, is now beginning, for whatsoever
we write concerning the Martyr happened shortly after his

---

[1] i. 531 "Castro quod Angli Divisiones vocant."
[2] "More gentis suae." The distinction is curious. Is the writer contrasting
a custom of the East with one of the West? Would such a distinction have
occurred to a poor man?   [3] "Qui castello praeerat."

martyrdom[4]—to work mighty works and acts of healing. So within a few days people flocked thither and the place became famous : and the blind man and the deaf man, whom the two Saints made their messengers, were the first to obtain compassion and restoration to health."

§ 26. St. Thomas among friends

[696] A slightly familiar or even comic colouring is given to the next group of miracles. The first tells how the Saint healed, first, Wicard, arch-priest[1] of Lyons (ridiculously deformed by a tumour on the nose), and, after him, an unnamed monk of Wenlock, who was liable to redness that made him look tipsy even before breakfast. The next[2] describes him as restoring speech to a former servant of his, by familiarly accosting him with the words " Brother Robert, speak to me : I am Thomas."

[697] Robert was a lay-brother of Pontigny, Becket's hospitable home in exile. Naturally, the Martyr would be supposed to retain a peculiar interest in the Abbot of that place. This was manifested in the case of one, Guarin by name, Archbishop elect of Bourges. It happened that, on the day fixed for his consecration, only two Bishops appeared, the canonical quorum being three.[3] It was, therefore, impossible to proceed. An Abbot comforted the clergy by saying he had seen in a vision a clerk of St. Thomas, namely, Alexander the Welshman, who had come in haste to give a message to the Archbishop elect and had then departed. The message was that St. Thomas would make a fourth at his consecration to-morrow. Next day, after long waiting in vain, they had well-nigh given up all hope of proceeding for

---

[4] There is a slight confusion. Logically, "we write" should be substituted for "happened." "Whatsoever (quicquid)" seems to imply more than this single narrative. It may be one of several stories communicated by some one writer to William.   [1] i. 532 "archipresbyter."

[2] i. 532.   [3] i. 533. Editor gives in margin the date A.D. 1174.

that day, and were on the point of going to dinner, when the Bishop of Cahors, riding in advance of his attendants, who had been detained by a flood, came galloping into the city. This made the canonical three. And it was inferred that the Martyr made an invisible fourth.[4]

§ 27. *The Saracen of Palermo*

[698] Next comes a unique story of a rich Saracen of Palermo,[1] to whom St. Thomas appeared in a dream "clothed in red garments[2] and with a red mitre,"[3] saying that, though he was a good man and zealous for his law, his works were barren because not sanctified by baptism ; wherefore he was to be baptized. The Saracen at once went to the Archbishop demanding baptism, and, on his not immediately conceding it, replied, " If I die meanwhile, the Lord require my soul at thy hand." Next day, the baptism took place, and he dedicated a church of his own to the Martyr.[4] " This," says the writer, " was related to us by the Bishop of Evreux, and his chaplain, who celebrated mass in the same church,"[5] presumably the church dedicated by the Saracen.[6]

§ 28. *St. Thomas kills a cow*

[699] After describing a miraculous restoration of money[1]—taken by a cut-purse from a poor pilgrim, and

---

[4] " Qui se tertium exhibuit, Sanctum quartum non deesse probavit."

[1] i. 534. Text " Palernae." But Editor, "more likely Palermo (properly *Panormus* in Latin) than Palerna near the Lake of Fucino."

[2] " pannis."

[3] [698a] " Mitre." The use of " mitra " to mean " mitre " indicates that, in the accounts of the Martyrdom, " pileus " means " cap," not " mitre." Most English and French folk saw the Archbishop in white. Why did the Saracen, or whoever originated the Saracen's story, see him in red ? Comp. 712a " in red and with a comely mitre (decenter *mitratus*)."

[4] " templum suum martyri consecravit."   [5] " in eadem ecclesia."

[6] It would be interesting to ascertain whether any light is thrown on this story by the name of any church at Palermo, or by any traditions connected with the city.   [1] i. 534-5.

heard tinkling some days afterwards in his phial—William
passes from this miracle of encouragement to one of chastise-
ment, inflicted on Helias, a rich man, and one of William's
own relations.[2]   It happened that Helias, who was a farmer,
had six fine bullocks.   Pointing to the finest of these,
a neighbour said to him, "This should be given to St.
Thomas."   "No," said the farmer, "not long ago I bestowed
one on his shrine."[8]   The writer does not accuse his
kinsman of lying.   Apparently Helias had really given a
bullock quite recently to the Martyr, and his only fault was
that he now declined to give another at a neighbour's casual
suggestion.   But William is very severe on him, and makes
him a shocking example: "Whoso lets his tongue play
freely, let him hear what happened.   Let him set a watch
on his mouth and a door to close his lips, lest his tongue
vent folly and words of naught."   Helias never saw that fine
bullock again till he found it in a corn-field, a putrefying
carcase.

§ 29.   St. Thomas revivifies a cow

[700] Against this dismal cow-story is another of
encouragement, very pretty and French.[1]   It happened in
Limousin, where a poor man, having lost his single cow,
skinned it, buried it,[2] and then poured tearful complaints—
nay, even demands for his "victualia"—into the ears of
St. Thomas.   Accordingly, "[The Martyr], wishing to
tread in the footsteps of the wonder-working St. Nicholas
('shall I speak out or be silent?'[8]), recalled the dead to
life.   The cottagers were in bed when the reanimated cow
approached the door of the poor plaintiff."   The mother,

---

[2] i. 535-6.   [8] "oratorium."   [1] i. 536-7.
[8] The cow had been good to him, says the writer, so he was good to her,
and spared her from "the sepulture of asses," *i.e.* the birds of prey.   This
perhaps was a French trait.   In England, a sucking pig and a gander, when
dead, are to be "thrown out of doors (projicienda foras)."   See above (633-4).
[3] Virg. *Aeneid*, iii. 39, quoted above (674).

hearing the lowing, bade her son let in the neighbour's cow, for fear the wolves should get at it. "What concern have we," said the sleepy fellow, "with other people's cows, now that we have lost our own?" "Get up, my son," she replied, "we must obey the Lord's word and do by others as we would have them do by us."[4] So the boy let the cow in, and she went at once to her stall. Next morning she was let out to pasture, and, instead of going to her owner, came back to the same stall! And this happened the second day, and the third day! How much longer, we are not told. The writer simply says "saepius," which may mean "rather often," or "more often." In any case, the father of the house seems to have taken several days to be astonished at the cow's conduct. But at last he was astonished. And now, examining the animal more closely and finding some traces of resemblance to his lost cow, he was beginning to bless St. Thomas for her restoration, when he reflected that it would be as well to look for her old carcass and her old skin. He looked for the first; it was not there. He went to the tanner for the second. The tanner, after saying he had it, could not produce it. "I knew," replied the poor man, in triumph, "that the skin could not be found. The cow that I had lost, and the skin that I had taken off her, have been gratuitously restored to me by the Martyr. See, I give you back your money."

[701] Less satisfactory, from the picturesque point of view, is another cow-story, also from France, from the diocese of Quimper.[5] The owner of two oxen recovers both of them from thieves. They had killed and partly skinned one of them, but the animal revives. It does not appear that the farmer gained anything from St. Thomas on this occasion. He had vowed his oxen to the Martyr if he

---

[4] The mother's meaning is clear, the Latin not so clear : "tenemur ex prae-cepto Domini velle idem alii quod nobis volumus fieri."

[5] i. 537 "e regione Lata Via."

recovered them, and to the Martyr he had to pay them. At first, he began to drive them back to his farm; but "seized by a sudden infirmity" he hastily repented and discharged his vow.

§ 30. *Miscellanea*

[702] One Roger (from Valognes in Normandy) is punished for neglect of pilgrimage (though his father had detained him). A second Roger, a notable knight (from Merlai, "de confinio Albaniae et Loegriae") recovers the use of his right little finger; but the candid scribe adds, " the hand, as it seems, is sound, but there are also traces of infirmity." [1]

[703] A lame man describes how he, alone out of five thousand (in the great flood of Holland in May 1173), was saved by St. Thomas. He adds a far more picturesque experience of a neighbour, who, when fleeing from the deluge, had been forced to leave in his cottage (entrusting them to the care of the Martyr) two little children and a cow. After the waters had abated, he returned, in dread of the cruelty of the flood, but in hope of the Martyr's aid. Everything was safe. "'A man in white clothes,' said the little ones, 'brought us bread for ourselves and hay for the cow.' And besides (to the best of their power), describing the Martyr, they also shewed, as a proof of their story, the remains of the bread and the hay." [2]

§ 31. *A story cut short*

[704] William's book concludes with two stories that come from his furthest points to East and West, Lund to the East and Ireland to the West. It will be remembered that Benedict's concluding pages similarly placed the East

---

[1] i. 538-9. For "Loegria," see **783**.   [2] i. 539-40.

and West in juxta-position.[1]   Before these, comes a story
about retribution on the Wends ; and, before that, a
prophecy of a Canterbury monk about the election of a
Canterbury Prior.   This miscellaneous collection is preceded by two miracles related in verse, one located in
Bamberg, the other in Wales.   The whole appears to be of
the nature of an Appendix, the last regular miracle being
one concerning a boy in Northamptonshire, revived when
seemingly dead.[2]

[705] This miracle appears to have been left incomplete.
We might be tempted to suppose that the last page of the
MS. had been torn off.   But the extant portion exhibits so
remarkable an indifference to facts as to suggest that the
writer may have been ill, or indisposed to write, or may
have been prevented by circumstances from finishing his
work.   " Some one," he says, "of good position in a village
of Northampton—*whose name we did not enquire, being
contented to know the miracle*—shewed us his son of about
three years old, whom he constantly asserted to have been
dead.   He also described the process of revivification.   The
boy had expired after a troublesome illness of some days[3] :
the exequies had been paid ; and he lay a corpse for about
three hours.   But by reason of his mother, mourning and
crying that she could not believe Thomas to be Saint or
Martyr unless he manifested his power in her child . . ."

§ 32. *Comic verses*

[706] We may hope that the two (apparently comic)
copies of verses[1] were not from William's hand.   His book,
in its present form, was certainly not presented by him to
the King, and may very well contain the labour of his later
years, perhaps left unfinished, with blank pages that invited
an insertion.   Such a phenomenon would not be half so

---

[1] See above, **587**.   [2] i. 540.   [3] i. 540 " Dies *aliquod* " (sic).
[1] i. 541.

remarkable as the abrupt termination of the Gospel of St. Mark with the words (Mark xvi. 8) " For they were afraid," followed by a fragment acknowledged by competent critics to proceed from a different hand.

[707] The first of these doggerel poems tells how Bortrad from Bamberg became a mother and ceased to be a mother on one and the same day, by the birth and death of her child. St. Thomas restored the babe to life, but the writer asserts that "the city of Bamberg might have seen it, but she sent very few witnesses of it."[2] The second tells how a Welsh leper was cured after apparent failure and tears, and presented himself at Canterbury quite altered, and was warned by the monks to lead a continent life, lest his disease should return.[3]

---

[2] " Urbs Babemberg videre potuit, Sed perpaucos testes adhibuit."

[3] Here is the last part :—

     " Agens ergo gratias venit alteratus
     Et nobis apparuit tanquam transformatus,
     Sic ad unguem faciem totam permundatus
     Ut in ea specie videretur natus.
     Haec videntes diximus, ' Vive continenter ;
     Nam si tibi fuerat (*sic*) dissolutus venter,
     Tollet a te Dominus quod dedit clementer.
     Sic male viventibus contingit frequenter.' "

SECTION V

[708] IT has not been thought necessary to call the reader's attention to occasional condensations or paraphrases of the original in the following parallel stories, as the whole of the Latin is given, in every case, at the foot of the page.

It may be well to add that, in some cases, it has been thought necessary to sacrifice the English to the Latin, where there was a special need to bring out the difference between the two writers, or to illustrate some play of words, antithesis, or other peculiarity, in either writer.

§ 1. *Sir Thomas of Etton is miraculously visited with quinsy and miraculously cured*

[709] Benedict (ii. 92)   William (i. 153)

(1) In the days when   (1) In the county of York, some still disparaged the   a knight, Thomas of Etton Christ of the Lord,[1] Thomas   by name, under the control

---

(1) Quibusdam tamen Christo Do-   (1) In territorio Eboracensi miles
mini [1] adhuc detrahentibus, quum   Thomas de Ectune sub martyris ditione

---

[1] For references, see 1a, and note particularly that black Arabic figures, followed by ordinary Arabics, refer to subsections and paragraphs in the Parallel Miracles. Thus, 709 (3) refers to paragraph 3, in subsection 709.

[1] "Christo Domini," *i.e.* the Anointed of the Lord, a term frequently applied to St. Thomas by Herbert of Bosham.

Benedict (ii. 92)

of Etton, a knight of the province of York, though he had once served the Saint when the latter was discharging the Provostship of Beverley, was himself not ashamed to derogate from his saintliness and honour.

(2) No sooner had he cast the venom of blasphemy against his lord, the Christ of the Lord, than he was smitten, and almost suffocated with what was thought to be a dangerous quinsy.

William (i. 153)

of the Martyr, had discharged the Provostship of Beverley while he himself also filled the office of secretary.[1]

(2) When the Martyr's miracles were noised abroad, he broke out into blasphemy with the glibness of a courtier, calling him a profligate spendthrift, thinking him to be such as he had remembered him to be in old days—if he ever had been so—or rather measuring another's con-

---

audiret hoc de provincia Eboracensi miles, Thomas videlicet de Ethonia, ipse quoque, licet ei olim praeposituram de Beverleia ministranti servierit, ejus sanctitati et gloriae derogare non erubuit.

(2) Non citius in dominum suum, christum Domini, blasphemiae venena jactaverat, quam, juxta quod scriptum est, " Flagellat Dominus omnem filium quem recipit," periculoso, ut putabatur, squinantiae morbo percussus paene praefocatus est.

praeposituram de Beverle ministraverat, dum et ipse scribatus impleret officium.[1]

(2) Qui enarratis vulgo miraculis quibus in martyre ad gloriam legitime certantium Dominus coruscabat, curiali facilitate in blasphemiam erupit, ponens in coelum os suum ; martyrem libidinosi et nebulonis elogio notans, talem nunc reputans qualem multis retro diebus vidisse meminerat, si talis unquam fuerat ; vel potius juxta propriam con-

---

[1] William seems to take the view that the knight of Etton *really* "discharged the duties of the Provostship," although, *in name and office*, merely a " secretary."

Benedict (ii. 92)

William (i. 153)

science by his own. He was therefore struck with a sudden *synanchy;* the avenues of breath were choked ; and he thought every moment he would be suffocated.

(3) Led by this sudden disease to see his guilt, he turned to the Lord with his whole heart, and combined the Martyr's rod with that of penitence and contrition.

(3) Feeling in himself the divine rebuke, he remembered his words, his want of reverence, his ignorant and shameless attack upon holy men. He beat his breast, confessed his guilt with sighs, and sought pardon.

(4) The wonderful justice of the Lord was followed by the wonderful pity of the Lord. No sooner had he offered the Martyr [2] the tears of a penitent heart, than per-

(4) The compassionate heart of the Martyr is unable, yea, unable to persist in punishing those who return to wisdom, and cannot spurn the truly contrite. For with

---

scientiam metiens alienam. Percussus igitur incontinenti synanchia, coarctato vitalis aurae meatu, per singula momenta suffocari putabat.

(3) Advertens autem ex repentina infirmitatis immissione derogationis se reum esse atque correptum, in toto corde conversus ad Dominum, flagellum martyris flagello poenitentiae et contritionis spiritus temperare non distulit.

(3) Sentiens autem in se supervenientem divinae severitatis animadversionem, recordatur quid dixerit, quam fuerit modestiae nescius, et pudoris ignarus in sanctos. Pectus itaque contundit, gemitu suspirioso reatum confitetur, et veniam petit.

(4) Miram Domini justitiam mira Domini pietas est subsecuta. Non enim citius reatus sui poenitens internas cordis lacrymas martyr [2] obtulerat,

(4) Nescit, nescit martyris misericordia resipiscentes insequi, vere contritos aspernari. Nam sub ea celeritate qua obloquentem percussit, resipi-

---

[2] "Martyr" must be a misprint for "martyri."

Benedict (ii. 92)	William (i. 153)
fect peace came back and all his pain vanished,	the same speed with which he smote he cured.
	For [the sin of] speaking anathema, the man was straitened in spirit [or, "*breath*," there is a play on the word "spiritu"]; for [the merit of] speaking in the holy spirit, he obtained free breathing through the throat that had been but now closed.
(5) and, when fit time occurred, hastening to the Saint's Memorial,[3] he testified that he had also in after times been freed from violent fevers by calling on the Martyr.	(5) omitted.

Little comment is required on these two narratives, as the facts are simple and the two agree. William's appears to be the later. He gives fuller details than Benedict's about the knight's office in Beverley, and about the nature and motives of his slander. (1) Where Benedict praises the Lord, William praises the Martyr; (2) the latter also prefers the manifestly Greek term " synanchy " to

quam omnimodo redeunte quiete totus ille dolor in nihilum evanuit,	scentem sanavit. Anathema locutus, spiritu arctatus est ; in spiritu sancto locutus, gutturis intercepti liberum spiramen consecutus est.
(5) et occurrente tempore opportuno ad sancti festinans memoriam,[3] etiam a febribus validis se postea per martyris invocationem liberatum testatus est.	(5) omitted.

[3] " Memoriam," often used for " tomb."

the French-Greek form, "squinantia," and (3) shews a greater proneness to playing on words. All these differences are characteristic of William's general style as compared with Benedict's. There is nothing to prove that William had seen the earlier narrative : but he gives the impression that he had read it and is endeavouring to improve on it.

§ 2. *Eilward of Westoning in Bedfordshire, mutilated for theft, is miraculously restored*

[710] (i.) Benedict (ii. 173-82)

William (i. 155-8)

(1) There was one of the common folk,[1] Eilward by name, in the king's town of Weston in the county of Bedford. One of his neighbours, Fulk, owed him a *denarius* as part of rent for cornland, and put off payment on the excuse of not having the money.[2]   One day, a

(1) This[1] Ailward had a neighbour in his debt. When, on demanding it, he met with a refusal,

---

(1) Erat plebeius[1] quidam in villa regia Westona in territorio Bedefordensi, Eilwardus nomine, cui ex vicinis suis quidam Fulco pro dimidii jugeris aratura duorum denariorum debito tenebatur. Qui, altero reddito, alterius solutionem usque in annum sequentem, sub non habentis specie, protelavit.[2]   Die

(1) Ordinem rei non ab re esse putamus ad confirmationem posteritatis in fide dilucidare. Huic igitur Ailwardo[1] vicinus tenebatur in nummo ; quem cum repeteret, et ille solvere recusaret,

---

[1] "*Plebeius*" is very seldom used in introducing the common folk who are the most frequent subjects of miracles in Benedict's treatise.   But this is one of the few instances where there seems to have been an anti-Norman feeling, or, at all events, a sense that a man of low degree had been unfairly treated by the authorities.
[2] The whole rent was two *denarii* for half an acre (pro dimidii jugeris aratura).

[1] William has placed at the head of his narrative a letter of attestation from the burgesses of Bedford.   This mentions Ailward by name.   Hence he begins thus abruptly with "this Ailward."   William spells the name "Ailward" (once "Ailword") ; Benedict "Eilward."

Benedict (ii. 173-82)

William (i. 155-8)

holiday, when they were going to the alehouse together, as is the English custom, Eilward asked for his money, and Fulk denied [the debt] on oath. Then Eilward bade him pay half, as he was going to have some beer, and keep the other half for himself for beer likewise. On Fulk's still refusing, the other said he would be even with him.

(2) After they had both got drunk, Eilward, leaving the ale-house before the other, turned aside to Fulk's cottage, tore away the bar, burst into the house, and carried away

(2) Ailward in a rage, rushing into his debtor's house—which the latter had fastened with a bar that hung down from the outside when he turned aside [2] to the tavern

---

quodam festo post beati martyris passionem, cum forte simul ad tabernam proficiscerentur (moris enim est Anglis feriantibus commessationibus et ebrietatibus indulgere, ut videant hostes et derideant sabbata eorum), exigente isto debitum, abjurat ille. Postulat iste ut eunti ad cervisiam saltem dimidium sibi solvat debiti, dimidio ad simile negotium sibi ipsi retento ; negante hoc nihilominus debitore, talionem se redditurum minatur exactor.

(2) Utroque ad tabernam inebriato, surgens praetaxatus Eilwardus debitorem suum praecessit, et ad domum ejus

(2) motus ira domum debitoris, quam sera exterius dependente ad tabernam digressus [2] obfirmaverat, ir-

---

[2] William perhaps argued that "turn aside" must mean going to the inn ("diversorium"). Benedict says that Eilward "turned aside" to Fulk's cottage, instead of going straight home.

Benedict (ii. 173-82)

a great grindstone and a pair of gloves, both scarcely of the value of a *nummus*. The boys, who were playing in the courtyard, cried out, and running to the tavern called their father out to reclaim his property. Fulk followed the thief, broke the man's head with the grindstone,[8] wounded him in the arm with a knife, brought him back to the cottage, bound him, and

divertens, avulsa ostii sera, tam impetuosus quam ebrius effractor, domum irrupit. Evolvens domum, quaerensque quid auferat, cotem magnam offendit, et chirothecas, qualibus ruricolae contra spinarum aculeos manus armare consueverunt ; sublatis utrisque vix pretium nummi praedo pauper asportavit. Exclamant pueri in atrio domus colludentes, et concurrentes ad tabernam, patrem suum evocant ut praedam excutiat. At ille hominem persecutus cotem extorsit, et eadem in caput praedonis vibrata, tam cotem in capite quam caput cote confregit.[3] Exserto quoque cuspidis acutae cultello quem ferebat, brachium ejusdem perforavit. Praevaluit adversus eum, miserumque, ut furem, ut raptorem, ut effractorem reducens, in domo, quam effregerat, colligavit.

William (i. 155-8)

—tore away the bar as a pledge, and seizing at the same time a grindstone placed on the roof of the cottage, together with an awl[3] and a pair of gloves, went off. Word was then carried to their father by the boys, who were shut up in[4] the house at play, that a thief had broken in and gone off with plunder. Fulk followed him, wrested the grindstone from his hand

rumpens, seram in pignus avulsit, arreptaque simul cote apposita tecto casae, cum terebro[3] chirothecisque, discessit. Nuntiatum est autem a pueris, qui infra domum ludebant inclusi,[4] patrifamilias, quia confracta domo, supellectilique direpta, raptor abscederet. Qui insecutus eum comprehendit, et cotem a

---

[3] Benedict, who is very diffuse here, and evidently takes great pity on "the poor robber," says that Fulk also broke the grindstone on Eilward's head. The version given above is condensed ; the original, though verbose, omits some facts mentioned by William.

[3] The "awl" is mentioned by Benedict (note 4) among articles *not* taken by the prisoner.

[4] William seems to think that Fulk would not have locked his cottage from the outside except to *shut the boys in* (? "infra" misprint for "intra"). This seems contrary to Benedict's "in the courtyard."

Benedict (ii. 173-82)

William (i. 155-8)

and wounded his head [with it]. Then, drawing a knife, he pierced his arm, and, bringing him back as a thief taken in the act, bound him in the house he had broken into.

(3) (he) called in Fulk the beadle of the village, to know what he must do with his prisoner. "The charge," said the beadle, "is not heavy enough. If you tie a few more things round the prisoner and produce him thus, you can accuse him of breaking the law." The debtor agreed, and fastened round his prisoner's neck an awl,[4] a two-edged axe, a net, and some

(3) When a crowd gathered,[5] with Fulk the beadle, it was suggested by the beadle —because stealing under the value of one *nummus* does not subject a man to mutilation—that he should add to the number of the things stolen. So there was placed close to the prisoner a bundle of skins, cloaks, napkins, gowns, with a tool commonly called a "volgonium." Next

manu bajulantis extorquens caput vulneravit. Extractoque cultello brachium transfigens, eum quasi furem manifestum cum concepto furto reductum ligavit in domo quam fregerat.

(3) Accersit deinde praeconem villae Fulconem ; quid facto opus sit interrogat. At ille, " Brevis," inquit, " et insufficiens est causa pro qua captus est ; si vero, aucto furto, aliis rebus quasi furtivis oneratum produxeris, plectendi eum sceleris poteris accusare." Acquievit ille, et terebro,[4] bisacuta, reti, vestibusque nonnullis simul cum

(3) Concurrente autem turba,[5] cum apparitore Fulcone, quia res furtiva pretii unius nummi hominem non mutilat, suggestum est ab apparitore ut furtum rebus aliis, quasi furtivis, augeret ; quod et factum est. Posita est itaque juxta ligatum sarcinula pellium, laenae, lintei, togae, cum ferramento quod volgonium vulgus appellat. Postera die

---

[4] "Awl." See note 3 on William's account.

[5] Why does William add these words ? Is it to convict Fulk the beadle of giving this infamous advice ? Without the presence of witnesses, he could not be convicted.

clothes, together with the grindstone and the gloves, and on the following day brought him thus before the king's officers.

(4) So having been taken to Bedford he was kept in the prison there for a month. He sent for a priest, in whose hearing (after confessing his sins) he vowed a pilgrimage to Jerusalem if he escaped, and he, begged that he might be branded with a cross on

day he was led to trial before one Richard, a viscount, and the knights with him, with the above-mentioned bundle fastened round his neck.

(4) The matter being doubtful, in order to avoid a hasty decision, the prisoner was remanded for a month to custody in Bedford. Meantime he secretly[6] sent for a village priest, who heard him confess, and advised him to appeal to the protection of

---

cote et chirothecis in collo illius colligatis, officialibus regis die postera praesentavit.

(4) Tractus itaque Bedefordiam in custodia publica mense uno tentus est, et accito presbytero quodam venerabili, Pagano, utpote periculis extremis expositus, ad mortem, immo et ad vitam, se praeparat, et omnia conscientiae suae secreta evolvens, quicquid saluti contrarium invenit in tutis presbyteri auribus effundit. Sed et de corporis sui liberatione spem suam divinae miserationi committens, "Domine," inquit, "carissime, terram quam Dei Filius, Dominus noster Jesus, et vita temporali sanctificavit et morte, pedes adibo, si necessitatis instantis articulum evasero. Unde et humero meo dextro candenti ferro signum crucis precor

ad cognitionem Ricardi cujusdam vicecomitis militumque comitatus cum praedicta sarcinula ductus est, quae et collo ejus appensa est.

(4) Ne autem de re dubia praecipitaretur sententia, in publica custodia Bedeford suspenso judicio per mensem tentus est. Interim clam[6] vocato Pagano presbytero suos excessus omnes ab ineunte aetate confessus est; a quo et

---

[6] Omitted here by Benedict, who however states that the priest's access was subsequently forbidden; and this suggests that it was secret from the first.

Benedict (ii. 173-82)	William (i. 155-8)
the shoulder. The Priest branded him accordingly, but also suggested that he should seek the protection of the Saints, and especially of St. Thomas, measuring his body for the length and thickness of a candle to be offered to the Martyr, and also giving him a bundle of rods that self-punishment might accompany his invocations. Then he left him, saying that the judges had forbidden any priest to have further access to the accused. However	the blessed Mary and all the Saints, and especially St. Thomas ; to put away anger; not to distrust God's compassion; and to bear patiently what he might have to suffer, looking to remission of sins : —and that, all the more earnestly because, having been christened on Whitsuneve, he could not sink in water or be burned in fire (according to the common belief) if he had to undergo either of these ordeals.[7] He also gave him a rod for self-

inuri, quod mihi, licet vestes auferantur, auferre nemo praevaleat." Fecit ille ut fuerat rogatus, commonens ut ad sanctorum suffragia devotus confugeret, maxime vero gloriosi martyris Thomae, quem Dominus tanta signorum gloria mirificavit. Filo praeterea longitudinem latitudinemque corporis ejus mensus est, unde factam candelam sancto martyri liberatus offerret. Flagellum etiam de virgis ei praebens, "Accipe," inquit, "virgas istas, et cum invocatione martyris quinquies quotidie priusquam gustes tibi ipsi tortor existe, nec cesses ad martyrem die noctuve genua flectere, martyrem invocare, nisi cum, importunitate somni gravatus, naturae deficienti cogeris succurrere." Diligentius igitur instructum dimisit, inhibitum esse a judicibus asseverans, ne ullus presbyterorum ulterius ad eum haberet accessum. Mittebat tamen saepenumero

monitus est suffragia Beatae Mariae sanctorumque omnium, et maxime beati Thomae, quem Dominus virtutum et signorum indiciis glorificare dignatus est, suppliciter implorare ; omnem iram et incentivum odiorum ab animo secludere ; de Dei misericordia non diffidere, et quicquid pati cogeretur, aequanimiter in remissionem peccatorum sustinere, et eo attentius quod vigilia Pentecostes ipse parvulus regeneratus aqua submergi vel igne cremari non posset, sicut vulgaris habet opinio, si judicium alterutrum subiturus esset[7]; virgamque dedit qua quinquies in die suscepta

---

[7] "Ordeals." See note 9, below.

Benedict (ii. 173-82)

the Priest still sent messages to his window to comfort and strengthen him in secret. Also the Prior of Bedford often supplied him with food, visited him and had him out for a breathing-space now and then, in the open air.

(5) At the beginning of the fifth week he was had up for trial. On his asserting that he took what he took, as a pledge, and that he did not take the other articles at

William (i. 155-8)

discipline. The man willingly heard him ; he also measured the thickness of his own[8] body, devoting himself to the Martyr, and promising a better life. Moreover, fearing that his clothes might be taken from him he imprinted the sign of the cross with a hot iron on his shoulder.

(5) It came to pass that, as the magistrates were meeting at Leighton Buzzard, the accused was taken thither. Thereupon he demanded trial by battle, or else ordeal by

---

qui eum occulte per fenestram ad indicta sibi vel negligentem excitaret, vel studiosum magis accenderet. Sed et prior canonicorum de Bedfordia Gaufridus, quem et hujus admirandi miraculi testem habemus, victus ei necessario saepius administrabat, saepius incarceratum visitabat, et ut saltem ad horam respiraret, eductum de carcere sub divo deambulare faciebat.

(5) Jam quatuor septimanis exactis, quintae principium advenerat, quum eductus miser de carcere ad concilium trahitur judicandus. Impetit eum accusator crimine furti ; impositum crimen constantius ille repellit, et omnibus quae sibi a collo pendebant longius excussis, de cote duntaxat fatetur et chirothecis, quod eas in pignus pro debito acceperit ;

disciplina Dei misericordiam in se provocaret. Qui monita libenter audiens, circumducto filo corpori suo[8] martyri se devovit, emendatiorem vitam promittens, timensque sibi panniculos suos diripi, in dextro humero calido ferro signum crucis impressit.

(5) Factum est autem ut convenientibus ad vicum Legtune magistratibus reus eo duceretur. Ubi cum impetitore suo Fulcone monomachiam inire aut judicium ignis subire postulavit ; sed

---

[8] The difference between Benedict and William is represented by the difference between "ejus" and "suum," which are often confused in these books.

Benedict (ii. 173-82)	William (j. 155-8)
all, he was again remanded to prison. In the fifth week he was again tried on the charge of stealing simply the grindstone and the gloves. For the accuser, fearing to undergo the ordeal of battle demanded by the accused, condemned by silence all his previous charges, and—having on his side the viscount and the judges—managed to free himself from obligation to fight, and to secure that the accused should be tried by ordeal of water.	fire ; but by the assent of the beadle Fulk—who had received an ox to bring this about—he was bound over to ordeal by water, lest he should by any possibility escape.⁹

furtum et scelus omnimodum inficiatur. Dilato judicio, carcerali rursus mancipatur custodiae. Itaque quinta post hebdomada extractus, et tractus item ad concilium, super cotis tantummodo et chirothecarum furto ab adversario suo impetitur. Ille enim, quia postulante reo monomachiam inire sibi metuebat, omnia quibus illum ante insimulaverat silentio damnavit, et vicecomitem judicesque habens sibi propitios, ut a duelli necessitate seipsum excuteret, et alter aquae judicio examinaretur, obtinuit.

annuente Fulcone apparitore, qui ob id ipsum bovem acceperat, judicio aquae adjudicatus est, ne quoquo modo evadere posset.⁹

⁹ Being born on Whitsun eve (see 710 (4) above), he could not "sink (submergi)." Being unable to "sink," he was sure to be condemned on this ordeal. This seems to be the meaning of the obscure passage : and hence William inserts mention of the Whitsun superstition in 710 (4).

Benedict (ii. 173-82)

(6) Now it was the Sab-
bath, and the examination
was put off till the third day
of the following week, he
himself being again kept in
prison, and not allowed by
the cruelty of his keeper to
keep vigil in the church—a
right conceded by the compassion of religion to all that
are to purge themselves [by
ordeal] from criminal charge.
In prison, however, he de-
voutly kept the watch that
he was not allowed to keep
in the church.

When brought out to the
water [-ordeal], he was met
by the village priest, who exhorted him to bear all pati-
ently, looking to remission of

William (i. 155-8)

(6) Then he was taken
back to Bedford for a month.[10]

(6) Erat autem sabbatum, et usque
in feriam tertiam hebdomadae sequentis
examinatio dilata est, ipso iterum con-
servato in carcere. Vigiliam in ecclesia,
quam seipsos a crimine purgaturis con-
cessit Christianae religionis pietas,
negavit ei custodis crudelitas. In carcere tamen excubias devotus celebravit,
quas ei in ecclesia celebrare non licuit.

Educto ad aquam obvius venit
presbyter praenominatus, Paganus,
commonens omnia aequanimiter in
peccatorum remissionem sustinere,

(6) Inde Bedeford reductus, in carcere mensem exegit.[10]

[10] Did William derive his "month"
from some corruption of Benedict's "in
feriam iii hebdomadae," e.g. "in fere
jam v hebdomadā"?

Benedict (ii. 173-82)

William (i. 155-8)

sins, to entertain no anger in his heart, to forgive all his enemies heartily [all they had done to him], and not to despair of the compassion of God.[5] He replied, "May the will of God and the Martyr Thomas be fulfilled in me."

(7) When plunged into the water he was found guilty. The beadle, Fulk, now seized him, saying, "This way, rascal, this way!" "Thanks be to God," said the other, "and to the holy Martyr Thomas!" Dragged to the place of execution, he was deprived of his eyes, and also mutilated according to law. As for his left eye,

(7) Thither the judges assembled, and after he had been delivered over to be tried by ordeal of water, he received the sad sentence of condemnation. He was then led to the place of execution. His eyes were gouged out. The privy members were also cut off in accordance with the law of mutilation and buried in the earth in the

---

odium et iram in animo non habere, omnibus adversariis suis omnia ex corde dimittere, et de Dei misericordia non desperare.[5] At ille, "Fiat," inquit, "Dei et martyris Thomae voluntas in me!"

(7) Demissus in aquam reus deprehenditur ; quem praeco praedictus Fulco arripiens, "Huc," inquit, "scelerate, huc venies ad me." Et ille, "Deo gratias et sancto martyri Thomae!" Tractus itaque ad locum supplicii, orbatur oculis, genitalibus mutilatur. Et oculum quidem sinistrum

(7) Quo convenientibus judicibus, cum judicio aquae traderetur examinandus, damnationis suae tristem excepit sententiam, eductusque ad locum supplicii, oculis effossis et virilibus abscisis mutilatus est, quae multitudine

---

[5] William has similar words above, in (4).

Benedict (ii. 173-82)

they at once extracted that, whole ; as for the right, after being lacerated and chopped to pieces it was at last with difficulty gouged out. The members of which he had been deprived by mutilation they hid under the sod ; and (in accordance with what is read about the man that " fell among robbers ") they stripped him, and, after inflicting wounds[6] on him as aforesaid, they " departed, leaving him half dead."

He was mutilated by his accuser Fulk, and the official of the same name (by whose suggestion and advice the man is believed to have been brought into this misery), and

William (i. 155-8)

sight of a multitude of the common folk.

All the time he was suffering, he ceased not to implore the help of God, and to invoke St. Thomas, forgiving the torturers all their cruelty towards him.

statim integrum eruerunt ; dexter autem, laceratus et in frusta concisus, vix tandem effossus est. Membra, quibus eum mutilaverant, sub cespite absconderunt, et, juxta quod de illo legitur qui incidit in latrones, despoliaverunt eum, et plagis,[6] ut praedictum est, impositis, abierunt, semivivo relicto. Confluxerat ad spectaculum non parva populi multitudo, quibusdam nomine publicae potestatis compulsis, quibusdam curiositate attractis. Mutilaverant eum accusator ejus Fulco et ejusdem nominis regis officialis, cujus instinctu consilioque in tantam creditur devenisse

vidente plebis terrae infossa sunt. Inter plectendum, divinum auxilium implorare non cessabat, et beatum Thomam invocare, remittens tortoribus quicquid in se crudeliter egerant.

[6] " Plagis " must mean the blows with the knife above-mentioned.

Benedict (ii. 173-82)

William (i. 155-8)

also by two other execu-
tioners with them : whom,
however, when they asked
pardon, for the love of God
and St. Thomas the Martyr
he freely forgave, crying aloud
that he would go to the Martyr's memorial, blind though
he was, and persisting in the
cry with a wonderful faith—
knowing that it was more
glorious for the Martyr to
restore eyes that had been
taken away than to preserve
them when not taken.

(8) He was attended by
none but his daughter, twelve
years old, who had also
begged food for him when in
prison. For, as all his goods
were confiscated, all his friends
spurned him, and there was
no one, of all those dear to

(8) After the infliction of
his punishment, he was led
into the town and hospitably
received by one Ailbricht.

---

miseriam, et cum iis lictores alii duo ;
quibus tamen veniam petentibus pro
Dei et sancti Thomae martyris amore
libenter indulsit, martyris memoriam
aditurum se, licet lumine orbatum,
admiranda fide inclamitans, de martyris
pietate virtuteque non diffidere ; martyri
sciens gloriosius esse oculos restituere
perditos, quam non ablatos conservasse.

(8) Secuta eum fuerat sola filia sua
duodennis, quae et incarcerato ali-
moniam mendicaverat. Confiscatis
enim omnibus quae habuerat, omnes
amici ejus spreverunt eum, nec erat qui

(8) Peracto supplicio, vicum in-
ductus est, et exceptus hospitio cujusdam Ailbrichti.

Benedict (ii. 173-82)   William (i. 155-8)

him, to take compassion on
him.   Such a stream of blood
gushed from his wounds that,
in fear of his death, those
who were present sent for a
priest.   To him he confessed.
By degrees, however, when
the flow of blood was as-
suaged, led by the little girl,
he returned to Bedford, where
he threw himself down against
the wall of a house ; and all
that day, till evening, no man
shewed him kindness.   But
at nightfall, one Eilbrict took
compassion on him, and willingly welcomed him into his
house from the cold and rain.

    (9) There, after many   (9) There ten days passed.
vigils and prayers, in the   One night, before sleeping-

---

consolaretur eum ex omnibus caris ejus.
De vulneribus ejus tanta sanguinis
emanavit copia, ut metu mortis sus-
pectae presbyterum accersirent qui
aderant; cui et confessus est.   Paulatim
tamen cruoris fluxu restricto, ductu
puellulae in villam   Bedfordensem
rediens, et juxta parietem domus se
projiciens, diem illum nullo sibi collato
humanitatis beneficio duxit ad vesperam.
Succedente   jam   noctis crepusculo,
misertus   ejus   vir   quidam   nomine
Eilbrictus, maxime quia aeris incle-
mentia et pluviarum inundatio sub divo
jacentem plurimum molestasset, excepit
illum gaudens in domum suam.

    (9) Fecit igitur in tenebris dies   (9) Quo decem evolutis diebus,
decem, vigiliis orationibusque dans   una noctium ante conticinium beatum

first watch of the tenth night, he whom he had invoked appeared to Eilward in his sleep, clothed in snow-white garments, with his pastoral staff painting the sign of the cross on his forehead and on his eyeless sockets. A second time he appeared, before dawn, bidding him persevere in watching and praying, and place his hope in God, and the blessed Virgin Mary, and St. Thomas who had come to visit him : " If, on the

operam. Nocte vero diei decimi, prima noctis vigilia, post luctus, gemitus, et suspiria in somnum resoluto apparuit quem invocaverat, nivei candoris vestibus indutus, baculoque pastorali signum crucis in fronte ejus et oculorum foraminibus depingens, sub silentio discedere visus est. Expergefactus ille et visionis negligens projecit se rursus et obdormivit. Iterum ergo ante lucanum rediit in albis qui in sanguine Agni vestes suas dealbaverat ; dixitque viro, " Homo bone, dormis ? " Vigilare se fatenti, " Noli," ait, " noli dormire, sed vigila, insiste orationibus. Noli diffidere, sed spem tuam in Deo

time, he saw St. Thomas (whom he had been constantly all the time invoking) clothed in white, imprinting, between his eyebrows, the sign of the cross with his pastoral staff, and again doing the same thing before dawn, and saying " Sleepest thou, good man ? Watch ! To-morrow must thou keep vigil at the altar of the blessed Mary with a light.[11] Lo, Thomas hath come to thee and thou shalt receive sight." [12] Also, after

Thomam, quem assidue vocabat, vidit in somnis, alba veste indutum, sibi inter supercilia baculo pastorali signum crucis imprimentem, denuoque ante lucanum idem facientem, et dicentem, " Homo bone, dormis ? Vigila ; die crastina tibi est ad altare beatae Mariae cum lucerna [11] excubandum. Ecce venit ad te Thomas, et visum recipies." [12]

[11] " Lucerna," see Benedict, footnote 7.

[12] Note that, whereas Benedict makes the recovery of sight conditional on the vigil in St. Mary's church, William does not. The next section will shew that he received his sight *before* that vigil. So that Benedict is inconsistent with himself.

Benedict (ii. 173-82)

night of the morrow, thou keep watch with a waxen light [7] before the altar of the blessed Mary in her church close by, and devote thyself to prayer, in faith, and without doubting, thou shalt be gladdened by the restoration of thine eyes." The maid-servant also had a similar dream. When she told it to Eilward, he replied, "So it may be when it shall please God and His blessed Martyr, Thomas."

(10) When it was growing toward evening and the

William (i. 155-8)

sunrise, the maid-servant told Ailward a dream to the same effect. He replied, "Even this is possible with the Lord, as indeed all things are possible."

(10) When the sun was toward setting, the left eye

---

et beata virgine Maria pone, et sancto Thoma, qui te venit visitare ; ei si nocte proxima in ecclesia beatae Mariae vicina, coram virginis ejusdem altari, cum lucerna [7] cerea excubaveris, et orationibus incumbens in fide non haesitaveris, oculorum restitutione gaudebis." Excusso somno tractat homo secum tacite quid visio talis portendere possit ; utrumve potius integumento remoto promissio sancti mancipetur effectui. Talia secreto volventi, quasi dextri ominis nuntia, respondit domus ancilla, "Videbam hac nocte in somnis, Eilwarde, te utriusque oculi visum recuperare." At ille, "Sic fieri poterit, cum Deo et beato martyri ejus Thomae placuerit."

(10) Cumque advesperasceret et

Orto autem sole dixit ancilla, "Videbam in somnis, Ailworde, te visum recuperasse." Respondit, "Possibile est hoc Domino, sicut et omnia possibilia sunt."

(10) Inclinata vero die, pruriente

---

[7] "Lucerna," rarely thus used in either treatise.

Benedict (ii. 173-82)	William (i. 155-8)
sun was toward setting,[8] the eyelids of his left eye began to itch. In order to scratch them, he removed a waxen poultice which had been applied, either for the purpose of drawing out the purulent matter of the empty orbs, or for the purpose of closing the eye-lids themselves : and, as by the wonderful power of God [9] he opened his eye-lids, there was seen to shine in on the house-wall in front of him as it were the brightness of a lantern : for it was the red sunlight, since the sun was by this time verg-	began to itch ; and in the act of scratching it, he removed some wax and a poultice that had been applied to draw out the purulent matter. Seeing the sun-light on the wall, he exclaimed, "Praised be God, I see." His host, dumb-founded, replied, " What is the matter ? You are mad " ; and, drawing [13] away (?) his hands before the man's eyes, "You see," said he, " that which I am doing ? " He replied, " I see your hand moved."

inclinata esset jam dies,[8] prurientibus sibi oculi sinistri ciliis, ut ea ungue scalperet, malagma cereum, quod sive ad extrahendas orbium vacuorum purulentias, seu ad ipsa cilia claudenda fuerat appositum, amovit ; ciliaque mira Dei virtute aperienti videbatur [9] in opposito domus pariete quasi lucernae splendor irradiare ; erat enim radius solaris rubens, sole jam ad occasum

sinistro oculo, scalpens ungue ceram summovit et malagma quod appositum fuerat ad purulentias extrahendas. Visoque radio solis in pariete, exclama-vit, " Adoretur Deus ! video." Ad quam vocem hospes obstupescens ait, " Quid est ? deliras." Et ante oculos ejus deducta [13] manu sua, " Vides," inquit, " quod ago ? " Respondit, " Video motam manum."

---

[8] "Inclinata dies" seems to have this meaning, since it (1) follows "advesperascere," and (2) precedes "vergente ad occasum."

[9] "Ciliaque *mira Dei virtute aperienti* videbatur." The italicized words seem misplaced. The sense demands "there was seen by the mighty power of God."

[13] See Benedict, note 10.

Benedict (ii. 173-82)

ing toward his going down.
But he, ignorant of the truth,
and distrusting himself about
the matter, called the master
of the house, and shewed
him his fancy. "You are
mad, Eilward, you are mad,"
replied his host: "be silent!
You know not what you
are saying." "Sir," he said,
"I assure you I am not mad:
but I verily seem to myself
to see as I say with my left
eye." Shaken in his mind,
and anxious to ascertain the
truth, his host spread out [10]
his hand before his eyes and
said to him, "Do you see
that which I am doing?" He
answered, "Your hand is

vergente. Ignarus tamen veritatis, et
sibi ipsi super hoc incredulus, dominum
domus vocavit, quid opinaretur ostendit.
Cui ille, "Insanis, Eilwarde, insanis:
tace, nescis quid loqueris." "Nequaquam," inquit, "domine, insanio; sed
ita revera oculo sinistro mihi videre
videor." Fluctuans autem hospes ejus,
certitudinisque sciendae sollicitus, manu
ante oculos ejus diducta,[10] dixit ei,
"Videsne quod ago?" Respondit,

[10] "Diducit," in classical Latin,
implies the outspread hand as distinguished from the closed fist. But
here it may mean "move in different
directions." William's "deducta" is
probably an error of transcription.

Benedict (ii. 173-82)

moved before my eyes and drawn this way and that." Then he told Eilbricht, in order, all about his visions, and the precepts or promises he had received.

(11) The thing was noised abroad. A multitude collected, and, among them, Osbern the dean—who had control, or rather service, of the above-mentioned church.[11] He brought the good man before the altar, instructed and strengthened his faith, and then placed a light in his hand. As soon as this was done, Eilward declared he distinctly saw the altar cloth ; then, the image of

William (i. 155-8)

(11) So they called the dean of the town. The crowd streamed together, and Ailward was snatched away and taken to the house of prayer. Now there began to grow up little eyes of extreme smallness, the right one perfectly black, the left parti-coloured, whereas he had both parti-coloured from his birth.

" Puto manum tuam motam ante oculos meos huc illucque duci." Tunc a principio primae visionis incipiens, quid viderit, quid sibi vel praeceptum fuerit vel promissum, seriatim enarravit.

(11) Exiit ergo sermo iste inter vicinos, et populi multitudinem non parvam novitatum novitas attraxit. Accurrit et Osebernus decanus, ecclesiae· praedictae dominus, aut potius minister [11] ; et audita viri visione, virum in ecclesiam introducit, collocat coram beatae Virginis altari, instruit et confortat ad fidem. Data in manu ejus lucerna, pallam altaris se perspicue

(11) Igitur vocato ejusdem villae decano, et confluente turba, direptus est, et in oratorium ductus. Succrescebant autem nimiae parvitatis ocelli, dexter penitus niger, et sinister varius, cum varios ambos habuerit a nativitate.

---

[11] i.e. St. Mary's. Benedict corrects the common phrase "dominus ecclesiae," as not being so seemly as "minister."

Benedict (ii. 173-82)

the blessed Virgin Mary; then, objects of smaller size.

The people marvelled more and more. Presently, testing the source of his sight, they detect two very small pupils latent, deep in the head, scarcely as large as the pupils of the eye of a little bird. These, also, incessantly increasing, prolonged by their slow augmentation the wonder of all that beheld them. The shouts of the people went up to heaven; they give God due praise; the bells are set ringing; crowds flock in from their beds; keeping vigil with their brother who had received the gift of light, they sleeplessly await the light of the sun.

In the morning, the whole of the town gathered together, and then, examining the man more closely, they found that whereas, before, both his eyes were parti-coloured, now he had one parti-coloured, but the other quite black. Now came, among others, the priest of St. John's church, the same who had received Eilward's confession after mutilation. When he beheld the wonderful miracle of God, " Why," said he, " do we wait for papal precept ? No more delaying for me ! This very moment will I begin, and conduct to the end, a solemn service, in the name

---

videre fatetur: deinde beatae Mariae virginis imaginem, postremo quaelibet alia minoris corpora quantitatis. Crescit stupor populo quantum viro gratia visus. Probaturi unde procedat vis illa videndi, ab oculis videlicet novis, an ab evacuatis foraminibus absque pupilla, deprehendunt pupillas duas parvulas profundius in capite latitantes, pupillis avis parvae vix quantitate coaequas, quae, etiam incessanter crescentes, omnibus intuentibus ineffabilem incredibilemque stuporem lenta sui augmentatione continuabant. Attollitur igitur ad coelum clamor populi, laudes Deo debitae persolvuntur, signa pulsantur ecclesiae, confluunt plurimi, qui jam obdormierant, et cum illuminato suo lumen solis insomnes expectant. Mane autem turba totius villae in unum conglobata diligentius clara luce intuentes, alterum oculorum varium, alterum prorsus nigrum adverterunt, quum natales ambos varios habuerit. Accurrit autem inter alios et presbyter de ecclesia sancti Johannis, qui mutilati confessionem susceperat, et mira Dei visa virtute, "Quid," inquit, "auctoritatis apostolicae praestolamur praeceptum ? Absit ut ulterius exspectem; jam nunc

Benedict (ii. 173-82)

of Thomas the glorious friend of God, since in truth he is a martyr beyond price. Who can hesitate to give the name of martyr to one who does such mighty and such merciful deeds?" So he ran to his church, set the bells ringing, and was as good as his word.

(12) Now no longer bereft of light but bedecked therewith, even as he had been dragged with ignominy through the midst of the town to endure his punishment, so now through the self-same street, amid the praise and applause of the people, he was led back to the church of St. Paul, where also he passed the eve of the Lord's day in vigil. Departing thence he hastened

(12) See the Latin below.

---

de glorioso Dei amico Thoma, utpote de martyre pretiosissimo, solenne inchoabo servitium, et ad finem usque complebo. Quis ambigat martyrem esse, qui tanta facit et talia?" et ad ecclesiam currens, pulsatis signis, dicta factis implevit.

(12) Vir autem, non jam orbatus lumine, dico, sed ornatus, sicut per medium villae cum ignominia fuerat tractus ad poenam, ita et eadem via cum gloria populi et favore reducitur ad sancti Pauli ecclesiam, in qua etiam noctem Dominicam duxit insomnem. Inde discedens ad salutis suae auctorem

(12) Genitalia vero, quae cuilibet palpanda praebebat, infra quantitatem testium galli poterant aestimari.

Benedict (ii. 173-82)	William (i. 155-8)

his journey to St. Thomas, the author of his restoration. Whatever gifts folk gave him, he bestowed on the poor, for love of the Martyr. . . .

(13) On his coming to London, he was received with congratulations by Hugh, Bishop of Durham, who would not let him go from himself, till he had sent a messenger to Bedford and had been certified of the facts after diligent inquiry.

(13) William omits this. [But he inserts, later in his treatise, a letter from this bishop, speaking of a similar miracle as (i. 420) " of a new kind conceded by the Divine munificence to our St. Thomas ; which we *heard to have taken place long ago at Bedford*, and know to have been afterwards repeated in our city of Durham."]

(14) But even after we   (14) The things that we

Thomam iter arripuit. Quacunque transibat, sequebatur eum multitudo plebis copiosa ; fama namque prae-volans in occursum ejus quoslibet ex-citavit. Quicquid ei muneris confere-bant, pro martyris amore pauperibus erogabat. Quasi quatuor passuum millia confecerat, cum prurientem sibi testium folliculum adjecta manu scal-pere coepit ; et etiam membra illa sibi restituta comperit, parva quidem valde sed in majus proficientia, quae etiam volenti cuilibet palpare non negavit.

(13) Londonias venientem episcopus Dunelmensis Hugo gratulabundus ex-cepit, nec ante a se dimittere voluit, quam misso Bedefordiam nuntio et diligenter inquisita veritate certificatus fuisset.

(13) omitted.

(14) Sed, et apud nos eodem sus-

(14) Quae vidimus et audivimus

Benedict (ii. 173-82)	William (i. 155-8)
had received him in our house at Canterbury, although he had been preceded by the testimony of very many witnesses, yet we did not feel satisfied till we heard the substance of the above-written statements confirmed by the letter and testimony [12] of the citizens of Bedford. For they directed to us a document of which the contents were as follows :	have heard and seen we speak and testify. For he of whom we speak, having been sent to Canterbury, remained many days with us, receiving an allowance from the Martyr's substance.

[711] "The Burgesses of Bedford [a] to the convent of Canterbury and to all the faithful in Christ, health ! Be it

cepto, licet plurimorum praecurrisset testimonium, tunc primo nobis satisfactum est cum praedictorum summam litteris et testimonio [12] civium Bedefordensium confirmatam audivimus. Direxerunt enim nobis apices in hunc modum continentes :	loquimur et testamur. Is enim de quo loquimur, Cantuariam transmissus, dies multos mansit apud nos, de martyris substantia stipem habens.

"Burgenses Bedefordiae [a] conventui Cantuariensi, et omnibus fidelibus in Christo, salutem.

[12] "Litteris et testimonio" might possibly mean "by an[other] letter and [also] by the testimony." But Benedict would have probably inserted "aliis" had that been his meaning. In the third miracle of this kind, Benedict has "litteras testimonii," see below, 737 (19). But the use of two nouns in the same case, instead of one noun qualified by another in the genitive, is common in Latin.

[a] William places this *before* the narrative and after a prologue enumerating the many evils healed by the Martyr. Consequently, he inserts "then" for connection's sake ("To come to facts then") "Burgenses *igitur* de Bedeford." This particle frequently introduces miraculous fact, after a moral preface.

In the next sentence, William has corrupted "sciat" into "sicut" (unless it

Benedict (ii. 173-82)

known to the convent of Canterbury, and further (" necnon,"
om. by W.) to all catholics, that God hath wrought in
Bedford a wonderful and illustrious miracle on account of
the merits of the most holy (W., " holy, sancti ") Thomas, the
Martyr.   For it happened that a countryman of Westoning,
Eilward (W. " Ailward ") by name, for some theft, of the
value of only one *nummus*, having been taken and brought
before the viscount of Bedford, and before the knights of the
county, and having been by them publicly condemned, was
deprived of his eyes and privy members, in the presence of
clergy and laity, [men] and women.   This is also testified by
the chaplain of St. John in Bedford, to whom the aforesaid
countryman confessed [after mutilation[b]].   And this same is
testified by his host, Eilbrict (W., " Ailbricht ") by name, in
whose house he was afterwards received—namely that he was
entirely without eyes and testicles when first he was received
in his house.   And afterwards, invoking oftentimes the merits
of St. Thomas the Martyr, by an apparition of the aforesaid
Martyr he was gloriously and wonderfully restored to health."[c]

" Sciat conventus Cantuariensis, necnon et omnes catholici, Deum in Bedefordia mirabile et insigne miraculum propter merita sanctissimi Thomae martyris
operatum fuisse.   Accidit enim quod quidam rusticus de Westonia, Eilwardus
nomine, pro quodam furto, pretii unius nummi tantum, captus et ante vicecomitem de Bedefordia et ante milites comitatus ductus, et ab eis in publico con-
demnatus, extra villam Bedefordensem oculos et pendentia, astantibus clericis et
laicis et mulieribus, amisit.   Quod etiam testatur capellanus de sancto Johanne
de Bedefordia, cui praedictus rusticus [post mutilationem[b]] confessus est.   Et hoc
idem testatur hospes ejus, Eilbrictus nomine, apud quem postea hospitatus fuit,
quod oculis et testiculis, quando primo apud eum hospitatus fuit, omnino caruit ;
qui postea, saepius invocans merita sancti Thomae martyris, gloriose et mirifice
apparitione praedicti martyris sanitati restitutus est."[c]

---

is the Editor's error).   B. has " Sciat conventus Cantuariensis " ; W., " Sicut
universitas conventus Cantuariae."   Also B. has " Bedefordia " ; W., " Bedeford."
   [b] William omits the bracketed words.
   [c] Benedict adds a lengthy comment on the novelty of this miracle, and the
circumstances precluding deception or collusion, etc., especially emphasizing the
fact that Eilward was mutilated by his enemies, who would not have spared him.

[712] (ii.) A second miracle of the same kind is described by William alone in an attesting letter from Hugh de Puiset, Bishop of Durham, who says that it happened in Durham, in December, 1174. On the 17th of September in that year, "one Roger, a simpleton,[1] having pleaded guilty, underwent mutilation of the eyes and *genitalia* as the penalty of theft ; and the parts extracted are known to have been buried in the ground, in the presence of many eye-witnesses, according to custom." After being kept some weeks in the Bishop's hospital, he had to leave and beg his bread ; so that his blindness was well known in Durham. On the eve of St. Thomas the Apostle, in answer to the poor man's repeated supplications, the Martyr appeared, clothed in red, and in a comely mitre,[2] and bearing three tapers in his hand, and saying that he had come to assuage his pain. Departing, after bestowing his blessing, the Saint left the man so endowed with supernatural light that, "although others in the house said nothing, he bade his hostess—who had hastily risen [from bed] to seize him, thinking him to be mad—fasten to her dress a needle (hanging from her bosom) for fear of losing it." Roger, called before the Bishop and Chapter of Durham, was found to have eyes, new but as yet of moderate size. Evidence on oath was received from him, from the executioners, and from the witnesses of the mutilation. The bells were set ringing, and a thanksgiving was celebrated.

[713] After giving the Bishop's letter in full, William says that, on the day when Roger came to the Cathedral, it happened that the knight who had sentenced him came also thither, not to testify, but to pray. On finding Roger there, Sir Richard of the Prickly Thistle, for that was his name, assured all the people that it was of the Martyr's grace, and not for any fault of the judges, that this miracle had been

---

[1] "hominem simplicissimum." The judge says that (i. 423) he could not induce the man to plead not guilty.

[2] [712a] "In red, and mitred " : see 698a.

worked. "Before sentence was passed on him," said the knight, "I asked him whether he had ever eaten of the flesh,[3] wishing him to deny it. But, whether because he was simple, or because the Martyr was destined to be glorified in him, the man could not be driven to a denial." He concluded by offering to swear that he had seen Roger with eyes different from those which he now had.

(iii.) A third miracle is recorded by Benedict alone (ii. 250-1). It deserves exact and full quotation, as the monks of Canterbury, in this case, sent a special messenger to ascertain the facts.

[714] "We also heard that a wonderful thing had happened in the town of Corbie, viz. that, by the aid of the blessed and glorious Martyr, a man had recovered his eyes after they had been gouged out. But, on sending a messenger thither, we heard that they had not been gouged out, but severely wounded with a sharp knife: for the executioner, when he found it very troublesome to extract them, being very angry, drew a sharp-pointed knife and pierced the eyes again and again with such cruelty that all thought it worse to have them thus wounded than [actually] extracted: they said he must be a thorough villain to murder the poor fellow in that way instead of blinding him." After ascertaining the facts from the men of the town who saw them with their eyes, our messenger, being unable to find at his residence the Abbot of Corbie to whom we had written

---

[714] Mirum quid etiam audivimus contigisse in villa Corbeiae; hominem effossos oculos per beatum et gloriosum martyrem recuperasse. Misso autem illuc nuntio, non effossos sed cultello acuto graviter sauciatos audivimus; tortor enim, cum in iis eruendis laboraret, iratus valde cultellum acuta cuspide extraxit, et oculis totiens totiensque crudeliter infixit, ut gravius esse arbitrarentur omnes sic eos esse vulneratos quam erutos. Grandis eum arguebant impietatis, qui hominem occideret potius quam excaecaret. Nuntius itaque noster, per ejusdem villae homines, qui haec oculis conspexerunt, cognita veritate, cum abbatem

---

[3] "Cane" should surely be "carne." See the same error above (361). Possibly it was a case of stealing flesh.

concerning an investigation into this great miracle, brought back to us a letter of testimony from the Prior and convent, with contents to this tenor :

[715] " To the venerable lord Odo, by the grace of God Prior of the church of Canterbury, A.,[1] called Prior of the Church of Corbie, and the convent, [send] health and respect.

" On the points about which you thought worthy to inquire by letter from us we write in return to you as follows. A young man named John, native of Valenciennes, was found in our town and proved [to have been engaged] in theft, and, in accordance with the decree of secular law, was adjudged to be hanged. And when he had been dragged to the punishment of terrible death, it pleased our burgesses that he should be only deprived of his eyes, and thus let go : and presently he was blinded and severely wounded in the eyes ; and so he was led to the infirmary, and received by Ralph the head of the hospital, who, for compassion's sake, washed his blinded eyes with hot water, that night and the next, and poulticed them to assuage the pain. But on the third day, when Ralph anxiously inquired of him whether he had still open any inlet of light,

Corbeiensis ecclesiae, cui super tanti inquisitione miraculi scripseramus, domi non invenisset, a priore conventuque litteras nobis testimonii reportavit, in hunc modum continentes.

[715] " Domino et venerabili Odoni, Dei gratia priori Cantuariensis ecclesiae, A.,[1] dictus prior Corbeiensis ecclesiae, et conventus, salutem et obsequium.

" Super his, quae per literas vestras dignum duxistis a nobis inquirere, talia vobis rescripsimus. Quidam juvenis, Joannes nomine, ortus de castro qued dicitur Valentianas, in oppido nostro repertus et probatus est in furto, ac juxta legis mundanae decretum adjudicatus suspendio. Cumque ad horrendae mortis supplicium traheretur, placuit burgensibus nostris ut oculis tantummodo privaretur, et ita dimitteretur ; moxque caecatus est et graviter in oculis sauciatus ; sicque ductus est ad domum debilium, et ab hospitario receptus, qui vocatur Radulfus ; qui caecata ipsius lumina ea et sequenti nocte aqua calida lavit, intuitu miserationis, et refovit, pro doloribus scilicet mitigandis. Die vero tertia, dum ab eo sollicite percunctaretur, utrum ei post excaecationem suam extremae saltem

---

[1] It is not uncommon for letters of this kind to contain in their superscription merely the initial of the name of the addresser.

even the slightest, he replied that in one of his eyes there was no light at all left, but in the other a very little brightness found admission, but in such slight measure that without a guide he could in no wise keep a straight path.

[716] " Meanwhile there came in a young poor clerk, who declared that he had in a glass vessel some of the very water of our most blessed Patron and Martyr, Thomas, glorified in these our days by God, by which, as almost all men know, many miracles have been wrought. So they took a little of this Water, and then, after reverently lighting tapers in honour of the Martyr, they carefully and thoroughly bathed the eyes therewith. But he received sight on the spot, so that even the scars of the very wounds that he had received when he was being blinded, were now healed. Next day, healed and happy, he returned to his home.

[717] " And, lest on these matters there should be some lingering doubt in the bottom of your hearts, we testify to you that one of our own brethren, drinking of that same Water, was delivered from a running at the nose."

[718] The third miracle throws light on the first two. It shews that (1) in the process of judicially blinding, it was possible to blind *for the time*, yet in such a way that the blinded man could recover ; (2) this was a fact so well

---

visionis aditus patuisset, respondit in uno quidem oculorum suorum nihil penitus luminis remansisse ; in altero vero parum quid claritatis admitti, sed tam modicae quantitatis, qua sine ductore nullatenus posset calle recti itineris incedere.

[716] " Affuit ibidem interea quidam puer clericus pauper, qui de ipsa aqua beatissimi patroni nostri et nostro tempore a Deo glorificati martyris Thomae, archiepiscopi Cantuariensis, in vitreo vase se ferre confessus est, qua plerique noverant facta fuisse crebra miracula. Acceperunt igitur illius aquae modicum, et ob honorem memorati martyris luminaribus reverenter accensis, oculos praedicti caeci ex ea diligenter abluere curaverunt. At ille visum illico recuperavit, adeo ut ipsorum etiam vulnerum vestigia sanarentur, quae inflicta fuerant ei dum excaecaretur. Postera autem die sanus et gaudens ad propria recessit.

[717] " Et, ne super his aliqua in vestro corde resideat cunctatio, testamur vobis quod quidam de fratribus nostris ex ipsa aqua bibens liberatus est a narium profluvio."

known to Ralph, the head of the Infirmary at Corbie, that he "anxiously asked" John whether he had any sight still remaining—whereas no one would ask of a man whose leg or arm had been cut off, "Have you any vestige of your arm or leg?"; (3) this temporary but not complete blinding was compatible with atrocious cruelty on the part of the executioner.

[719] This last fact partly meets Benedict's argument that Eilward must have been effectually blinded because he was blinded by his enemies. The answer is, that their very cruelty may have led them unwittingly to save their victim's sight by lacerating his eyes instead of extracting them. And indeed Benedict himself tells us that one of the eyes was not regularly extracted, but "chopped in pieces." It is true, he adds that the fragments were afterwards buried : but, in the flow of blood, in the excitement and haste of the revolting process, and (not improbably) amid the murmurs from an angry crowd of spectators, it is not difficult to perceive that one of Eilward's eyes may not have been extracted. There is nothing in Benedict's description of the evidence as to sight regained to shew that he saw with *both* eyes.

[720] Benedict alone has preserved the facts that give an apparent clue to an explanation of this alleged miracle from natural causes. William's narrative appears to be either a condensation of Benedict's, or a shorter account written on the basis of the same notes (kept in the Cathedral) which Benedict had used. In any case William probably had Benedict's narrative before him, correcting errors in it, and inserting explanations or new facts necessary for clearness (see footnotes 2, 3, 4, 9, 10, 12). As regards the shorter utterances of the characters in the drama, and especially those of St. Thomas, the two are in considerable agreement. But as regards the facts, William, while toning down the resentment against the judges, and laying most of the blame on the two Fulks, subordinates sentiment and pathos to proof of miracle.

§ 3. *The ship that came back by herself*

[721] Benedict (ii. 212-3)

William (i. 301-2)

A man named Ailwin from Bristol brought a gold piece as an offering to the Martyr and went away. The monk that was sitting at the tomb, noting that the gift was very large for one so poor (for he was but meanly clad), called him back and questioned him. " I vowed this to the Martyr," he replied, "and now I have paid it. Sailing of late from Ireland, my ship fell on a quicksand. The more we toiled to get her off, the more the sand

Some sailors from Ireland fell on a sand called Colresand,[1] and there stuck fast. What was to be done? The ship was heavy laden with hides and bound for her customary port enriched to her own loss. What was to be done? [*He proceeds to quote Lucan ix.* 335-9, *slightly altered.*] The wretched sailors, seeing inevitable shipwreck before them (for as the tide went down the sand came up and the prow plunged deeper and deeper

Ex oblatione viri alterius inusitatum et magnae pietatis apprehendimus miraculum. Venit enim vir unus de Bristo ad martyrem, nomine Ailwinus, qui aureum obtulit et recessit. Quumque intueretur monachus, qui ad tumbam residebat, quod oblatio ejus longe discordaret ab habitu (erat enim homo habitus valde abjecti), revocatum interrogavit quare pauper aureum sancto praesentasset? "Votum," inquit, "vovi martyri et reddidi : dum enim nuper ab Hibernia navigarem, navis mea in sabulum incidit vivum, et in sabulo fixa consedit. Quanto vero amplius labora-

Navigantes quidam de Hybernia in sabulum quod nautae Colresand [1] appellant inciderunt, et stetit navis fixa in vado, velo suspenso. Quid faciat? Deprimit eam onus suum ; nam coriis et aliis rebus venalibus onerata, et dives damno suo, ad navale solitum redibat. Quid faciat?
" Obvia consurgit tellus . . . . . .
. . . atque interrupta profundo
Terra ferit proram, dubioque obnoxia fato,
Pars sedet una ratis, pars altera pendet in undis."
Videntes igitur miseri nautae sibi naufragium irremediabiliter imminere (nam refluente mari succrescebat arena, et

[1] Perhaps an attempt to express the English "quicksand."

Benedict (ii. 212-3)

sucked her in. The water had well-nigh covered the deck when we leapt into the boat to save our lives ; for we had given up all hope of the vessel. Then said I, 'O Thomas, Martyr of God, if thou hast any power with God, and didst ever work miracle, give me back my ship. Then will I visit thy tomb and offer a gold piece.'

" So we let the ship shift for herself and rowed for the shore. We got about eight furlongs from her : but after rowing some while longer, the ship was still as near as ever. We cheered one

William (i. 301-2)

into it), leapt into their pinnace to save their lives, leaving their ship and substance to the care of Thomas.

When they had fled a long way from the ship, the ship (an unprecedented novelty !) began to follow the fugitives, and on she came approaching them without crew of human kind. But meanwhile their eyes were holden, that they should not recognize in the coming vessel the one that they had left sinking in the shallows. They beheld the sail set and the substance they had left behind them, but knew not

---

bamus ut de periculo instanti ejiceretur, tanto eam absorbebat arena. Jam fere usque ad supremum tabulatum videbatur submergi, quum desperantes omnes in cymbam parvam desilivimus, saltem vitae nostrae volentes esse consultum ; nam de navis vel rerum nostrarum recuperatione spes nulla supererat. Tunc ego, 'Martyr Dei Thoma, si cujus meriti es apud Deum, si quid potes, si miraculum aliquod unquam fecisti, navem meam mihi restitue. Sepulchrum tuum visitabo, si feceris, aureum tibi oblaturus.' Navi itaque dimissa navigavimus in navicula ut evaderemus ad terram, et quasi stadiis octo a navi elongati sumus ; cumque diutius in remigando vexaremur, a navi semper aeque distare videbamur. Hor-

magis magisque illidebatur prora), exsilierunt in scapham, salvantes animas suas, navi rebusque derelictis, martyri Thomae custodiam delegantes. Cumque procul a navi fugissent, navis inaudita novitate fugientes subsequebatur, et sine humano remige ferebatur appropinquans. Oculi autem eorum interim tenebantur, ne agnoscerent venientem quam reliquerant vadis insidentem. Velum suspensum et sua quae dimiserant aspiciebant, sed

Benedict (ii. 212-3)

another on to row our hardest, but the more we rowed the closer came we to the ship. So we gave it up and waited a little: and behold, the vessel that we had left— sails set, and well-nigh sunk —we now beheld bearing down on us. When she came up, we welcomed her as God's own gift. On board we went, and reached home after a prosperous voyage. This was the cause why I came on my pilgrimage to the Martyr and offered him the gold piece."

He had no witnesses. But we believed his story on the strength of his simplicity and the rich offering from one so poorly clad.

William (i. 301-2)

as yet that it was theirs: for they had no hope that what had been taken *away* was now taken *to* them. So they hailed the vessel and asked who were on board and whence and whither they were bound, and there was none to answer. However, the Guardian to whose care they had entrusted the vessel opened their eyes. It was by his powerful hand that she was extricated from the Syrtes, and by his steering that she was borne after her former crew. So when they recognized their own ship they leaped on board and returned with prosperous course to the town of Bristol whence they had come.

---

tabamur ergo nos invicem ad laborem, sed quanto amplius navigavimus, tanto ad navem accessimus. Cessantes tandem ab inani labore, modicum exspectavimus, et ecce, navem, quam velo expanso et fere absorptam reliqueramus, absque rectore venientem advertimus; venientem quasi a Deo oblatam nobis recepimus. Ascendimus; prospere absque damno applicuimus. Hac de causa martyrem visitavi, aureum obtuli." Haec cum dixisset, licet testibus careret, credidimus ei, ex simplicitate ipsius, et oblatione vestibus ejus male respondente, veritatis argumentum trahentes.

sua esse nondum advertebant; non enim ablata sperabant oblata. Unde acclamantes interrogabant quinam intus essent, quo et unde vectarentur; et non erat qui responderet. Aperuit autem oculos eorum custos navi delegatus; cujus impulsu a Sirtibus eruebatur, cujus et regimine post remigem suum ferebatur. Igitur navim suam recognitam insilientes prospero cursu ad vicum Bristov, unde venerant, revecti sunt.

In this story, Benedict has preserved the mariner's simple tale, while William has adorned it with a quotation from Lucan, and with remarks of his own, increasing the miraculousness by representing the mariners as *losing sight* of the ship, so that, when she returns, *they mistake her for a strange vessel.*

§ 4. *How St. Thomas pushed a ship off a shoal*

[722] Benedict (ii. 214)	William (i. 302-3)
For this cause we deemed him [*i.e.* the above-mentioned Ailwin] no less worthy of credit than three others who testified to a miracle no less wonderful. For they affirmed that they, too, had been on board a ship that had fallen into the same danger as his. In fear of death, they all cried to the Saint, and knelt down on the deck, and said the Lord's prayer. Then the man [of God] visibly appeared to them in glistening white garments, and walking on the rolling waves.	There had gone forth into the deep other sailors, drawn to their fate by love of gain, and by desire to catch herrings, and by the flattery of calm weather—and destined to have been drawn on to utter destruction had not their perishing lives been preserved by Him who willeth not the death of a sinner. For while they are catching fish they are themselves unwittingly caught; and while they fix their eyes on their prey, under the guidance of greediness, they

---

Unde nec minus ei credendum esse censuimus, quam aliis tribus, qui signi non minoris dederunt testimonium. Aiebant namque et se in navi exstitisse, quae per noctem in simile devenit periculum ; cumque omnes metu mortis ad sanctum clamassent, et flexis in navi genibus Dominicam dixissent orationem, apparuisse illis hominem visibiliter in vestibus candidis, et super mobiles ambulasse maris undas. Qui,

Exierant in altum alii nautae, quos amor lucri et allecis capiendi cupido, tempusque serenum, quod blandiebatur, in fata trahebant, et usque in exitium pertraxissent, nisi Qui non vult mortem peccatoris vitam pereuntium servasset. Nam dum pisces inescant, imprudentes inescantur, dumque praedae inhiant, praevia duce aviditate, vadis insident et

Benedict (ii. 214)

William (i. 302-3)

Catching the ship by the prow, he drove her far on into the deep, so that the noise of her rush could be heard a great way off: and then he vanished away from their eyes. The three worthy men above mentioned stood forward as witnesses of this ; and they were also prepared to lay their hand on the sacred elements and to certify us that they stood at that instant on the vessel and saw with their own eyes that figure through the shades [of night].

settle down on a shoal and sink till the water almost reaches the deck.   Earth and sea were so confused that the nature of the elements could not be distinguished, and, as the poet describes [*here he quotes Lucan, Pharsalia, ix.* 305-9].

So the ship stood, projecting only with her stern, and with her prow on the point of going down under the water to meet the sea as it came up.   As the wretched skippers [1] made diverse vows in accordance with their

apprehensa navis prora, navem longius in profundum impegit, ita ut sonus fluctuum ejus longe valde posset audiri, et ipse evanuit ab oculis eorum.   Hujus rei testes astiterunt tres viri praedicti, parati etiam, tactis sacrosanctis, nos certificare quod in navi eadem tunc exstiterint, et oculis suis personam illam per umbras conspexerint.

usque ad foros ferme immerguntur. Erat autem terra pelago commixta, ut elementarum natura discerni non posset, et, sicut poeta describit,

> Tum "neque subsedit penitus, quo stagna profundi
> Acciperet, nec se defendit ab aequore tellus,
> Ambigua sed lege loci jacet invia sedes ;
> Aequora fracta vadis, abruptaque terra profundo,
> Et post multa sonant projecti littora fluctus."

Stetit igitur carina, puppi duntaxat exstans, et prora ad ascensionem maris descensura sub undas.   Miseris naucleris [1] diversa voventibus pro diversitate

---

[1] [722a] "Naucleris." William is fond of using Greek terms, not always intelligently (611a).

William (i. 302-3)

diverse minds, and at last called to mind the last of the Martyrs, the man of God, compassionating their affliction, deigned to exhibit himself visibly. And walking on the waters, he seized the ship by the figurehead and drove her back into the waves : and she brought her crew prosperously into port.

William, while again adorning his story with quotations and plays on words, makes a mistake by representing St. Thomas as pushing the vessel *back*, instead of driving her *on*. But "reppulit in fluctus" is probably a quotation, and to this William sacrificed truth of fact.

§ 5. *Recovery of anchors*

[723] Benedict (ii. 215)	William (i. 300-1)
Eilwecher[1] of Dover was sailing to lesser Britain. A storm arose and he cast out	One Girard of Dover, while sailing the ocean, let down an anchor on the rising

animorum, novique martyris novissime reminiscentibus, dignatus est vir Dei miseratus afflictos se visibiliter exhibere. Ambulansque super aquas, arreptam a rostro navem repulit in fluctus, quae felici navigio nautas suos produxit ad portus.

Navigabat in Britanniam minorem Eilwecher[1] Dovrensis, et orta tempe-

Dovrensis quidam Girardus oceanum navigans orta tempestate a navi

---

[1] Al. Eilweker, or Ejuneker. The last reading suggests a corruption of "ein junker." William has "Girard."

Benedict (ii. 215)	William (i. 300·1)
three anchors, but lost all of them through the cables breaking. However, he came safe to land, after invoking the Martyr. On the return of fair weather he returned with his companions to the sea to seek the anchors ; for the place where he had lost them was not far from the land. For three days they sought and found nothing. So said one of them, " Let us promise also² to the Martyr of Canterbury a waxen anchor that he may give us back our iron ones." All	of a storm. Wishing to draw it up again, two of the sailors, in the usual way, stood in the prow and tried to haul in the rope ; and they could not wrench up a certain barbed hook,¹ until they all pulled together. None the less, in spite of it all, their efforts were vain and they gave it up. So, in the last resort, they tried what sailors call a " windas,"² . . . But still the tenacious hook felt not the hands of the panting [men]. So being deserted by human aid, they seek divine, saying,

state tres anchoras emisit, quas et funibus ruptis omnes amisit ; ad terram tamen evasit, invocato martyre. Redeunte serenitate rediit cum sociis suis in mare anchoras quaesiturus, eo quod locus, ubi eas amiserat, non longa (*sic*) a terra distabat. Tribus diebus quaesitum est, et nihil inventum. Ait ergo unus ex ipsis, " Promittamus et martyri² Cantuariensi anchoram ceream, ut ferreas nostras nobis restituat." Con-

anchoram demisit. Quam cum vellet reducere, duo ex nautis, sicut moris est, stantes in prora attrahebant funem, et non poterant uncum quendam mordacem avellere,¹ donec omnes conatum suum communicarent. Nihilominus tamen omnes casso conatu defecerunt. Unde ad ultimum refugium confugientes ligno quod nautae windasium vocant caput rudentis circumposuere, ut suffragante ligno conatus efficacior esset.² Est

² " Et martyri." The meaning may be that they had already made vows to other Saints.

¹ " Non poterant *uncum quendam mordacem* avellere." William, who is fond of technical terms, not knowing the word here, substitutes the italicized phrase. Note below, his introduction of the term "windasium," the "windas" of Chaucer, *C. T.* 10498 (see Skeat, *Etymolog. Dict.*).

² Here William gives a long description of a " windas."

Benedict (ii. 215)

agreed : and straightway letting down into the water the instrument with which they were searching the bottom, they drew out all the anchors. So they turned back to England and came to the Martyr. They brought to him the gift they had promised.

William (i. 300-1)

" Restore, O Thomas, genuine martyr, powerful over land and sea, what our frailty cannot [restore]. Loose the cable,[3] preserve our ship from damage, . . . We promise a visit to thy memorial and a waxen model of our iron implement. Restore the instrument by which we are detained." So approaching [the task, or the place],

---

senserunt omnes ; statimque demisso in aquam instrumento, quo maris fundum scrutabantur, omnes anchoras ex-traxerunt. Reversi itaque in Angliam venerunt ad martyrem ; munus attule-runt quod promiserant.

autem lignum ex transverso puppis positum, et ex latere perforatum, cujus usus est in majoribus navibus ad sus-pendendum velum. Nam foraminibus immittuntur radii, et quod non potest per se vis humana, potest innitens radiis ; dum enim circumducitur lignum funibus circumvolutum, provenit ex ligno facile suffragium. Sed nondum tenax uncus sensit anhelantium manus. Igitur humano adminiculo destituti petunt divinum, dicentes, " Redde, vere martyr Thoma, potens maris et terrae, quod non potest infirmitas nostra. Retinacula solve ;[3] conserva navem indemnem. Scimus quoniam bonorum nostrorum non eges, vis tamen tibi reverentiam exhiberi, vis mortalium devotionem votis et precibus augeri. Unde memoriam tuam visitaturi pro ferreo armamento ejusdem formae ceram promittimus. Redde quo retinemur

---

[3] " Retinacula." What the sailors really wanted was the loosing of the *anchor*: but "loose the *cable*" is Virgilian, and this suffices for William.

William (i. 300-1)

after the fulfilment of their vow,[4] they easily got back the hook.

But they, going forth again,[5] cast forth two anchors in different places,[6] with the one that had been restored to them ; and thus they tossed about, kept where they were by their hold on the bottom. After a short time, they stood again near the prow to recal that anchor which they had recovered by the gift of heaven. And behold, pulling in the cable broken, they began to cry aloud, " Martyr Thomas, wherefore have we lost that which through thee we recovered? Restore that which thou restoredst ! We, too, will render that which we promised."

Well, they had given up hope of regaining it. But by the providence of the Martyr, beyond hope, that which they had lost was returned. For in the act of haul-ing up the other anchors they recovered also that which was the object of their solicitations. A fragment of the cable of the lost anchor had stuck fast, having been fastened in a celestial knot with the cables of the other

---

instrumentum." Voto igitur expleto [4] accedentes, levi conatu uncum recepe-runt.

Procedentes autem rursus [5] duas anchoras diversis locis [6] cum ea quae restituta fuerat projecerunt, et fluctuabant ab imo retenti. Post tempus iterum modicum stabant ad proram revocaturi anchoram quam divino munere receperant. Et ecce ruptum legentes rudentem clamare coeperunt, " Martyr Thoma, quare perdidimus quod per te recepimus ? Redde quod reddidisti ; reddemus et nos quod promisimus." Igitur a spe recuperationis exciderant ; sed procurante martyre praeter spem restituitur quod amiserant. Nam dum alias anchoras reducunt, et eam de qua solliciti erant recipiunt. Adhaeserat namque fragmen-

---

[4] That is, they first went to Canterbury and "fulfilled" their vow, and then "approached" the place of the lost anchor and recovered it.

[5] The ambiguous English expresses the original, in which, (1) "procedentes" may mean "proceding *from that place*, or *out to sea*," and (2) "again" may refer to "proceeding," or to "casting."

[6] " In, or from, *different places* (*of the vessel*)." See remarks below.

two, so that the ship was preserved from damage and
the Martyr was manifested to have power in the waters.

_____

[724] The two narratives agree enough to make it pretty
certain that both refer to the same event. It is impossible
to explain their divergence with certainty, but there are good
grounds for conjecturing that William, in the attempt to
improve, has corrupted, Benedict's story.

According to Benedict, the facts are these. Three
anchors were thrown out in a storm ; the three cables broke ;
and the men, after invoking St. Thomas [to save their lives],
got safe to land. Benedict does not add, but he almost
certainly assumes, that the invocation was accompanied by a
promise of a pilgrimage and an offering. This promise may
be supposed to be now paid. Afterwards, fair weather
having set in, they return to seek their anchors. They fail
till they promise a waxen anchor to the Martyr. Then they
succeed.

[725] This being, probably, the true tale, William finds
it unsatisfactory on the following grounds : " If *three* anchors
were lost, *three* anchors of wax ought to have been vowed.
But we know that only *one* anchor was offered. It follows
that only *one* anchor was lost."

[726] " But," says an objecting monk, with the Canterbury notes in his hand, " was there not *something* said by the
pilgrims about *three* anchors ? " William replies, by resorting
to the common subterfuge of Harmonizing Apologists, " *There
were two voyages*. In the *first* voyage, one anchor was lost,
and one waxen anchor vowed ; and, after the vow had been
paid, that anchor was recovered. Then came a *second*
voyage, which has been erroneously regarded by my pre-
decessor Benedict as a mere expedition to search for lost

_____

tum funis amissae anchorae, funibus aliarum coelesti nodo colligatum, ut et puppis
servaretur indemnis, et martyr potens ostenderetur in undis.

anchors. In this voyage, they took with them the recovered anchor, and two others. When a storm came on, they cast out the first *at the prow* (ad proram). Now if they had cast out the others 'at the prow,' *there would have been no great miracle in the recovery of the three together.* Therefore mark that the two others were cast out *at different places* [*of the vessel*] (diversis locis).

"In hauling up the anchor at the prow, the cable snapped again. Again they prayed to St. Thomas. At first, it seemed as though their prayer was unheard : but presently, in hauling up the two others, they hauled up the first also, which, *in spite of its distance from the others,* had been entangled with the others—clearly the result of 'a celestial knot,' entwined by the hand of the Martyr! Thus you are right in saying that there was '*something* about three anchors'; but three anchors were not *recovered.* Three anchors were *hauled in,* and, of these, one was recovered for the second time."

William's story appears to exemplify, 1st, *the Fallacy of Duplication,* 2nd, *the Fallacy of Improvement,* or, *the Fitness of Things* (**365-8, 379**).

§ 6. *How the son of Yngelrann of Golton was visited with paralysis by the Martyr and then healed*

[**727**] Benedict (ii. 219-20)   William (i. 195-8)

(1) Benedict omits this.   (1) One Stephen[1] had made a feast for a rich man

---

(1) om.   (1) Stephanus quidam[1] de villa Huerveltuna fecerat diviti cuidam con-

[1] "De villa Huerveltuna": Ed. adds, "This place appears from the sequel to have been at some distance from Canterbury so that it cannot be identified with Harbledown. Possibly

William (i. 195-8)

named Robert. While the latter was seated at meat with Stephen, Hugh of Morville, one of the Martyr's murderers, who knew him, demanded a visit from his old friend,[2] naming time and place. Robert, much disturbed, and unwilling to consort with the murderer,[3] was persuaded to accept the invitation by the mother of the family, who (seeing her guest's dejection) scoffed at the Martyr and bade Robert go and feast and make merry with Hugh of Morville.

As time went on, this woman's husband [Stephen],

---

vivium. Apud quem dum dives ille pranderet, Robertus nomine, misit ad eum [2] Hugo de Morvilla, dicens in haec verba: "Miror super dilectione mutua veterique societate nostra, quae sic de facili tepuit ut multo tempore non videris faciem meam. Mando igitur ut te mihi locuturum exhibeas"; locumque constituit et tempus praefixit. Hoc audito mandato concidit vultus ejus, et non bibit neque manducavit, revocans ad animum atrox et immane flagitium quod perpetraverat, declinansque, sicut decet Christianum, detestabile consortium, quod vel solo colloquio praecisionis ecclesiasticae maculam aspergit.[3] Quid, nostri infamia saeculi, candidatorum petis colloquium? Quid, civis Babyloniae confusionis, gregem dominicum contaminas? Nescis quia

> "Grex totus in agris
> Unius scabie cadit et porrigine porci?"

Materfamilias vero, videns hospitis sui tristitiam, ait ei, "Quae cura si mortuus est presbyter ille Thomas? Quis inde moveatur? Supra modum clerus dominabatur, in tantam prorumpens arrogantiam ut etiam principum colla suppeditare tentaret. Regemne putavit inquietare et subjugare? Epulare, precor, et laetare." His et hujusmodi verbis illota delirabat.

Procedente tempore, vir ejus de consuetudine saeculari ad saecularia

---

Warbleton in Sussex." But, if this story refers to the same facts as Benedict's, may not "Huerveltona" be a corruption of "Goltona" 727 (2)?

This section, though full of unnecessary details, has some value in placing before the reader the causes that may have led the man and his wife to talk about propitiating the Martyr.

[2] What follows indicates that it is Robert (not Stephen) who is thus invited.

[3] William intervenes with an apostrophe ("Why, O infamy of our age, dost thou seek colloquy with those who are in white robes? Why, O citizen of the shameful Babylon, ...") concluded by a quotation from Juvenal, *Sat.* ii. 79, 80, that one pig may infect a herd.

Benedict (ii. 219-20)

William (i. 195-8)

in the course of his occupa-
tion,[4] heard a good deal
about the mighty works of
healing performed by the
Martyr's merits. So on
returning home he related
what he had heard, and
added that he wished to
visit the Martyr's tomb.

(2) At the time when
crowds began to rush, and
folk from the cities to hasten,
towards the tomb of our
Martyr, the same desire came
into the mind of the wife
of Yngelrann[1] of Golton, a
knight of Yorkshire, which

(2) The mother and the
elder son conceived the same
desire. "I have no need of
it," said the younger, "for I
am neither dumb, nor lame,
nor suffering from any infirmity." But it came to
pass that, while he was giving

negotia profectus[4] audivit multa dici
de illuminatione caecorum, auditu sur-
dorum, mundatione leprosorum, caete-
risque magnalibus quae meritis beati
martyris Dominus operari dignatus est ;
rediensque domum narravit quae
audierat et vulgo dicebantur, et adjecit
se velle visitare sepulchrum martyris.

(2) Cum turbae multae irruerent ad
martyrem nostrum et de civitatibus
properarent ad eum, incidit in mentem
uxoris Yngelranni[1] de Goltona, militis

(2) Capitur eadem voluntate materfamilias et filius ejus major natu.
"Non," inquit minor, "necesse habeo
ire, quia neque mutus neque claudus
sum, neque corporis alio detineor incommodo." Factum est autem, dum

[1] The Editor has "Ingelram."
This somewhat resembles the son's
name as spelt by William in (7)
below, "Engelram." But see note
there. The text has "Yngelranni" as
the genitive. Golton (Ed.) is in
Craven.

[4] "De consuetudine saeculari ad
saecularia negotia profectus." Perhaps
the object of this addition is to shew
that the Martyr's miracles were now
so famous that even a man of the
world could not fail to hear about
them.

Benedict (ii. 219-20)

she also intimated to her lord, adding, "Let us also take our son." The boy, who stood listening to his parents, replied, "I am whole and healthy; what should I have to do with the Martyr?" The father raised his hand to chastise the boy for his foolish answer; but he escaped, and went away, and gave his time to scholar's tasks, recking naught of the sin of his mouth. And on that night his arm was made as if dead, and quite insensible, so that it could not feel fire placed near, or knife placed on it: for it was actually often pricked and

William (i. 195-8)

his time to scholar's discipline, he was struck with paralysis and lost the use of one of his arms. After being detained [at school] by this for some weeks, he was brought home. Thence he was taken round through the different convents [5] of the diocese and consulted the physicians, who pricked his arm with a needle and found it quite insensible.

Eboracensis, voluntas eadem, quam et domino suo intimavit; addiditque mulier dicens, "Ducamus nobiscum et filium nostrum." Stabat autem puer auscultans parentes, verbisque maternis ita respondit: "Sanus sum et incolumis; quid cum martyre facerem?" Increpat pater stultum pueri responsum, manuque ad eum castigandum extensa, effugientem nec laesit nec tetigit: et abiit puer scholisque vacavit, nullipendens quod ore deliquit. Et mortificatum est nocte illa brachium ejus et prorsus insensibile factum, ita ut nec ignem appositum nec ferrum impositum sentire valeret; nam et acu saepius

scholari disciplinae vacaret, ut paralysi percussus officium alterius brachiorum amitteret; qua cum per hebdomades aliquot detineretur, domum reductus est, et inde per coenobia [5] comprovincialia circumductus medicos consulebat; qui brachium ejus acu transfigentes, insensibile penitus repererunt.

[5] "Coenobia," which had hospitals or infirmaries attached to them.

Benedict (ii. 219-20)

William (i. 195-8)

pierced through with a needle,
but no feeling was found in
it. The boy was sent by his
parents on a round of visits [2]
to many physicians, who were
consulted about him but were
found useless.

(3) " See," said his
parents, " see, you have something [now] ' to do with the
Martyr' of Canterbury:
promise at once what but
lately you presumed to
refuse." And he gave the
pledge.

(3) At last the woman,
whose furious outburst against
the Saint was described
above, returned to her senses.
Recognising that her son
was being punished for his
mother's offence, she punished
her wild speech by scourging
and fasting.

(4) So on the following
night he saw the Saint in
his dreams—with that same
blood-streak obliquely de-
scending from his forehead

(4) And God had regard
to her penitence and con-
trition. For St. Thomas,
appearing to her sick son,
said, " Be thou whole. See

compunctum et perforatum est, sed
nihil in eo sensibilitatis inventum.
Mittitur a parentibus puer per loca
diversa ; [2] medici plures super eo con-
suluntur : nihil reperitur auxilii.

(3) "Ecce," inquiunt parentes,
"ecce habes quid agas cum Cantuariensi
martyre ; cito promitte quod pridie
praesumpsisti negare." Et spopondit.

(4) Vidit itaque nocte sequenti
sanctum in somnis, habentem illum
sanguinis tractum per obliquum nasi

(3) Resipuit tandem mulier quam
diximus in sanctum saevisse, cogno-
scensque quia filius suus in materno
delicto puniretur, linguae suae delira-
menta jejunio virgaque castigavit.

(4) Et respexit Deus contritionem
poenitentis ; nam patienti filio ejus
apparens beatus Thomas dixit, " Esto

[2] " *Per* loca diversa," *i.e. through*
one to the other, on a round of visits.
The " loca " are defined by William.

Benedict (ii. 219-20)

across the nose and left cheek, with which we saw him when he lay in his own church killed by the swords of the impious. And he said to the boy, " See, boy, that thou betake thyself this year to religion. Arise, be thou whole."

(5) He spake, and it was done. When sleep was banished from his eyes, he shewed that the death of his arm, if I may so say, was banished from his arm. He stretched out his arm,

(6) and began in health

William (i. 195-8)

that thou change thy condition of life this year, and put on the habit of a monk."

(5) Then the house— what with the splendour of the figure and with the flood of light from heaven—was so illumined that every nook and corner was as clear as day : and the young scholar —startled from sleep by the rays—leapt from his bed, and seizing a garment with the hand that was but now torpid, cried out again and again, " Father, I am healed."

(6) Astonishment fell on

---

sinistraeque maxillae a fronte descendentem, quem et vidimus illum habere cum in ecclesia sua jaceret, gladiis impiorum occisus. Dixitque ad puerum, " Vide, puer, ut hoc eodem anno ad religionem te conferas : surge, esto sanus."

(5) Dixit et factum est. Excusso enim ab oculis ejus somno, excussam a brachio brachii, ut ita dixerim, mortem ostendit ; brachium extendit,

(6) et itineris laborem, quem per-

sanus. Vide ut vitae tuae statum mutes hoc anno et monachum induas."

(5) Domus itaque ex claritate personae et multo coelesti lumine serenata est, ut omnes anguli perspicui viderentur ; ad cujus radios somno abrupto, lecto pupillus exsiliit, arripiensque vestem ea manu quae torpuerat, ingeminat, " Pater, pater, sanus sum ! "

(6) Excitati parentes obstupescunt,

Benedict (ii. 219-20)	William (i. 195-8)
that very journey which he thought to accomplish in sickness.	his awakened parents, and also on some of the King's servants, who happened to be guests there at the time—on account of whose presence, perhaps,[6] this dispensation of mercy came from Him who will have all men to be saved and to come to the knowledge of the truth. And [these], on learning the history of the matter in order, in that same hour entered the chapel and gave thanks, which they afterwards offered up more fully at the Martyr's tomb with him who had obtained this mercy.
(7) We afterwards heard from the Priest of that town	(7) When they came home, the youth, who had

---

ficere putabat infirmus, sanus inchoavit.

et quidam de ministris regis, ea tempestate hospitio suscepti, ob quorum forsan praesentiam[6] dispensavit hanc misericordiam qui vult omnes homines salvos fieri et ad cognitionem veritatis venire. Seriemque rei discentes, eadem hora capellam ingredientes, gratias egerunt, quas post cum eo qui misericordiam consecutus est ad sepulchrum martyris plenius exsecuti sunt.

(7) Audivimus postea ab ejusdem villae presbytero puerum praedictum

(7) Unde cum domum redissent, factus est adolescens mansuetissimus et

---

[6] *i.e.* in order that the King might be awakened to a sense of the Martyr's holiness and power. William elsewhere alleges this as a reason for St. Thomas's action (619).

Benedict (ii. 219-20)

that the boy assumed the habit of a monk at Fountains Abbey. For on his return home, the Saint, appearing to him in his sleep, again warned him to betake himself to a monastic order. And the boy kept answering him, and putting questions to him, with little intervals between,[3] "When, my lord?" "Where, my lord?" and many more of the same kind. And the parents happened to hear[4] the boy talking at intervals thus—but the voice of him that spoke with their

William (i. 195-8)

before been given to mirth and sport as youths are, became now most mild and sober, and begged, through the Priest—not venturing to ask it in his own person—that he might be allowed to cast off the secular garb. But his father put him off, fearing that, with the fickleness of youth, he might hastily take an arduous and difficult path from which he would afterwards shrink back, impatient of the toil, and repenting of his penitence.

And it came to pass that,

---

apud Fonteines religionis habitum induisse. Domum namque reverso iterum sanctus in somnis apparuit, iterum, ut ad ordinem monasticum se conferret, commonuit. Et respondebat ei puer, et intervallis parvis intercurrentibus[3] interrogabat, "Ubi, domine? quando, domine?" aliaque plura in hunc modum. Et audiebant[4] parentes puerum per intervalla temporum

maturae conversationis, qui lascivus fuerat, ut id aetatis habet. Et cum non auderet in propria persona, praemium petiit per presbyterum, ut liceret sibi saecularem habitum mutare. Pater autem differebat, timens ne puerili levitate rem arduam et arctam viam arriperet, a qua postmodum oneris et laboris impatiens, et poenitentiae poenitens, resiliret. Et factum est uti puero

---

[3] "Intervallis parvis intercurrentibus," *i.e.* so as to give time for the Saint to answer. The parents heard the questions; but, when the Saint was replying, they only noted a "little interval."

[4] "Audiebant." Probably they were by the boy's bedside, when he was in this disturbed condition. This suits what follows better than "used to hear," which is grammatically admissible.

Benedict (ii. 219-20)

Benedict (ii. 219-20)

son was quite inaudible, nor was his figure seen—when, however,[5] the darkness of night was dispelled, and a marvellous splendour lighted up all the house so that they saw both their son and everything else in the house. And they said to one another, "Let us wait. He sees something that we cannot see."

When the splendour departed and the youth awoke, he related to his parents what he had seen and heard ; and, after a few days, he betook himself to monastic religion in the convent assigned to him by the Saint.

William (i. 195-8)

while the youth was meditating about turning to a life of religion, the Martyr Thomas appeared to him one night, as before, with his insignia,[7] and stained with blood. And his parents heard him in his sleep answering the Martyr thus, "Which monastic habit ? " "Where ? " "When ? " "O my lord, have pity on me." And they said to one another, "Let us wait ; let us not rouse him ; he has a vision." But when his vision and sleep had fled, he cried aloud, "Did you see St. Thomas ? He was here but now. He

loquentem, vox autem loquentis cum eo penitus non audiebatur, nec videbatur persona ; cum tamen,[5] caligine nocturna repulsa, mirabilis quidam splendor totam domum illuminaret, ita ut puerum ipsum, et caetera omnia quae in domo erant, perspicue viderent. Dicebantque ad invicem, "Sustineamus ; aliquid videt quod videre non possumus." Discedente vero splendore, cum puer evigilasset, quae viderat et audierat parentibus retulit, paucisque diebus interpositis, in coenobio, quod ei sanctus assignaverat, religioni se monasticae contulit.

de conversione sua meditanti una noctium martyr Thomas sicut et prius apparuerit, infulatus[7] et cruentatus. Et audierunt parentes eum in somnis martyri respondentem, "Cujus habitus monachus ? " "Ubi ? " "Quando ? " "Domine, miserere mei"; dixeruntque ad invicem, "Sustineamus, non excitemus eum ; visionem videt." Cum autem visio somnusque fugissent, clamavit, "Vidistis beatum Thomam ? Hic

[5] "Cum tamen." We should have expected "suddenly," but the writer is illogically influenced by the parenthesis.

[7] Literally, "with the *fillet*," perhaps here "with the *mitre*" (712*a*), implying all the insignia of the sacrificial office.

William (i. 195-8)

has but now departed.[8]   He said to me, 'Engelram,[9] I have twice spoken to thee in secret.   The third time I will appear unto thee, and the whole region round about shall know it.'"

[728] In William's narrative, the youth is punished, not merely for a boyish flippancy disrespectful to St. Thomas, but also for his mother's sin ; the miraculous healing is ordained (in part at all events) to recall King Henry to a better mind ; moreover, lest the reader should suppose that the Martyr takes from the father his only son and devotes him to a life of celibacy, it is pointed out that there was an elder brother.

[729] The graphic description of the poor boy in his troubled sleep holding converse with the Martyr—in which William and Benedict closely agree—was probably taken by both from the priest of Golton whom Benedict mentions as

modo fuit, modo abscedit.[8] Dixit mihi, 'Duabus vicibus tibi, Engelrame,[9] occulte locutus sum.   Tertio tibi apparebo, scietque tota regio.'"

[8] "Abscedit," (?) an original error for "abscessit."

[9] "Engelrame." Here the son is called "Engelramus." According to Benedict (727 (2)), "Yngelrannus"—according to William (727 (1)), "Stephen"—was the *father's* name. The editor identifies the two names. The instances where father and son have the same name (*e.g.* "William" in *Mat.* i. 200) are rare, and this is not a common name like "William."

his informant: and the information (in view of the close similarity) probably came by letter.

[730] The miraculous brightness by night is connected by Benedict with the second vision, and witnessed by the parents; by William with the first vision, and witnessed only by the youth, who is awakened by it. On the other hand, the blood-streaked appearance of the Martyr is connected by Benedict with the first vision ; by William, with the second. Possibly, William thought that the brightness was most appropriate to the promise of healing, the blood-streak to the threat of punishment. A sudden outburst of moon-light through dark clouds might very well impress the excited parents—hearing their son hold converse in the dark with an invisible Saint—as though it were a flood of miraculously celestial light.

[731] William has probably modified the narrative for reasons of style. But the impression left on the reader is that he had come to the knowledge of some antecedent facts, unknown to Benedict and shewing that Benedict's account, perhaps following the story as told by Yngelrann's wife at Canterbury, was far too favourable to her. It seemed to William that the mother's tongue had encouraged her boy to his ruin, had he not been saved by the Saint. His severity to " the foul woman " (" illota ") is perhaps increased by his sense that she had *imposed on the monks for a time as a pious matron, who had actually suggested a pilgrimage to her husband, of her own motion* (Benedict (2)).

§ 7. *Jordan, son of Eisulf*

[732] Benedict (ii. 229-34)   William (i. 160-2)

(1) The hand of the Lord was heavy on a knight

(1) There came to Canterbury a knight, Jordan, son

---

(1) Aggravata est manus Domini   (1) Venit Cantuariam miles Jordanus,

Benedict (ii. 229-34)

of great name,[1] Jordan, son of Eisulf, and smote his house with plague from August to Easter.[2] Very many were sick in his house, and there was none to help. And the nurse of his son William (the boy was also known as Brito) died of acute disease and was buried. But on the third day after the decease of the nurse the Lord also smote the boy himself (being about ten years of age) with that same sickness, and he was

William (i. 160-2)

of Heisulf, from a town which he called Pontefract,[1] with his wife and a son of about ten years old, whom he asserted to have died and to have been restored to life by the Martyr St. Thomas, offering thanks for this blessing.

For on the death of the boy's nurse the boy likewise[2] died, and, as being dead, received all the last rites except sepulture,

---

super militem nominis magni[1] Jordanum Eisulfi filium, et percussit domum ejus plaga a tempore Augusti usque ad dies Paschales.[2] Et infirmati sunt multi valde in domo ejus, nec fuit qui adjuvaret. Et mortua est nutrix filii ejus Willelmi, cognomine Britonis, morbo acuto, et sepulta est. Tertio vero die post decessum nutricis percussit Dominus et puerum ipsum fere decennem eodem incommodo, et sub-

filius Heisulfi, de villa quam nomine Fracti Pontis appellabat,[1] cum uxore et filio decem circiter annorum, quem mortuum fuisse, et per beatum martyrem Thomam suscitatum asserebat, pro gratia gratias agens. Nutrix (prob. " nutrice ") siquidem pueri hujus rebus humanis exempta, puer pariter[2] decessit. Cui sicut mortuo caetera justa praeter sepulturam exhibita sunt,

---

[1] Contrary to his usual custom, Benedict omits the domicile of this knight. Is it possible that "nominis magni" may be a remnant of some expression like William's "quam nomine Fracti Pontis," which has been corrupted here?

[2] "Dies Paschales." This is to be understood as including *all* the deaths mentioned in the narrative, not the first two deaths merely (which took place some time before the middle of Lent, see below (7)).

[1] "Quam nomine Fracti Pontis appellabat," a curious statement (if the text is correct). Did William think the name "Broken Bridge" so strange that it could not be the regular name?

[2] "Pariter," here implying approximate, but not complete, simultaneousness.

Benedict (ii. 229-34)

taken on the seventh day, about the third hour.[3] A priest came, and commended his soul to the hands of the Creator, and celebrated for the deceased the appointed exequies in accordance with the custom of the church. All that day and the following night, vigil was kept over him as over one deceased. Concerning the unbounded sorrow of the parents, I say nothing : any one, however simple, can imagine it.

(2) There arrived on the same day pilgrims returning from the Martyr's memorial, in number about twenty, all of whom the father hospitably entertained for love of the Martyr : and on the morrow,

William (i. 160-2)

(2) , because the father would not permit him to be carried out for burial. For he said, as though an angel spoke within him, [My] spirit promises me that my son will be restored,[3]

---

latus est de medio die septimo, hora quasi tertia.[3] Affuit presbyter, qui et animam in manus Creatoris commendavit, et pro defuncto constitutas ecclesiastico more celebravit exsequias. Toto illo die et nocte sequenti super eum utpote super defunctum vigilatum est. De luctu parentum immoderato sileo, quem quilibet etiam simplex imaginari valebit.

(2) Supervenerunt eodem die peregrini a martyris memoria revertentes, numero circiter viginti, quos omnes paterfamilias pro martyris amore sus-

(2) patre ad sepulturam eum non permittente deduci. Aiebat enim, tanquam in se loquente angelo, " Mihi filium meum restituendum [3] spiritus promittit ;

[3] i.e. at 9 A.M.

[3] " Restituendum," a constr. common in William for fut. passive.

Benedict (ii. 229-34)   William (i. 160-2)

when they would have de-
parted, he made them rest
and refresh themselves. Now
came the Priest to carry the
corpse to the church that it
might be buried. But the
father said, " In no wise shall
my son be carried to the
grave, for my heart prophe-
sies to me that the Martyr
will not let me lose him : for
indeed, while he was in the
body, I was his man,⁴ and
his familiar friend."

(3) And having received   (3) , and if I had even a
the Water of the Martyr   little of the Water of the
from the pilgrims, he said to   glorious Martyr Thomas, to
the Priest, " Pour it into his   pour it into his mouth, it
mouth, in case perchance the   seems to me that I should
Martyr may give me back   not be—in the righteousness
my son."   of my faith and the firmness
                             of my hope—a father be-

cepit hospitio : quos etiam in crastino,
quum vellent abire, recumbere fecit et
refici.   Venit presbyter ut corpus
exanime ad ecclesiam ferret et traderet
sepulturae.   At pater, " Nequaquam,"
inquit, " efferetur filius meus, quia
vaticinatur mihi cor meum nolle martyrem Thomam quod illum amittam ;
nam et homo⁴ ejus fui, dum esset in
corpore, et familiaris ejus amicus."

(3) Et accepta a peregrinis martyris   (3) et si vel modicum aquae gloriosi
aqua, ait presbytero, " Infunde in os   martyris Thomae, quod in os ejus in-
ejus, si forte reddat mihi martyr filium   funderetur, haberem, videor mihi non
meum."   in fide recta et spe firma pater or-

⁴ " Man," *i.e.* vassal.

Benedict (ii. 229-34)	William (i. 160-2)
	reaved of his child. So having received the Water from pilgrims whom he had hospitably entertained,
(4) Wondering at the faith, or rather suspecting the insanity, that dictated this request, the Priest poured it in: and the boy did not arise. So the funeral was delayed to the tenth or eleventh hour,⁵ while the father was awaiting what the Lord would do. The Priest, suspecting that this strange craving sprang from something wrong in his reason, said, "Why, my lord, is the funeral thus deferred? This is now the second day since the boy died."⁶ And	(4) , he poured some of it into the mouth of the deceased, which there was great difficulty in opening, owing to the *rigor* [*mortis*], inasmuch as from the third hour of the day till the eleventh hour of the following day he had lain lifeless. At first nothing went down into the stomach through the closed passages,

bandus." Aqua igitur a peregrinis hospitio susceptis accepta,

(4) Admiratus jubentis fidem, immo potius suspicatus insaniam, infudit, et non surrexit puer. Dilata est ergo corporis exanimis sepultura usque ad horam decimam sive undecimam,⁵ expectante patre quid Dominus esset facturus. Suspicatus sacerdos hanc non sani capitis esse voluntatem, ait illi, "Utquid, domine, sepultura differtur defuncti? ecce jam secunda dies defluxit, postquam puer decessit."⁶

(4) orique defuncti, quod vix rigor aperiri permiserat, infusa (nam ab hora diei tertia usque quasi in undecimam diei sequentis exsanguis jacuerat), primo nihil per interceptos meatus in praecordia descendit ;

⁵ 4 P.M., or 5 P.M.
⁶ A remarkable testimony to the prevalence of speedy burial in those times.

Benedict (ii. 229·34)   William (i. 160-2)

he replied, " In no wise shall my son be buried : for verily my heart testifies to me, that he is to be given back to me by Thomas the Martyr. Bring hither the Water of my lord."

(5) It was brought. He approached the corpse and uncovered it. Then, slightly raising the head and separating with a small knife the clenched teeth, he poured in the Water. And there appeared, immediately after the infusion, a small spot of red in the middle of his left cheek, which gladdened the father not a little. So he poured some in again, in such a way that, the boy being placed upright, the Water might pass through the throat.

(5) but by degrees the natural channels were loosened, and, as a proof of the Divine power at work, a redness tinged the cheek.

Et contra ille, " Nequaquam sepelietur filius meus ; revera namque testificatur mihi cor meum, quod per martyrem Thomam mihi reddendus sit : afferte aquam domini mei."

(5) Quae cum allata fuisset, accessit corpusque detexit ; sullevavit caput, dentesque cohaerentes cultello interposito separans, aquam infudit. Et apparuit continuo post infusionem aquae in medio faciei ejus sinistrae nota ruboris modica, et patrem non modicum laetificavit ; infudit ergo iterum, ita ut erecti guttur pueri aqua transiret.

(5) sed laxatis sensim naturae canalibus Divinae virtutis indicium rubor maxillam infecit.

Benedict (ii. 229-34)

(6) And he opened one eye, and seeing his parents in floods of tears, he said these words, " Why lament, father ? why weep, lady ? Be not sad.   See, Thomas the Martyr has given me back to you."

After this he was silent and said nothing more till late in the evening.

(7) And his father said, " Quick !   Bring hither four silver   pieces " ;   and   he fastened to [the child] two for himself and his wife, and two   for   the   resuscitated [child], placing one in his right hand, the other in his left, promising that the boy should be presented to the Martyr   in   the   middle   of

William (i. 160-2)

(6) And after a short interval, the boy opened one eye, and said, " Do not weep ! Thomas the glorious Martyr has given me back to you."

(7) So both the parents, together with the boy, vowed a pilgrimage to the Martyr's memorial,

---

(6) Et aperuit alterum oculorum, vidensque parentes suos in lacrymas effluere, haec verba locutus est, "Cur ploras, pater ? quare fles, domina ? nolite tristari ; en, reddidit me vobis beatus martyr Thomas." Haec quum dixisset, obmutuit, et usque ad vesperam amplius non est locutus.

(7) Et ait pater ipsius, " Cito afferte argenteos quatuor"; et complicuit duos pro se et uxore sua, duos autem pro resuscitato, ponens alterum in sinistra ejus, alterum in dextera, promittens offerendum martyri puerum

(6) Parvaque interveniente mora, unum oculorum aperiens, " Nolite," inquit, " flere.   Reddidit me vobis gloriosus ille martyr Thomas."

(7) Vovens itaque parens uterque cum puero memoriam martyris adire,

Benedict (ii. 229-34)	William (i. 160-2)

Lent.[7]   Then, sitting down, they watched him.   So when it grew late in the evening, the boy sat up, tasted [food], spoke, was restored to his parents, and [ultimately] recovered (convaluit).

(8) The time appointed for paying the vow passed on, and payment was delayed, owing to some impediment. So the Martyr appeared to a leper named Gimpe,[8] who lived three miles from

(8) But they prolonged their preparations for the journey till the day of *Rejoice Jerusalem*.[4]   Then, when everything was ready, they were hindered by the arrival, in that neighbourhood, of the

in medio Quadragesimae :[7] et sedentes observabant eum.   Cum ergo ad-vesperasceret, resedit puer, gustavit, locutus est, et redditus parentibus suis convaluit.

(8) Transiit terminus voto solvendo praefixus, et intercurrente impedimento in aliud tempus voti solutio dilata est. Apparuit itaque martyr Domini Thomas cuidam leproso in somnis, tribus passuum millibus a militis domo distanti,

(8) usque in *Laetare Jerusalem*[4] procinctum itineris protelarunt.   Tunc vero paratis necessariis, in via aliud subiit impedimentum.   Nam comes

[7] This, then, could not have been later than the second or third week in Lent, and might have been before. The sun would set about 6 P.M., and probably earlier.   The funeral is said above to have been delayed till 4 or 5 P.M., which may be called the early evening.   The applications of the Water, and the subsequent waiting, would bring the time to late in the evening.

[8] Al. "Gympe." This section is condensed from the original, in which the dialogues are given at great length.

[4] i. 161, Ed.   "This is the beginning of the introit for the Fourth Sunday in Lent."

Benedict (ii. 229-34)

Jordan's house *and knew nothing of what had happened*,[9] bidding him go and warn the knight to hasten to Canterbury : "Unless he speedily haste, I will bring evil on him and his wife, and as much joy as he has received through me, through the bringing to life of his son, so much sorrow shall he

William (i. 160-2)

Earl Warrenne, in whose name the knight possessed lands. But it came to pass that St. Thomas appeared to a leper on the lands of the knight bidding him go and warn the knight to-morrow not to delay his pilgrimage any longer. "Otherwise let him know he shall lose something else which[5] he loves

---

et *rem gestam prorsus ignoranti*,[9] et ait, "Gimpe,[8] dormis ?" (hoc enim leproso nomen esse audivimus). "Dormivi," inquit, "sed jam excitasti me ; tu quis es ?" Et martyr, "Ego sum Thomas Cantuariensis archiepiscopus : Jordanum Eisulfi filium nosti ?" "Optime," inquit, "domine, utpote virum | optimum, qui multa mihi bona impendit." Tunc sanctus, "Vade et dic ei ex parte mea transisse terminum quem posuit, et vota reddita non esse quae promisit. Acceleret ergo et ad Cantuariam eat, et pro filio suo, quem Dominus interventu meo vitae restituit, vota persolvat. Nisi citius iter arripuerit, inducam super uxorem ejus malum ; quantumque de filio suo resuscitato per me suscepit laetitiae, tantundem de alio, quem amittet, obtinebit moeroris."

Warennensis, cujus nomine res soli miles praetaxatus possidebat, eo loci veniens peregre profecturos detinebat. Factum est autem ut beatus Thomas leproso in fundo praedicti militis habitanti appareret, dicens, "Dormisne, frater ?" "Dormiebam," inquit, "priusquam dormientem excitasses. Quisnam es tu?" Respondit, "Thomas, Cantuariensis archiepiscopus. Perge crastina die nuntiatum militi huic ut peregrinationem et votum suum ulterius non differat. Alioquin aliud, quod[5] non minus diligit quam filium quem ei reddidi, se noverit amissurum."

---

[9] The italicized words are omitted by William : and it certainly seems strange that the leper should know nothing of such a marvel. It is all the stranger because the leper says to St. Thomas that he knows the knight as being "a very good man who bestows many benefits on me."

[5] Benedict's "alio quem," if written "alio quē" in the Canterbury archives, may have been corrupted into "alio quod."

Benedict (ii. 229·34)	William (i. 160·2)
obtain for another [son] whom he shall lose."	not less than the son that I have restored to him."

Benedict (ii. 229·34)

obtain for another [son] whom he shall lose."

(9) The leper replies that, being blind as well as confined to his bed by disease of the feet, he cannot obey the Saint: and, when he awakes, he takes no notice of the dream. The Saint, appearing a second time, and again receiving the same excuse, bids him entrust the message to his Priest.

(10) He did so. But the Priest replied, "It is a

William (i. 160·2)

not less than the son that I have restored to him."

(9) The leper feared [6] to deliver such a message. So the Saint appeared again on the following night and rebuked him. " Thou knowest, my lord," he replied, "that I am diseased in the feet and cannot walk." He (?) replied,[7] "Call thy Priest that he himself may at all events carry my message."

(10) He did so, and when the Priest excused

(9) Respondit ad haec leprosus, "Jam anni ferme viginti praeterierunt, domine, ex quo lumen coeli non vidi, et pedes debilis jaceo lecto affixus; et quomodo possem ad militis domum pervenire?" Et evigilans, nec magni pendit quae audierat, nec fecit quod ei martyr injunxerat. Apparuit ergo ei iterum martyr, et ait; "Quare non fecisti quae dicta sunt tibi?" "Non potui, domine," inquit, "caecitate et debilitate praepeditus." Et ait ad eum sanctus, "Voca presbyterum tuum, et pone verba mea in ore ejus, ut annunciet militi omnia quae praecepi."

(10) Accersivit presbyterum leprosus, et ait illi; "Haec et haec

(9) Eo autem timente [6] nuntium hujusmodi perferre, denuo postera nocte martyr adest. "Heus," inquit, "mandato non paruisti." Respondit, "Novisti, domine, quia infirmus pedes incedere non possum." Adjecit,[7] "Voca sacerdotem tuum, ut vel ipse perferat mandatum."

(10) Quod cum faceret, praetendente sacerdote timoris excusationem,

[6] It is not clear whether William regards the "fear" as the only real reason. William makes no mention of the "blindness" of which Benedict speaks.

[7] "Adjecit" would naturally mean "added."

dream. Should I tell a great man like that such fancies and idle dreams ? He is a man of rank and power, and if I tell him, he will ridicule and despise both tale and teller. You will not catch me bearing such a message."

For the third time the Saint rebuked the leper, who told him that the Priest scorned even to listen to him : " What could I do more ? " Then the Saint bade him send his daughter

himself on the ground of fear and of the proneness to anger in a man of such high rank, the Martyr manifested himself for the third time— not counting him unclean whom the Lord had hallowed in the water of regeneration —and, convicting his inter- mediary [8] of contempt, he called and bade him send his daughter to take the message to the knight and his lady.[9]

mandat tibi martyr Cantuariensis." At ille ; "Somnium est ; ergone viro tanto fabulas et somniorum naenias recitarem ? Vir magnus et potens est, et tam recitantem quam recitata sub- sannando contemneret ; non me habebis talis nuncii bajulum." Tertio astitit sanctus eidem leproso, et dixit, "Quare factum non est quod praecepi ? " " Domine," inquit, " pertuli mandata tua presbytero, et audire contempsit ; quid ultra facerem ?" Et contra sanctus, " Mitte mane filiam tuam

hominisque privilegiati facilem indig- nationem, tertio martyr suam exhibuit praesentiam, non immundum reputans quem Dominus lavacro regenerationis sanctificarat, arguensque contemptus interpretem,[8] vocans ait, " Per inter- nuntiam filiam tuam militem et uxorem ejus nuntia [9] quae in mandatis ac- cepisti " ;

[8] " Interpretem " ought to mean the Priest, who should have been the " intermediary," but had despised the message. The leper cannot be said to have " despised " it.

[9] " Militem et uxorem nuntia " is, no doubt, a mistake for the dative. William does not say (as Benedict does) that the daughter *fetches* them.

Benedict (ii. 229-34)

to fetch the knight and his lady. When they came, he was to tell them the whole truth, hiding nothing.

(11) They came, and heard the story, and were filled with wonder. So they fixed a date that should positively not be overpassed, viz. the last week of Lent: but owing to the unexpected arrival of the Earl Warrenne, the knight's lord, they put off the pilgrimage, and turned themselves away [10] and did not keep their covenant.

(12) But on the last day of the appointed limit, namely the holy Sabbath (*i.e.* Saturday) that precedes the day of

William (i. 160-2)

(11) This was accordingly done. But as they still put it off,

(12) Easter being close at hand, the elder son, whom the father loved the more tenderly because he was the

---

pro milite et pro uxore ejus, et proculdubio venient ad te; cave ergo, cum venerint, ne celaveris ab iis vel unum verbum ex omnibus quae locutus sum tibi."

(11) Mane vocati sunt; venerunt; audientes admirati sunt. Terminum ergo posuerunt quem non transgrederentur, hebdomadam videlicet Quadragesimae ultimam : sed superveniente comite Warennensi, militis domino, peregrinationem distulerunt, et averterunt se,[10] et non servaverunt pactum.

(12) Ultimo autem constituti termini die, sabbato videlicet sancto,

(11) quod et factum est. Veruntamen illis adhuc differentibus,

(12) imminente solennitate Paschali, filius familias major natu, quem pater

---

[10] "Averterunt se," *i.e.* from following the Martyr's bidding.

Benedict (ii. 229-34)	William (i. 160-2)
the Lord's resurrection, the Lord smote with a sore disease another son of the knight, more loved than the one that had been restored to life, and a little older. On the morrow the parents themselves fell sick and took to their bed, and were despaired of: and the sickness grew strong on the boy, and he fell asleep and so passed into death [11] on the seventh day, the sixth day of Easter week. The death of their son increased the sickness of the parents, especially that of the father, who loved the boy all the more for being an exact image of himself. So he urged his	image of his father's ancestors in form and figure, was seized by disease and died. And the knight and his lady, with the whole of the household, were kept to their beds by such a disturbance of health that they despaired of life. So fearing death, or some worse visitation, they set out on their pilgrimage.

qui Dominicae resurrectionis diem praecessit, percussit Dominus acuto morbo alium militis filium, resuscitato magis dilectum, et natu paulo majorem. In crastino parentes ipsi infirmati sunt et ceciderunt in lectum, et desperati sunt ; et invaluit morbus in puero, et obdormivit in mortem [11] die septimo, feria sexta paschalis hebdomadae. Aegritudinem parentum filii obitus augmentavit ; patris maxime, qui eum tenerius dilexerat eo quod vultus paternus elimatius in eo videretur

tenerius diligebat, quia genus paternum corporeis lineamentis elimatius expressit, correptus infirmitate rebus humanis excessit. Miles autem cum uxore tanta corporis inaequalitate detentus est, sicut et domus ejus tota, ut de vita diffiderent. Timentes itaque vitae exitum, vel gravius dispendium, peregre profecti sunt,

[11] "Obdormivit in mortem" : I am not sure whether "obdormire" is here used literally or to mean "fell asleep in death." If the latter, "in mortem" seems superfluous.

Benedict (ii. 229-34)	William (i. 160-2)

wife to an immediate pilgrimage, "lest something worse
befall us."

(13) In that instant, the
disease in both of them somewhat abated. Some of their
friends, hearing of their in-
tention, begged them to delay,
especially for the sake of the
mother, who seemed likely to
die on the way. But the
knight replied, "Living or
dead, we will both go to the

(13) And they were
escorted by their twenty-one
servants, of whom some,
having been long sick, had
recovered on that very day,
by drinking the healing Water.
But the mother, having fainted
nine times within a short
interval in the journey,
despaired because of the

---

expressus. Qui, videns completum iri
quae per leprosum sanctus pronuntia-
verat, dixit uxori suae: "Ecce,
domina, quid nobis attulit mora nostra
doloris: proh dolor! certe nimis
tardavimus; mentiti sumus martyri,
en, secundo, et ecce, filium nostrum
amisimus: nos quoque comprehende-
runt mala quae promisit, et exitum
similem praestolamur. Oravi pro
alio martyrem, et reddidit eum nobis;
sed quomodo orabimus vel pro isto vel
pro nobis? nihil ulterius martyrem
offensum rogare praesumam antequam
vota persolverim: acceleremus itaque,
ne deterius nobis aliquid contingat."

(13) Mirum dictu, in eodem instanti minorata est utriusque infirmitas;
audito vero quod ad iter se praepara-
rent, convenerunt ex amicis eorum,
suggerentes ne infirmi et debiles tanto
se darent labori, maxime propter
matrem familias, quae periculosius
laborabat, metuendum esse ne labor
itineris aegrotantium mortem maturaret.
At miles, "Sive vivi sive mortui,
utrique veniemus ad martyrem. Aut

(13) et a viginti et uno domesticis
suis, quorum quidam diu languentes
aquae salutaris potatione ipsa die
convaluerant, deducti sunt. Mater
vero familias, infra modicum itineris
intervallum novies in extasim lapsa, de

Benedict (ii. 229-34)

Martyr. . . ." About twenty of the household had been confined to their beds for periods reaching from seventeen to thirty weeks. On the point of starting, the knight gave each of them a draught of the Martyr's Water. Not one but was so far strengthened by it that he rose from his bed and escorted his master at least to the gate, and some a good way beyond the gate. His wife, who had

William (i. 160-2)

length of the way. But her husband adhered to his purpose. " Living or dead," said he, " she shall be carried into Canterbury." And their journey prospered under the protection of the merits of him whom they were seeking [*i.e.* St. Thomas], according to the saying, " For them that love God all things work together for good, for them who are called according to His purpose " [10] :—so that the

vivus ibo, aut ferar mortuus ; uxor mea vel vivens martyri adducetur vel afferetur defuncta : si noluerit viventes, certe habebit nos vel exanimes." Languebant autem de familia militis viri numero quasi viginti, quorum aliqui hebdomadis decem et septem, quidam viginti, alii viginti et sex vel septem, nonnulli viginti et novem vel triginta lecto affixi jacuerant. Profecturus igitur martyris aqua, quam habebat, singulos salutis gustum administravit. In singulis aqua virtutis effectum ostendit ; singulos de lecto erexit, ita ut nec unum jacentem relinqueret, qui

viae longitudine desperabat. Sed vir animi constans, " Aut viva," ait, " vel mortua Cantuariam efferetur." Et prosperatum est iter ipsorum suffragantibus meritis ejus quem petebant, juxta quod dictum est, " Diligentibus Deum omnia cooperantur in bonum, his qui secundum propositum vocati sunt sancti " ; [10] adeo ut mulier tria

[10] The text has " qui secundum propositum vocati sunt *sancti*," which might either mean "called (to be) holy," or " called according to the purpose of the holy one, or Saint."

William seems to mean that they were called by St. Thomas, but he may quote St. Paul's words (Rom. viii. 28) as applicable to his purpose because God may be said to call those whom He calls through another.

Benedict (ii. 229-34)	William (i. 160-2)
fainted seven times and more on the first day of the journey, dismounted from her horse on seeing the pinnacle of Canterbury Cathedral, and walked barefoot as far as the Martyr's tomb, a distance of about three miles, without any fatigue. So,[12] together with the boy, the parents came barefoot, rendering to the Martyr with floods of tears the vows which their lips had specified.	woman, when entering Canterbury, came three miles on her feet at a rapid pace.

[733] Here William ends, but Benedict has a long discourse on the glory of this miracle, in which he says, " We also wrote secretly to the Priest of the knight on these points, and he testified to the truth, writing back that the boy was

dominum suum exeuntem longius extra portam vel usque ad portam non deduceret. Uxor ejus, quae primo die prae labore· itineris septies et eo amplius in exstasim lapsa est, videns pinnaculum templi Cantuariensis de equo descendit, nudisque pedibus usque ad martyris sepulchrum, quasi milliaria tria, nullo gravata labore perrexit. Simul [12] ergo cum puero parentes pedibus nudis venerunt, reddentes martyri cum uberrima lacrymarum copia vota, quae distinxerunt labia sua.

milliaria Cantuariam ingressura pedes arriperet.

[12] This sentence looks as if it had been composed before the insertion of the preceding one—which describes how the mother entered Canterbury barefoot—and had been left unaltered after the insertion.

certainly dead, and was raised from the dead by the Water of the Martyr."

This probably explains many of the differences between the two writers. Benedict inserts the coming of the Priest to perform the burial ; his futile attempt (at the father's request) to resuscitate the child ; his remonstrance with the father ; his suspicions that the father was not quite right in his mind; his dialogue with the leper[1] and his contemptuous treat-ment of the leper's dream—all of which are omitted by William. Some of these points are of importance, and especially the failure of the Priest, and the action of the father in lifting the boy's head, and then raising the body to a sitting position.

[734] As regards other details, it is curious that William should differ from Benedict as to the precise number of times the lady fainted (B. " seven times and more," W. " nine times "), and as to the precise number of servants ill (B. "about twenty," W. " twenty-one ") : but perhaps here, too, Benedict copied the Priest's letter, and William the knight's testimony as set down in Canterbury. A more important difference, concerning these servants, is this. Benedict says they were all able to leave their beds and to escort their master, *some a good way* (longius), *and all as far as the gate.* If this was the fact, William's statement that they " were *escorted* by their twenty-one servants—some of whom had on that same day *recovered* (convaluerant)"—though literally correct, is mis-leading, as it ignores the fact that some *could only get as far as the gate.* On the other hand, Benedict represents the whole twenty as being benefited, more or less, by the Water : William mentions only " some of them."

[735] It is interesting to find William approximating to Benedict in some striking utterances of the father, *e.g.* about

---

[1] [733a] This assumes that Jordan's priest would also be the priest of the leper, who was on Jordan's land, three miles away. Even if the two Priests were different, the details are such as might naturally be emphasized by any one who subsequently became a convert to St. Thomas.

his "heart prophesying to him" (William, "his spirit
promising "). Also we can well understand that one or
both of the parents may have told the monks that the elder
child whom they had lost irrevocably was "the image of his
father," or (as perhaps the knight had put it) "the image of
his ancestors on his father's side."

[736] William has the advantage of Benedict in brevity.
Yet the former omits some things of dramatic vividness, too
natural to have been invented, as for example when the
knight, who appears to have been of a hasty temper,[2] instead
of simply saying that they will go to Canterbury alive or
dead, adds, "I will go living, or I will be carried dead. My
wife shall be either led to the Martyr living, or brought to
him lifeless. If he won't have us alive, he shall certainly
have us dead." Such sayings as these, treasured in the ears
of the knight's friends, and especially perhaps recalled by
the wife and her relations, may have been repeated to
Benedict by Jordan's priest : and they are extremely
characteristic. It must be added, however, that Benedict
inserts them elsewhere (**741** (5)), where William omits them.
Did the omission arise from a sense that they betokened a
want of faith ? Probably such words were often uttered.
Stanley (p. 223) mentions "a wide cemetery" in which
"were interred such pilgrims as died during their stay in
Canterbury." It would be interesting to know whether
those who died on the way thither were also interred there,
and whether this often happened.

Some stained glass in Canterbury Cathedral still
commemorates this miracle. One of the scenes represents
"the mother caressing her son with one hand, whilst with
the other outstretched she gives to the father "[3] the four
silver pieces which he vows to the Saint.

---

[2] See William (10) above.

[3] Stanley, p. 297. Another picture represents the parents as coming to the
leper (*ib.*). Both these points are omitted by William.

§ 8. *Cecily, daughter of Jordan of Plumstead, is restored, when supposed to have died from cancer*

[737] Benedict (ii. 234-7)

(1) Well then,[1] in the diocese of Norwich, a girl, Cecilia [by name], daughter of one Jordan of Plumstead,[2] about fifteen years old, was smitten with cancer.

William (i. 190-3)

(1) I remember that I spoke above of one Jordan[1] whose son we saw recalled from the dead. I have now also to speak of another of the same name, but of inferior rank, whose daughter we saw liberated from a double death by a prodigy not inferior [to the other].

Well then,[2] in the diocese

---

(1) Igitur[1] in diocesi Norwicensi puella Caecilia, Jordani cujusdam filia de Plumstede[3] quindecim circiter habens aetatis annos, cancro percussa est.

(1) Memini me dixisse de quodam Jordane,[1] cujus filium vidimus revocatum a mortuis. Dicendum est et nunc de quodam alio ejusdem nominis, sed inferioris conditionis, cujus filiam non inferiori prodigio vidimus a duplici morte liberatam. Igitur[2] in diocesi Norwi-

---

[1] "Igitur." The last miracle, that of Jordan of Pontefract, concluded thus : "I will subjoin two miracles, not less wonderful and not much inferior in importance (magnitudine), concerning two who are believed to have died." After such a preface, "igitur" is often used as an introduction. When the introductory "igitur" is used without an introduction, we may often assume that it once existed, but has been omitted.

[3] "De Plumstede." Ed. adds "in Norfolk." The similarity of the name "Jordan" to that in the last narrative makes it all the more remarkable that Benedict omitted the domicile there (732 (1)).

[1] "Jordane" (for "Jordano") both here and below, in section (15).

[2] "Igitur." See note (1) in Benedict. William includes in his story a Preface similar to that which Benedict has written to do double duty,—being an Appendix to the preceding narrative and a Preface to this one.

	of Norwich, a girl, Cecilia [by name], about fifteen years old, was smitten with cancer.
(2) While maidenly modesty induced her to bear her pain rather than publish what caused her shame, the disease gradually spread till it ate away the thighs and hinder parts so that the joints of the bones, and the muscles lay open to view.	(2) In a short time, while maidenly modesty induced her to bear her pain rather than publish what caused her shame, the thighs were eaten away so that the joints of the bones were laid bare and the muscles lay open to view.
(3) At length her pale face shewed that she was out of health : her parents asked what ailed her and received most painful reports.[3]	(3) William omits this.
(4) The ulcers were a foot in breadth, emitting such	(4) The wounds were a foot in breadth, and there

---

.

censi puella Cecilia, quindecim circiter habens aetatis annos, cancro percussa est.

(2) Quae dum virginali verecundia maluit perferre dolorem quam proferre pudorem, serpente paulatim morbo exesa sunt femora ejus et nates, ut ossium juncturae nervorumque colligamenta paterent.

(2) Cujus in brevi, dum virginali verecundia mavult perferre dolorem quam pudorem proferre, exesa sunt femora, ut denudarentur ossium juncturae nervorumque colligamenta paterent.

(3) Tandem vero sanam non esse eam vultus indicabat exsanguis; quaerunt parentes quid patitur, et magni doloris rumores [3] excipiunt.

(3) om.

(4) Ulcerum latitudo pedis mensuram aequabat ; tanti foetores inde

(4) Nam vulnerum latitudo mensuram pedis aequabat, intolerabilesque

---

[3] "Magni doloris rumores " (?), "reports of great pain (in the patient)," or, "that caused the parents great pain."

Benedict (ii. 234-7)	William (i. 190-3)
a stench that even her mother desired her death and her familiar friends avoided her presence. The neighbours loathed to enter the house where she lay. The ulcers of the devouring cancer were wrapped in cloths that had to be changed every hour owing to the mass of putrid matter that came forth thence as it were in steam.	came forth thence as it were in steam mephitic vapours, intolerable, so that even her mother desired her death and familiar friends avoided her presence. For the corrupt matter used to consume[3] every day the strips of cloth in which the devouring plague was swathed.
(5) Sit, or lie, she could not ; but leaning on her knees and elbows she kept the attitude of one falling on her face.	(5) William omits this.

---

prodibant, ut et mater mortem ejus optaret, et familiares ejus declinarent praesentiam ; vicini quoque domus in qua jacebat abhorrebant ingressum. Edacis ulcera cancri pannis obvolvebantur, quos tabis evaporantis copia singulis horis mutari cogebat ;

(5) sedere seu jacere non poterat, sed genibus innitens et cubitis procumbebat in faciem.

mephites evaporabant, ut et mater ejus mortem optaret, familiaresque praesentiam declinarent. Corruptio quippe panniculos quibus pestis edax involvebatur omni die consumebat.[3]

(5) om.

[3] MSS. "consume*bant*." Ed. reads "consume*bat*" (which might have been changed to "consume*bāt*"). The original meaning probably was that the disease "wasted," or "consumed," the cloths that were continually applied, because they had continually to be taken off and destroyed, and new ones applied. William's words suggest that the "devouring disease" literally "consumed" them (Sophocl. *Trach.* 695); but that is perhaps the result of his attempt at brevity and force.

Benedict (ii. 234-7)

(6) Suffering thus from harvest-time up to the month of March, she was at last quite brought to extremity. For three or four days, taking neither food nor drink, but remaining still [4] in bed, leaning against the wall, with her knees drawn together, her eyelids open and motionless, she seemed to present the aspect of one neither living nor dead.

(7) So her friends, beholding her [thus], thought she had been carried [in ecstasy] out of her body : calling to mind a woman in the neigh-

William (i. 190-3)

(6) Tortured [4] by this pest, from about harvest-time to the first of March, she was brought down to extremity. So from Tuesday to Friday she took neither food nor drink, but all the time remaining still in bed, leaning against the wall, with her knees drawn together, her eyelids open and motionless, she presented the appearance of one neither dead nor living.

(7) So the servants of the house,[5] beholding her [thus], thought she was being led out of her body : calling to mind a woman in the

---

(6) A tempore messis usque ad mensem Martium laborans tandem ad extrema perducta est ; tribus aut quatuor diebus non edulio, non potu, refecta est, sed residens [4] in lecto, accumbens parieti, genibus contractis, ciliis patulis et immotis, nec viventis nec mortui speciem exhibere videbatur.

(7) Unde sui contemplantes arbitrati sunt eam extra corpus raptam, reminiscentes cujusdam mulieris vicinae, Ag-

(6) Hac autem lue vexata [4] quasi a tempore messis in kalendas Martias, ad extrema deducta est. Igitur a tertia feria usque sextam non edulio, non potu reficiebatur, sed usque residens in lecto, accumbens parieti, genibus contractis, ciliis patulis et immotis, nec mortui speciem nec viventis exhibebat.

(7) Unde domestici [5] contemplantes eam arbitrati sunt extra corpus duci, reminiscentes cujusdam mulieris vicinae,

---

[4] " Residens" sometimes means "sitting *up*," sometimes "sitting *to rest*," but here seems to mean " remaining still " as in 737 (10).

[4] " Vexata," used of torture in Purgatory by William in section (8), below.

[5] In 732 (13), William has " domestici," where Benedict has "familia," and where the sense and context indicate that " servants " (not " family ") are meant.

bourhood, Agnes by name, who, a few days before, on falling into a deep sleep, had been carried in the spirit [out of her body], and, with the guidance and revelation of St. Catharine, had for five days beheld the rewards and punishments of the departed.

(8) Benedict omits this.

neighbourhood, Agnes by name, who, on falling asleep, had been carried in the spirit through divers regions with the guidance of St. Catharine; and the rewards and punishments of the departed had been revealed to her.

(8) Among whom she [*i.e.* Agnes] saw also one Godwin, a priest—who had departed life a few days before—with his knees grievously ulcerated by repeated blows from a nail.[6] It was thought that he was tortured with this punishment because,

---

netis nomine, quae paucis ante diebus cum obdormivisset in spiritu rapta est, et beata Katerina ducente et ostendente, diebus quinque praemia poenasque defunctorum contemplata.

(8) om.

Agnetis nomine, quae cum dormisset ducente beata Katerina per varia loca in spiritu rapta est, et ostensa sunt ei praemia et poenae defunctorum ;

(8) inter quos et presbyterum vidit Godwinum quendam, qui paucis antea diebus a corpore exierat, genua sua assidua repercussione clavis unius graviter exulceratum.[6]   Quo supplicio vexari putabatur quia vivens in corpore

---

[6] " Genua *sua* assidua repercussione clavis *unius* graviter exulceratum." Does the bad Latin (" unius ") indicate that William is adding a local tradition told in local language?   It appears probable that "sua "= "ejus."   Godwin did not wound himself thus in penitence.   He was punished thus,— we may suppose, in Purgatory.

Benedict (ii. 234-7)	William (i. 190-3)
	when living in the body, he had taken away and kept the key of the Church of St. Mary while another priest was celebrating mass therein.
(9) So, thinking that she, too, like [Agnes], had been led out of the body, they watched her in the hope of her return.	(9) William omits this.
(10) But it came to pass, while the girl remained [thus] unmoved, there came in to [see] her, toward night-fall, a woman from the neighbourhood, who loved her very dearly. And she, believing her to be really dead, exclaimed, " What a sin it was for you to let this girl die in	(10) But it came to pass, while the girl above-mentioned remained [thus] unmoved, there came in [to change all this] a woman from the neighbourhood for the sake of paying her a visit—one that had loved her. And seeing[7] her dead, she exclaimed, " Why, in your[8] sight and with your

---

(9) Putantes itaque et hanc de corpore similiter eductam, spe reversionis ejus servabant eam.

(10) Factum est autem, dum sic puella resideret immota, ut introiret ad eam sub noctis initio mulier vicina, quae tenerius eam diligebat, credensque revera mortuam, exclamavit dicens, " Quam male egistis, qui puellam hanc

clavem ecclesiae beatae Mariae sibi praeripuerat dum quidam alius sacerdos in ea solennia missae celebraret.

(9) om.

(10) Factum est autem, dum sic puella praedicta resideret immota, ut interveniret mulier vicina visitandi gratia, quae dilexerat illam. Quam videns[7] mortuam exclamavit, " Quare nobis[8] videntibus et dimittentibus in

[7] Stronger than Benedict's " believing her to be dead."

[8] Text " nobis," an obvious error of the scribe (or modern misprint) for " vobis." William's words do not appear (like Benedict's) to say that she

Benedict (ii. 234-7)

her bed! Why, like [all] catholics on the point of death, was she not laid out in a hair-cloth? You have acted foolishly."

(11) She was carried, then, into an outer building, and laid out on the floor:—her limbs stiff, her body cold, and eyes wide open; the muscles of the knees contracted, and stiff, and quite hardened, as [might be expected] in one dead: the legs could in no wise be straightened out or stretched—a linen sheet was also laid on the corpse, and,

William (i. 190-3)

permission, dying in her bed, was she not—like [all] catholics on the point of death— laid out in a hair-cloth? You have acted foolishly."

(11) She was carried accordingly into an outer building and laid down on the floor, with limbs stiff, and eyes wide open. There was also placed under [9] the corpse a linen sheet, and, after the custom of funerals, tapers were kindled.

---

in lecto suo mori permisistis; quare, de more morientium catholicorum, exposita non est in cilicio? imprudenter egistis."

(11) Elata est ergo in exteriorem domum et in aream exposita, membris rigidis, frigido corpore, oculisque patentibus, contractis poplitum nervis, et utpote in mortuo rigidis et prorsus obduratis. Crura nullatenus erigi poterant aut extendi; superpositum est

lecto mortua de more morientium catholicorum exposita non est in cilicio? Imprudenter egistis."

(11) Elata est itaque in exteriorem domum, et in area deposita rigidis membris et patulis oculis. Suppositum [9] est et cadaveri linteamen, et in morem funeris accensa sunt luminaria.

---

ought not to have been allowed to die in her bed, but that, if she died in her bed, she ought to have been clothed with hair-cloth. But probably he meant the same a Benedict; only he has disarranged the words.

[9] "Suppositum," apparently a corruption of Benedict's "superpositum." See 793a.

Benedict (ii. 234-7)   William (i. 190-3)

after the custom of funerals, tapers were lighted.

(12) But the father—who had thrown himself down [to sleep] in a separate chamber, worn out at once by sorrow and by labour—roused from slumber, rushed in, crying aloud,

(12) But the father—who had thrown himself down [to sleep] in a separate chamber, worn out at once by sorrow and by labour—shaking off slumber, rushed in, crying aloud,

(13) "Is my daughter really dead?" "Indeed," said his wife, "she is dead."

(13) "If the Lord is propitious unto me, my daughter is not dead.

(14) Then said he, "O St. Thomas, Martyr of God, return me now my service, which in bygone days I zealously paid you. Return me my service. Now am I in sore need.

(14) "O, St. Thomas, return me now my service, which in bygone days I zealously paid you." And with lamentable outcry he kept on repeating, "Return me my service. Now am I in sore need. Return me my service."

(15) "Once I served you with zeal before you were

(15) Now as to his reason for saying this, we deem

---

etiam cadaveri linteamen, et in morem funeris accensa sunt luminaria.

(12) Pater autem, qui se seorsum projecerat, vexatum dolore pariter et labore, excitatus a somno cum clamore irruit,

(12) Pater autem, qui se seorsum projecerat, vexatum dolore pariter et labore, excusso somno irruit cum clamore,

(13) "Nunquid mortua est filia mea?" "Revera," inquit mulier, "mortua est."

(13) "Si Dominus mihi propitius est, filia mea mortua non est.

(14) Tunc ille, "O beate Thoma, Dei martyr, redde mihi nunc servitium meum quod tibi olim sedulus impendi; redde mihi servitium meum! Urget nunc necessitas.

(14) "O beate Thoma, redde nunc mihi servitium quod tibi sedulus olim impendi!" Et iterat lugubri clamore, "Redde mihi servitium! urget nunc necessitas; redde mihi servitium meum!"

(15) "Olim tibi sedule servivi ante-

(15) Quod quare dixerit, non credi-

Benedict (ii. 234-7)

exalted with this world's honours. Return me my service! Remember, blessed Martyr, how you were sick long ago in Kent in Clerk Turstan's house, and what good service I gave you there. You could not touch wine, or spirits, or beer, or any intoxicating liquor, and I used to scour the whole neighbourhood to find you whey. Return me my service! Then you had but one horse, and I had charge of that, too. Return me my service, bearing in mind all

William (i. 190-3)

it not beside the purpose to append an explanation of succinct brevity.

Well then, St. Thomas, before being exalted with this world's honours—before by fortune's smile he was enlarged both in resources and in reputation [10]— was entertained as a guest by a clerk, Turstan by name, a native of Kent, who, in a place called Croindenne,[11] under Archbishop Theobald, being appointed Proctor, was energetic in business and

quam saecularibus efferreris honoribus; redde mihi servitium meum! Memento, beate martyr, quam infirmus dudum in Cantia in domo Turstani clerici exstiteris, qualiter illic tibi servierim. Vinum et siceram et cervisiam, et omne quod inebriare potest, gustare non poteras; et ego tibi per totam viciniam serum perquirebam, quod biberes; redde mihi servitium meum! Unicum tunc habebas equum, cujus et ego curam agebam; redde mihi, martyr, servitium meum, reminiscens

mus ab re succincta brevitate subnectere.

Beatus igitur Thomas, priusquam saecularibus efferretur honoribus,[10] priusquam risu fortunae facultate dilataretur et nomine, hospitio susceptus est apud quendam clericum Turstanum nomine, Cantianum natione, qui in loco qui dicitur Croindenne [11] sub archiepiscopo Theodbaldo procurator constitutus rem strenue gerebat, et in-

[10] "Before . . . reputation" looks as though it were an ornate paraphrase (of Benedict's "before . . . honours") which William inserted along with the original. In any case the insertion is an amusing comment on William's "succinct brevity."

[11] "Croindenne." Ed., in marg., "(Croydon ?)."

Benedict (ii. 234-7)	William (i. 190-3)
the trouble I had in waiting on you. Return me my service! You [surely] do not wish me to have served you for naught."	diligent in his service. In his house—when Thomas, who was sick, could drink neither wine, nor spirits, nor any intoxicating liquor [12]—it was by the procurement and diligent search of this valet of his (" vernaculo "), Jordan,[13] all through the neighbourhood, that he used to drink whey, as his disease required. The man also had charge of his single horse, for, as a private man, he [*i.e.* the Saint] had but one. It was because of this liberal [14] service thus bestowed that the man presumed, repeating again and again, " Return me my service."
omnium laborum, quos circa te perpessus sum ; redde mihi servitium meum ! non indiges quod gratis tibi servierim."	dustrie negotia ministrabat. Ubi cum Thomas infirmatus nec vinum nec siceram [12] nec aliquid quod inebriare possit biberet, vernaculo isto Jordane [13] procurante et disquirente per viciniam, serum bibebat, sicut morbus exigebat. Qui etiam curabat equum quem unicum privatus habebat. Huic de impensa liberalitate [14] praesumens replicabat " Redde mihi servitium."

[12] William omits Benedict's " beer," perhaps as too common for St. Thomas, even in the flesh.

[13] " Jordane," (?) misprint for " Jordano."

[14] " Liberal service." Perhaps a play on the word as meaning also

Benedict (ii. 234-7)

William (i. 190-3)

(16) In such outcries as these the man spent nearly half the night. So, when he had reiterated "Return me my service" so often as to stop his windpipe with hoarseness, the pity of the Martyr assented to the prayers of the suppliant, and, lest he should seem ungrateful for all his services, he restored his daughter to her original health.

(17) For straightway, under the linen sheet with which she lay covered,[5] she

(16) And when he had reiterated this so often as to stop his windpipe with hoarseness, the Saint, moved by pity, resolved not to be thought ungrateful. For he restored the woman to life.[15]

(17) And immediately, drawing her hand towards her, she spoke ; although she

---

(16) In hujusmodi clamoribus fere dimidium noctis expendit.   Quum igitur totiens inculcasset "Redde mihi servitium meum !" ut raucitas ei arc-taret arterias, annuit martyris pietas precibus supplicantis, et, ne omnibus servitiis ejus videretur ingratus, puellam pristinae sanitati restituit ;

(17) statim namque sub linteo, quo tecta[5] jacebat, manum porrectam

(16) Quod cum totiens inculcasset ut raucitas arctaret arterias, noluit beatus, pietate motus, ingratus haberi. Nam mulierem vitae[16] restituit,

(17) quae confestim manum ad se trahens locuta est, quamvis nondum

---

[5] William, who (737 (11)) regarded the linen sheet as "suppositum," in-stead of "superpositum," here omits all mention of it.

"the service of a free man." This mere domestic servant, this "vernacu-lus," *presumed* on his service as though it had been a free gift ! And St. Thomas rewarded his presumption, instead of chastising him !

[15] William perhaps feels that she was restored *first* to "life," and only *afterwards* to her "original health." By this alteration, he emphasizes the deliverance from what he called above (1) "a double death."

Benedict (ii. 234-7)

put her hand forth and then drew it back (or, drew back her outstretched hand). But, though she attempted to speak, she could utter nothing intelligible, owing to her excessive weakness.

(18) On the morrow she gained strength by food and drink. Even the cankered thighs were dried up within three days; and, in three weeks, without any medicine of this world, they were made quite whole.

(19) After this wonderful termination, the man

William (i. 190-3)

did not as yet utter any intelligible sound, reduced as she was by leanness and death.[16]

(18) On the morrow she took food and drink. Even the cankered thighs — the purulent matter being dried up [17]—were made quite whole within the space of three weeks.

(19) After this wonderful ending, the man above-

---

ad se retraxit, sed loqui conata prae debilitate nimia nihil intelligibile valebat exprimere.

(18) Postero die cibo potuque refocillata est ; ipsa vero femora cancerosa infra diem tertium desiccata sunt, et in hebdomadis tribus absque omni medicina carnali redintegrata.

(19) Quibus mirifice completis adiit

intelligibilem vocem exprimeret, macie[16] et morte confecta.

(18) Postera die cibum sumpsit et potum. Ipsa vero femora cancerosa infra trium hebdomadarum spatium purulentiis desiccatis [17] redintegrata sunt.

(19) Quibus mirifice expletis, adiit

---

[16] " Macies " is nowhere used for " hunger " as William seems to use it here. He probably sacrifices sense to alliteration. Above, he omits Benedict's " porrectam " perhaps as superfluous. But Benedict seems to see the arm *first stretched out from beneath the face-cloth*, and then drawn back again. Comp. 741 (6).

[17] William perhaps objects to the expression " femur desiccatum."

Benedict (ii. 234·7)

above-mentioned, the girl's father, sought the presence of William, Bishop of Norwich, informing him of the event and asking for a letter of testimony.

But the Bishop did not at once [6] credit the story, but first called the Priest and the eye-witnesses, and ascertained all the facts in order, so that, when certified by their testimony, he might come forward as a witness. Moreover, after calling in two respectable matrons to examine any traces of cancer, he proved that the girl was [now] in perfect health.

William (i. 190·3)

mentioned, the girl's father, sought the presence of his lord, the Bishop of Norwich, informing him of the event and asking for a letter as testimony,[18] lest — when he came to Canterbury and prepared to tell his story—he might be thought to say things that passed supposal and belief, without authority.

But the Bishop did not at once credit [19] the story, until—after calling the Priest and the eye-witnesses and two respectable matrons to examine any traces of cancer—he ascertained all the facts in order.

---

vir praedictus, pater puellae, Norvicensis episcopi Willelmi praesentiam, rem gestam indicans et litteras testimonii petens. Episcopus vero non de plano [6] fidem adhibuit, sed sacerdote vocato, iisque qui rem praesentes viderant, rem totam didicit ex ordine; quorum testimonio certificatus rei gestae posset testis existere. Duabus etiam vitae probatae matronis ad se vocatis, quae cancri vestigia considerarent, sanissimam esse probavit.

praedictus vir, pater puellae, praesentiam domini sui Norwicensis episcopi, rem gestam indicans, petensque litteras testimonia, [18] ne Cantuariam veniens et rem narraturus supra opinionem et fidem, citra auctoritatem, loqui putaretur. Episcopus vero non de plano [19] fidem adhibuit, donec vocato sacerdote et eis qui rem praesentes viderant, et duabus matronis probatae vitae, quae vestigia cancri considerarent, rem omnem didicit ex ordine.

---

[6] "De plano," like the French "sur le champ," here means "right off," or "as a matter of course."

[18] "Litteras testimonia," perhaps a corruption of Benedict's "l. testimonii." But see above (710 (14)), for variations of this phrase.

[19] Ed. suggests "de pleno." But see note on Benedict.

Benedict (ii. 234-7)	William (i. 190-3)
(20) So he addressed to us a letter sealed with his seal testifying that she had been laid out on the floor as dead, but touching too briefly on the points treated by us, as we believe, with sufficient fulness. The tenor of the letter is as follows :—	(20) And it was divinely provided that [this] careful inquiry should remove all doubt. So he made the matter known to the brothers worshipping God in the church of Canterbury in a document signed with his seal, of which the tenor is as follows :—

"William, by grace of God Bishop of Norwich, to his venerable brothers in the Lord, the Prior and sacred convent of Canterbury, eternal salvation in Christ.

"The wonderful works of God, which in our diocese come to pass concerning those afflicted with divers infirmities, from their earnest devotion to St. Thomas (W., *to the Saint of God, the most saintly Thomas*), and (W. om. *and*) from the pure invocations of their hearts, which of their free will they proffer—these we desire with all our heart[a] to make known unto you. For what God, glorifying His Saint, would not have to lie hid, how shall man presume to keep secret?

(20) Litteras ergo sigillo suo signatas nobis destinavit, quod tanquam mortua in aream exposita fuit testimonium perhibens, sed breviter nimis tangens quae superius a nobis sufficienter, ut credimus, tractata sunt. Litterarum autem forma haec est :

(20) Divinitusque procuratum est ut diligens inquisitio omnem removeret ambiguitatem. Igitur apicibus caractere suo signatis fratribus in Cantuariensi ecclesia Deum venerantibus factum innotuit, quarum forma haec est :

"Willelmus Dei gratia Norwicensis episcopus, venerabilibus in Domino fratribus suis, priori sacroque conventui Cantuariae, aeternam in Christo salutem :

"Magnalia Dei, quae in nostra eveniunt diocesi circa oppressos variis aegritudinibus, ex attenta devotione quam habent erga sanctum Thomam, et ex pura mentium invocatione, quam ipsi porrigunt, vestrae sanctitati innotescere omni desiderio desideramus ;[a] quippe quae Deus mirificando sanctum suum latere non vult, qualiter apud homines occultari praesumetur? Ut itaque ex testimonio

[a] Lit. "we desire with all desire," as in Luke xxii. 15 "with desire have I desired."

Benedict (ii. 234-7), William (i. 190-3).

[738] "As, then, we have received from the testimony of William, a priest in our domain, and of very many [b] of our men, the bearer of these presents, Cecilia, daughter of one that is a man of ours, having been long kept to her bed by the disease of cancer, while that disease was painfully creeping round her thighs, at last, under the increasing pressure of the disease, was brought so low that she was thought to be lifeless, and laid out on the floor as being dead. Wherefore her father's soul, turned to bitterness,[c] yet still trusting in the Divine compassion and in the merits of the most blessed Martyr, [*bursting out into exclamations of sorrow, invoked the Saint of the Lord with perfect devotion of heart ; and, through the co-operation of Divine grace, obtained the restoration of her original health for his daughter. Wherefore this girl, restored to her original health by the merits of the most blessed Martyr,[d]*] is sent by us to you together with the testimony of our writing, because of (W., for) the glory of this great miracle. Farewell."

Willelmi sacerdotis cujusdam terrae nostrae et plurimorum [b] hominum nostrorum accepimus, latrix praesentium Caecilia, filia cujusdam hominis nostri, aegritudine cancri diu detenta, dum morbus iste circa femora sua anxie serperet, tandem eo usque morbo aggravante oppressa est, ut exanimis reputaretur, et tanquam mortua in area exponeretur ; unde anima patris sui in amaritudinem [c] conversa, confidens tamen de Divina misericordia et de meritis beatissimi martyris, [*in vocem doloris prorumpens, mente devotissima sanctum Domini invocavit, et pristinae sanitatis restitutionem filiae suae, gratia Divina cooperante, impetravit. Unde eam pristinae suae sanitati meritis beatissimi martyris*][d] restitutam cum scripti nostri testimonio ad vos ob gloriam tanti miraculi transmittimus. Bene valete."

[b] Benedict, "plurimorum," W., "plurium." "Men," and "man" below, mean "vassals."

[c] No doubt this is right ("in amaritudinem "). But W. has "amaritudine," either an error of transcription, or possibly interpreted thus "turned [to God] in its bitterness." Note that both above ("pluriorum "), and here ("amaritudinē "), W. may have been misled by abbreviations. In i. 416, editor corrects "amaritudinem " to "amaritudine," which is manifestly right.

[d] Benedict omits the italicized passage, all except the word "restored (restitutam)." The reason for the omission is that, after copying the Bishop's letter up to the *first* "merits of the most blessed Martyr," the copyist's eye, in

[739] The similarity between Benedict and William is very close in the description of the disease, which is too well written to represent exactly what Cecilia or her father said at Canterbury. It may well have proceeded from the priest William whom the Bishop called in to give evidence. Perhaps his handwriting was crabbed, for William seems to have misread it in several places. Also William seems to have thought that Benedict's account was more than "sufficiently" full. At all events, he in several passages condenses it, and sometimes omits important, or even essential, details. He also improves the style by changing "foetores" to "mephites," omitting "cerevisia," and softening the "vernacular" expostulation of Jordan (whom he expressly calls "vernaculus") by giving it as Reported Speech in the Third Person. On the other hand he goes off into digressions—about Priest Godwin, who stole a church-key, and Proctor Turstan, who was an excellent man of business—that do not give point to his narrative.

[740] As regards the cure, it is remarkable that in this case there was no resort to the Water of Canterbury. This indicates that it was an early miracle. So does the absence of any offering of coin, or vow of pilgrimage. The emotional shock that raised the poor girl from her lifeless condition would be explained by some in modern times as the result of sympathetic "brain-wave"—and not as the mere result of outcry. Experts must decide how far a disease of the kind described above could be permanently cured by a mere shock of emotion.

---

returning to the original, fell on the *second* "merits of the most blessed Martyr." So he passed on, as if he had written the *second*, and also what preceded it. Occurring in a letter, which might seem to need no revision, such a mistake might more easily remain uncorrected than in its own narrative. This scribal error is commonly called the error of *Homoioteleuton*, i.e. "similar endings."

§ 9. *The son of Hugh Scot is restored after drowning*

[741] Benedict (ii. 238-9)	William (i. 200-2) [1]
(1) In a manor of the county of Warwick, called Benedega,[1] Hugh, known as Scot, is testified by his neighbours in the county to be of good name and unblemished reputation. His son Philip, about eight years old, while by a	(1) In the county of Cheshire, the man Hugh, known as Scot, was of good name and repute among his fellow tribesmen.[2] His son Philip, about eight years old, sitting by an ironstone quarry while he had been overwhelming[3] with

(1) In praedio territorii Warwicensis, quod Benedega[1] dicitur, Hugo cognomento Scotus boni nominis et opinionis integrae a comprovincialibus suis esse perhibetur. Filius hujus Philippus, annorum circiter octo, dum ad ferrifo-

(1) In[1] territorio Cestrensi vir Hugo, cognomento Scotus, boni nominis et opinionis fuit inter contribules[2] suos. Cujus filius Philippus, octo circiter annorum, dum ad ferrifodinam residens bufonem a lutosis emergentem puerili studio lapidibus obruerat,[3] conatus suos incircum-

---

[1] Or, "Beneclega." William has "Cheshire." In ii. 245 Benedict has "Cheshire" for "Gloucestershire." Perhaps, where the first letters of the name of a county were obscured, the termination "-censis" was likely to cause the name to be corrupted into "Cestrensis."

[1] William prefixes to his story a reference to his preceding one (which is also about revivification): "Why wonder, reader? Wonder at what follows . . . the facts themselves and the Martyr's power should persuade you."

This way of connecting two stories by remarks that may either be called an epilogue to the preceding or a prologue to the following, has been noted above (737 (1)).

[2] William prefers "contribules," as being better Latin than "comprovinciales." Both are rare words; but the latter is the rarer, the former is an old word revived by the Fathers.

[3] "Obruerat," probably an error for "obrueret," the imperf. subjunct. being frequent, in these treatises, with "dum (while)," whereas the pluperf. indic. is very rare.

Benedict (ii. 238-9)

William (i. 200-2)

deep pool in an ironstone quarry, overwhelming with stones (as boys will) the frogs that rose to the surface, happened to fall in, and was himself in turn overwhelmed by the waters.[2]

stones (as boys will) a frog that rose from the mud to the surface, continuing his attempts without circumspection, was himself in turn overwhelmed by the waters.

(2) When his father, on coming home, could not find the boy, he looked for him in every direction. At last he finds him under the water, and draws him out while the sun was setting, distended by the abundance of the water [he had swallowed], and, as he [still] believes, lifeless.

(2) When his father, on coming home, could not find the boy, he looked for him everywhere [at home] and [also] in different farms. He found him under the water, and drew him out, dead, and distended by the abundance of the water [he had swallowed]. It was now inclining towards twilight.

(3) The corpse was carried into the house : the

(3) So the father gave vent to sighs and groans, the

dinam profundam et aqua repletam bufones emergentes studio puerili lapidibus obrueret, casu incidens et ipse aquis obrutus est.[2]

(2) Quem quum pater domum veniens non invenisset, quaquaversum quaesitum, reperit tandem aqua submersum, et extrahit, occidente jam sole, aqua multa distentum, et ut adhuc credit exanimem.

(3) Infertur in domum cadaver ;

specte prosecutus et ipse aquis obrutus est.

(2) Quem cum pater domum veniens non invenisset, ubique et villitim quaesitum, reperit aqua submersum ; et extraxit mortuum, et aqua multa distentum. Vergebat jam dies in crepusculum.

(3) Igitur pater suspiriis et gemitu[i],

[2] "Et ipse" seems to mean "in retribution for his treatment of the frogs." He had "overwhelmed" them with showers of stones : now, "he himself, too," was "overwhelmed" in the flood.

Benedict (ii. 238-9)

people flock in, expressing their sympathy with the agonising grief of the parents. They try — but all in vain —whether human exertions might possibly in some respect avail the child.

The boy's coat, which happened to be very wide, big enough for two boys— since it could not be taken off, being so tightly filled by the distension of the stomach—they rip from top to bottom. They hang him up head downwards, and beat the soles of his feet. But no water flowed out, so they quite gave up hope. Finally, the boy was stretched out on a table, a fire lit at each end of the room, and watch kept till morning.

William (i. 200-2)

mother to tears and wailing. They take the first steps that are supposed expedient in such cases.

The coat was ripped up, since, owing to the distension of the body, it could not be drawn off; they beat the soles of the feet and hang up the corpse head downwards ; but they give up hope, for no water flowed out. And when they found all this labour of no avail, placing some planks under him, they light a fire at each end of the room, and pass the night without sleep.

---

vulgus glomeratur in unum et anxio parentum dolori compatitur ; tentatur conatu inutili si ei posset in aliquo sedulitas humana succurrere. Tunica pueri lata valde, duorumque puerorum capax, quia ventre distento impleta exui non poterat, a summo usque deorsum scinditur. Suspendunt puerum a pedibus ; plantas tundunt, sed aqua non effluente, a spe sua decidunt. Extentus deinde puer super tabulam, accenso hinc inde foco, usque mane custoditur.

mater lacrymis indulget et planctui. Prima quae ad hujusmodi expedire putantur exsequuntur. Tunica scissa, quae propter distensionem corporis detrahi non poterat, contundentes plantas cadaver a pedibus suspendunt ; sed cadunt a spe sua, non effluente aqua. Et cum nihil hac praevalerent industria, substernentes ei tabulatum, hinc inde focum accendunt, et sine somno spatia noctis transmittunt.

Benedict (ii. 238-9)

(4) But at sunrise, by the mother's advice, they sent to the next village (or, farm), and fetched the Water of St. Thomas the Martyr. Opening the closed mouth and fast-clenched teeth with a spindle or some such thing, she happened to put in her finger; and, as the spindle slipped out, the finger was caught fast and almost pierced to the bone by the meeting teeth. Hearing her cry out, the father placed a small knife between [the teeth] : but, before he could extricate her finger from their grip, he had to break two front teeth, those called "incisive."[8]

William (i. 200-2)

(4) At sunrise, by advice of the mother—whose anxiety made her more earnest[4] for action—the Water of St. Thomas was fetched from the next village (or, farm). Desiring, herself with her own hands, to pour it in between the child's cold lips, and unfastening (with the aid of a spindle) the closed mouth and fast - clenched teeth, she happened, along with the spindle, to insert her finger too : but, as the spindle slipped out, the finger was caught fast and almost pierced to the bone by the meeting teeth. Hearing her cry out, the father applied a small knife to [the

(4) Orto vero sole, matris consilio ad villam proximam missum est, et aqua beati martyris Thomae allata est. Quumque mater clausum os pueri dentesque cohaerentes, fuso quodam intruso, disjunxisset, casu immisit et digitum : resiliente autem fuso digitus interceptus est, et dentibus concurrentibus fere transfixus. Clamante illa interponit pater cultellum ; sed, antequam interceptum mulieris digitum possit eripere, duos dentes anteriores, qui incisivi dicuntur, confringit.[3]

(4) Orto sole, consilio matris, cujus diligentior[4] erat sollicitudo, a proxima villa allata est aqua sancti Thomae ; quam cum propriis manibus ipsa gelidis labiis instillare satageret, fusique suffragio clausum os dentesque cohaerentes disjungeret, cum fuso immisit et digitum. Sed resiliente fuso interceptus est digitus, dentibusque concurrentibus fere transfixus. Et cum clamaret, apposuit

[3] The teeth in front of the "canines" are now called "incisors." William has "praecisores," which does not

[4] We may supply "than the father." But it may mean "specially, or unusually (earnest)."

teeth], and struck out two
front teeth, those called
" praecisors."

(5) Others, who were   (5) William omits this :
standing by, desired to have   but see (9).
a priest called to say a funeral
mass for the boy, that the
boy might be buried ; but
the father loudly refused,
saying, " So may God help
me, as St. Thomas, if he will
not restore him to me here
alive, shall have him at
Canterbury dead.   For I will
either lead him thither alive
or carry him dead.[4]   In no
wise shall he be buried here."

(6) So the first time, and   (6) When therefore the
the second time, the Water,   health-bestowing drop was

---

pater cultellum, et duos dentes anteriores, qui praecisores dicuntur, excussit.

(5) Volentibus aliis qui astabant ut   (5) om.
presbyter vocaretur, ut fierent pro
puero exsequiae, ut puer sepeliretur,
reclamavit pater dicens, "Adjuvet me
ita Deus, nisi eum beatus Thomas
hic mihi restituerit vivum, habebit
illum Cantuariae mortuum.   Illuc enim
eum vel vivum ducam vel mortuum
portabo ;[4] nequaquam hic sepelietur."

(6) Et semel igitur et secundo aqua   (6) Cum ergo primo stilla salutaris

---

correspond to anything now, or perhaps
ever, in use : it would mean "teeth
cutting off abruptly."   "Confringit,"
"breaks (perforce)," *i.e.* "has to
break."

[4] These words are very similar to
those of the knight Jordan (736).

Benedict (ii. 238-9)

poured into [the mouth], finding no penetrable channels, flowed back again. On the third injection, by the Divine will, it went down into the inner parts, and suddenly the muscles seemed to move. The boy unfolds his hand, which was before clenched : after unfolding it, he by degrees draws it towards him; he opens one eye.

(7) In inexpressible joy the father cried, " My son, do you wish to live ? " " Father," he replied, " I do wish [it]." [5]

William (i. 200-2)

first poured into [the mouth], finding no pervious passages, it began to flow back again. But on the third occasion, the faith and devotion of the parents caused it to flow in ; and the muscles seemed to move ; and the boy began to draw his hand towards him, and to open one eye.

(7) Leaping from his seat, the father asked him whether he could live, and he replied, " I wish to live."

---

infusa meatus pervios non inveniens refluxit ; tertio injecta, nutu divino in interiora descendit, visaeque sunt subito fibrae moveri ; puer manum prius clausam explicat, explicatam paulatim attrahit, alterum oculorum aperit.

(7) Pater inexplicabiliter laetus, " Visne," [5] ait, " fili, vivere ? " " Volo," [5] inquit, " pater mi."

infunderetur, non pervios commeatus inveniens refluebat. Sed tertia vice fides et devotio parentum obtinuit ut influeret, visaeque sunt fibrae moveri, et coepit puer manum attrahere, et alterum oculorum aperire.

(7) Exsiliente patre et interrogante utrumnam vivere posset, respondit " Volo vivere."

---

[5] " Vis " and " volo " are difficult. We should have expected " Art thou indeed alive, or, going to live ? "

Can some confusion have arisen from the Old French " Vis tu de voire ? Dost thou live in truth ? " or from a misrendering of " vas (going to)"? A translator may have mistranslated Benedict's (404a) French, and William may have partly (and wrongly) corrected him.

Benedict (ii. 238-9)

William (i. 200-2)

(8) Those who were present crowded round, still lamenting, however, the frightful inflation of the stomach: but by degrees the stomach subsided and recovered its natural symmetry and condition before the eyes of all, and this though not a drop of water flowed forth from the body above or below.

(8) Wonderful is the Lord, and there is no numbering his mercies: for first he restored what was absent [*i.e.* life], and subsequently consumed what was superabundantly present [*i.e.* water].

For while those who were present were lamenting the inflation of the stomach, the stomach began by degrees to reduce its swelling before their eyes, and to recover its natural size and condition, and this in such a way that not a drop of the imbibed waters flowed forth from the body, either from the parts above or from those below.

(9) That this [boy] therefore, as well [as Cecilia],[6] was

(9) In this narrative we are telling the actual fact—

(8) Circumstantibus qui aderant, et de horrido ventris tumore adhuc ingemiscentibus, paulatim venter subsidit, omnibusque intuentibus naturalem gracilitatem statumque recepit, ita tamen quod a corpore nec gutta aquae superius inferiusve profluxit.

(8) Mirabilis Dominus, et misericordiarum ejus non est numerus, qui quod non erat primo restituit, et consequenter quod erat ex abundanti consumpsit. Nam ipsis qui aderant de tumore ventris ingemiscentibus, coepit venter in oculis eorum paulatim detumere, naturalemque grossitudinem et statum recipere, ut nec gutta bibitorum fluctuum superiori vel regione inferiori proflueret a corpore.

(9) Et hunc ergo[6] proculdubio

(9) Haec dicimus rem gestam nar-

---

[6] " As well," *i.e.* as well as Cecilia, mentioned in the last narrative. Benedict said, at the end of the story

Benedict (ii. 238-9)	William (i. 200-2)
undoubtedly dead, we have ascertained not only from the testimony of the father but also from that of very many others—and indeed finally by a testifying letter from his Priest.	not magnifying by figments of our own the mighty works of God, which need no such aid—as we learned it from the boy's father in person when he offered up thanks in company with the boy: for, as he repeatedly said, if St. Thomas had not restored him alive, he would have conveyed him dead from his neighbourhood to his [the Saint's] resting-place.[5]

[742] The last sentence explains the close similarity between the two narratives in many passages. Where they agree, the two probably used the Priest's "testifying letter." Benedict makes more use of the letter, and hence inserts

---

fuisse mortuum, non solum patris sui sed et aliorum plurimorum assertione, tandem vero et presbyteri sui litteris testimonioque, cognovimus.

rantes, non figmento nostro magnalia Dei, quae non egent hujusmodi, magnificantes, sicut ab ipso parente pueri cum puero gratias agente didicimus; qui, sicut aiebat, nisi beatus Thomas vivum eum restituisset, de partibus suis ad locum requietionis ejus mortuum transvexisset.[5]

---

of the knight Jordan (737 (1)) that he would append *two* other instances of revivification. He now claims that death, in this instance, is proved no less conclusively than in the last.

"Therefore (ergo)" seems to mean "because of the miraculous evanescence of the water," which made it natural to believe that the whole event was miraculous. The sentence is confused: but that this is the meaning is made likely by William's remarks (741 (8)).

[5] "Ad locum requietionis ejus" has this meaning also in 758 (3) (William).

William places here, as uttered at Canterbury, what Benedict records (741 (5)) as uttered at home.

(**741** (5)) the advice to send for the Priest, beside calling attention to it at the end.

[**743**] William—laying more stress on a few striking words and very small details in the evidence of the father (and perhaps of the child, whom he alone mentions as coming to Canterbury)—tells us that the boy was " sitting " at the edge of an ironstone pit (presumably with his legs dangling over) and that he was pelting *a* frog, not (as Benedict) " frogs " ; and that the father sought the boy " from farm to farm." Perhaps it is from the same source, and not from the nature of things, that William tells us how the father " groaned," while the mother " wept," and that the latter was " more anxiously restless " than the former. Again, the Priest would say that the instrument used by the mother to open the mouth was "quidam fusus," " some sort of spindle," or " something of the nature of a spindle " ; but the father would say definitely " spindle " ; the Priest would report what the father actually said when the proposal was made to bury the boy in the churchyard, viz. " I *will* bury him at Canterbury if at all " ; but the father, giving thanks afterwards at Canterbury, might tell William that he *would have* buried him at Canterbury : and this may explain why William ends his narrative with these words.

§ 10. *Elias, a monk of Reading, after [pretending to] resort to Bath for the cure of leprosy, is cured by St. Thomas*

[**744**] Benedict (? see note 1) (ii. 242-3)	A monk of Reading (see note 1) (i. 416-7)
(1) Let any one go to the holy convent[1] of Reading,	(1) Elias, a monk of Reading, suffered from

---

(1) Sanctum Radingensis ecclesiae conveniat conventum[1] qui monachi sui	(1) Radingensis ecclesiae monachus Helyas lepra vel morphea labora-

[1] Note the play on "conveniat" "conventum." Al. "conventui."

Benedict (ii. 242-3)?	A Monk of Reading (i. 416-7)
who would fain know the disease of the monk Elias and the manner of its healing.	leprosy or morphew[1] — so full of ulcers that he might have been called a second
A frightful leprosy had attacked him — so it was asserted by many of the highest skill in medicine; it was proved by his eyes, dropping and flowing with rheum, by the ulcers on his limbs, and the scales on his whole body. (You might have seen his bed covered with them when he rose in the morning.) The [exact]	Lazarus; for, from the sole of his foot to the crown of his head, there was not a spot spared by the host of tubers or ulcers.

Helyae et morbum modumque cura-tionis ejus nosse desiderat. Horrida lepra percussum illum dicebant multi, maxime medicinalis artis periti : indicio erant oculi lacrymosi atque fluentes, ulcerosa membra, corpus totum squa-mosum; mane quando surgebat, lectum ejus squamis videres contectum. Ipsis

bat,[1] sic ulcerosus ut Lazarus alter diceretur; nam a planta pedis ejus usque ad verticem capitis non erat vel minimus in eo locus cui tuberum turba vel ulcerum pepercisset.

The whole narrative is more in William's style than in Benedict's.

[1] This was probably not written by William but by a monk of Reading, whose letter William has adopted with-out alteration or preface, except that he inserted the words "A monk of Reading." See note 5, below.

The monk indicates a *doubt* whether this was a case of leprosy : the account in Benedict's treatise says there was *no doubt* of it among experts. The difference indicates that the case had excited attention and discussion at Canterbury.

"Morphew" is used by Elizabethan writers to represent Fr. *morphée*, a scurfy eruption.

description of it I leave to the monks themselves,[2] for what is manifest needs no proof.

(2) This brother, therefore, being in extreme pain,[3] and not knowing how to come to St. Thomas — for he feared that if he asked leave the Abbot would refuse it — at last obtained leave under pretence of a journey to the hot baths of the City of Bath.

(2) Thinking that hot baths might do him good and that his pains might be mitigated by the heat of sulphur, he spent forty days at the baths of [the City of] Bath.

But inasmuch as he set his hope on hot sulphur, and not on the wonder-working Martyr whom the Lord

---

Dei servis[3] descriptionem ejus relinquo; res manifesta enim probatione non indiget.

(2) Anxius[3] itaque frater ille, et quomodo ad beatum Thomam veniret nescius (metuebat enim ne postulanti sibi ab abbate suo negaretur licentia), itinere tandem ad balnea calida Bathoniensis urbis simulato licentiam impetravit.

(2) Existimans autem calidis balneis sibi posse subveniri, suumque per sulphureum calorem mitigandum dolorem, abiens balneis Batensibus xl. diebus incubuit. Sed quia spem posuit in calido sulphure, non in mirifico martyre quem Dominus vulneravit

---

[2] Lit. "to the servants of God themselves," *i.e.* his fellow monks. These remarks indicate that some doubted whether the disease was true leprosy. The writer, while clearly believing that it was leprosy, sends the doubter to the monks for a "descriptio," or scientific description. The enumeration of the symptoms is natural for William, who elsewhere has a learned discussion on different kinds of leprosy (767 (8)).

[3] "Anxius" has this meaning elsewhere in these treatises.

Benedict (ii. 242-3)?

A Monk of Reading (i. 416-7)
wounded for our iniquities that we might be healed by his stripes,[2] he was not as yet counted worthy of better health. So when he had spent on physicians all that he could collect, [then]—like the woman in the Gospel who was counted worthy to touch the border of the Lord's vesture—he began to sigh [for a journey] to the Martyr.

(3) He was to go westward : but he turned back and went eastward, to the city of the newly-risen Martyr.

This was the time when the glory of the Martyr was beginning to display itself in his earliest miracles ; while the storm-blast still lasted [4]—before Iniquity had

(3) William omits this.

---

propter iniquitates nostras, ut ejus livore[3] sanaremur, nondum meliorari promeruit. Postquam itaque erogavit in medicos quicquid corrogare poterat, tanquam mulier evangelica quae fimbriam Dominici vestimenti tangere meruit, ad martyrem suspirabat.

(3) Ad occidentem perrecturus, reflexo gressu ad orientem tetendit, ad nuper orti martyris urbem. Erat autem hoc cum primis martyr coruscaret miraculis ; dum adhuc staret [4]

(3) om.

---

[4] "Staret," of a fixed wind. Unless it is an error for "flaret."

[3] "Livore," lit. "black and blue marks." Comp. Is. liii. 5.

Benedict (ii. 242-3) ?

A Monk of Reading (i. 416-7)

shut her mouth, before any one dared publicly to speak of the mighty works of the Lord, before many came and "went up" to the Martyr of the Lord and "to the house of the God of Jacob" (Micah iv. 2). And hence this narrative might have been written among the earliest of the Martyr's illustrious signs, had it not been put off till now, either through forgetfulness, or for the sake of inquiry and ascertainment.

(4) The writer omits this.

(4) So, under pretence of seeking medicinal aid, he set out for London [3]—because [4]

---

spiritus procellae, antequam os suum oppilasset iniquitas, antequam publice loqueretur quis potentias Domini, antequam multi venirent et ascenderent ad martyrem Domini et ad domum Dei Jacob; unde et istud inter prima martyris insignia conscribi potuit, nisi vel oblivione vel inquisitionis et certitudinis causa usque in praesens dilatum fuisset.

(4) om.

(4) Igitur sub obtentu quaerendae medicinae Londonias [3] profectus, qua [4]

---

[3] "Londonias": the sense rather demands "Londoniis":—on pretence of seeking medicine in London he set out [for Canterbury]. But the writer probably means "he set out for London [*but really to go through London to Canterbury*]."

[4] The translation adopts the Editor's "quia" for "qua."

Benedict (ii. 242-3)?	A Monk of Reading (i. 416-7)
	our [5] Abbot did not [at that time] pay adequate respect to the Martyr, and would not give his monks leave to go on pilgrimage [to him]—expecting to steal time enough for going as a pilgrim to Canterbury.
(5) Well, the monk was met by a knight between whom and himself there was a strong mutual affection. When the knight asked and heard whither his friend was journeying, he dissuaded him, saying, " Go not, dear sir, go not to Canterbury, lest, if the great lords hear of it, you bring evil on your convent. See, I carry with me Water of St. Thomas the Martyr. Taste on this spot,	(5) Meanwhile, as some pilgrims were returning from the Martyr's memorial, he begged for his Water, drank it,

---

	citra quam decebat abbas noster [5] martyri deferebat, suis peregrinari non permittens, peregrinandi Cantuariam furtivum tempus exspectabat.
(5) Obviavit itaque monacho miles quem diligebat, plurimum dilectus ab ipso. Quaesivit quo tenderet, audivit, disuasit : " Noli," inquit, " domine mi, noli Cantuariam proficisci, ne, si inter magnates auditum fuerit, inducas super ecclesiam tuam malum. Ecce, aquam sancti martyris Thomae porto ; hic	(5) Interim redeuntibus peregrinis a memoria martyris, aquam ejus petiit, bibit,

---

[5] " Our " indicates that *the writer is a monk of Reading*

Benedict (ii. 242-3)?

A Monk of Reading (i. 416-7)

if you will.   On this spot
will the merciful Martyr be
able to give ear to your
prayer."

The monk alights from
his horse, prostrates himself
on the earth in adoration of
the Water, tastes [it], washes
his face [in it]—to the best
of my remembrance [5]—after
having first washed [his
heart] in streams of tears.

(6) Afterwards, turning
aside to St. Edmund the
Martyr,[6] he obtained from a

(6) The monk omits this.

gusta, si volueris; hic te poterit
martyris exaudire benignitas."   Descendit de equo monachus, aquam
in terra pronus adorat, gustat, faciem
(ut memini)[5] lavat, lacrymis prius
lotus uberrimis.

(6) Deinde ad beatum martyrem
divertens Eadmundum,[6] a quodam

(6) om.

[5] These details are such as Elias
alone would be likely to give, and they
may have been given by him later on
to the monk in charge of the Martyr's
tomb.   They are described more in
the style of William than of Benedict :
comp. **674**, "*If I remember right*,
Walter, etc."

[6] Presumably, Elias had more faith
in a pilgrimage than in the Water, and
thought that, if he could not go to the
new Martyr, it would be well to try the
old one : but the writer appears to
regard the fact as an instance of man's
ends being "shaped" by Providence.
Elias went to *St. Edmund:* but cure
came through *St. Thomas.*

Benedict (ii. 242-3)?

friend of his a strip [from the clothes] of the Martyr Thomas, tinged with his blood. This he squeezed out in water, [with which] he washed his infected body,

(7) and cleansed away the leprosy. After some days,[7] therefore, he came home, and his friends received him, absolutely free from ailment.

(8) The wonderful change led the Abbot to suspect that he had not been to Bath but to Canterbury, and he asked him how he had been cured. At first, Elias feared to confess. But by kindness of voice and manner

A Monk of Reading (i. 416-7)

(7) and recovered his health, so that he retains not a trace of the disease, but has a most agreeable countenance, as all may [6] see.

---

amico suo pannum martyris Thomae cruore tinctum obtinuit, quo in aqua expresso, corpus tabidum lavit,

(7) lepram abluit. Post aliquot igitur dies [7] domum venit, et sui eum receperunt, nihil prorsus mali habentem.

(8) Suspicatur abbas ex mira leprosi corporis mutatione Cantuariam illum perrexisse, non Bathoniam; quaerensque qualiter curatus fuerit, confiteri metuentem vultu seniore alloquitur, et

(7) et convaluit, adeo ut morbi vestigia non retineat, sed vultu gratiosus, sicut videntibus liquet,[6] appareat.

---

[7] "After some days." Why did he delay? Perhaps to disarm the suspicion of a miraculous cure. He had received leave to go to Bath for a medical cure, *which would take time:* he had not received leave to be miraculously cured in a moment.

[6] This confirms the view (see note 5) that the writer was one of the monks of Reading, among whom Elias was residing at the time when this letter was written.

Benedict (ii. 242-3)?
the Abbot at last elicited the
method of the cure, which he
accepted in all faith and
wonderment.

[745] The conclusion to be drawn from the interesting differences between the two preceding narratives is that Monk Elias was not a veracious person. He probably told his Abbot that he had been to Bath and that he had spent forty days there and a great deal of money, and subsequently told him that he intended to go to London whereas he really intended to go to Canterbury. On the other hand he told the monk in charge of the Martyr's tomb that he had never gone really to Bath, but had merely pretended to go; he had intended to come to St. Thomas the Martyr, but, having received, on the way, the Water of the new Martyr, he thought he could use his leave of absence by going to the shrine of the old Martyr St. Edmund. No doubt, he said to the monks at Canterbury that he had confessed his fraud to the Abbot of Reading. So he had, in part; but he had not made a clean breast of it. If he did not really go to Bath, what account was he to give of the money spent during these forty expensive days? Perhaps the Abbot had paid it. If so, would he not want it back again? These considerations (and others) may have induced Elias, when confessing much, not to confess all. And hence the two stories.

[746] Such unveracities would not greatly affect our belief in the cure. That Elias was grievously ill and rapidly recovered, may be accepted as satisfactorily proved. But whether the disease was leprosy or not; whether the cure resulted simply from the emotional shock produced by the

tandem modum curationis ejus audit et
admiratione plenus credit.

Water of St. Thomas ; or whether the strip of St. Thomas's \
vesture also contributed to it ; whether the shrine of St.
Edmund might allege a reasonable claim ; and whether the
effect of forty days at Bath or elsewhere, with fresh air, and
travelling, had something to do with the result :—these
questions must be left unsettled. Only our suspicions of
Elias's character must not lead us to deny the possibility of
an intense and (for the purpose) efficacious faith. He may
not have believed in veracity : but he may have believed in
the Water of St. Thomas.

[746*a*] The narrative in Benedict's treatise was probably
not written by Benedict. Notes 1, 2, and 5 give reasons for
thinking that *it may have been written by William, during the
period when the latter was* (415) *assisting the former.* If
this was the case, it is easy to understand why William, when
compiling a book of his own, resorted to a letter from a
Reading monk. He did not care to repeat the account
already given to the world in Benedict's treatise, although it
was of his own composition. Close and continuous verbatim agreement is never found in the two Books on Miracles
except where two narratives are derived from one letter.
In this case, William may have thought that, next to repeating his own story, the best course was to transcribe the letter
on which it was based. See also 754*a*.

§ 11. *Queen Eleanor's Foundling*

[747] Benedict (ii. 245)	William (i. 213-4)
(1) Eleanor, Queen of the English, found an out-cast infant and committed	(1) Eleanor, the venera-ble Queen of England, finding a little child cast forth on

(1) Infantem abjectum invenit Alienor Anglorum regina et episcopo	(1) Invenit venerabilis regina Angliae Alienor parvulum unum in via

Benedict (ii. 245)

its breeding and training to Godfrey Bishop of St. Asaph. The boy was taught letters.[1]

(2) After a few years he was covered from head to foot by a foul leprosy. They separated him from intercourse with the scholars; and, at last, by the decision of the Bishop himself, he was prevented from entering the court of Abingdon.

(3) In the course of four years the tubers on his face grew more and more numerous and prominent, and his whole body more and more infected.

William (i. 213-4)

the road, abandoned by his mother, gave charge that he should be reared in the monastery of Abingdon. When he had spent several years there learning letters,

(2) he was seized with a disease of the nature of elephantiasis and removed from the school and the monastery by the command of Godfrey, Bishop of St. Asaph, who managed the monastery's affairs.

(3) For the tuberous face, the running eyes, the broad ulcers on the arms and thighs, so deep as to go down to the bones, provoked nausea [in those who saw him]; his hoarse voice scarcely reached

---

de Sancto Asaph Godefrido educandum commisit. Ad literas[1] puer applicatur.

(2) Post annos paucos sordida lepra totus obvolvitur; segregatur a communione scholarium, tandemque ipsius episcopi sententia ab introitu curiae Abindoniensis arcetur.

(3) Tractu annorum quatuor tubera in facie magis magisque excrescunt, totumque corpus magis magisque tabescit.

projectum, materno gremio destitutum, et praecepit quod in coenobio Abendoniae nutriretur. Ubi cum plures annos litteras discens explesset,

(2) elephantico morbo correptus, amotus est a scholis et a coenobio, jubente episcopo Godefrido de Sancto Asaph, qui res coenobii ministrabat.

(3) Facies enim tuberosa, oculi fluentes, rara supercilia, ulcera brachiorum et femorum lata, et ad ossa pertingentia, nauseam provocabant. Vox rauca vix

---

[1] "Letters," i.e. a lettered, or liberal, education.

Benedict (ii. 245)   William (i. 213-4)

those who were standing close at hand ; his bandages had to be changed daily, or at least every other day, owing to the flow of matter. All these things deterred people from living and holding intercourse with him.

(4) In secret, the boy departs, flees to the Martyr, is purified by flux of the stomach, comes back in sound condition.

(4) Trusting, however, in the compassion and merits of St. Thomas, whom the grace of heaven deigned to glorify in the healing of similar diseases, he set out for Canterbury. On the way, in excessive purgation of the stomach, he felt a beginning of his cure. Furthermore, after two days, returning from the tomb of St. Thomas, he brought back the [mere] vestiges of the now healed disease.

---

ad aures prope stantis perveniens, panni quoque singulis diebus vel alternis propter saniem effluentem mutandi, convictum et cohabitationem dissuadebant.

(4) Clam puer abscedit, ad martyrem convolat, ventris fluxu mundatur, sospes regreditur.

(4) Confidens autem adolescens de misericordia meritisque beati Thomae, quem superna dignatio glorificabat in consimilibus, Cantuariam proficiscens obiter in nimio ventris obsequio curationis suae praesensit initia. Porro post biduum rediens a tumba Sancti Thomae sanati vestigia morbi domum reportavit.

Benedict (ii. 245)

(5) On his return, his acquaintances were amazed at his face so altered, the leprosy so annihilated, the tubers so banished, the flesh so like a child's.

Up to that time, the Bishop had remained incredulous of the reports about the Martyr's power. But when he saw thus cleansed the boy whom he had seen before a leper, whom he had ejected from the court [at Abingdon], whom he had [actually] loathed—he was compelled to believe that St. Thomas was [indeed] of high merit, venerable excellence, and marvellous power. What

William (i. 213-4)

(5) One day, while the Bishop was walking up and down, the boy caught hold of his gown, and said that he had been cleansed by the merits of St. Thomas of Canterbury. Not recognizing him after his sudden transformation, the Bishop asked who he was and what was his name. By uttering his name, he at the same time defined who he was, to the utter astonishment of him whom he was addressing. Well, after considering the issue of the affair, and the length of the disease (for it had been gathering strength for two years), the Bishop consulted the physicians; and then, when he could by no possibility refute those who asserted his recovery—and

---

(5) In reditu ipsius obstupescunt, qui eum noverunt, sic alteratam ejus faciem, sic lepram annullatam, sic evanuisse tubera, sic carnem ejus refloruisse. Usque ad tempus illud incredulus exstiterat episcopus his quae dicebantur de martyre. Videns autem mundatum puerum, quem viderat ante leprosum, quem de curia ejecerat, quem abhorruerat, credere compulsus est beatum Thomam magni esse meriti, excellentiae venerandae, mirandae po-

(5) Qui cum una dierum episcopum deambulantem per vestem apprehendisset, ait se per merita beati Thomae Cantuariae mundatum.   Episcopus vero subito transformatum non agnoscens, personam et nomen interrogat. Ille nomen edicit, eademque responsione personam determinat, stupidum reddens quem compellabat. Igitur episcopus, eventum rei considerans, et diuturnitatem morbi, qui per biennium invaluerat, consultis medicis, postquam sanitatis

Benedict (ii. 245)	William (i. 213-4)
is more, the Bishop of Salisbury, on seeing the boy, was converted to the love of the Martyr.	indeed the evidence of his own eyes,[1]—he recalled him from his outcast condition to the court of the monastery and to general intercourse.
	Moreover he brought the boy along with him, when coming to the Martyr's tomb to pray, and exhibited him to public view.

[748] The two accounts do not appear to borrow from any common document. William's, which is the later and was written after the Bishop of St. Asaph had come to Canterbury, is not, in appearance, so severe upon the Bishop as Benedict's is. Indeed, William perhaps borrows from the Bishop the details about the boy's disease, which made it

tentiae. Sed et episcopus Saresberiensis, eodem viso, ad martyrem diligendum animum convertit.	illius assertoribus[1] et fidelibus oculis refragari non potuit, abjectum in curtim coenobii et convictum popularem revocavit ; quem et secum pariter, ad tumbam martyris veniens oratum, videndum exhibuit.

[1] In "sanitatis illius assertoribus," "illius" is hardly needed, but we almost need "illis," if the "assertores" are the physicians. Perhaps they are not. The text leaves it doubtful. The "faithful eyes" may mean "the fidelity of his own eyes," but it may be ironically used about the eyes of the physicians, which the Bishop regarded as preeminently "faithful." William, who loses no opportunity of attacking physicians, is here manifestly scoffing at the Bishop—so ready to believe in them, so unready to believe in St. Thomas.

necessary to remove him from the convent. But while also
fully giving an account of the Bishop's cautious deliberation
before giving his adhesion to St. Thomas, he apparently
indulges in a little irony at his expense. Benedict's tone is
one of severe reproach. The Bishop was "compelled to
believe" that St. Thomas had certain powers and qualities.
The Bishop of Salisbury began to "love" the Martyr: not
so the Bishop of St. Asaph.

[749] The mention of (Benedict (3)) "four years" may
be reconciled with that of (William (5)) "two years" by
supposing that the former period includes the whole time from
the commencement of the disease ; the latter, only the stage
during which (long after it had become apparent) it had
been "gathering strength."

[750] Why did not Benedict record in its place this very
early cure of leprosy, which almost certainly took place
before the end of 1171? Probably the boy had returned, as
he came, "in secret" ; and so the miracle was not recorded at
the time in the Cathedral archives. Benedict may have been
informed of it by letter some time afterwards. The style is
rather more terse than that of most of Benedict's narratives.

§ 12. *Geoffrey, a monk of Reading, is restored, when in
extremity*

[751] Benedict (ii. 251-2)   William (i. 210-1)

(1) Benedict omits this.   (1) Let the church of
Shrewsbury[1] and Reading
declare, without labour of
mine, what propitiation it
found in the Martyr.

---

(1) om.

(1) Dicat absque labore meo Salopes-
beriensis[1] et Radingensis ecclesia quid
propitiationis invenerit in martyre.

---

[1] This Preface introduces *two*
miracles, one of which is attested by a

Benedict (ii. 251-2)	William (i. 210-1)
	"To the venerable Lord Odo, Prior of Canterbury, brother Aug[ustine], a monk of Reading, health and much love in Christ.
	"We have thought it fitting to make known to your holiness a great and renowned miracle [wrought] in [our] house at Reading.
(2) Geoffrey, a monk of Reading, being suddenly attacked by a very violent disease, and brought, as was supposed, to extremity, was deprived of the use of all his senses and limbs.	(2) "For a brother of our congregation, Geoffrey of Warengford by name, an able man and a good singer, and one among the chief of our house—being suddenly attacked by a very violent disease, and brought, as was supposed, to extremity—was deprived of the use of all his senses and limbs.

	"Venerabili domino Odoni, priori Cantuariensi, frater Aug[ustinus], Radingensis monachus, salutem et multam in Christo dilectionem.
	"Dignum duximus vestrae sanctitati magnum quoddam et celebre in domo Radingensi pandere miraculum.
(2) Ecclesiae Radingensis monachus Gaufridus, gravissima infirmitate praeventus, et ut putabatur ad extrema deductus, omnium sensuum omniumque membrorum corporis officio privatus est.	(2) "Nam quidam frater nostrae congregationis, Gaufridus de Warengeford nomine, vir fortis et bonus cantor, et de prioribus domus nostrae, gravissima infirmitate praeventus, et, ut putabatur, ad extrema deductus, omnium sensuum omniumque membrorum corporis officio privatus est.

letter from Shrewsbury, which follows the letter from Reading.

Benedict (ii. 251-2)

(3) What need of many words ? The brethren all assembled to anoint him, according to custom, with the extreme unction. He communicated, became speechless, was entirely given up.

William (i. 210-1)

(3) " What need of many words ? The brethren all assembled to anoint him, according to custom, with the extreme unction. But when it came to receiving the sacred communion, and our Prior exclaimed, " Sir Geoffrey,[2] open thy mouth to receive thy salvation," he desired, and was not able ; and yet with difficulty he succeeded so far that a very small particle was received within his teeth.

" Presently, when he had been replaced in his bed and still remained in the same grievous condition so that we thought he would that same day depart, the Prior, after

(3) Quid plura? convenerunt fratres omnes ut eum ex more oleo sanctae unctionis perungerent. Communicavit, obmutuit, penitus desperatus est :

(3) "Quid plura ? Convenerunt fratres omnes ut eum ex more oleo sanctae unctionis perungerent. Cum autem ad receptionem sacrae communionis perveniretur, clamante priore, ' Domine[2] Gaufride, aperi os tuum ad tuae salutis susceptionem,' voluit et non potuit, et tamen vix obtinuit ut parvissima quaedam particula intra dentes ipsius reciperetur. Mox illo in proprio strato recepto, et in eadem invaletudine permanente, ita ut putaremus illum eodem die exiturum a corpore, non longo postmodum intervallo advenit prior cum paucis fratribus, tentans si

[2] "*Domine* Gaufride." One would have expected "*brother* Geoffrey."

Benedict (ii. 251-2)

William (i. 210-1)

no long interval, came to [him] with a few of the brethren, in the attempt to elicit perchance some word of confession from the mouth of the patient. Absolutely nothing could be anticipated now for him except death.[3]

(4) Knowing absolutely nothing to do [for him], the Prior said, "If there is some one of you who knows that there is in some place at hand the Water of St. Thomas the Martyr,[1] in the faith of Christ let him bring it here this moment."

(4) "Knowing absolutely nothing to do [for him], the Prior asked the brethren if they kept among them the Water of St. Thomas the Martyr. The Water of healing was presently brought— some that I had brought from the Martyr's memorial.

---

forte aliquid verbum confessionis de ore ipsius infirmi exigere valeret. Nil prorsus de illo nisi mortem exspectare potuerunt.[3]

(4) quid ageret prorsus prior ignorans, "O fratres," inquit, "si est aliquis vestrum qui sciat alicubi aquam sancti martyris Thomae,[1] in fide Christi modo afferat eam." Mox

(4) "Quid ageret prorsus prior ignorans, fratres interrogat si apud se servaretur aqua sancti martyris Thomae. Mox allata est aqua salutaris, quam de memoria ejusdem martyris attuleram ;

---

[1] The Abbot of Reading did not at this time favour St. Thomas, and any monk who had the Water, had it secretly, and was liable to be rebuked, comp. (744 (2)). But the Prior, being in despair, resorts to this question as a last hope, "If *some one* of you should *by chance* have it in *some place*, or even know that it is hidden *in some place*." A few months later, every monastery, even the most obscure, would have plenty of the Water.

[3] The meaning seems to be that they could not now anticipate any words of confession. It was the absence of confession that drove the Prior to his next step.

Benedict (ii. 251-2)	William (i. 210-1)
Presently a phial with the water was brought by one of the brothers.	
(5) After it had been poured into the patient's mouth, the string of his tongue was straightway loosed, all his senses returned in full strength, and all his limbs received their original health, so that he said, " I feel well," [2]	(5) " In the moment when it was poured into the sick man's mouth, the string of his tongue was straightway loosed, all his senses returned in full strength, and all his limbs received their original health, so that he said, ' I feel well.'
(6) and, just afterwards, exclaimed in a powerful voice, " Thanks be to God who, through the merits of His Martyr St. Thomas, has perfectly delivered me from the evil one, who was forcibly constricting my throat and nose."	(6) " Just afterwards, he exclaimed in a powerful voice, ' Thanks be to God, who, through the merits of His Martyr St. Thomas, has perfectly delivered me from the evil one, who was forcibly constricting my throat and nose.'

allata est a quodam fratrum ampulla cum aqua,	
(5) quae postquam labiis infirmi infusa est, statim solutum est vinculum linguae ejus, omnesque sensus illius convaluerunt, omniaque membra corporis ejus pristinam sanitatem ceperunt, ita ut diceret, " Bene [2] est,"	(5) "quae dum labiis aegrotantis infusa est, statim solutum est vinculum linguae ejus, omnesque sensus ejus convaluerunt, et omnia membra corporis pristinam receperunt sanitatem, ita ut diceret ' Bene est.'
(6) postmodum valide exclamaret, " Deo gratias qui me per merita sancti Thomae martyris sui a maligno perfecte liberavit, qui guttur meum et nasum vehementer constringebat." Itaque	(6) " Postmodum valide exclamavit, ' Deo gratias, qui me per merita sancti Thomae, martyris sui, a maligno perfecte liberavit, qui guttur meum et nasum vehementer constringebat.'

[2] " Bene est mihi" means " I am well off," " I am doing well"; and this meaning is suitable here.

Benedict (ii. 251-2)	William (i. 210-1)
And so the monk escaped both the hands of the demon and the loss of life.[3]	"This miracle is attested by the whole of the convent of Reading and almost all the inhabitants of our town."

[752] The comparison of these two narratives shews that Benedict's account, which a reader might have naturally anticipated to be from his own pen, is really a condensation of an unacknowledged letter from a monk of Reading, with two brief insertions. Benedict's version omits what is personal to the sick man Geoffrey, but somewhat emphasizes what concerns the Water of Canterbury.

[753] Above, when inserting the story of Elias of Reading, Benedict's book tells us that it might have been inserted long before, but was neglected either through forgetfulness or through the desire of further investigation. Possibly, the same causes operated here: but there may have been another, namely, the hostility of the Abbot of Reading in the early days before St. Thomas's fame was recognized. This may have induced Prior Odo of Canterbury not to publish, in the form of a letter from a mere private monk of Reading, a miracle that ought to have been attested by the Abbot of Reading himself. So Odo may have caused the letter to be entered in the records of Canterbury not as a letter but as a narrative. In William's later book, there was no need of this reticence.

[754] The conclusion to be drawn is an instructive one.

---

evasit monachus et manus daemonis et dispendium mortis.[3]	Hujus miraculi testes sunt totus Radingiae conventus et fere omnes villae nostrae habitatores."

[3] Lit. "loss of, *i.e.* consisting in, death."

Wherever there is close agreement between William and Benedict, we are not justified in inferring that the former borrowed from the latter ; but we are justified in thinking it probable that they borrowed from a common document.[4]

§ 13. *Deliverance from the fall of a wall*

[755] Benedict (ii. 252-3)	William (i. 206-7)[1]
(1) I know a man of good position[1] in the city of Winchester, whose son Geoffrey, about a year and a half old, was delivered by the Water of Canterbury from acute disease.	(1) The boy named Geoffrey, a native of Winchester, son of Robert and Laeticia, about sixteen months of age, was in the heat of a raging fever. After drinking the Water of St. Thomas, he gladdened his parents by an immediately reduced temperature.

(1) Novi virum honoratum[1] de urbe Wintoniensi, cujus filium Gaufridum, quasi annum et dimidium aetatis habentem, aqua Cantuariensis a morbo acuto eripuit.

(1) [1] Audisti puerum vulneratum ; audi puerum aetate minorem, a majori periculo liberatum. Puer Gaufridus nomine, Winthoniensis natione, patre Roberto natus et matre Laeticia, habens a nativitate quasi xvi. menses, fervore febris exaestuabat. Qui bibita aqua sancti Thomae, statim sumpto refrigerio parentes laetificavit.

---

[4] [754*a*] It is quite possible that this narrative, like the last, though found in Benedict's book, proceeded (in that condensed form) from William's pen. It is not like Benedict, but it is like William, to omit the clause of attestation (William (6)) and to substitute the antithetical jingle about "the hands of the demon and the loss of life." See 746*a*.

[1] "Honoratus," below (758 (8)), applied to a chaplain, seems to mean "respected." Here, it may refer to official "honour."

[1] William begins with one of his usual appendix-prefaces : "You have heard [, reader,] of a boy wounded : hear [now] of a boy lesser in age but delivered from a greater peril."

Benedict (ii. 252-3)　　　　　William (i. 206-7)

(2) But after some days, when the boy's mother was sitting alone in the house, and he, opposite her, quiet in the cradle, a great stone party-wall fell with a crash, burying the child in a heap of rubble.

(2) But the sudden joy[2] was clouded with sorrow. For when his mother was sitting by herself,[3] a party-wall of the house was shaken down and fell from top to bottom, under which the boy lay quiet in the cradle.[4] Now it was of stone, thirteen feet high.

So the cradle (which was made of solid boards, squared

---

(2) Post dies autem aliquot, cum sederet sola pueri mater in domo, et puer e regione in cunabulo quiesceret, corruit ejusdem domus paries magnus lapideus, et caementi tumulo sepelivit.

(2) Sed repentina laetitia[2] tristitia obnubilata est. Nam cum mater ejus sederet seorsum[3] in domo sua, ruit concussus paries domus a summo usque deorsum, sub quo infans quiescebat in cunis.[4] Erat autem lapideus, tredecim pedes habens in altitudine. Contritum est itaque cunabulum in decem et octo partes, quod erat ex solidis lignis quad-

---

[2] "Joy (laetitia)." William has also taken the trouble to tell us that the mother's name was "Laeticia." These two insertions make it hardly uncharitable to suppose that William is here punning on the name. The words may mean : "But Laetitia was clouded with a sudden sorrow."

[3] "Seorsum," in the story of Cecilia (737 (12)), meant "in a separate room."

[4] "Sub quo quiescebat" seems to be taken by William to mean "under which" (that is, "by the side of which") the boy "had been sleeping." Taken literally, his words mean that the boy still remained quiet or sleeping under the fallen wall.

Benedict (ii. 252-3)

William (i. 206-7)

like embossed work[5]) was shattered into eighteen pieces : some fragments, too, were driven deep into the ground. Now it was thought that the wall fell in owing to a storm the day before : but *we* believe that the Holy of Holies ordained this to the glory of His Holy one [*i.e.* St. Thomas].

(3) The mother cried out : " My lord, St. Thomas, save me my son whom thou didst [but] yesterday [2] restore to me." Then she fainted for excess of sorrow. But some of the house-servants

(3) The mother, seeing her little one overwhelmed in the chasm, cried, "St. Thomas, save me my boy whom thou didst give back to me," and fainted for sorrow in the moment of her cry.

---

ratum, instar toreumatis.[5]   Nonnulla quoque fragmenta humi pessum infossa sunt.   Putabatur autem paries propter praecedentis diei tempestatem procu- buisse.   Nos vero credimus ad glori- ficandum Sanctum sanctorum haec dispensasse.

(3) Exclamavit autem mater : " Domine," inquit, "sancte Thoma, conserva mihi filium meum, quem mihi pridie [2] restituisti." Haec cum dixisset, prae nimietate doloris in ex- stasim lapsa est ; introierunt autem aliqui ex servientibus domus, et videntes

(3) Videns autem mater quia chas- mate parvulus obrueretur, clamavit, "Sancte Thoma, conserva puerum quem mihi reddidisti" ;[6] et prae dolore cum clamore in extasim lapsa est.

---

[2] "Yesterday (pridie)." See the same phrase uttered by a mother below, 758 (5). Here William omits "pridie." There he substitutes "pridem." In 727 (3), William omits a passage that contains "pridie" used in this loose sense to mean "lately."

[5] "Instar toreumatis." The bear- ing of the phrase on the context is obscure, but see 757.

Benedict (ii. 252-3)

came in, and, seeing her lying on the floor as one dead, they applied the usual remedy of cold water.

(4) When she came to herself and sat up, they said,

William (i. 206-7)

Wonderful the kindliness of the Saint! Wonderful the power of the unconquered Martyr! Quickly did he give ear to the affectionate [6] mother, and preserve the boy too young to have merit [of his own], in the very jaws of death, with four cart-loads, or three [at all events], pressing upon him.

For when on the one hand the son was being snatched [from life] by the falling mass, and on the other hand the mother [was being snatched] out of herself by grief, two men entered just in time, and set the woman on her feet,

(4) and asked and heard the cause of her sorrow.

---

eam in area jacere quasi mortuam, aquae frigidae, ut fieri solet, apponunt remedium.

(4) Quae cum ad se rediens resedisset, "Quid," inquiunt, "habes, do-

---

Mira benignitas sancti ! Mira potentia martyris invicti, qui et piam [6] matrem celerius exaudivit, et puerum citra meritum in ipsa morte conservavit illaesum, quem quatuor aut tria presserunt onera quadrigarum ! Nam cum filius hinc ruina, inde mater sibi moestitia praeriperetur, intervenientes viri duo mulierem jacentem in pedes[*] statuunt,

(4) causam doloris interrogant et accipiunt.

[6] "Piam" would mean "affectionate" in classical Latin. But perhaps it is here "pious."

"What ails you, mistress?"
"Woe is me," she replied,
"my son is dead. See!
Beneath yonder heap of rubble
and stones, he lies crushed
to pieces."

(5) Invoking the name
of God and the Martyr, and
calling in plenty of men to
help, they tear asunder the
mound, and at last, though
not without much toil, reaching the boy, they find him
not only unhurt but actually
laughing—and this, though
the boy's cradle, which was
of stout and solid boards,
had been shattered and splin-
tered into eighteen parts.
But the infant's tender body
was absolutely intact, with
the exception of a very slight
blueness under the eye : [and

(5) Calling in helping
hands, casting down the vast
mass of rubbish from the
wall, finding the cradle splin-
tered into the smallest fragments, they raise the boy not
only unhurt but actually
bright and laughing—won-
derful to say—not having
any sign of hurt on his whole
body beyond a slight blueness near one of the eyes—
and this could hardly be
noticed.

---

mina?" "Proh dolor!" inquit, "mortuus filius meus est ; ecce sub acervo illo
caementi et lapidum jacet confractus."

(5) At illi, nomen Dei et martyris
invocantes, et plurimum hominum con-
vocantes auxilium, aggerem illum
diruunt, et ad puerum tandem, licet
labore plurimo, pervenientes, non
solum illaesum sed et ridentem reperiunt,
cunabulo pueri, quod de lignis erat
grossis et solidis, confracto et in partes
decem et octo dissipato. Infantis vero
caro tenera prorsus intacta. fuit, livore
permodico excepto, quem habebat sub

(5) Qui vocatis auxiliis, ruinosam
congeriem dejicientes, cunabulum com-
minutum frustatim invenientes, puerum
non modo illaesum, sed et laetum et
ridentem, attollunt, mirabile dictu, non
habentem laesionis signum in toto corpore, praeter modicum livoris in altero
oculorum, qui vix poterat adverti.

Benedict (ii. 252-3)

this] while there lay [just] over the infant one stone bigger than the infant himself.

But they [8] wondered at the sight and astonishment seized them.

(6) Benedict omits this.

William (i. 206-7)

(6) As time went on, and they deferred paying the thanks to which they were bound by the Martyr's kindness, the boy began to sicken and to be required to pay the debt publicly announced [by the parents].[7]

And it happened that one day a woman came to the boy's grandmother and said, "It is revealed to me concerning this boy that he ought

---

oculo ; cum super infantem lapis aliquis jacuerit, ipso infante major. Ipsi [3] vero videntes admirati sunt, et stupor apprehendit eos.

(6) om.

(6) Procedente tempore, et gratias differentibus eis qui ex beneficio martyris tenebantur, coepit puer aegrotare, et ad debita praeconiorum reposci.[7] Et accidit in una dierum ut mulier quaedam veniens ad aviam pueri ingrederetur dicens, " Revelatum est mihi de puero

---

[8] "Ipsi" in classical Latin would mean "they themselves" ; but in this Latin it so often means "the above mentioned," that this is probably the meaning here.

[7] "Ad debita praeconiorum reposci" may possibly mean that the boy's life would be required to pay the debt.

William (i. 206-7)

to be conveyed to the Memorial of St. Thomas. Know that this revelation has proceeded from the Lord. For I say not this for the sake of gain, or some [8] other dishonourable reason : but I come to bring you word of a Divine warning."

So after a short time they conveyed the boy to Canterbury and told us what we tell [you].

---

[755] Benedict appears to have received his account from the father, who was an acquaintance of his, and who may have written to him at once about it. Perhaps the father took the facts as they were given him by the servants, who rescued the boy, and who would be able to give him a more connected account than the mother, on the day on which she received so terrible a shock. The servants, suddenly entering the room, would notice the mother's chair in one place and the heap of rubbish (now covering the poor child's cradle) "over against" it, shewing how the mother had escaped :

hoc quod ad memoriam beati Thomae transmitti debeat. Noveris hanc revelationem a Domino processisse. Non enim hoc dico vel lucri gratia vel alia quadam [8] minus honesta causa, sed nuncia divinae admonitionis existo." Igitur post modicum tempus puero Cantuariam transmisso, didicimus quae dicimus.

[8] We should have expected "quaquam" instead of "quadam."

they would know (but the mother would not) that they had
applied cold water to her, whereas she would remember
nothing till she found them "setting her on her feet." The
servants' narrative, following the order of the events, would
not describe the cradle or the number of pieces into which it
was smashed, till they actually found it : and the fact that
some of the pieces were driven into the floor would not
impress them at the time so much as the fact that "just
over the baby there was one big stone lying, as big as the
baby himself." The wonder of the rescuers, with which
Benedict's narrative concludes, is very naturally emphasized
if it was from them that he derived his account.

[757] On the other hand, Laetitia, the mother, appears to
have inspired William's narrative. It was very natural for
her to pass over what she said when she came to her senses,
of which she probably had a very vague recollection ; she
is also very woman-like in describing the child's cradle as
something rather above the average, "like embossed work,"
and in mentioning the number of the fragments so early, out
of the historical order ; and very mother-like in telling us
that the child was " bright " as well as " laughing," and that,
as for the "blueness" near "*one of* the eyes," "*one could
hardly notice it.*" Of course, also, the warning of the
prophetess to the grandmother, coming from the grandmother
to the mother, would lose nothing in the telling, and we
cannot be surprised that William gives it at considerable
length.

The one statistical point peculiar to William is that the
wall was thirteen feet high. This William might ask her ;
and she might naturally know the height of her own room.
If she exaggerated at first the number of cart-loads of rubbish, she might perhaps, when pressed by the monk to be
careful, correct herself as in William's narrative, " four, or,
say three." But it might fairly be argued that this, and the
height of the wall, may have come, not from her, but from

one of her servants. In the main, however, the style of the two narratives favours the view above suggested, that Benedict's account came from the father, William's from the mother. Contrast the story of the son of Yngelrann (**731**), where the mother appears to have influenced Benedict, but not William.

§ 14. *Miracles wrought on James, son of the Earl of Clare*

[758] Benedict (ii. 255-7)

(1) The powerful also are not cast away by God, since He too is powerful. For the powerful and the noble have received their dead by resurrection. Concerning one in particular of these,[1] mention was made above, and now a second time mention must be made of one in particular.

William (i. 228-30)

" There is no acceptance of persons before God, but in every nation whoso feareth God, he is accepted by Him."[1]   He casts not away the powerful, since He too is powerful: He does not always give access to a poor man [merely] because he is poor. Hearts, not rank, He notes ; possessors, not possessions. For if rich and poor are

---

(1) Potentes etiam Deus non abjicit, cum et ipse sit potens ; potentes enim et nobiles acceperunt de resurrectione mortuos suos.   De quorum aliquo[1] superius specificatum est, et nunc iterum de aliquo specificandum.

(1) " Non est acceptio personarum apud Deum, sed in omni gente qui timet Deum, hic acceptus est illi."[1] Non abjicit potentem, cum et ipse sit potens ; non admittit quandoque pauperem quia pauper est.   Corda, non conditionem, attendit ; possessorem, non possessionem.   Si enim dives et

---

[1] " De aliquo," probably referring to the knight Jordan, above (**732**). This miracle on one of noble birth seems to have been made the subject of a discourse in Canterbury, on the basis of the words "Potens potentes non abjicit." Both writers have them.

[1] Acts x. 35.

Benedict (ii. 255-7)	William (i. 228-30)
	strong in merit of good deeds,[2] they deserve to be heard impartially, when making requests of the Lord. Against the latter there is no prejudice from his poverty, nor against the former from his wealth.[3] Therefore, let each one study to please God in mind ; let him make it his business to work for God in word,[4] that God also may work for him.
(2) He that makes all breath, first sent away the breath of life, and then sent	(2) Matilda, countess of Clare, bore her husband a son named James.

---

	pauper merito virtutum[2] polleant, petentes a Domino indifferenter exaudiri merentur. Non praejudicat huic paupertas, non illi facultas.[3] Igitur unusquisque studeat placere Deo mente, verbo[4] satagat operari Deo, ut et Deus operetur pro eo.
(2) Qui flatum omnem facit, Jacobo, Rogerii comitis Clarensis filio, adhuc	(2) Matildis comitissa de Clara suscepit filium Jacobum e viro suo.

---

[2] " Virtutum " so frequently, in these treatises, means "mighty works," that it probably means " works " here.

[3] William elsewhere (688) frankly avows a prejudice in favour of the rich, so far as concerns veracity as to miracles.

[4] So the text "mente, verbo." But (?) " mente *et verbo* ; satagat," *i.e.* " let him study to please God in mind *and word* ; let him make it his business to work for God that God may work for him. "

Benedict (ii. 255-7)

it back, to James, son of Roger Earl of Clare, while still a babe at the breast. The same innocent one was succoured by the merits of the innocent Martyr, not once alone but a second time.

Born about the feast-day of St. Michael, the little infant numbered but forty days when, owing to over-violent crying, the intestines were ruptured and filled the follicle of the testicles. Everything being thus disordered, that which ought to have been the contents of the stomach became the contents of the follicle, which was so distended as to reach almost to the knees.[2]

William (i. 228-30)

A short time after his birth, he was afflicted with hernia, and the intestines flowed into the vessels of the testicles.

His father, seeing that his child was destined from tender years to a life of protracted pain, and [to pass] from the cradle to care,[5] called a consultation of physicians, promising them a large sum in ready money if they would cure him. Ascertaining that the cause of the rupture was a violent outburst of screaming and struggling, they said they must use incision. But the mother, feeling (as for herself) the danger for a child of such tender years, would

---

lactenti vitalem flatum remisit amissum. Eidem innocenti innocentis martyris merita non solum semel, sed et secundo succurrerunt. Circa solennitatem beati Michaelis natus, quadraginta dies habebat infantulus, cum rupta prae clamore nimio intestina genitalium folliculum impleverant ; ordine confuso, quae ventris esse debuerant habebat folliculus distentus, et ad poplites pene porrectus.[2] Quadraginta, aut eo amplius,

Qui parvo tempore post nativitatem hernia percussus est, et fluxerunt intestina in sacculos testiculorum. Cujus pater videns quia a tenero protraheretur ad poenam, et a cunis ad curam,[5] medicos convenit, multam spondens numeratam pecuniam si ipsum curarent. Qui rupturae causam in nimio motu et vagitu deprehendentes, opus esse incisione dicebant. Mater vero, puerili

---

[2] The contents of this and the preceding section, with the antithetical use of "aliquis," " remitto " and "amitto," "flatus," and "innocens," are not in Benedict's ordinary style.

[5] "A cunis ad curam" seems an intended jingle ; "care" is used in the sense of "cares," gnawing the heart.

Benedict (ii. 255-7)

Forty silver marks, or
more, did the father offer for
a cure : but no one was found
venturous enough to accept
the offer unless he might
make an incision into the
little infant. But the parents,
fearing for his tender age,
would by no means consent
to the application of the
knife : so the infant remained
for a year and some months
suffering from hernia.

(3) At length, in the
second year from his birth,
on the day of the Purification
of the blessed Virgin and
Mother, Mary, he was brought
by his mother to the Martyr,
washed with the Martyr's
Water, and within three days

William (i. 228-30)

not permit any incision,
but

(3) placed all her hope
in the Lord and St. Thomas.
And going to the place of
his rest[6] on the day on which
the blessed Virgin and Mother,
Mary (as we read in Scripture)[7] presented her Son in
the Temple, she, too, herself,

marcas argenti, quas ob ejus curationem
pater offerebat, non erat qui accipere
praesumeret, nisi infantulum incidere
liceret.   At parentes, aetati tenerae me-
tuentes, ut ferrum admitteretur minime
consenserunt ; permansit itaque infans
herniosus anno uno et mensibus aliquot.
   (3) Tandem anno nativitatis suae
secundo, in die Purificationis beatae
virginis et matris Mariae, a matre sua
martyri allatus, et martyris aqua lotus,
infra diem tertium dimissus est ab

teneritudini compatiens, non permittebat incidi, sed

   (3) spem totam in Domino beatoque
Thoma constituit.   Et abiens ad locum
requietionis ejus,[6] die qua beata Maria
mater et virgo Filium suum legitur[7] in
templo praesentasse, curavit et ipsa

   [6] *i.e.* the Martyr's tomb (741 (9))
(William).
   [7] " Legitur," lit. " is read to have
presented."

Benedict (ii. 255-7)

William (i. 228-30)

released from his disease, so that no trace of the disease remained.

took care to present her own son to the Martyr to be cared for.[8]

There, too, she received advice (for she had not presumed [before]) to wash the boy's diseased parts with the healing Water. By merely washing she gained complete health for him whom she washed. No other kind of cure was employed. Faith alone reduced the intestines into their place.

(4) After some weeks, in the middle of the following Lent, being seized by another disease, he at length breathed forth his spirit.

The mother had gone to church and was attending

(4) After this, some considerable time passed on, and the boy was withdrawn from life by disease. Great was the sorrow of those in charge of him. When the limbs became so stiff as to make

---

infirmitate sua, nullo infirmitatis remanente indicio.

suum martyri curandum[8] praesentare. Ubi et in consilio accepit; (non enim praesumpsit), infirma pueri aqua salubri lavare. Lavit [tantum], et ei quem lavit omnimodam sanitatem promeruit. Non aliud genus curationis adhibitum est ; sola fides in locum suum intestina reduxit.

(4) Post hebdomadas aliquot, in medio videlicet Quadragesimae sequentis, alia aegritudine correptus, tandem spiritum exhalavit. Mater ad ecclesiam profecta divinis intendebat

(4) Inde aliquanto tempore profluente correptus idem puer infirmitate vitae subtractus est ; et facta est tristitia magna tutorum. Qui cum rigor membrorum certissimam vitae prae-

---

[8] *i.e.* "to be cured," a play on the words "curavit—curandum."

Benedict (ii. 255-7)	William (i. 228-30)
divine service: the household had remained at home.	death certain, they carried the body into an outer building, reserving for the mother's anxious care the arrangements for the burial and the funeral rites. But as no one dared to afflict her with the sad news, a little brother of the deceased, running out [of the house], brought word to the mother of what he had seen.
No one was found willing to bear to the mother's ears the news of her son's death, lest he should be called the cause of the calamity. At last, a little boy (brother of the deceased) ran to the church, unable (like a boy) to keep a secret, and cried out repeatedly to his mother, " Lady, my brother is dead. Lady, my brother is dead."	
(5) She immediately turned pale, started up, threw off her mantle, and, running back to the house, found the infant carried out from his chamber to an outer hall,	(5) Casting off her garment, and hurrying back from prayer, she raises [9] the corpse in her hands, presses it to her breasts, cherishes it in her arms, not fearing to apply

obsequiis; domi familia remanserat. Non est inventus qui pueri mortem maternis auribus nuntiaret, ne calamitatis ejus causa diceretur fuisse. Currit tandem puerulus, pueri frater defuncti, ad ecclesiam (nescit quippe puer aliquis celare secretum), et matri clamat ingeminans, " Domina, frater meus est mortuus; domina, frater meus est mortuus."

(5) At illa statim expallens exsiliit, domumque indumento rejecto recurrens, infantem reperit a thalamo in aulam exteriorem elatum, extensum in area,

dicasset absentiam, in exteriorem domum corpus transferentes elationem et ritum funeris maternae sollicitudini reservarunt. Nemine tamen audente matrem tristi nuntio sollicitare, procurrens fraterculus defuncti quod viderat matri nuntiavit.

(5) Quae veste rejecta cursim rediens ab oratione cadaver manibus attollit,[9] premit ad ubera, fovet inter brachia, vultus vultibus suis admovere non

[9] "Attollit" might mean, with emphasis, "raises *towards herself*," but is used by William elsewhere without any such emphasis.

Benedict (ii. 255-7)

William (i. 228-30)

stretched out on the floor—the mouth open, but no breathing whatever, the tongue and lips drawn inwards, the eyes deep sunk, and turned up so that only the white could be seen —absolutely cold and stiff, and, to speak briefly, in very truth dead.

the child's face to her own,[10] and crying aloud, "St. Thomas, long ago [11] you gave me back my son : why did you resolve to give [him] back,—merely to cause sorrow to a mother ? You healed the disease that caused him such frightful tortures : woe is me, how have I sinned, what command have I transgressed, that I am now condemned to be-reavement ?   Give back, even now, holy Martyr, him whom you [then] gave back."

And snatching him up into her arms, "St. Thomas," she cried, "restore me my son ; but yesterday,[3] when he was afflicted with hernia, you brought him back to health. Now he is dead; holy Martyr, restore him to life."

---

ore aperto, sed penitus absque spiraculo, lingua labiisque in se retractis, defossis oculis, et ita ut albugo sola videretur eversis, frigidum penitus rigidumque, et, ut breviter sit dicere, revera mor-tuum.   Et arripiens eum in ulnas, "Sancte Thoma," inquit, "restitue mihi filium meum ; pridie [3] herniosum redonasti sanitati ; nunc mortuum, sancte martyr, vitae restitue."

trepidat,[10] clamans, "Sancte Thoma, pridem [11] puerum mihi reddidisti ; cur ad maternum luctum reddere voluisti? Morbum, quo misere cruciabatur, curasti ; vae mihi, quo nunc peccato, qua transgressione mandatorum, dam-nor orbitate?   Redde, martyr sancte, etiam nunc quem reddidisti."

---

[3] "Pridie," a hyperbole natural to a mother, but not understood by William, who alters it to "pridem." Suspicions may occur that Benedict, who assigns this ¹ phrase to another mother above (755 (3)) may be writing what he thought the mother *might have* said rather than what she did say. But both here and there the circum-stances make the phrase highly natural, and the fact that William alters it here, and omits it above, shews that the

[10] "Not fearing." This seems a strange thing to need to say. Does the writer imply that the disease was infectious, or of some specially revolt-ing character? The: carrying of the corpse "into an outer building," here mentioned by William, is not, I think, often mentioned by him except in the supposed death of Cecilia, from cancer (see above, 737 (11)), whose condition was exceptionally repellent.

[11] See note 3 on Benedict.

Benedict (ii. 255-7)

(6) She also ran and fetched from a writing case relics of the Saint which she had brought from Canterbury. Some of the blood of the Saint she poured into the mouth of the dead child, and pushed a small portion of his hair-clothing right into the throat,

(7) incessantly exclaiming, " Holy Martyr, Thomas, give me back my son. He shall be brought to your tomb if he lives again : I myself will visit you on my bare feet. Hear my prayer."

William (i. 228-30)

(6) Placed by William in section 10.

(7) " Do but place me under a [second] debt, and then, clothed in woollen attire, barefoot, as an outcast, will I again seek your tomb in devotion. Give back, holy Martyr, him whom you long ago gave back." Thus did she alternate [vows and supplications [12]] fixing her knees on the ground.

---

(6) Currens etiam, reliquias sancti, quas a Cantuaria detulerat, a scrinio extraxit ; sancti cruorem in os mortui infantis infudit, et portiunculam cilicii ei usque in guttur intrusit,

(7) incessanter clamans et dicens, "Sancte martyr Thoma, redde mihi filium meum ; ad sepulchrum tuum adducetur si revixerit ; ipsa te nudis pedibus visitabo ; exaudi me."

(6) vide (10).

(7) " Voto obnoxia, laneis induta, nudis pedibus abjecta, tuum repetam devota sepulcrum. Redde, martyr sancte, quem pridem reddidisti." Hujusmodi loquens invicem [12] in terra genua sua defigebat.

---

phrase is unlikely to have been invented. It seemed to William difficult.

[12] " Hujusmodi loquens invicem—defigebat " could hardly mean " she spoke and knelt by turns " : for surely she would speak while she knelt. Benedict connects (758 (8)) " iterum iterumque " with

Benedict (ii. 255-7)

(8) But all the knights that were standing near, the countess of Warwick, too, and the other ladies, "kept chiding her that she should hold her peace."[4] But she, bending her bare knees again and again on the ground, cried so much the more, "Holy Martyr, have pity on me."

Then Lambert, her chaplain, expostulated with her, a man of a good old age and honoured [by all],[5] "Madam, what possesses you? You are behaving like a simpleton. You are become a fool. What you are doing and saying

William (i. 228-30)

(8) But the men and ladies that were standing near "kept chiding her that she should hold her peace,"[13] especially the chaplain Lambert, saying, "What is the matter with you, Madam? What is this you are doing? what is this you are saying? Such conduct does not savour of sanity or wisdom. A funeral demands funeral supplications, not such as these. Render the body to the ashes,[14] commit the spirit to its Creator who according to His pleasure infuses and withdraws the soul. Do not

---

(8) Milites vero omnes qui astabant, comitissa etiam Warwicensis et reliquae mulieres, increpabant eam ut taceret;[4] at illa genibus nudis iterum iterumque in terram flexis multo magis clamabat, "Sancte martyr, miserere mei." Tunc capellanus ejus Lambertus, vir honoratus[5] et senectutis bonae, "Quomodo te habes, domina? insipienter agis; stulta facta es; amentiam sapiunt

(8) Viri autem et mulieres qui astabant, increpabant eam ut taceret,[13] et praecipue capellanus Lambertus, dicens, "Quid est, domina? quid agis? quid loqueris? Non haec sapiunt mentem sanam et sapientem. Funus funebria, non hujuscemodi, precamina poscit. Redde corpus cineri,[14] spiritum Creatori suo commenda, qui creaturae suae prout vult animam infundit et aufert. Noli

---

[4] Mark x. 48.
[5] "Honoured (honoratus)." See 755 (1).

"genibus flexis." Perhaps there was a French original capable of both translations. Comp. 741 (7).
[13] Mark x. 48.
[14] "Redde cineri" seems to mean "to the *ground*," as in our Burial Service ("ashes to *ashes*"). Elsewhere "imponere cineri" means, *literally*, "lay (a dying person) on ashes."

Benedict (ii. 255-7)	William (i. 228-30)
savours of insanity. Is the Creator not to be allowed to do what He wills with His creature? Cease! Cast away[6] the infant, and let the infant be treated as one dead. It betokens great folly that you should wish to struggle for that which is impossible to obtain." Likewise also said they all:	anger the Divine mercy by fatuous speech."
(9) But she answered, "Certainly I will in no wise cease. In no wise will I cast away my babe: for I am confident that he is to be given back to me. Martyr most	(9) None the less the mother continued her lamentation: "I will not stop," she said, "till the Martyr is propitiated to me and my son is restored to me from death."

quaecunque agis et loqueris. Nunquid non licet Créatori de creatura sua quod vult facere? desine; projice[6] infantem, fiatque de infante utpote de mortuo; stultitiae grandis est ad hoc te niti velle quod impossibile sit impetrare." Similiter et omnes dicebant:	fatuo sermone divinam clementiam exasperare."
(9) at illa, "Certe nequaquam," inquit, "cessabo; nequaquam infantem projiciam; confido enim quod mihi reddendus sit. Martyr," inquit, "glo-	(9) Nihilominus illa plangens, "Non," ait, "omittam priusquam martyr mihi propitietur, et de funere filius restituatur."

[6] "Projice," a very strong word. But the whole of Lambert's language is coloured with an exaggerated bluntness, almost brutal, apparently intended (perhaps by the Countess herself) to shew the strength of the obstacles that she had to contend with in persisting in her prayer to the Martyr.

Benedict (ii. 255-7)

William (i. 228-30)

glorious," she cried, "Martyr most pious, Martyr beloved! Shew pity to me! Give me back my son!"

(10) Placed by Benedict in (6).

(10) And furthermore she opened the lips of the deceased and dropped in some of the Martyr's Water; she also pushed in a piece [15] of the hair-cloth garments of the Martyr.

---

riose, martyr," inquit, "piissime, martyr dilecte, miserere mihi; redde mihi filium meum."

(10) vide (6).

(10) Et adjecit labiis defuncti reclusis aquam martyris instillare, tomumque [16] cilicinum de vestibus ejusdem martyris intrudere.

---

[16] "Tomum," mostly used of paper. Benedict has "portiunculam." William likes Greek words (722).

It is out of the question that the use of the hair-cloth and the water should have been so long delayed. Benedict inserts it in its right place.

William is also wrong in speaking of the mother as "opening the lips," whereas Benedict described (5) "the mouth open."

The fact is, that William, or perhaps his informant, not having, or not following, the mother's account, assumes that here, *as is expressly stated in many other cases*, the mouth was shut fast and had to be opened before St. Thomas's Water could be poured in.

Also it appeared more seemly that the application of the relics and the use of the water should come as a climax and be closely followed by restoration. Benedict places the application early,

Benedict (ii. 255-7)

(11) When she had spent about two hours in thus calling [on him], the Martyr took compassion on her and restored her babe to life. First there appeared a spot of red on his face : soon afterwards he began to roll his eyes and burst out crying.

(12) And they blessed the Lord, who maketh dead and maketh alive, bringeth down to the grave and bringeth back. And there was great gladness in the house, and joy supplanted the agony of sorrow; for "they obtained

William (i. 228-30)

(11) While she [thus] groans and calls [on the Martyr], she noticed a spot of red break out on his face,

(12) perceived it to be the sign of the Divine compassion, and, [? moved by] the tidings of returning life, rose from her knees with thanksgiving.[16]

---

(11) Cumque ita quasi per duas horas clamasset, misertus martyr ejus infantem vitae restituit ; et apparente primitus in facie illius nota ruboris, post modicum oculos circumducens in ejulatum prorupit.

(12) Et benedixerunt Dominum qui mortificat et vivificat, deducit ad inferos et reducit ; et facta est laetitia magna in domo, et extrema luctus occupavit gaudium ; ·"gaudium enim et laetitiam obtinuerunt ; fugit dolor et

(11) Dum gemit et clamat, advertit in facie notam ruboris erumpere.

(12) Signum divinae miserationis intelligit, nuncioque [16] vitae redeuntis cum gratiarum actionibus assurgit.

---

and says that after this, the mother's prayers were unavailing for "two hours." William places the application late and omits the "two hours."

[16] "[(?) Moved by] the tidings (nuncio)." Possibly we ought to read "nuncia (as messenger)."

Benedict (ii. 255-7)

joy and gladness, and sorrow and sighing fled away."[7]

And the Countess, the mother of the boy [thus] restored, readily undertook[8] an unwonted task, and, setting out with the boy for Canterbury, performed the promised journey bare-foot. She was followed by the Countess of Warwick and many other ladies; also by Lambert, the Chaplain above - mentioned, and by many knights, all of whom testified that they had seen the boy and that he had been in very truth dead, and in very truth restored from the dead.

------

[759] As in the case of Geoffrey of Winchester above-mentioned, so here, one account seems to be derived from the mother, one from some other source, probably the Chaplain. Benedict represents the former; William (who has a predilection for the testimony of the clergy), the latter.

[760] The Countess describes the child as the Earl's son, the Chaplain (so we will call William's unknown informant) as the son of "Matilda, Countess of Clare." The mother gives *maternal details, e.g.* "at the breast," "born about Michaelmas," "only forty days old"; and we can fancy her saying that *her husband* offered "forty marks" for a cure, but that "*we* would not allow the physicians to use the knife": on the other hand, the Chaplain—who had (doubtless) talked over matters with the Earl—lays stress

------

gemitus."[7] Et apprehendit[8] comitissa, pueri mater suscitati, laborem inusita-tum, et Cantuariam cum puero properans nudis pedibus iter promissum perfecit. Secuta est autem eam comitissa Warwicensis et aliae mulieres multae; capellanus etiam praenominatus Lambertus, et milites multi, qui omnes vidisse se puerum et vere mortuum et vere a morte resuscitatum testificati sunt.

------

[7] Isaiah xxxv. 10.

[8] "Apprehendit," lit. "seized." Not "suscepit," which would be the regular word for "*undertaking* (a task)."

on the father's anticipations of a life of misery for the poor child and says that it was *the Countess who would not allow the operation.*

[761] Both record the day of the Purification as the day when the Countess took the little one to Canterbury. But the mother alone mentions the date *relating to her child* ("he was *in his second year*"): the Chaplain (or perhaps here William) dilates on her faith, and on her reverence for the Water of Canterbury, and her employment of no other means.

"After *some time*," says the Chaplain—"in the *middle of Lent*," adds the mother—the child died. Thenceforth the Chaplain follows the course of events among the servants *in the house;* the mother tells her tale *as things came to her.*

[762] At home, they lay the body out in an outer building. A few words describe it. The mother is uppermost in their thoughts. Things must be left to her. No one dares tell her. The narrator does not stop even to say where she is. Their minds are not with her: the fear of her passion is with them. They did not suppose that the babe's little brother realized the meaning of death: but he runs out and tells the mother "what *he had seen.*"[1]

[763] The mother begins her account by saying she had gone to church; and what more natural, in the middle of Lent, and her son ailing, too? But "the household had remained at home." While on her knees, she hears her son say twice, "My brother is dead." There is a mother's sense of wrong in the phrase about a boy's "not keeping a secret," as though the servants had tried to prevent even her son from coming to tell her the news, and as though forsooth, she would have treated a mere messenger as "the cause of the death"! So absurd—it seems to her; so certain—though absurd—to the servants.

---

[1] [762a] For another instance where the mother apparently tells the story in one order and the servants tell it in another, as things occurred to them, see **756, 757.**

She *felt* " pale," as she " started up," and this little detail (which must have come from her, for it was not in Benedict's nature to invent it) is not unnaturally inserted in the narrative, as well as the statement that she threw off her " mantle "—vaguely called by the male witness her " garment." She came back " at a run from praying " says the Chaplain, as though the point were that she did not stay to the end of the prayers ; and then he describes what she *did*, adding that she did not even "*fear to place her face close to the child's.*" But the mother describes not what she came *from* (*i.e.* praying), but what she came *to* (*i.e.* home), and not what she *did*, but (first of all) what she *saw*—the little pitiful corpse, not in its bed, but in an " outer hall," and " lying on the floor " ! And then the ghastly features of death ! The mother thinks it needless to describe that she "*cherished*" the child : the point was, to *save* it. If she catches it in her arms, it is to offer up a prayer over it to St. Thomas. Then to the relics at once, the " blood "— she will not call it Water ; for her, it is " blood "—and the little scrap of cloth which she " pushes right into " the little one's throat.

[764] Is it not also very womanly that in mentioning the painful expostulations of those who would fain have prevented her from saving her child's life, she should single out the Countess of Warwick ? From the " knights," it was natural enough. They were men, and did not understand things. And the worthy and venerable old Chaplain, she did not mind his plain frankness. It was even a pleasure to recollect that, with the best possible motives, he had told her she was " a fool," and was acting like a simpleton. But from a woman it was so different. She has no good epithet for her.

[765] As for the Chaplain, here, it is amusing to note how cleverly, without denying, he softens his expostulations. He merely alters " insanity " into " not . . . sanity," and " fool "

into "not wisdom"—a very pardonable extenuation: but the Countess's version represents the unextenuated truth.

[766] Benedict's account of the conclusion is in his own sensible, earnest, and accurate manner. He recognizes that there was a delay of "two hours" before the child revived (whereas William leads readers naturally to infer that the revival followed almost immediately on the application of the Martyr's relics): he adds some interesting details about the accompanying signs of the revivification; and he makes us realize, in the words of Isaiah, how, in that household, "sorrow and sighing fled away." Also, his concluding sentence adds attestation to the miracle, and incidentally affords a slight probability to the conjecture, above thrown out, that Lambert the Chaplain may have originated William's account. The Countess of Clare, he says, came first to the Memorial. Benedict might naturally write his narrative from her story. Afterwards came the Chaplain, and his account suggested another version of the miracle to William.[2]

§ 15. *The cure of Hugh of Ebblinghem, a leper ; William adds another*

[767] Benedict (ii. 259-60).

(1) The Almighty Father who smites His children with His rod and delivers their souls from death, who visits

William (i. 332-4).

(1) "Never in my life," says Galen, "have I seen a man perfectly cured of leprosy —unless indeed he has drunk

---

(1) Pater omnipotens, qui percutit filios suos virga et liberat animas eorum a morte, qui visitat in virga iniquitates

(1) "Nunquam," inquit Galienus, "vidi in vita mea hominem a lepra plenarie sanatum, nisi qui vinum biberit ubi tyria inciderit et ibidem

---

[2] [766a] The Prologue, in both narratives, suggests that this miracle had been made the subject of "Canterbury Discourses" such as the monks might naturally make to the pilgrims. Comp. 758 (2) and 767 (1): it is natural that, in compiling his Book, Benedict should take any striking utterances from such a Discourse, and use them as an Introduction.

Benedict (ii. 259-60)

their iniquities with a rod and their sins with stripes,

(2) Benedict omits this.

William (i. 332-4)

wine into which a viper has been dropped and allowed to rot, for under those circumstances I *have* seen him peeled and stripped of the diseased skin, upon drinking that wine." But *we* have seen two men perfectly cleansed and not retaining a sign of leprosy, though they had not received any medicine other than the Water and blood of the Martyr.

(2) One of these stayed for a long time near the Martyr's tomb, "eating and drinking such things as were with us."[1] His name was Richard, and he was beheld by kings, counts, natives and foreigners, who came to pray.[2]

eorum et in verberibus peccata eorum, misericordiam autem suam non dispergit ab eis,

(2) om.

computruerit. Hunc enim vidi excorticari et cute exspoliari cum vinum illud biberet." Nos vero vidimus duos ad unguem mundatos nec signum leprae reservantes, qui non aliud medicamen acceperant quam aquam et sanguinem martyris ;

(2) quorum alter diutius circa tumbam ejusdem martyris conversabatur, edens et bibens quae apud nos erant,[1] Ricardus nomine, et erat spectaculum regibus, comitibus, indigenis et alienigenis oratum venientibus.[2]

---

[1] Luke x. 7.
[2] This may have been Queen Eleanor's foundling (747), who was

Benedict (ii. 259-60)

(3) smote Hugh of Hembegim [1]

(4) with a sudden leprosy in harvest time; and his whole body was deformed by prominent tubers. And the man thought over his sin, and confessed his unrighteousnesses that were against him in the eyes of the Lord, and, after invoking the Martyr, feeling within ten days that he was better, he bent his way to Canterbury. And he saw in a vision of

William (i. 332-4)

(3) Another, named Hugh, of the village of Hemblenguiem, about fifteen furlongs from a great town commonly called by the name of the Confessor St. Omer,

(4) we saw as a leper,

---

(3) percussit Hugonem de Hembegim [1]

(4) lepra repentina messionis tempore; totumque corpus ejus tubera prominentia reddidere deforme. Et cogitavit homo pro peccato suo, et confessus est adversus se injustitias suas Domino, et martyre invocato infra diem octavum meliorari se sentiens, Cantuariam tetendit. Et vidit in visu

(3) Alterum vero quendam Hugonem, de vico Hemblenguiem, quasi quindecim stadiis a vico grandi distante quem nomine confessoris Audomari vulgus appellat,

(4) leprosum vidimus

---

[1] Or, "Amblengim."

brought by the Bishop of St. Asaph to Canterbury "to be exhibited." As being under the Queen's protection he might naturally have been shewn to "kings." On the date implied by "kings," see **441**, note 2.

Benedict (ii. 259-60)

the night the face as of one crucified, touching with his hand the place of the leprosy and saying, " Behold, thou art made whole."[2]   And he came on,[3] even unto us. And when we saw him, " he had no form nor comeliness.[4] For though in several places there remained only the traces of the leprosy, yet in some the prominent tubers had not been driven away.

(5) Benedict omits this.

William (i. 332-4)

/

(5) and we sent (him) away from our house cured,

noctis quasi crucifixi hominis vultum, manu sua locum leprae tangentis, ac dicentis, " Ecce sanus factus es."[2]   Et venit usque ad[3] nos ; et vidimus eum non habentem speciem neque decorem.[4] Nam, licet in locis pluribus sola leprae remansissent vestigia, in aliquibus tamen tubera prominentia fugata non fuerant.

(5) om.

(5) et sanatum a nobis dimisimus,

[2] The words seem taken from John v. 14, with a special allusion to what follows, viz. "sin no more." It is implied by both writers that Hugh had special reasons for penitence. William appears to connect them with the fact that he was "a merchant." Elsewhere (627) he says that a trader's gain is mostly another man's loss.

[3] " Usque ad " perhaps means that, though he had received a sort of promise of cure, yet he went *on*, till he had reached his original destination.

[4] Isaiah liii. 2.

Benedict (ii. 259-60)	William (i. 332-4)
	warning him to carry on his business without fraud (for he was a merchant) or to give up business altogether. For in other points he was respectable above the average, with a good presence, and strong, and not past the prime of life.
(6) So he washed himself in the wonder-working Water of the Martyr, who was washed in his own blood and [he] is wholly clean. The man was unclean when he came to the Martyr and was made clean through him; for we sent him away part-cleansed,[5] and, after the lapse	(6) He was cured easily, though his disease was difficult—and all the more difficult because a year had elapsed since it had spread over his skin. He spent two nights in prayer with us, and departed after his face had been sprinkled with a little of the Water. On departing, ,

monentes ut negotiationem suam sine fraude prosequeretur (erat enim mercator), vel ex toto negotiationi renuntiaret. Nam ad aliam conditionem honestiorem satis habebat idoneam personam, et vires corporis quae nondum metas virilis aetatis excesserant.

(6) Lavit itaque se mirifica martyris aqua, qui in sanguine proprio lotus est, et est mundus totus. Immundus erat homo cum veniret ad martyrem, et mundus per ipsum factus est; emendatum[5] enim dimisimus, et post aliquot

(6) Sanabatur autem facili modo in difficili morbo, quem et difficiliorem reddiderat annus exactus ex quo creverat in cute. Duas noctes in oratione pernoctavit apud nos, et discessit aquae modico faciem perfusus. Discedens

[5] "Emendatum," lit. "amended," but rendered as above in order to suggest the play on "mundus (clean)" and "mundus (the world)," "immundus," "emendatus," "emundatus."

Benedict (ii. 259-60)	William (i. 332-4)
of some months, received him again whole-cleansed.	he shortly perceived its mighty and wonder-working virtue. When he returned to give thanks, he informed us of its efficacy; and we believed him because his face, [now] cleansed, deserved to be credited.
(7) Blessed be in all things the kind Providence of God, which stole away our clean Martyr from the [unclean] world, that by his cleanness [freeing us] from worldly uncleanness he might cleanse the unclean.	(7) William omits this.
(8) For great indeed is the multitude of those whose skin, roughened with the tubers of leprosy, has been smoothed by the Martyr; but to set forth the accounts of single cases singly, and [of all] collectively, presents	(8) [William devotes a page to the two points briefly touched on by Benedict: (1) the special mission of the Martyr, the great High Priest, to cure leprosy, (2) leprosy collectively as typifying sin, whether in the

mensium decursum recepimus emun-
datum.

ejus magnificam mirificamque virtutem
sensit in brevi; de cujus efficacia, cum
rediret ad gratias, nobis indicavit, et
credidimus, quia mundata facies fidem
promeruit.

(7) Benedicta in omnibus benigna
Dei providentia, quae martyrem mundo
mundum surripuit, ut mundus a mundi
sordibus mundaret immundos.

(7) om.

(8) Multi enim sunt valde, quorum
hispidam leprae tuberibus cutem martyr
complanavit; sed de singulis singulatim
conjunctimque explanari non congruit.

(8) Quid, putas, agit impraesenti-
arum Dominus curando tot leprosos?
nemini videatur onerosum si super hoc
dixero quid sentiam. . . . . Curat

Benedict (ii. 259-60)

an incompatibility. For even a sweet song oft repeated causes, sooner or later, weariness. Lest therefore we wear a well-worn subject to the point of disgusting our readers, let us await something new.[6]

William (i. 332-4)

" viper - form (tyriam)," the " lion-form (leoninam)," " the elephant-form (elephantiam)," and the " fox-form (alopeciam)," or in " any other genus of leprosy excogitated by the physical student."

" By benefits such as these," he concludes, "the good are invited onward to [new] goodness, the bad are called back from evil : and modern ages (God be thanked !) see such a [spiritual] progress as has not been from the time when the apostles ceased to be seen on earth."]

[768] There is a remarkable contrast between these two narratives. Both agree, indeed, in making the cure of this Hugh an occasion for some remarks on leprosy in general ; but, whereas Benedict says he cannot treat of leprosies singly and collectively at the same time, William attempts this very task, giving two accounts of completely cured lepers, one from abroad, one at home, and at the same time entering into a disquisition on the kinds and cures of leprosy and on their spiritual meanings. It would seem that William was attempting to improve upon Benedict.[1]

Nam et dulcis cantus frequentatus adducit quandoque fastidium. Ne ergo usque ad taedium trita teramus, novi aliquid exspectemus.[6]

igitur omnem lepram, non modo tyriam, leoninam, sed elephantiam et alopeciam, et siquid aliud leprae genus physicus excogitat. Curat et spiritualem lepram, etc.

[6] Here ends Benedict's Fifth Book (see **584**).

[1] If we knew the history of this miracle we should probably find that, like the case of William of Horsepool (**565**), it had been exaggerated by some who (ii. 224) " de parvis magna loquebantur."

[769] William's narrative must have been written after 1174.[2] Almost certainly, therefore, he had Benedict's facts before him. If so, he suppressed one important fact, (1) that the leper was in great measure cured before he reached Canterbury. He does not suppress, but he does not emphasize as Benedict does, the fact (2) that he was not completely cured when he was sent back from Canterbury.

[770] As in other instances, Benedict's narrative shews two distinct styles, (1) the Hebraic, in which the sentences, introduced by the monotonous "and," are thrown into simple and Scriptural forms, and (2) the monkish, or jingling antithetical, mostly reserved for the prologue and epilogue, but occasionally emerging in the body of the story. These two styles may imply two different hands (Benedict being the chronicler and some one else the retoucher and dramatic adapter), or merely the two different moods of the historical narrator and the monkish moralizer. The "jingling" style will be found exemplified in the opening of Benedict's next story.

§ 16. *William of Gloucester is saved from a fall of earth*

[771] Benedict (ii. 261-3)

(1) We sighed for something new. By something new we are kindled anew to a new love of the Martyr (see 770).

William (i. 253-6)

(1) Roger, Bishop (*sic*) of York, a man of the first rank in learning, human and divine, if only his knowledge had been "according to knowledge,"[1] once a rival of

---

(1) Nova suspiravimus. Novis jam de novo in novi Anglorum martyris amorem accendimur.

(1) Aemulum suum martyr Thomas Rogerium, Heboracensem episcopum, virum in humanis rebus et divinis apprime eruditum, si secundum scientiam[1]

---

[2] The date of King Henry's visit to St. Thomas's tomb.

[1] Rom. x. 2 "a zeal for God, but not *according to knowledge*."

Benedict (ii. 261-3)

William (i. 253-6)

the Martyr Thomas, received a warning as to the need of charity among brethren and peace between members of the Church, from a miracle of a very novel kind.

(2) A new thing hath the Lord wrought on the earth, yea, under the earth. For the earth fell in and compassed a man round, and pressed him sore on all sides yet pressed him not to death. A man, unharmed, supported what might have overwhelmed a multitude of oxen.

This came to pass in a village near Gloucester, called in English Churchdown, in the case of a man whose name was William. The man was

(2) For the Archbishop Roger was bringing water into his town of Churchdown from the brow of a hill about five hundred paces off. Now the ground midway swells into a small hill looking down on the surrounding level from a steep top, about twenty-four feet high. The work being at its height,[2] this hill was dug through so that it might receive the aqueduct direct through the opening in its depths. The work was

---

sciens esset, novitate mirandae rei fraternae charitatis admonuit et ecclesiasticae pacis.

(2) Novum fecit Dominus super terram, immo sub terra. Terra enim corruens circumdedit virum, et undique comprimens non oppressit. Portavit homo illaesus quod boves multos posset obruere. Apud villam hoc factum est Gloecestriae vicinam, quae Anglice Cherchesdun appellatur, in homine cui nomen erat Willelmus. Faciebat homo ille aquaeductum, et stans in defosso

(2) Duxit siquidem aquam antistes Rogerius in villam suam Cherchesdune a supercilio montis quasi quingentis passibus remoto. Tumet autem collis in medio, circumjacentium aequora camporum erecto vertice despiciens, altitudinis viginti quatuor circiter pedum. Qui, cum ferveret opus,[2] transfossus est, ut aquae ductum patulo sinu receptum traduceret per directum.

---

[2] This seems the most probable meaning.

Benedict (ii. 261-3)

making an aqueduct. It was about the tenth hour.[1] The depth of the pit is said to have amounted to twenty-four feet : and the impending earth fell with a crash upon him as he worked [below], filling the pit to the level of the surrounding soil.

(3) Benedict omits this.

William (i. 253-6)

being pressed on by one William, who had hired out his services[3] from the neighbouring town of Gloucester. Just when he was laying the leaden pipe at the bottom of the cutting in the hill, the vast mass of earth thrown out from the work fell forward on the top of him.[4]

(3) His companions leapt away to right and left, and would have made an effort to dig him out, buried as he was all round,[5] when lo, once more, the earth on the brink of the cutting broke clean away, and the impending heap rolled down and cut off

---

terrae calamum plumbeum protendebat. Hora erat quasi decima ;[1] foveae profunditas pedum viginti quatuor dicitur exstitisse. Et corruit terra pendula super operantem, foveamque repletam reliquae terrae coaequavit.

(3) om.

Instabat operi quidam Willelmus, qui locaverat operas[3] suas ex oppido Gloecestria vicino. Super quum,[4] cum plumbeam fistulam in imo transfossi collis collocaret, proruit moles ruinosa telluris egestae.

(3) Dissilientibus hinc inde sociis, et volentibus eum jam circum[5] obrutum effodere, ecce rursus abrupta crepidine fragilis et pendula congeries devoluta

---

[1] *i.e.* 4 P.M.

[3] " Locare suam operam " (sing.) is used by Plautus in this sense. Perhaps the plural here means "his services and those of his workmen."

[4] " Super quum," an error for " super quem."

[5] *i.e.* not yet *covered up*, but "all round " up to the armpits, or neck.

Benedict (ii. 261-3)

William (i. 253-6)

the young man from all aid. The earth - fall might be reckoned at about a hundred small cart-loads.[6]

(4) But before [this] burial, as though he were [already] dead,[2] he cried, " St. Thomas, glorious Martyr, if the tales told of thee are true, succour me that I may be snatched hence living. If thou wilt save me alive, I will visit the place where thou didst live and die."

He was standing, bowed

(4) He remained standing, leaning forward, his hands spread before his face, with nothing but a shirt on, for he had been hard at work. So seeing that all means of getting out[7] were closed against him, he sought the first and last refuge of all who are in sore need, by sighing unto the Lord. He invoked also the blessed

---

juvenem intercipit. Poterant in casu quasi centum onera bigarum [6] aestimari.

(4) Ille vero ante sepulturam, quasi mortuus,[3] " Sancte Thoma," inquit, "gloriose martyr, si vera sunt quae de te dicuntur, succurre, ut hinc vivus eripiar. Si vivum me conservaveris, locum ubi et vivus et mortuus fuisti visitabo." Cumque incurvatus staret et in

(4) Stabat autem ille pronus, faciei manibus oppansis, solaque vestitus interula, sicut operi se studiosus applicaverat. Qui videns quod sibi praecluderetur effugium,[7] primum et postremum cujuslibet necessitatis refugium, suspiravit ad Dominum.

---

[2] " Ante sepulturam, quasi mortuus" might also mean " As though all but dead, he repeated a prayer, *as a preliminary to interment.*" But the prayer to St. Thomas would surely be uttered in the faith that he would *not* die and that he was *not* already dead. Hence the Editor ingeniously suggests "ante sepultus quam mortuus," "interred before he was dead." Sense would also be made by "ante . . . mortui," "before this interment, so to speak, of the dead."

[6] " Bigae." Benedict, in (4), says "quadrigae."

[7] The translation does not keep the play on the words " effugium," " refugium."

Benedict (ii. 261-3)	William (i. 253-6)

forward, and, as he prayed thus, his breath was being at every instant cut shorter and shorter, when there came an unexpected eructation, and the eructation was followed by vomiting, and the vomiting by a free power of breathing.
 	
   So he cried without ceasing to the Martyr, being interred all that night, and during the following day up till the third hour.[3] About his death there was but one opinion in all those who had been on the spot. No one at all could doubt the death of one crushed under such a mass.   Yet by the virtue [that went forth] from the Martyr this one frail creature was enabled to support the
	Virgin Mary, who, according to her name, is a star unto those who are tossed in the troubled sea of human calamity, guiding them to the haven of eternal bliss. But the Lord did not send succour at the invocation of His own name, because He purposed to glorify His own Martyr.
	
	   What should the poor man do, cut off from help by the fall of so vast a mass ? Breath was denied by the interception of air ; all aid of man was shut out by the mass heaped on him. So he began to feel distended by the breath pent up within him : and when he was in such agony as almost to

hunc modum oranti jam jamque praecluderetur anhelitus, ex insperato eructavit, eructationem vomitus secutus est, vomitum anhelandi facultas libera. Clamavit igitur incessanter ad martyrem sepultus nocte illa tota, die etiam sequenti usque ad horam tertiam.[3] De morte ejus omnibus, qui affuerant, una eademque sententia. Nemo penitus ambigeret mortuum, quem tanta moles oneraret ; sed martyris virtute centum et eo

Invocavit et beatam virginem Mariam, quae, secundum nomen suum, fluctuantibus in turbulento salo calamitatis humanae, stella est ad portum felicitatis aeternae. Sed non succurrit Dominus ad invocatum nomen suum, quia mirificaturus erat martyrem suum. Quid faciat miser, ruina tantae molis interceptus ? Spiramen negat aer interclusus, excludit congesta moles omne juvamen humanum. Coepit igitur incluso spiritu distendi ; cumque

[3] *i.e.* 9 A.M.

Benedict (ii. 261-3)	William (i. 253-6)
weight of a hundred large cart-loads and more.	breathe his last, the name of Thomas the Martyr came into his mind, and he said, "St. Thomas, men say that thou hast power with thy Lord and that thou canst easily obtain [from Him] that which thou art asked [to obtain]. If thou art so holy and great as men's mouths declare, aid me in my extreme need ; loose me from this miserable trap ; lead me out of this dungeon, restoring me to my former place. [Then] shalt thou be for a refuge to me, and I will seek the place consecrated by thy precious blood, where for the liberty of the Church thou didst contend while living, and conquer when dead."

amplius quadrigarum onus unus homuncio supportabat.

ad exspirandum vexaretur, incidit in os ejus nomen martyris Thomae. Et ait, " Beate Thoma, homines aiunt quia potens es apud Dominum tuum, et facile quod rogaris potes impetrare. Si ita sanctus es et tantus ut ore populi praedicaris, adjuva me in extremis constitutum ; absolve miserrime deprehensum ; educ me de carcere isto, restituens in gradum pristinum. Eris mihi in refugium, et petam locum pretioso sanguine tuo consecratum, ubi pro libertate ecclesiastica vivus decertasti et mortuus evicisti." Haec dicens

Benedict (ii. 261-3)

William (i. 253-6)

Saying these words—for we do not invent such words as he *might* have said, but we say the very same words that he *did say*, preferring to set down less [than the truth] rather than to speak beyond the truth—he breathed forth (in copious eructation) the wind with which his stomach had been distended, and was further relieved by vomiting. From that time he regained the power of breathing.

(5) The Priest of the town became anxious[4] about the soul of the dead man, not

(5) This was what was going on in the heart of the earth. And there was raised

(neque enim confingimus quae potuit dixisse, sed dicimus haec eadem quae dixit, malentes minus apponere quam praeter veritatem loqui)—ventum quo distentus intumuerat multis eructationi-bus efflavit, et vomens alleviatus est. Ex tunc praestita est spirandi facultas.

(5) Fit sollicitus[4] ejusdem villae sacerdos de anima mortui, ignorans

(5) Haec in corde terrae gerebantur. Factus est autem clamor "Sacerdos,

[4] "Became anxious." This frivo-lous sentence is contrary to the fact (as stated by William) that the Priest was "sent for." The fact that it uses "sacerdos" while the next uses "pres-byter" suggests that it may have been an insertion, for the sake of a joke, by a humorous Editor. It must be ad-mitted, however, that the next sentence partakes of jocosity, and "presbyter" may have been used for "sacerdos" for the sake of variety. But is this Benedict's style (770)?

Benedict (ii. 261-3)	William (i. 253-6)
knowing that the man's soul was more anxious about his body, which was still living. So the Priest celebrated the exequies for him, not the last, as he supposed, but the first.[6]	a cry "Priest! Priest! For he is dead." So the Priest was called, and paid the funeral rites, after the discharge of which he returned to his home. But the man underground, for the space of that night, left to himself and the earth,[8] awaited the Martyr's compassion.
(6) Benedict omits this.	(6) Fifty-one days had now run their course since the summer solstice, and as the sun was on the point of passing from the Lion to the Virgin, the nights were growing longer. Yet in the length of the nights[9] the Lord sent

quod anima hominis sollicitior esset de corpore suo, adhuc vivente. Celebrat igitur pro ea presbyter exsequias, non ultimas, ut putabat, sed primas.[6]	[sacerdos], quia mortuus est!" Unde accitus exsequialia impendit, quibus expletis in propria recessit. Obrutus autem, per spatium noctis sibi soloque[8] dimissus, misericordiam martyris exspectabat.
(6) om.	(6) Jam ab aestivali solstitio quinquaginta dies et unus excurrerant, solemque Leo transmissurus in Virginem nocturnis spatiis indulgebat. In tanta tamen noctium longitudine[9] factus est

---

[6] Perhaps he means that this man was destined to have the funeral service *twice* read over him. This was his *first* funeral.	[8] "Sibi *soloque*," not improbably intended as a pun. "Sibi *solique*" might mean, in bad Latin, "to himself, and (that) *alone*."
	[9] The meaning seems to be that the longer night, affording scope for dreams, was made instrumental for the man's deliverance through a dream.

Benedict (ii. 261-3)

William (i. 253-6)

help to him in his tribulation. For a woman, a native of the village, saw a vision and said to her son in the morning, " I think, my son, that the man underground lives still ; for I saw in my sleep that he drank milk and slept in milk."

(7) Now when morning came, it happened that a young man of that town, led by the Divine will, passed across the spot and heard a subterraneous sound. And by chance meeting the town-crier (? bailiff) he said to him, " Assuredly that man buried in the earth-fall yesterday is alive." " What you say," replied the other, " is impossible. He died on the instant." The young man

(7) Forthwith, contrary to his wont, the youth rose from his bed and went out into the fields, not of any set purpose but as chance led him ; and, as though guided by the Spirit, he reached— I will not call it the water-place but the sighing-place ; and, putting his ear to the ground, he heard as it were a groaning. And shouting to the man in charge of the fields—who had gone out early

ei Dominus adjutor in tribulatione. Nam vidit mulier indigena visionem, et ait mane filio suo, " Puto, fili, quod obrutus ille vivit adhuc ; nam vidi per somnum quod et lac potaret et in lacte requiesceret."

(7) Mane autem facto, contigit juvenem de villa eadem, nutu divino ductum, per locum illum transire et sonum audire subterraneum. Casuque occurrens villae praeconi, " Vere," inquit, " homo ille hesterna die obrutus vivit." At ille, " Impossibile est quod ais ; in momento exspiravit." E contra

(7) Ille protinus praeter consuetudinem surgens a lecto in agros egrediebatur, non de industria, sed quo casus ferebat ; et tanquam deductus Spiritu pervenit ad locum, non jam aquaeductus, sed luctus ; et aurem solo defigens tanquam audivit gemitum. Exclamansque ad agrorum custodem, qui ad considerandum jumentum matu-

Benedict (ii. 261-3)	William (i. 253-6)
retorted, "If you doubt it, come and listen."	in the morning to look after the cattle which he had turned out at nightfall—"Hulloa," he said, "he still lives: for I hear something like a man groaning and lamenting." "It is naught," said the other: "and if all Gloucester said the contrary, I would not believe them." The boy rejoined, "Come and listen": and when they heard it,
He agreed, and applied his ear to the earth's surface; and his hesitating doubt [6] was banished from his heart.	
(8) Benedict omits this.	(8) the other carries word to the Priest that the man was alive. Forthwith the Priest broke off divine service and came to the spot with all the people.
(9) The report of it was noised abroad in the town.	(9) And word was carried likewise to Gloucester that

---

juvenis, "Si haesitas, veni et audi." Adquievit, et auribus ad superficiem terrae admotis, amota est a corde ejus cunctatio, qua dubitavit.[6]

(8) om.

(9) Rumor in villa insonuit. Con-

tinus exierat quod sub divo nocte dimiserat, "Heus!" inquit; "vivit adhuc; nam tanquam lacrymabilem gemitum hominis ego audio." Respondit, "Nihil est, et si omnes Gloecestrenses assererent, non crederem." Subjunxit, "Veni et audi"; et cum audissent,

(8) nuntiavit alter sacerdoti quia viveret; qui protinus cum populo venit ad locum, intermisso divino officio.

(9) Et nuntiatum est similiter Gloe-

---

[6] "Cunctatio qua dubitavit" is a strangely superfluous phrase. Moreover, it is asserted above that he did not merely "doubt," but absolutely disbelieved.

Benedict (ii. 261-3)

William (i. 253-6)

The people flock together with prongs, (?) mattocks, and digging tools of divers kinds ; the soil is removed ; the man is released from his grave. When drawn out, living, and unhurt,

the man still breathed.   And they came—all that had a liking and affection for their neighbour—grey-beards, boys and women, with besoms, pans, tubs, and other rustic utensils, setting to work to clear away the soil.

The man underground, hearing them at their noisy work, each striving to get to him before the others, began to accost those who were standing above,[10] both those close at hand and those far off—lest they [*i.e.* the former] should either hurt him with their tools or [the latter should] keep at too cautious a distance.   And the day wore on to the third hour.[11]

---

currit populus cum vangis et ligonibus et generis diversi fossoriis.   Tollitur humus ; extumulatur homo ; vivus et illaesus extractus,

cestriae quia spiraret adhuc.   Vene-runtque quotquot erant pronae devo-taeque mentis in proximum, senex, puer, mulier, solumque scopis, paropsidibus, alveolis, et aliis rusticanis utensilibus incumbentes   rejiciebant.   Obrutus autem, tumultuantes audiens et invicem se labore praevenientes, ad prope longeque stantes desuper [10] obloquebatur, ne vel ipsum ferramentis laederent vel se nimis absentarent ; et processit dies in tertiam.[11]   Tum tandem sepultus

---

[10] "Desuper."   Editor suggests "desubter."   But perhaps "desuper" may modify "stantes."

[11] *i.e.* 9 A.M.

Benedict (ii. 261-3)	William (i. 253-6)
	Then at last the buried man appeared, with his cheeks badly bruised and his arms crushed almost to breaking, his body stiff and frozen with the cruel subterranean cold.
(10) Benedict omits this.	(10) So he was restored to the living that sinners might emerge from the dead. For, as we believe, it was for the purposes of reformation that the Martyr saved the [bodily] life of [this] innocent man that the guilty also might save their [spiritual] life.[12] And this you may conjecture from the fact that when he had (?) previously [13] delayed

| (10) om. | apparuit, genas collisus citraque fracturam brachia contritus, subterranei frigoris asperitate rigidus et congelatus. (10) Restitutus est itaque superis, ut peccatores emergerent ab inferis. Ad correctionem enim credimus martyrem salvasse animam innocentis, ut et nocentes salvarent animas [12] suas. Quod inde conjicias, quia cum praecedente [13] tempore distulisset se Can- |

[12] "Animam . . . animas"—"life . . . souls."

[13] "Praecedente." But this is extremely abrupt. It assumes some previous vow, of which we are told nothing, and moreover a vow in return for some deliverance granted by

Benedict (ii. 261-3)

William (i. 253-6)

to present himself publicly at Canterbury, some woman was told in a dream that he was rash in delaying to manifest at the Martyr's tomb this manifestation of the Divine pity, and that he would not escape punishment if he presumed to delay further.

(11) he proclaimed to all the mighty work of the Martyr Thomas ; and, visiting the Martyr, he certified us with a letter of the following nature, anticipated, however, long before, by the arrival of rumours and reports about the matter :

(11) All this was related to us by the very man that had endured it, and he brought us a letter worded as follows :

---

tuariae palam facere, dictum est alicui mulieri in somnis quia temerarius esset qui divinae pietatis ostentum apud sepulchrum martyris differret ostendere, et quia supplicium non esset evasurus si ulterius differre praesumeret.

(11) martyris Thomae virtutem praedicavit omnibus, et martyrem visitans litteris nos certificavit hujusmodi ; quas tamen rei hujus fama longe ante praevenerat.

(11) Haec idem vir qui pertulerat retulit nobis, et obtulit litteras in haec verba :—

St. Thomas which required a "public" acknowledgment.

Almost certainly we should read "procedente," i.e. "when *time passed on* and he [still] delayed."

Benedict (ii. 261-3), William (i. 253-6)

(12) "To his venerable lord and father, Prior of Holy
Trinity of Canterbury [William omits "of Canterbury"],
and to the whole convent, Godfrey, Dean of Gloucester,
[sends] health.

[772] "Know that the bearer of this, William [by name],
was buried in the bottom of a pit twenty-four [William, "twenty-
three"] feet deep, while all his companions escaped ; and that he
remained interred for the space of one night and the following
day up to the third hour [*i.e.* 9 A.M.], and the whole of the
obsequies were performed, as for one dead.   But when the
man perceived that death was imminent, he invoked God,
and prayed that, for love [William, "by the merits"] of His
most glorious Martyr Thomas He would deliver him from
such peril ; and he made a vow aloud that he would go to
the place where St. Thomas fell.   These sounds being heard
by some that happened to cross the place, they brought
word to the whole of the town that they had heard a man's
voice in the pit.   Then the Priest, and more than a hundred
men, went thither and drew him out.

"But many other miracles, besides, are wrought daily
among us through Christ's most glorious Martyr, Thomas,
which, intending to come to you shortly, if God will, I will
relate to you."

---

(12) "Venerabili domino et patri suo priori Sanctae Trinitatis Cantuariae
totique conventui Gaufridus decanus Gloecestriae salutem.

"Sciatis latorem praesentium Willelmum in profundo cujusdam foveae, quae
erat viginti quatuor pedum, sociis suis ;fugientibus obrutum fuisse, et per unius
noctis spatium et in crastino usque ad tertiam ibi fuisse sepultum, et pro eo
sicut pro mortuo obsequium totum factum fuisse.   Hic autem, sentiens sibi
mortem imminere, Deum invocavit, et oravit ut pro amore gloriosissimi martyris
sui Thomae a tali eum periculo liberaret, et votum clamando fecit iturum se ad
locum ubi sanctus Thomas occubuit.   Quem cum audissent quidam ibidem
transeuntes, nunciaverunt toti villae se vocem humanam in fovea illa audisse.
Sacerdos vero et plusquam centum homines illuc pergentes extraxerunt eum.   Sed
et alia multa miracula fiunt quotidie apud nos per gloriosissimum Christi martyrem
Thomam, quae vobis in brevi iturus ad vos, Deo annuente, narrabo."

Benedict (ii. 261-3)	William (i. 253-6)
(13) This was the tenor of the document, agreeing in all points with the testimony of the people who had been on the spot. And accordingly he,[7] with many others, came for a testimony, that he might bear testimony concerning the light.[8] If we receive the testimony of men, the testimony of God is greater.[9] And this is "the testimony of God" which is "greater"—[namely,]	(13) William omits this.

(13) Hic erat tenor apicum, testimonio populi qui affuerat per omnia concordantium. Et is itaque cum aliis multis[7] venit in testimonium, ut testimonium perhiberet de lumine.[8] Si testimonium hominum accipimus, testimonium Dei majus est ;[9] hoc est autem

[7] "Et is itaque cum aliis multis" seems needless, if it refers to the man buried : for his visit has been mentioned above in (11). It ought naturally to refer to the Dean of Gloucester, and "accordingly" would then mean ."*in accordance*" with the promise in his letter.

[8] John i. 7, 8.

[9] 1 John v. 9. The writer's meaning seems to be that the oral and documentary evidence of this particular miracle is, as it were, merged in the collective evidence as to the Martyr's power, and as to its harmony with the Divine dispensation for the later ages of the Church.

Benedict (ii. 261-3)

that with which he had lately [10] testified concerning His Martyr.

[773] By his graphic account of the place, and nature, of the accident; the man's attitude when caught (" with his hands spread before his face "); his exact words (which he professes to record as being what the man *did* say, not what he *might* have said); the poor fellow's fears lest some of his deliverers should come too close and wound him with their tools, and lest others should keep too far off, and not get him out soon enough; and, above all, the man's pitiable condition, when rescued, with his cheeks and arms bruised and crushed almost to breaking, and frozen with the sub-terranean cold—William justifies his claim that he received his account from the buried man himself.

[774] Benedict (or his scribe)—who alone (incidentally) tells us that the letter from the Dean of Gloucester brought by the buried man was anticipated by " reports and rumours " —seems to have composed an earlier rough draft from these reports, which, he says, had reached him " long before." This may have been afterwards revised in the light of a letter from the Dean of Gloucester, and perhaps of oral com-munications from him. But Benedict does not appear to have taken notes, in such full detail as William, from the sufferer's own account. He received from him, or from some of the " reports and rumours," the account of the prayer and

---

testimonium Dei, quod majus est, quo nuper [10] testificatus est de martyre suo.

---

[10] " Nuper " may refer not to this miracle alone, but to all the Martyr's miracles, which, when compared with the miracles of the apostolic age, are sometimes described as " moderna," and here as occurring " nuper," *i.e.* in these last times.

vow to St. Thomas, the " eructation," followed by the " vomiting," and then by power to breathe : and he also gives us
the details of depth (" twenty-four feet ") and of time (" all
night till the third hour next day "), from the Dean's letter.
But he does not make us clearly see, as William does, why
the unfortunate plumber was so many feet beneath the
earth, owing to the need of cutting through a hillock with a
steep top ; he exaggerates slightly by speaking of the falling
earth as levelling the pit with the surrounding earth, and (if
William is right) more than slightly when he speaks of a
" hundred four-horse carts " instead of " two-horse." Also,
he does not know that, the man being from Gloucester, the
Gloucester people turned out to his rescue, and that, besides
men, there were women, and children too.   As clerics might
do, the Dean and Benedict spoke together about spades,
mattocks, and " digging implements " : but they forget that the
earth was loose and that even women and children could do
much with " besoms," " pails," and " tubs," as William says
they did.   Again as clerics, they indulge in a little clerical
amusement at the expense of the Churchdown parson who
was anxious about the buried man's soul, while the buried
man's soul, all the time, was more anxious about his body :
but they omit the fact that it was the man's companions
themselves, and the poor villagers, who raised the cry of
" Priest !   Priest !   He's dead ! "

[775] On the whole, we ought to be grateful to William
for having taken careful notes from the sufferer, for making
us realize the poor plumber's position when he was trapped,
along with his pipes, under the earth-fall—and, we must add,
for helping us to see that the man's deliverance may be
explained without resort to the miraculous.   In the first
place, whereas the Dean of Gloucester says "the *pit* was
twenty-three (or, twenty-four) feet *deep*," the plumber simply
says that the *hillock* through which he was cutting was
" twenty-four feet *high* "—which is not quite the same thing.

Also William tells us that he was laying his pipes at the moment of his fall: and it is quite possible that the piping may have given some access to the air. The fact that his voice was heard at the surface indicates that, either through the loose soil, or through the piping, some air penetrated to the man underground.   .

[776] Nevertheless, if the man had not had faith to continue crying to St. Thomas, he would not have been heard ; and if he had not been heard, he would not have been saved. And again, if the woman of Churchdown had not dreamed about the plumber, her son would not have got up early that morning, "contrary to his wont," and gone out into the fields ; and if he had not done both these things, he would not have heard the plumber in time. So we may say that the buried man was saved by St. Thomas, and also saved by the woman, or by her dream, or by the causes of her dream. It is of course true that, all through that night, thousands of ailing and troubled people in England and France were calling on St. Thomas to save them, and calling in vain. Still the fact remains, that this one did call, and was saved.

§ 17. *Salerna of Ifield, after throwing herself into a well, is preserved from death*

[777] Benedict (ii. 263-6)

(1) Led astray by the instigation of the servants in her father's house, one Salerna, daughter of Thomas of Yffeld, stole a cheese from her mother and passed it on to them. The mother, by

William (i. 258-61)

(1) In an estate of Canterbury Cathedral is a village called in the English language Yfeld, where happened a wonderful matter worthy of relation.

For in the house of one

(1) Famularum paternae domus seducta instinctu Thomae filia de Yffeld, Salerna nomine, caseum matri suae surripuit, eisque contradidit. Mater

(1) In fundo quodam Cantuariensis ecclesiae vicus est dictus Anglica lingua Yfeld, quo res admiranda contigit, digna relatu. In domo namque cujusdam

Benedict (ii. 263-6)

chance noting that the cheese had been taken away,[1] accused the girl of doing it, and threatened her severely when she denied it. As threats did no good, she tried blows, declaring that the girl should be whipped to death next day, unless she confessed her guilt.

William (i. 258-61)

Thomas, a man of no mean rank according to [this] world, during the mother's absence, the servants (greedy for a good breakfast, as servants are) asked two of the daughters for some cheese to flavour their bread. Thus they took advantage of the thoughtlessness of the younger of the two —she was called Salerna— who, having got the keys, went at will in and out of the larder.

On her return home, the mother, not finding the full number of the cheeses, called the daughters to account, and, on their denial, suspecting the younger, she whipped her soundly and threatened her with something worse.

caseum casu [1] advertit sublatum ; impetit commisso puellam, neganti comminatur. Minis non proficiens, apponit et verbera, asserens eam usque ad exhalationem spiritus flagellandam in crastino, nisi reatum confiteatur.

Thomae, viri non ignobilis secundum saeculum, absente matrefamilias, familia, sicut fit, jentaculum liguriens rogabat duas filias-familias caseum sibi dare ad condiendum panem. Eo circumvenerunt imprudentiam minoris natu, Salerna vocabulo, quae clavibus acceptis licenter ingrediebatur et egrediebatur promptuarium. Rediens autem domum materfamilias numerum caseorum non inveniens, convenit filias ; quibus rem furtivam inficientibus, minorem natu suspectam habens, flagris cecidit, et saeviora minabatur.

[1] Probably a pun is intended in "caseum casu."

Benedict (ii. 263-6)

(2) It was the Sabbath on that day, [but not for her].[2] Then the girl, more anxious about the future than sorry for the past, spent almost the whole of the following night, without sleep, in tears and lamentations, saying, " St. Thomas, guard me ! St. Thomas, aid me ! Aid me, St. Thomas ! Guard me, St. Thomas ! "

Next morning, when she

(2) Erat autem sabbatum in die illa, sed non illi.[2] Tum illa, futuri mali magis sollicita quam dolens prae-teriti, noctem subsequentem fere totam duxit insomnem, flens et ejulans, ac dicens, " Sancte Thoma, consule mihi ; sancte Thoma, adjuva me ; adjuva me, sancte Thoma ; consule mihi, sancte Thoma." Mane vero, cum matrem

William (i. 258-61)

(2) When next morning came, the mother went to prayers at a chapel about three furlongs from her house. Now it chanced that a servant from the mill had come sooner than was expected—so Providence had ordained—and had gone to sleep on a heap of fodder.

But the girl, bent on self-destruction, which she had planned during the fears and

(2) Mane facto petiit oratorium quod tribus circiter stadiis distat a domo sua. Advenerat autem citius solito famulus a molendino, disponente Domino qui providet quae ventura sunt, et incumbens farragini somnum petebat. Puella vero, circa perniciem suam sollicita nocte praemeditatam, quam prae

[2] As her mother goes to church *next* day, it seems that Benedict, by " Sabbath," means Saturday, as he certainly does elsewhere, *e.g.* 732 (12), when speaking of the Saturday in Holy Week. If so, it seems a meaningless play on the double meaning of " Sabbata," (1) " Saturday," (2) " Sabbath," or "rest."

The words " but not for her " are not in one of the MSS. ; and they may be an addition by some early scribe who hastily took the Sabbath to mean the day of rest.

The only alternative is to suppose that the " Saturday half holiday " had in those days some sort of recognition. See 710 (1) (Latin) "derideant *sabbata* eorum."

Benedict (ii. 263-6)

knew her mother had started
for church, she stepped out of
doors, and went straight to a
well with water in it,[3] intending to throw herself headlong
into the well, in the hope
that, if she could not avoid
death, she might at least
change the nature of the
death.

(3) Now as she drew
near to the well, she saw
close beside her a form as of
a woman going with her;
and it sought to constrain
the girl (for indeed it was
seeking the girl's soul), pushing her on to the brink and

William (i. 258-61)

anxieties of a sleepless night,
went by herself into an inner
chamber, as though to seek
her little brother, who was
entrusted to her charge. And,
shutting the door behind her,
she stepped out into an
orchard, where, crossing the
hedge, she kept walking up
and down, shrinking from the
deed that she was planning.

(3) On one side was the
fear of death saying No : on
the other was the instigation
and impulsion of the enemy
of the human race trans-
formed into the appearance
of one of the maid-servants.
At length, leaping across the

suam ad ecclesiam profectam fuisse cog-
novisset, egressa perrexit ad puteum
aquae,[3] in puteum seipsam praecipita-
tura, quatenus, si mortem declinare non
posset, saltem mortis genus mutaret.

(3) Ad puteum autem appropinquans videbat juxta se quasi mulier-
culam aliquam commeantem ; et vim
faciebat quae quaerebat animam suam,
impingens eam ad praecipitium ac

timore duxerat insomnem, secessit in
penitiorem domum, tanquam ad fratrem
suum parvulum, cui custos deputabatur.
Et accludens ostium post se egressa est
in pomoerium, transiensque sepem ibat
et redibat, facinus abhorrens quod
meditabatur.

(3) Prohibebat hinc timor mortis ;
hinc instigabat et propellebat eam
hostis humani generis, in speciem unius
famularum transfiguratus. Tandem
sepem transsiliens recludit os putei, et

---

[3] "Puteum *aquae*," perhaps intended to indicate that the well was
not empty, or to distinguish it from
(**440**, note) a cesspool.   It cannot
mean "*full* of water," as this will be
seen below not to have been the case.

Benedict (ii. 263-6)	William (i. 258-61)
saying, "Go, go ; you shall go in, you shall go in."	hedge, she opened the well's mouth, and, putting her legs in, she hung suspended by her arms.
At last she sat down above the well, and then, hanging by her hands from the well's edge,	
(4) at the instigation of him who is from below, she cast herself headlong [4] below, crying out with a loud voice, "Almighty God and St. Thomas be my guard !"	(4) Seeing this from a field in the distance, a swine-herd shouted [to her] ; and the girl, suspecting hindrance, let herself down into the well, exclaiming "The Lord and St. Thomas be my guard !"
(5) Benedict omits this.	(5) Ah, how watchful and diligent the Shepherd, snatching the lost sheep from the jaws of a present and eternal death, lest his flock should be robbed of a portion

dicens, "Vade, vade ; introibis, introibis." Super puteum tandem consedit, et manibus ab ora putei pendens,

(4) ejus instinctu qui de deorsum est, misit se deorsum praecipitem,[4] voce magna proclamans, "Deus omnipotens consulat mihi et sanctus Thomas !"

(5) om.

cruribus suis immissis a brachiis pependit.

(4) Quod ab agro prospiciente subulco, et clamante, suspicans se impeditam, se demisit in puteum, dicens, "Consulat mihi Dominus et beatus Thomas."

(5) O pastorem vigilem et diligentem, perditam ovem de praesentis et aeternae mortis faucibus eripientem,

[4] "Praecipitem" ought to mean this. But obviously the writer means nothing by it, inserting it contrary to the fact, as a mere expletive. The girl drops feet foremost. "Below" is repeated to indicate that the girl, as it were, gave herself to Satan in act, though not in word.

Benedict (ii. 263-6)

William (i. 258-61)

of its body![1] Ah, how pitiful and propitious the Father, saving a soul—though unwilling, and hostile to Himself—lest the enemy should exult over the damnation of His household! The forethought of the Good Shepherd took heed for his successors, and for the shepherds that should come after (lest the envy of detractors should triumph over them as sluggards not doing their pastoral duty), and for the diocese of Canterbury, lest it should be branded with infamy.

(6) And into the abyss

(6) Well, with many a

ne grex sui corporis portione[1] vastaretur! O patrem pium et propitium, salvantem animam invitam et hostem sui, ne de damno familiae suae inimicus exsultaret! Cavit prudentia boni pastoris successoribus suis et posteris pastoribus, ne livor eis obtrectatorum tanquam desidibus et pastoralem curam non agentibus insultaret. Cavit diocesi Cantuariensis ecclesiae, ne notaretur infamiae.

(6) Et cecidit in abyssum et non

(6) Igitur virgo multis circumacta

[1] The metaphor of the flock is combined with that of a body, so that a sheep corresponds to a limb.

It is not clear, in what follows, whether "Father" and "Shepherd" (which often mean St. Thomas) mean the Saviour or the Martyr. Probably they mean the latter. Benedict (7) ("God *and* the Martyr") perhaps intends to meet doubts of this kind.

Benedict (ii. 263-6)

she fell and was not utterly destroyed,[5] because the Lord placed His hand beneath her. For He heard her and her cry, and went down with her into the pit, and took her up out of many waters, that the depth of the abyss might not swallow her up, nor the deep waters of Satan close fast their mouth over her.

Three or four times was she immersed, and as often did she emerge. But when, fetching her breath, she called out, "St. Thomas, aid me!"

William (i. 258-61)

whirling revolution, the girl was plunged in and went down thrice to the bottom of the water. Emerging for the fourth time,[2] she seemed to have heard St. Thomas saying[3] "Thou shalt not die. Thou shalt ascend from the well."

est collisa,[5] quia Dominus supposuit manum suam. Audivit enim eam et vocem ipsius, descenditque cum illa in foveam, et assumpsit eam de aquis multis, ne absorberet eam abyssi profundum, neque urgeret super eam inferni puteus os suum.

Immersa itaque tertio vel quarto, totidemque vicibus emersa, cum respirans clamasset, "Sancte Thoma, adjuva me !"

rotationibus ad fundum aquae ter submersa est. Quarto [2] emergens, visus est beatus Thomas dixisse,[3] "Non morieris ; ascendes a puteo."

[5] "Collisa": probably an allusion to 2 Cor. iv. 9 "Cast down, yet *not destroyed.*"

[2] A confusion of thought. The writer forgets that (as Benedict says) every "emerging" must have been preceded by an "immersing." The third "immersing" would be followed by the *third* (not "the fourth") "emerging."

[3] "Dixisse," lit. "to have said." Benedict places these words of St. Thomas later, in (10).

(7), [straightway], by some pressure of the Divine hand, the whole of the girl's body, even to the feet, was pressed upwards out of the water, and, through God, or the Martyr—nay, through God *and* the Martyr—her feet were set upon some sort of staff, and another staff was placed in her trembling hands to be a support for her. So she took her stand on the former, at the surface of the water, and stretched the latter against the side of the well, and leant upon it—not knowing at all either how she had come upon the first, or who had put the second into her hands.

(7) Wonderful, and scarce credible, is the tale I must now tell, yet without a touch of falsehood.

The well was twenty-five great cubits high from the water up to the top, and eight from the water down to the bottom ;[4] and yet, though the depth was so great, the girl who cast herself headlong down, was preserved unharmed. For the Divine Hand placed a beam across the well and set the poor shipwrecked creature on it, and gave into her hands a staff whereby to sustain herself against the well's side.

(7) impulsu quodam divino totum puellae corpus usque ad pedes de aquis expulsum est, et statuit Deus vel martyr, immo et Deus et martyr, super baculum quendam pedes ejus, et alium baculum in manus ejus tremulas administravit. Super alterum igitur in superficie aquae consistens, alteri contra putei parietem porrecto innitebatur, ignorans prorsus et qualiter super baculum venisset, et quis baculum secundum manibus ejus imposuisset.

(7) Mira loquar et vix credenda, impermixta tamen falsitati. Puteus altus erat viginti quinque cubitis magnis ab aqua sursum, octo vero penetrabat ab aqua deorsum ;[4] et cum tanta esset altitudo putei, quae se praecipitem dedit illaesa conservata est. Nam lignum per transversum putei divina manus imposuit, naufragaeque superimpositae manibus baculum dedit, quo se sustentaret a latere putei.

[4] See Benedict's different dimensions below (19).

Benedict (ii. 263-6)	William (i. 258-61)
(8) Benedict omits this.	(8) This is the Hand that is placed under the righteous man, so that, when he falls, he may not be utterly destroyed: for, as [the Scripture] says, "He will send help to him, and His arm shall strengthen him, that the enemy may not prevail against him,[5] and the son of iniquity may not proceed to do him more hurt." This is the Hand that brought the children of Israel forth from the bondage of Egypt, Jonah from the whale's belly, Daniel from the lion's den,[6] Peter from prison, Paul from the depth of the sea—which also created the climbing gourd to give shade to the prophet from the noonday heat: this same created also

| (8) om. | (8) Manus haec est quae viro justo supponitur cadenti ne collidatur; sicut enim ait, "Auxiliabitur ei, et brachium ejus confirmabit eum, ut non proficiat inimicus in eo,[5] et filius iniquitatis non apponat nocere ei." Manus haec est quae filios Israel eduxit ab Aegyptia servitute, Jonam de ventre ceti, Danielem de lacu[6] leonum, Petrum de carcere, Paulum de profundo maris; et quae creavit hederam ad umbraculum |

[5] Lit. "in him," Ps. lxxxix. 21, 22.
[6] "Lacu," Vulgate, Dan. vi. 7.

Benedict (ii. 263-6)

William (i. 258-61)

the beam for the help of the shipwrecked girl.

(9) But this we have ascertained, and know to be absolutely true, that this very well had been cleaned out a few days before by a man who had left in it neither staff, nor stick, no, not even of the smallest.[6]

(9) Be not beguiled into supposing[7] that the beam had been purposely placed as a support for people going down into the well [to clean it]. For their custom was, whenever anything fell into the well, to draw it out in the usual fashion, searching the bottom with a hook.

(10) Moreover, while the girl was standing thus, she heard the voice of one con-soling her and repeating over and over again the words of consolation : " Fear not, my daughter, thou wilt come safe

(10) [William places above, in (6), some words of St. Thomas, but mentions no visible figure.]

---

(9) Hoc autem constans habemus atque certissimum, quod ante dies pau-cos puteum eundem juvenis purgaverat, qui nec baculum nec virgulam, sed neque festucam,[6] in ipso reliquerat.

aestuantis prophetae, creavit et lignum in subsidium naufragantis puellae.

(9) Non tibi subripiat[7] ut putes lignum de industria tanquam suppe-daneum descendentibus in puteum fuisse impositum. Habebant enim hi con-suetudinem, siquid in illum incidisset aliquando, sicut solet, extrahere, un-coque fundum scrutari.

(10) Audivit etiam puella, dum ita staret, vocem consolantis se, eademque consolationis verba saepius replicantis : "Noli timere, filia, bene venies sur-

(10) vide (6).

---

[6] "Festucam," lit. "a small wand."

[7] "Non tibi subripiat." Perhaps some words are missing : "Let not [any one] filch from you [the truth]," or "Let not [the truth] be filched (sub-ripiatur) from you."

Benedict (ii. 263-6)

to the top. Safe to the top
wilt thou come, my daughter.
Fear not." She testifies that
she also saw the figure of the
speaker standing near, clothed
in the whitest linen.

And so much for what
was going on in the well.[7]

(11) Benedict omits this.

William (i. 258-61)

(11) And as far back as
the time when the well was
first dug, no such beam could
ever be perceived by the
master or by a single one of
his servants. Well then,[8] let
any one say what he pleases,
and maintain that it had
been placed there, and that,
after being long forgotten,
there it was, at one time
under the water, at another

---

sum ; bene sursum venies, filia, noli
timere." Testatur se etiam personam
loquentis prope se stantem vidisse, lino
candidissimo vestitam. Et haec quidem
in puteo ita gesta sunt.[7]

(11) om.

(11) Per tantum autem tempus quo
fossus est puteus, lignum tale non a
domino, non ab aliquo famulorum
adverti poterat. Dicat igitur [8] quivis
quidlibet, et controversetur illud fuisse
pridem impositum, et longa oblivione
dimissum nunc aquae subesse, nunc

---

[7] For a similar transition, common
in Greek writers, comp. above in
William's (771 (5)) story of the plumber
"So much for what was going on in
the heart of the earth."

[8] "Igitur" seems to be an error
for some other word such as "however."

Benedict (ii. 263-6)

William (i. 258-61)

time just touched by the water's surface, according as the well happened to be full or empty—yet still, let this [caviller] tell me how a girl of thirteen (for that was her age), who had thrown herself headlong from such a height, could mount the beam and plant her feet on it! What agent, except the Divine pity — which wills that none should perish—placed in her hands such a support ?[0]

(12) Now the cry of the girl, at the moment when she fell in, had been heard by

(12) So the swine-herd, seeing that the maid had thrown herself down, rushed

ejusdem lambere superficiem juxta defectum vel incrementum ejus. Respondeat et ipse quomodo virgo tredecim annorum (id enim aetatis agebat) quae se ex tam sublimi praecipitem dedit, lignum ascenderit et pedibus presserit. Quis nisi divina miseratio, quae neminem vult perire, podium manibus[0] immisit ?

(12) Audierat autem puellae corruentis vocem quispiam de familia in

(12) Videns igitur subulcus quia virgo se dejecisset, irruit cum clamore,

[0] " Podium " is properly a support for the *feet*, hence "balcony" etc. Perhaps this is an instance where William (**146** note 9, **611***a*) misuses Greek terms. He seems to apply the word to the "stick" and not to the "beam."

We should also have expected some conjunction : "[*And*, even though he may explain away the beam, *yet*] who . . . supplied the *stick* ?"

Benedict (ii. 263-6)	William (i. 258-61)
one of the servants at his work in a neighbouring field. He had seen her before sitting over the well, and had blamed her for it, wondering [at her strange conduct]. So he now ran and called (?) by name [8] a young man sleeping in the house, dinning it in his ears that Salerna had fallen into the well. But the sleeper, as though in a waking dream, while hearing all that the other shouted, could not shake off slumber. For he saw before him a figure as of a hideous man, vast of	in with loud cries, calling the sleeping servant. Now the servant saw in his sleep a man with clenched fist threatening him and saying, "Lie still! If you get up, you will have this fist in your face. Sleep on, lest you wake to your destruction."

campo vicino constitutus, qui et puellam super puteum sedentem vidit et admiratus increpavit ; currensque juvenem in domo dormientem vocavit ex nomine,[8] Salernam in puteum corruisse ingeminans. At ille, quasi per somnum vigilans, et audiebat yociferantem et somnum excutere non valebat. Videbat enim coram se quasi hominem quendam deformem, statura procerum,	vocans famulum dormientem ; qui videbat per somnum hominem sibi constricto pugno minitantem, et dicentem "Accumbe ; si surgis, pugnus iste tibi protinus haerebit in mala. Dormi, ne in exterminium tuum exciteris."

[8] "Juvenem . . . ex nomine," we should have expected "juvenem *quendam* (a young man)." But perhaps the participle may have an indefinite force. William calls the man a "servant" from "the mill," and previously describes his unexpectedly early arrival as providential.

I do not understand the force of "ex nomine." It is not classical Latin. But it seems here to mean "by name."

Benedict (ii. 263-6)

stature, and of a terrible countenance, holding a great club in his hands, and repeating without ceasing, " If you get up, you are a dead man. Move, and I kill you."

(13) Benedict omits this.

William (i. 258-61)

(13) Say, impious devil,[10] what now avails thy deceit? Thy manifold devices prevail not against the simple and innocent. Author of [all] guile, thou didst deceive an innocent young maid ; thou didst count her thy prey ; but thou didst not obtain her for a possession, for thy deceit was swallowed up in the Martyr's victory. Thou didst lull the servant to sleep and didst forbid his waking : but these and all thy other

---

vultu terribilem, clavam grandem tenentem in manibus, et incessanter dicentem, "Si surrexeris, mortuus es ; si te moveris, occidam te."

(13) om.

(13) Dic, impie Zabule,[10] quid valet nunc fraus tua? Non praevalet adversus simplices et innocentes machinationis tuae multiplicitas. Virginem juvenculam, auctor doli, decepisti, praedam putasti, sed in possessorio non obtinuisti; nam absorpta est in victoria martyris fraus tua. Mancipium sopisti et subvenire prohibuisti, sed et

---

[10] "Zabule," a form of "Diabole," used by Lactantius.

Benedict (ii. 263-6)   William (i. 258-61)

plots turn out to thy disgrace. Thou dost press sore on the Shepherd's lambs, but the forethought of the Shepherd defeateth thy deceits.

(14) At length, roused by the outcry that would take no denial, he ran with the lad to the well, and began to descend the well ; but he was dismayed at the great depth, and came out again. So there they both stood, sore distressed at the mishap and not knowing what to do. Then said one to the other, " Make haste, and mount, and ride to the church: and tell our mistress of this lamentable

(14) For, aroused by the shouting servant, the [other] servant hears the mischance of the hapless woman.[11] And forthwith, stripping off his clothes, he prepared to go down the well, and was let down (?) some way. But, seeing that nothing effective could be done, he took horse in haste and carried the tidings to the mother and those who were at church.

---

haec et cuncta quae moliris tibi foeda eveniunt. Instans et impugnans pastoris oviculas, at Pastor providus expugnat fraudes tuas.

(14) Tandem vero importunitate clamantis excitatus, ad puteum cum puero cucurrit, in puteum descendit ; sed metu praecipitii tanti correptus exivit. Stabant itaque ambo super infortunio anxii, et quid facto opus esset ignari. Tunc alter ad alterum, " Festina, equumque ascendens ad ecclesiam propera ; et dominae nostrae

(14) Excitatus enim clamore famuli famulus accipit casum miserandae mulieris ;[11] qui continuo pannos suos abjiciens, et nudans se, puteum penetrare parabat, et demissus est. Sed rem videns carere effectu, caballum arripiens matrifamilias et eis qui in ecclesia erant quod acciderat innotuit.

---

[11] " Mulieris," though he has just told us that she is but thirteen years old. But having so often used " puella," " virgo," " virgo juvencula," etc., he craves something new.

Benedict (ii. 263-6)

William (i. 258-61)

mischance." So he mounted, and galloped off, and, after very long delay, brought back with him

(15) not only the mistress, 'but also the whole parish, which had on that day flocked to church according to custom.

(15) The mother, groaning over her own fault, and over the terror she had caused the timorous maiden, arrived at the well with a stream of the hastening villagers, bringing with them one Ralph, an active and vigorous young man, who (by Divine will) had come that day to that chapel, contrary to his custom. No one except him, among those then present, would have dared to descend to these subterranean recesses. So, on arriving, they let down a bladder, which settled on the transverse beam close to the place where the girl stood.

miserabile infortunium quod accidit manifesta." Qui ascenso equo acceleravit, et post moram plurimam,

(15) non solum dominam, sed et parochiam totam, quae ad ecclesiam eo die, ut moris est, confluxerat, secum reduxit.

(15) Quae reatum suum, et timorem quem formidolosae virgini incusserat, ingemiscens, cum convicaneis irruentibus pervenit ad puteum, assumpto quodam Radulfo, juvene strenuo et expedito, qui divino nutu ea die praeter solitum venerat ad aediculam illam ; praeter quem nemo tunc praesentium subterraneis recessibus auderet illabi. Venientes itaque demiserunt utrem, qui subsedit in ligno transverso juxta stantem puellam.

Benedict (ii. 263-6)

William (i. 258-61)

(16) The (or, a) young man [9] was let down by a rope into the abyss of the well, and while he himself remained on the staff,[10] the girl was drawn out, calling aloud and saying, " Measure me for St. Thomas ! Measure me for St. Thomas ! "—meaning that she wished a candle to be made, of the length of her body, as an offering to the Martyr for her rescue.

(17) When drawn out, she was found unhurt, but chilled almost to death with the cold, and

(16) When Ralph was let down by a rope, he found the girl standing, as we have described [above], and he himself stood on the beam by her side, while fastening her to [the rope]. On being drawn out, she exclaimed, " Take the measure of my body, to make a vow [of a candle] to the blessed St. Thomas."

(17) Thus was preserved the soul [12] of this innocent and simple girl ; and, after being drawn away by the

---

(16) Demissus est juvenis [9] in abyssum putei per funem, et ipso interim super baculum [10] remanente, puella extrahitur, vociferans, ac dicens, " Metimini me ad sanctum Thomam ; metimini me ad sanctum Thomam " ; volens videlicet, ut ad mensuram longitudinis corporis ejus candela fieret, quam martyri pro ereptione sua offerret.

(17) Extracta autem illaesa inventa est, sed frigore pene usque ad mortem afflicta ;

(16) Ipse autem juvenis Radulfus, per funem demissus, puellam stantem, sicut diximus, invenit, et ligno pariter institit ipse alligans eam: Quae cum extraheretur proclamavit, " Praeparate mensuram corporis mei, voventes beato Thomae."

(17) Igitur salvata est anima [12] innocentis et simplicis puellae, malig-

---

[9] " Juvenis " here would most naturally mean the " juvenis " above-mentioned (12).

[10] " Baculum," called by William " beam (lignum)." Benedict uses the same word both for the " beam " and the " staff."

[12] " Anima," as above, means also " life."

Benedict (ii. 263-6)	William (i. 258-61)
	evil spirit, she was drawn out [again], free from all harm to limb.
(18) she began to say, " Lo, he was with me but now in the well. Lo, he has but now departed." Then said they, "Who was with thee?" And she replied, "The blessed Martyr Thomas, clothed in white, and he spoke to me in the well, after this and this manner." And all that stood by blessed the Martyr of the Lord who doeth whatsoever he will, in heaven and in earth, in the sea, and in all abysses.[11]	(18) William omits this.
(19) And indeed the	(19) [William omits all

	noque spiritu seducta educta est, a laesione membrorum immunis ;
(18) dicebatque, " Ecce modo mecum fuit in puteo, modo abiit." "Quis," inquiunt, "tecum fuit?" Et illa, "Beatus Thomas martyr in vestitu candido, et sic et sic mihi in puteo locutus est." Et benedixerunt omnes qui astabant martyrem Domini, qui facit omnia quaecunque vult, in coelo et in terra, in mari et in omnibus abyssis.[11]	(18) om.
(19) Et quidem abyssi praetaxatae	(19) vide (7).

[11] This perhaps may explain why this miracle is placed so late, as exemplifying the last of the four classes described, i.e. the miracles in "the waters under the earth."

Benedict (ii. 263-6)

wonderful depth of the abyss above-mentioned makes this a wonderful miracle. For I have myself measured [it] and have found the distance from the surface of the earth to the surface of the water about fifty feet, while the water itself is more than sixty feet in depth.[12] This [then] I have confidently set forth among the other wonderful signs of the Martyr, being certified by the testimony of no others [i.e. none less competent] than the girl herself, and her parents, and the neighbours, men of worth

William (i. 258-61)

this except the statement of dimensions, which he places above, in (7).]

---

mira profunditas mirum reddit miraculum.   Ipse   enim   profunditatem
mensus sum, et a terrae superficie
usque ad superficiem aquae circiter
quinquaginta pedum inveni distantiam,
ipsam vero aquam plusquam sexaginta
pedum habere profunditatem.[12] Istud
inter caetera martyris insignia fidenter
proposui, non aliorum quam ipsius
puellae et parentum suorum vicino-
rumque virorum fidelium testimonio

---

[12] One MS. has 150 feet (instead
of 100), and probably rightly. William
has (see (7) above) 25 "great cubits,"
and 8 "great cubits"; Benedict (if we
adopt 150) has "150 feet" and "more
than 60 feet," respectively. The pro-
portions are different, and the statements irreconcilable.

Benedict (ii. 263-6)	William (i. 258-61)
and credit. For with their own eyes they saw the works of the Lord and His wonders in the deep.[13]	
(20) Benedict omits this.	(20) Blessed be God and the Martyr for ever and ever! Let us therefore say, " O God, who dost manifest thy mercy most chiefly in bestowing thy grace on the unworthy, grant, we beseech thee, that we, who cannot be saved by our own merits, may ever be aided by the favour of thy Martyr St. Thomas, through the Lord, etc." [13]

[778] Benedict's account professes to be drawn from the testimony of the girl, the parents, and the neighbours : and, though shorter than William's, it indicates a special attention to the girl's evidence. For example, it describes the girl's

---

certificatus. Ipsi enim viderunt opera Domini et mirabilia ejus in profundo.[13]

(20) om.

(20) benedictus Deus et martyr in saecula ! Dicamus igitur, " Deus, qui maxime clementiam tuam ostendis dum indignis gratiam tuam largiris, praesta, quaesumus, ut qui nostris non possumus salvari meritis, sancti martyris tui Thomae semper adjuvemur suffragiis ; p. Dominum [&c.]." [13]

---

[13] Psalm cvii. 24.

[13] The writer concludes his sermon —for apparently it was a sermon—with a Collect, ending with the words "through Jesus Christ our Lord," which are not fully given in the text.

feelings on the Saturday night and her first prayer to St. Thomas, and, in particular, her being (as she might confess to the Priest) " more anxious for the future than sorry for the past ": and how she was pushed, as it were, up out of the water (on coming up for the third time), and saw the Martyr in white garments, besides hearing his consoling voice. Characteristically, perhaps, the girl may have spoken of standing on one " stick " and holding another " stick " in her hand : but the former name was very inappropriate for a transverse beam fixed to the two sides of the well ; and William, who gives us more of the evidence of the farm-labourers, more fitly calls it a " beam." The girl's words when she was drawn up to the top are given by Benedict as, " Measure me for St. Thomas," simply ; by William, as " Take the measure of my body to make a vow to St. Thomas ": there can be no question that Benedict is the more exact, and that William has, rather clumsily, inserted in the girl's words an explanation that Benedict appends to the words. " Measure me for St. Thomas " was a common phrase everywhere among the English poor, and this girl was on a farm belonging to the Cathedral : she could not possibly have used the longer phrase assigned to her by William.

[779] On the other hand, William is much clearer and fuller as to some details supplied by the servants on the farm. He knows that the poor things only had dry bread for their breakfast, and how Salerna got into the larder, and how she escaped the notice of the servants and got out of doors under pretence of looking after her little brother ; and then how the swine-herd in a neighbouring field saw her strange behaviour in the orchard, and marked her getting over one fence and leaping over another, and finally sitting with her legs over the uncovered well, and how he shouted to her, and all to no purpose. He, too, has told us how a providential miller's man came unexpectedly early, so that,

having to wait till the family returned from church, he had nothing to do but to go to sleep on a heap of fodder. Then, too, he is diffuse on the beam and the stick in the well. The former was clearly felt by the farm-servants to be a weak point in the miracle. At any rate, they protested a great deal about it. It had not been there, they said, since the well was made. At least neither they nor the master could ever see it. But perhaps they felt that this was a very miraculous beam indeed, not only having held Salerna up, but also remaining there after Salerna's rescue to support the brave young Ralph, and, even after Ralph had been hauled up, remaining there still permanently to serve the purpose of keeping the sides of the well from falling in, just like an ordinary joist! So William, while grappling as best he can with the sceptical view by alleging negative evidence (" no one had ever seen it "), nevertheless prudently concedes the sceptical view as to the beam or joist in order to concentrate attention on the question, Who set the girl on the joist? Who set the staff in her hands? Who prevented her from being destroyed by the fall?

[780] When we speak of " William " as doing this, it is not to be supposed that the narrative originated from him. It reads like a sermon—and it must have been a wonderfully interesting and stimulating one—addressed to some village congregation in the neighbourhood of Ifield, and in the diocese of Canterbury. This William may have adapted for his purpose.

[781] Whether William had Benedict's account before him, it is difficult to say with confidence. His statement of the dimensions of the well is irreconcilable with Benedict's (whatever MS. reading of the latter be adopted); but, if he had been correcting the latter, would he not have said that he, too, had measured it, or that he had ascertained the true measurement, or something at all events to maintain his position against Benedict's authoritative assertion? On the

other hand, the interesting statement about the "juvenis," Ralph, who went down so bravely into the well, looks like a correction of the false impression left by Benedict that the "juvenis" who went down was the same as the "juvenis" who was sleeping in the house, *i.e.*, according to William, the miller's man.

[782] It is probable that William, in the latter point at all events, is correcting some previous error or misunderstanding, and possibly one in some edition of Benedict's book. But we are now dealing with a part of Benedict's work that was probably added in later editions of it. If William had Benedict before him, would he not have borrowed from the latter the account of Salerna's seeing, as well as hearing, the Martyr? On the whole, it is probable that Benedict's account, or at all events the last paragraph, was written, or published, so late that William had not the benefit of it. To ascertain dimensions by actual measurement on the part of the writer was such an unusual proceeding in dealing with miraculous narratives that we seem justified in inferring that Benedict did not resort to it till there had been a great deal of discussion about Salerna's well.

§ 18. *John of Roxburgh is saved from the Tweed*

[783] Benedict (ii. 266-7)   William (i. 296-8)

(1) Another[1] unusual miracle, ascertained by us to have happened near the city of Roxburgh in the

(1) There is a great town that they call Roxburgh, in the boundaries of Loegria.[1]

---

(1) Inusitatum[1] quoque signum, quod apud urbem Rokesburch in

(1) Vicus grandis est quem Rochesburgum nuncupant, in finibus Loegriae,[1]

---

[1] "Quoque" rather abruptly connects this miracle with that of Salerna. That had to do with a deep well; this with the depths of a river.

[1] "Loegria." The editor gives no note. Another "Loegria" is mentioned in 702.

Benedict (ii. 266-7)	William (i. 296-8)
river Tweed, must by no means be passed over.	It is washed by the Tweed, a deep river, abounding in fish.
(2) It was wrought by the Lord on a house-servant of Sweyn, Provost of the city. His name is John.[2] This man happened to be washing or watering a horse of his master's in the above-named river toward evening. Now the horse was timid ; and, taking a great fright at a hurdle it happened to see in its way, it shied and leapt down into deep water. Throwing off the young man, it left him in the stream, and made its own way, by swimming, to the dry land.	(2) It happened that a young man, named John, was in the act of turning back from the river bed a horse that he had been watering, when the nervous animal was frightened beyond measure by a hurdle standing straight up, through which the sand was passing ; and, leaping forward into deep water, it threw off its rider and rushed back " to the familiar stall."

flumine Tuede accidisse cognovimus, nullatenus reticere debemus,	quem fluvius Thuidus alluit, profundus et piscosus.
(2) quod fecit Dominus in ejusdem urbis praepositi Swani vernaculo ; Johannes est nomen ejus.[2] Hic domini sui equum in flumine praenominato lavabat sive adaquabat ad vesperam. Erat autem equus timidus, et de crate, quam forte prae se videbat, perterritus, aversus in profundum desiliit. Juvenem abjectum in amne reliquit, ipse nando evasit ad aridam.	(2) A cujus alveo cum caballum juvenis Johannes adaquatum retorqueret, exterrebatur animal formidolosum ex crate erecta per quam transfundebatur arena ; et profundum insiliens, a se sessore dejecto, ad notum praesepe recurrit.

[2] Luke i. 63.   It would seem fanciful to regard this as a quotation, but for (1) the rarity of this way of giving the name ; (2) the fondness of the writer for short Scriptural quotations of this kind, where his own words would have done as well.   See the next note.

Benedict (ii. 266-7)

(3) Benedict omits this.

William (i. 296-8)

(3) "Woe unto him that is alone, because, if he fall, he has none to lift him up." For when the man was thrown off, the hurrying torrent was too strong for him and pulled him inward into the deepest parts of the swollen flood, and he began to sink down.

(4) And the young man exclaimed as he fell into the river, " O, St. Thomas, as truly as I have already been thy pilgrim, and have visited, and will again, if it please thee, visit thy tomb, so do thou now succour me lest I die."

(4) So having no hope, because the darkness of night had now come on and cut off all human aid, he resorted to prayer in these words, "Succour me, Thomas, Martyr most excellent, let not thy servant perish: for I have but lately visited the sacred threshold of thy martyrdom. Come to my aid, thou Champion of God, let not thy pilgrim die."

(3) om.

(3) "Vae soli, quia cum cecidit non habet sublevantem" (Eccl. iv. 10). Dejectus enim praevalente raptu gurgitis, introrsum tractus ad ima voraginis undosae, demergi coepit.

(4) Et exclamavit juvenis, cum in flumen corrueret, "Sancte Thoma, sicut vere peregrinus tuus exstiti, teque adii, iterumque, te volente, adibo, succurre ne moriar."

(4) Exspes igitur, quia jam tenebrae noctis incumbebant et omne humanum sibi praecludebant auxilium, conversus ad preces ait, "Succurre, martyr egregie Thoma, ne pereat servus tuus, qui sacrosancta martyrii tui limina nuper adivi. Subveni, athleta Dei, ne peregrinus tuus intereat."

Benedict (ii. 266-7)

(5) Benedict omits this.

(6) The horse, returning [to its stable], was found without its rider, and a sad report arose that he had been

William (i. 296-8)

(5) "In life's each stage, goodness must be the goal,
Through boyhood's sports or
manhood's graver quests,
Service is due : this debt
owe young and old." [2]

For unless the hapless subject of our story—"pre-vented " by that Grace which "freely justifieth the un-righteous " [3]—had, by the grace of pilgrimage, "pre-vented " [4] his peril, what good work could he have put for-ward for the sake of which he could have asked succour?

(6) William omits this (all but the first sentence, of which he gives the substance at the end of (2)).

---

(5) om.

(6) Reversus autem equus absque sessore suscipitur.   De submersione

(5) Quamlibet aetatem niti decet ad pro-
bitatem.
Vel pila ludatur vel serior annus
agatur,
Latria debetur, major, minor, inde
tenetur. [2]
Nisi enim miser iste de quo dicimus,
gratia praeventus quae gratis justificat
impium,[3] periculum suum gratia pere-
grinationis praevenisset,[4] quod bonum
proponeret cujus intuitu sibi succurri
postularet ?

(6) vide (2).

---

[2] I do not know whence these verses are quoted.
[3] Rom. iv. 5.
[4] " Praevenisset": as in our Collect,
"*Prevent* us, O Lord, in all our doings."

Benedict (ii. 266-7)	William (i. 296-8)
drowned. So the neighbours, hearing the reports, came out forthwith. But it was night. And they passed this way and that way, and, lo, "he was not " ;³ they sought him, and "his place was not found."	
(7) For by this time the water had drawn him further in, and was now keeping him at the bottom of the river under the hollow of a great rock. So they returned, each to his home, each having lost all hope of finding the drowned man.	(7) So after this brief prayer—uttered as well as the boisterous waters and his failing breath would allow— he was sucked down and forced into a kind of rock-built hollow, either fashioned by Nature, or hollowed out by the Martyr for his ship-wrecked one.⁵

---

ejus rumor flebilis subsecutus est. Cum ergo accepissent vicini rumores istos, exierunt continuo, erat autem nox. Et transierunt huc atque illuc, et ecce non erat³; quaesierunt et non est inventus locus ejus.

(7) Jam enim eum longius unda protraxerat, et in fundo fluminis sub petrae grandis concavo retinebat. Reversi sunt igitur in sua singuli, spe singulis ablata submersum inveniendi.

(7) Cum itaque paucis orasset, quatenus gurges fluctivagus et halitus suspensus permittebat, absorptus est, et in quoddam concavum lapideum, quod vel natura construxerat vel suo naufrago⁵ martyr excavaverat, intrusus est.

---

³ "Non erat," hardly classical Latin, but probably a quotation from Matth. ii. 18 (quoting Jeremiah) "mourning for her children because they *were not*." His "*place* was *not found*" is also Biblical, Rev. xii. 8, etc. Probably (under these circumstances) "But it was night" is also an allusion to the similar short sentence in John xiii. 30.

⁵ Salerna, above (777 (7)), is also called the Martyr's "shipwrecked one." This miracle is placed by William with others which are instances of regular "shipwreck," and perhaps he uses the term as a convenient one to use for any one in danger of perishing in "the deep."

Benedict (ii. 266-7)

(8) And when he had lain there till midnight in the bottom of the river, there appeared unto him eight men as if in the act of crossing close to him.

(9) He imagines that he arose and followed them as they preceded; but in truth he was borne up to the surface of the waters and was following by swimming. At last, nearing the bank,

(10) he catches hold of a willow bough. [But] in the act of drawing the willow towards him he tore away the bough; [moreover] a great

William (i. 296-8)

(8) While he was thus out of sight, deep down, fixed in the mud, it being now midnight, behold, eight figures of reverend presence were borne upon the waters, walking side by side.

(9) On their approach forthwith the drowned[6] man was brought out from under the stone and came to the top, and, by favour of the seconding current, was drifted towards a willow that leant forward and just touched the water near the bank.

(10) He grasped with his hands a little bough that hung down: but — either because the Martyr so foreordained, or because the man's

---

(8) Cumque usque ad noctis medium in fluminis fundo jacuisset, apparuerunt ei viri octo, quasi transitum juxta ipsum habentes.

(9) Surgere se aestimabat et subsequi praecedentes, sed revera ad superficiem aquarum elatus sequebatur natando. Ripae tandem appropinquans

(10) salicis ramum apprehendit, salicem attrahens ramum avulsit, ruente

(8) Ubi cum lateret infixus in limo profundi, nocte jam media, ecce octo personae venerabiles sub taciturnitate collateraliter incedentes super aquas ferebantur.

(9) Ad quorum adventum continuo de sub lapide eductus submersus[6] emersit, fluctusque subvehentis obsequio ad salicem, quae prona lambebat aquas marginales, appulsus est.

(10) Cujus cum ramusculum dependentem manibus apprehenderet, fracto ramusculo, vel dispensatione martyris,

---

[6] Note "submersus" as a noun with the article, and also "de sub."

Benedict (ii. 266-7)　　　　William (i. 296-8)

stone from the bank fell on him ; and he again fell right into the stream.

weight was too heavy, or rather because of the contrivance of an evil spirit—the little bough broke, and he was driven back anew into the stream.   For a stone, too, rolling forward on him from the bank, as he was floating in the waves, drove him back still farther from the land, until he was carried down to a bridge, which with its arm-like arches embraces the river-bed, more than a bow-shot from the place where the horse had thrown him.

(11) And behold, after a little, [there appeared] the men described above (,) as though crossing close to him,[4]

(11) [O, how] wonderful the love and diligence of the Saints in the protection of mortals !   Once more there

super ipsum de ripa lapide grandi rursus in amnem corruit.

vel gravi pondere appendentis, vel fragilitate ligni, vel potius molimine spiritus maligni, in fluctus denuo repulsus est. Nam et lapis a littore super fluctuantem provolutus eum longius a terra repulit, donec ad pontem deduceretur, qui brachiis arcuatis alveum fluminis amplexatur, distans a loco quo ab equo deciderat majori spatio quam jactus sagittae percurrat.

(11) Et ecce post pusillum viri memorati, quasi juxta ipsum transeuntes,[4]

(11) Mira dilectio et diligentia sanctorum circa tuitionem mortalium !

[4] It is not clear whether "as though crossing" goes with (1) "described," or with (2) ["appeared"]. But the writer seems to be describing two

Benedict (ii. 266-7)	William (i. 296-8)
and he followed them. Imagining himself to be walking, he was [in truth] swimming in the waters, until, [just] when he was under the bridge, he felt himself to be in the waters. And suddenly, by the wonderful power of God, he found himself lying on the bridge, not knowing at all in what way he had been raised from the waters or in what way he had come upon the bridge, since the bridge was at no small distance from the surface of the water, and no one could easily climb up from the water to the bridge.	appeared to the drowning man,[7] from under the bridge, those who had before appeared to him ; and at the moment of his extremity they rescued and placed him on the bridge, which stands three or four cubits above the water.
(12) He was [still] distended with the water that	(12) One of them, of fair aspect, and clothed in priest's

---

et secutus est eos ; ambulare se aestimans, super aquas natabat, donec sub ponte positus in aquis se esse sentiret ; et subito mira Dei virtute super pontem invenit se jacentem, omnino nescius qualiter de aquis fuisset elevatus, vel qualiter super pontem venisset, cum pons ab aquae superficie spatio distaret non parvo, nec posset cuiquam facilis esse ab aquis super pontem ascensus.

(12) Turgebat aquis quas biberat invitus ; sed eodem resiluerunt aditu

Apparuerunt naufraganti[1] denuo qui prius apparuerant de sub ponte, jam in extremis constitutum eripientes, et ponti, qui tribus aut quatuor cubitis undae supereminet, imponentes.

(12) Quorum unus, decorus aspectu, sacerdotaliter indutus, familiari colloquio

---

repeated actions :—" They appeared crossing (as before) ; he followed (as before)." If so, the constr. is (2).

[7] Lit. " the shipwrecked one."

Benedict (ii. 266-7)	William (i. 296-8)
he had unwillingly imbibed ; but it leaped back by the same passage by which it had flowed in ; and while he was painfully vomiting, he heard one of the men above-mentioned, one clothed in pontifical attire, saying to him, " To thine own good wast thou mindful of me yesterday when thou didst fall in. Behold thou hast been snatched from death. Be thou a good man : and do good while thou art able."	vestments, comforted him with familiar speech, saying, " Arise, go home. Thou hadst regard to thine own good yesterday,[8] when thou wast mindful of me ; for the rest, give thy mind to good deeds."
On raising his eyes to see who spoke with him, he, too,[5] vanished from his eyes.	When the vision of the Saints faded from his eyes, he vomited forth the water he had imbibed,

---

quo influxerant ; cumque anxie vomeret, audivit unum ex viris praetaxatis, ornamentis indutum pontificalibus, sibi dicentem, " Bono tuo mei memor heri fuisti cum caderes ; ecce a morte ereptus es, esto bonus homo ; et fac bene dum potes." Cumque elevasset oculos ut videret quis secum loqueretur, et ipse[5] evanuit ab oculis ejus.

eum consolatus est, dicens, "Surge, vade domum. Bono tuo cavens heri[8] mei memor fuisti ; intende de caetero bonis operibus."

Ille, elabente ab oculis visione sanctorum, fluctus bibitos evomuit,

---

[5] " Et ipse " may perhaps mean that the speaker vanished as well as the seven silent Saints.

[8] The Editor punctuates thus, "Go home, having regard to thine own good." But Benedict's version shews that it must be punctuated as above.

It is however possible that " cavens " is for (Benedict) " cadens (when falling)."

Benedict (ii. 266-7)

(13) Numbed by the cold, he was unable to rise [and walk] : but creeping on his hands and feet he reached a house abutting on the bridge.

(14) When he sought entrance, it was hardly granted him ; for those in the house at first supposed that it was the ghost of the drowned man that was groaning outside.

William (i. 296-8)

(13) and recovering some strength, he crept for the nonce[9] on hands and feet, and knocked at the door of the toll-keeper, who had his cottage adjoining the bridge.

(14) Marvelling who could be knocking at that early hour, the toll-keeper asked who it was. He replied he was John. "John's not enough for me," said the other, "there are many of that name." The man that sought entrance rejoined, "I am John, grandson of Sweyn the merchant." "In no wise shall he enter," said the toll-keeper's wife, "for he is dead." For by this time word had spread everywhere that he had died

---

(13) Frigore pressus surgere nequiebat ; sed manibus reptans et pedibus domum attigit ponti contiguam.

(14) Aditus petenti vix patuit, putantibus primo, qui in domo erant, spiritum submersi esse, qui foris gemeret.

(13) datoque vigore tantisper[9] manibus et genibus reptans ad ostium cujusdam pulsavit qui teloneo praefuit et ponti casam affixerat.

(14) Qui matutinum pulsatorem admirans quaerit quis est. Respondit se Johannem esse. "Nondum," ait, "scio ; multi censentur hoc nomine." Subjunxit his qui pulsaverat, "Johannes sum, nepos Swani mercatoris." "Nequaquam," inquit uxor telonarii, "intrabit, quia mortuus est." Jam enim sermo percrebuerat quia submersus in-

---

[9] "For the nonce." "Tantisper" generally means "meanwhile."

Benedict (ii. 266-7)   William (i. 296-8)

by drowning.[10] "Dead or alive," retorted her husband, "from what the man says, he shall come in."

(15) The limbs that were quite chilled with the cold of the water were [soon] quite warmed and strengthened with the aid of fire.

(15) On his opening the door, the man suddenly fell in a heap, as though dead— bereft of sight, strength, and hearing, so that no word could be drawn from him. But he was carried thence to his home, and, as the day wore on, he opened his eyes and spoke.

(16) Benedict omits this.

(16) William, King of Scotland, was in the town that day ; and, being struck by the strangeness of this re- markable miracle, he would fain have seen in his own person and on the testimony of his own eyes a matter like

---

teriisset.[10] Adjecit vir ejus, "Sive mortuus sive vivus sit, ex quo loquitur, ingredietur."

(15) Membra frigoribus aquarum congelata ignis beneficio confota robo- rantur.

(15) Et cum aperuisset, corruit ille subito quasi mortuus, visu, viribus, et auditu destitutus, ut non posset ab eo verbum extorqueri. Reportatus autem inde ad propria, procedente die aperiens oculos locutus est.

(16) om.

(16) Erat illo die illo in vico rex Scotorum Willelmus, qui tanti miraculi novitate percussus in propria persona et oculata veritate quod super opinionem

---

[10] Or, "that the drowned man was dead," "submersus" being perhaps used for "the man in the water," as in (9).

Benedict (ii. 266-7)

William (i. 296-8)

this, beyond ordinary belief. But as the [royal] purple does not pass into lowly cottages, he sent the Bishop of Glasgow with his Archdeacon to inquire into the facts. So they called on the man,[11] and, on peril of anathema and interdict, forbade him to say anything that should vary from the truth and mislead the people. Then he related about himself what we have related about him :

(17) When he regained his original strength, he and his master, Sweyn, visited Thomas, the Lord's Anointed,[6] and paid back to him the gratitude due for his grace.[7]

(17) which he related also to us a very little time afterwards.

erat cupiebat intueri. Sed quia purpura non in humiles migrat tabernas, misit episcopum Glesgucensem et archidiaconum ad inquirendam veritatem. Qui, cum naufragum [11] convenirent, et sub anathematis interminatione prohiberent ne quid diceret quod a vero deviaret, populumque seduceret, narravit de se sicut narravimus de eo.

(17) Vigorem pristinum adeptus una cum domino suo Swano christum [6] Domini Thomam, juxta quod voverat, adiit, et gratias ei pro gratia rependit.[7]

(17) Quod et nobis narravit post aliquantulum temporis.

[6] Lit. "the Lord's *Christ.*" See above, 709 (1).

[7] A play on the words " *Gratias* pro *gratia.*"

[11] Lit. "the shipwrecked one," as above (7).

[784] Similarity of sequence, as well as of fact, in these two accounts, co-exists with great difference of expression. For example, where Benedict says, "when he had lain there till midnight in the bottom of the river," William has, "he was out of sight, deep down, fixed in the mud, it being now midnight." The latter is more like what the man would say. No clerk, or monk, would be so likely to insert mention of mud, if there was no original mention of mud, as the man who had stood in the mud half the night would be likely to remember and record it. The same applies to the two narratives throughout : Benedict's is like a clerical statement taken down from the man's lips, omitting what the clerk thought unimportant and correcting occasionally what the clerk thought unseemly ; William's, like a second version of that statement, amplified after hearing oral evidence from John of Roxburgh himself.

[785] This view agrees with an antecedent probability suggested by the fact that the Bishop of Glasgow and his Archdeacon came first to hear the man's account, and that afterwards the man himself brought it to Canterbury. It would be only natural, indeed it is almost certain, that the Bishop, having taken down notes from John's deposition, would send to the monks at Canterbury a letter based on them. In such an interview, he, or the Archdeacon, might naturally make slight errors or omissions that John himself might afterwards amend. For example, they took the youth to be the "house-slave" of Sweyn "the Provost " : but he was really the grandson ; and Sweyn himself was better known, to the toll-keeper at all events, as "Sweyn the merchant."

Again, the Archdeacon is vague as to whether the horse was to be "washed" or "watered " ; John is definite that it is to be "watered," probably assuming that the term implies walking the horse into the water so as to wash his legs. John also more clearly explains the position of "the hurdle" and the noise made by the pebbles passing through it, which startled his horse.   The Bishop and the Archdeacon, lodging as they were in Roxburgh on that memorable night, would hear the talk in the town and perhaps actually see the Roxburgh men coming back after sunset from their fruit-less quest for the drowned man, having given up all hope. On this, therefore, they, and Benedict, are diffuse, while John, and William his representative, know nothing of it.

[786] No dimensions are given by Benedict, usually so exact in these matters ; and the reason probably is that none were given by the Bishop.   But William—vague in these points where he writes on his own account—tells us that the bridge was more than a bowshot farther down than the place where John fell in, and three or four cubits (not vague this, but exact, according to the state of the river) above the level of the water.

[787] The Bishop rationalizes a little, in his description of John following the guidance of the eight Saints.   Probably John actually said to the two ecclesiastics that he " arose and walked on the waters," as the eight Saints were walking, and as St. Peter was said in the Gospel to have " walked."   But they do not accept this.   " He *imagined*," they write, " that he rose up [erect],[1] and followed them, but in reality he was borne up and followed by swimming," and again, "*Imagin-ing* that he was walking, he was swimming."   Perhaps, how-ever, the ecclesiastics were not really rationalizing, but only toning down for edification.   It was scarcely seemly that a house-servant of Sweyn the Provost should have actually done what the Apostle St. Peter tried to do and failed !

[788] The final words of St. Thomas are placed far more naturally by William—immediately after John's being set on the bridge, and before he awoke to the sense of pain and the need of action—than by Benedict, who describes them as uttered while the poor man was painfully vomiting.   William's

---

[1] " Surgere " seems used here, as in Benedict (13), for "arise and *stand*."

graphic account of the dialogue on the bridge, between the shivering man outside and the toll-keeper and his wife inside, is naturally condensed by the Bishop; who also omits mention of the interdictory " anathema " with which he bound John to tell the whole and exact truth. The ecclesiastics might naturally pass over this, as being a matter of every-day occurrence: but, no less naturally, it would make a deep impression on John and, through him, would find a place in William's record.

[789] The conclusion from this miracle, as from that of Salerna, is that it would be highly misleading to lay down a general rule as to the superior trustworthiness of a narrative in Benedict's treatise to a parallel narrative in William's. Where the two writers write about what they observed at the Martyr's tomb, Benedict is the better authority ; but, where they write about things at a distance, the superiority lies with that one of the two who happens to have access to the best evidence. Benedict, when not an eye-witness—like Grim, when not an eye-witness—is liable to all the errors of his informants as well as those that may accrue from his own interpretation (392).

CHAPTER I

LEGENDS RECORDED BY AUTHORITATIVE WRITERS

§ 1. *St. Thomas's fish*

[790] ALAN writes that when the Archbishop, at the beginning of his exile, was making his way to the Monastery of St. Bertin's, hungry as well as weary, his companions began to speculate on the possibility of a good meat dinner at the end of their journey, if only he would dispense with the obligation of fasting on that Wednesday.[1] The Archbishop refused. They urged him, adding, " Perhaps they may have no fish, and we ought to stoop to accommodate them." "The Lord will provide," was Thomas's reply. Straightway " from the water " (for they were in a boat) "there leapt a great fish violently into the lap of the man of God, the fish, I say, called bream ; and that journey was made agreeable to them in the praise of the Lord."

[791] Garnier, Grim, and Fitzstephen all mention this journey, yet are silent about the fish. Their narrative. however, is somewhat brief, so that their silence may be explicable from their ignorance about the details of the journey. But their ignorance about this particular detail— so interesting, picturesque, and providential or miraculous—

---

[1] *Mat.* ii. 336.

tells heavily against its historical accuracy.   What, however, is needed for the practical demonstration of the falsehood of the story is the silence of some companion of the Archbishop's about it : and this negative evidence is afforded by Herbert of Bosham.   He had been waiting at St. Bertin's for four or five days to welcome the Archbishop, and in all probability dined with him on the evening of his arrival.   Moreover, Herbert tells us that on that very night the Archbishop gave him a minute account of all his wanderings and sufferings ; and some of these Herbert records at great length.   It is quite impossible that this striking little miracle, or quasi-miracle, should have been omitted from Herbert's pages had it been historical.

[792] The origin of the legend is probably a linguistic error.   This is rendered probable by the fact that Alan has misunderstood some words in the context.   He tells us that Thomas journeyed on foot " with *a monk's hood placed on his shoulders* (super scapulas posita)."   But the fact was that, for a few miles, being utterly tired out, he rode a horse hired from a village, without a saddle, *on which a " hood (cappa) " was placed.*   The mention of the monk's hood is meaningless *on the traveller's head* (or, *shoulders*), but intelligible *on the bare-backed horse.*   Garnier says that the Archbishop's friends " made *him* ride for two leagues : there was no more than a hood which they caused to be folded *under him* (suz lui)."   Possibly, some confusion arose, when Garnier's narrative was expanded, as it is in some of the prose writers, into " they made him ride *on a horse, which* . . . under *him*."   For then transcribers might say, " Did Garnier's second 'him' mean 'the horse'?   If so, 'suz (under)' must be a mistake for 'sur (over).'"   And, as a fact, Anon. I. seems to shew traces of such confusion.   For he has, in his text, "they put a hood *under* (subjecta) *the aforesaid horse*," [2] where one MS.

---

[1] [792a] *Mat.* iv. 56 " *subjecta* eidem jumento cappa beatum virum desuper sedere fecerunt."   The Editor adds " *superjecta*, G. (which seems right)."   One

reads "put *over* (superjecta)." There seems to be confusion between "*over* the horse" and "*under* the Archbishop."

[793] The same author, Anon. I.—who tells us that he ministered to the Archbishop in foreign parts, and who is very full of detail at this point—has a remarkable story about a woman who did the exile a good turn. Seeing the tired traveller pass through her village, she bustled into her house to give him a staff to support him. So she "caught up and gave him a 'spit-stick,' begrimed, besmoked, moist, and greased through and through with *the fat of fishes which had been hung from it*." The Archbishop, he adds, thankfully received this offering. It is just possible that some monkish verses about this "fishing-staff" suddenly bestowed for the "support" of St. Thomas, may have been interpreted —in view of the familiar "staff of life," as a metaphorical name of bread—to mean that Providence sent the Saint a "fat fish."[3]

[794] If this, or some similar explanation, is correct, the origin of this fish-legend will be of the same kind as that of the rescue of Thomas from drowning related above (397-401) —that is to say, (1) linguistic error seconded by (2) a prejudice for the marvellous. There, a falcon flying astray *across* a stream and in danger of being *lost*, was apparently confused with a falcon stooping on its prey *upon* a stream, and in danger of being *drowned*. Then Thomas "tumbling" was confused with Thomas "leaping." Lastly, a "miller turning off the water" was dispensed with, so that the mill-wheel was simply said to "stand still," apparently by miraculous agency.

---

or two cases occur above of "sub" for "super," *e.g.* 737 (11). Do they arise from French or Latin origin?

[3] That this journey was made the subject of early poems appears from the fact that, at this point, William (*Mat.* i. 42) quotes nine lines of poetry, descriptive of the Archbishop's wanderings.

§ 2. *The Vision at Pontigny,* (i.) *the statements*

[795] William tells us that the Archbishop, when departing from Pontigny, related to the Abbot of that monastery a vision of his martyrdom.[1] After describing a trial-scene, in which he himself was the accused, and relating how he was "left alone in the court," the Archbishop continues, "And behold, *four of the King's servants,* rushing in against me, sheared off with their swords the crown of my head."

Grim gives a similar account,[2] mentioning "the breadth of the crown" as being "sheared off," but not stating the number of the murderers, nor saying anything about the relation of the story to the Abbot. Grim also mentions another vision [3] at the conclusion of his description of the Archbishop's life at Sens, where he remained four years *after leaving Pontigny.* This vision is similar to that recorded in the next paragraph.

Some of the MSS. of Fitzstephen [4] describe a vision as occurring "at Pontigny," but quite different from William's, to this effect: while St. Thomas was celebrating Mass, "he heard a voice: 'Thomas! Thomas!' 'Who art thou, Lord?' he replied. And the Lord said to him, 'I am Jesus Christ, thy Lord and brother, my Church shall be glorified in thy blood, and thou shalt glory (gloriaberis)[5] in me.' Rising from the spot, he saw the Abbot behind a pillar, and exacted from him a promise not to reveal the vision during his (the Archbishop's) life."

---

[1] *Mat.* i. 52.   [2] Ib. ii. 413.   [3] Ib. ii. 419.

[4] Ib. iii. 83. It is omitted in the MS. J. (15a) which contains the earliest version of Fitzstephen's narrative, and it is found with marks of cancelling in another MS. The fact that "the Archbishop," as Fitzstephen usually calls him, is here called "St. Thomas" indicates that it is a later addition.

[5] "Thou shalt glory." The *Saga* (i. 317) has "*thou shalt be honoured by me,*" perhaps taking the deponent as a passive verb. Or is there an error in Fitzstephen's text?

Benedict[6] simply says that, while the Archbishop was in France, he had predicted to the Abbots of Pontigny and Val-luisant that he would suffer martyrdom and that he must be killed in a church.

Herbert of Bosham, who was with the Archbishop at Pontigny, describes him as being dejected when he rode thence with his host, the Abbot, and when he bade farewell to the latter; and then he adds a dialogue between the two in which the former describes the vision, exacting a pledge of secrecy.   The description resembles William's in mentioning "*four* soldiers," and "in a church (but I know not where)." A few days afterwards, continues Herbert, he revealed the vision to the Abbot of Val-luisant "that in the mouth of two [witnesses] this word of revelation might be confirmed."[7]

[796] Garnier mentions a vision of a trial-scene, followed by the entry of the murderers who shear off the crown of the Archbishop's head; but he does not give the number as "four," nor does he place the murder in a church. It is "in the court (el consistoire)"; so, too, William ("in consistorio").   Garnier adds, as a comment of his own, "Right well did God promise unto him that he should be slain in His cause, for holy Church."   He proceeds to add a story of a monk in Pontigny, suffering from dropsy, who was commanded by the Virgin Mary to apply to Thomas for a remedy and was cured by him.   This was followed by other cures, and the poet concludes by saying, "There was not in that country any man so full of fever as not to receive entire and certain health from his relief."[8]

Giraldus Cambrensis (born 1146, and therefore twenty-four years old at the time of the Martyrdom) gives a vision

---

[6] *Mat.* ii. 12.
[7] Ib. iii. 406 "ut . . . in ore duorum staret verbum revelationis hoc."
[8]   "N'out el pais nul home si plein de fièvre vaine,
                Par sun relief n'oüst santé tote certaine."
                                                                ll. 3599-3600.

somewhat resembling the *second* of the visions recorded by Grim, adding that he has not yet found the story set forth in any writing that he has read.[9]

§ 3. *The Vision at Pontigny*, (ii.) *the silence of Anon I., commonly called " Roger of Pontigny "*

[797] Among "statements," there ought perhaps to be included a non-statement, namely, the silence of the author commonly called Roger of Pontigny, who passes over the two years at Pontigny thus: " But the inmates of [the convent of] Pontigny [1] rejoiced beyond measure at the arrival of their distinguished guest, thanking him for turning aside to lodge with them, ... And as for the most reverend man himself, how saintly and how religious was his life, we forbear to relate, for fear of wearying our brethren with repetitions of what they know already,[2] and of exceeding the limits prescribed by brevity."

[798] Some have argued from this that the writer must have been a monk of Pontigny, and that he passed over what his Pontigny " brethren " knew. But does this satisfactorily explain his passing over in silence the remarkable miracles alleged by so early a writer as Garnier—*and by none of our*

---

[9] *Mat.* ii. 282. His preface is: "Whence also I have thought it worth while to append here a few notable facts that I have ascertained on good evidence about the end of the illustrious Martyr, which I have not yet found set forth in such writings as I have read of other authors (unde et pauca, quae circiter finem martyris insignis valde cognovi, et aliorum scriptis, quae legi, nondum expressa repperi, hic apponere dignum duxi)." The prediction there is simply, "Thomas, my Church shall be glorified in thy blood"; there is nothing about "thou shalt glory in me, or, be glorified in me."

This indicates that the writer had not read (or did not remember) Grim, nor the passage above quoted from some of Fitzstephen's MSS.

[1] *Mat.* iv. 64, " Pontiniacenses," probably does not refer to any but the hosts of the Archbishop, *i.e.* the people in the convent.

[2] " Know already." The text has "ne et fratribus nostris *notam* ingeramus, et veritatis metas excedamus." But Mr. Magnusson's emendation, "nota," is absolutely necessary (28*b*).

later writers—to have been wrought by the Archbishop at Pontigny? In his preface this author (Anon. I.) says that he writes [3] " because there is nowhere found a full history of his [St. Thomas's] life and acts," and because " some have held opinions about the Saint, not only divergent from, but even contrary to, the real truth." There is nothing at all to indicate that he is not writing for the world at large. That he would omit the details of the Archbishop's extreme asceticism at Pontigny, and of the illness that followed from it, and of the remonstrances of his friends—this is natural enough, first because St. Thomas's asceticism no longer needed any vindication, from the time when the " brethren " of the Canterbury Minster, unclothing his body for burial, had discovered his secret self-mortification, and secondly, perhaps, because the saintly self-mortification at Pontigny seems to have been reported so fully by Garnier, Grim, and later on by Herbert of Bosham, that our author may well have thought this point had received more than sufficient mention.

[799] But what is to be said as to the silence of this anonymous writer about the *miracles* recorded by Garnier? Though the former was probably not a monk of Pontigny— and indeed he speaks of " the inmates of the convent of Pontigny above " in a manner that indicates an absence of connection with them—yet he tells us that he [4] ministered to the Archbishop during his exile, so that he must (one would suppose) have known of such miracles, if they had been wrought. The silence of this writer, who was *almost certainly* present at Pontigny—when combined with the silence of Herbert, who was *certainly* present there—practically demonstrates the falsehood of Garnier's accounts of miraculous cures. What his silence about the visions may mean, will be considered in the next section.

---

3 *Mat.* iv. 1.   4 Ib. iv. 2.

§ 4. *The Vision at Pontigny*, (iii.) *all evidence from
Pontigny to be regarded with suspicion*

[**800**] From whom did Garnier procure his evidence
as to the miracles wrought by the Archbishop during his
stay at Pontigny? The most probable answer is, from the
Abbot and monks there. As Garnier went to Canterbury,
so he would naturally go to Pontigny, to obtain facts about
the Saint. He as good as tells us this when he relates the
story above-mentioned about the man suffering from the
dropsy. Apparently he would have liked to ask him some
questions, but "they did not tell me his name," he says.[1]

[**801**] This at once indicates, and reduces to a very low
level, the source of Garnier's information as to the miracles.
A monk, moved by a command from the Virgin Mary given
in a dream, seems to have asked St. Thomas to place his
hand upon his stomach that he might be healed. The
Saint complied, and he also gave him some potion, followed
by vomiting; but again Garnier could not ascertain the
facts. "He gave him somewhat to drink, but I know not
what."[2] On the strength of such testimony, Garnier records
not only this particular cure, but that of many others
afflicted with fever.

That St. Thomas—especially when asked in the name
of St. Mary—may have acted as Garnier describes, and that
others of the brethren, encouraged by the monk's cure or
improvement, may have also asked the Saint to give them
medicine or to pray for them, is quite possible: but the
combined hypothesis that there was "no man in the country,"
suffering from fever, who did not obtain complete cure from
the Archbishop, and that Herbert of Bosham—the Arch-

---

[1] Garnier, l. 3576.
[2] Ib. l. 3591-5 "E beivre li dona, mès ne sai quei, de fi. Guerres ne
demora que li frères chai, Venim et purreture grant merveille vomi, Et jut mult
lungement tut greilles sussailli, Par les mains al saint home de s'enferté guari."

bishop's tutor in Scripture, at that place and time, and Anon. I. his chaplain—should both be silent about such a testimony to his saintliness, amounts to an impossible absurdity. The conclusion is, not only that Garnier's narrative about miracles is false, but also that evidence proceeding from Pontigny is to be regarded with suspicion.[1]

§ 5. *The Vision at Pontigny*, (iv.) *the probable facts*

[802] The basis of fact appears to be that the Archbishop, when at Pontigny, had a dream, about a struggle in a "consistory" in which he had been pleading before the Pope. This may have ended with a scene in which he saw himself assassinated. Probably it did not.

The dream, in its original form as given by Garnier, represented "all the Cardinals" as attacking St. Thomas, "seeking to gouge his eyes out of his head and tear them in pieces." The Pope, who was sitting in judgment with the Cardinals by his side, favoured the Archbishop, but could not hear him, and could not make himself heard for hoarseness, by reason of the uproar of his assessors.[1]

Some such dream as this was confided by the Archbishop to the Abbot of Pontigny when the two parted ; and the former not improbably added that it was his destiny to "die for the Church." He is reported to have said on the night before his death, "that he knew he should not be killed out of church."[2] It is not improbable that on many occasions toward the end of his life he used some such words as these, meaning that he would come to a violent end, doing battle for his Lord, like a knight in harness, that is to say, in the discharge of his archiepiscopal work ; and this he may have expressed in the words " in the church and for the

---

[3] For another very picturesque miracle connected with St. Thomas's residence at Pontigny, see below, **815**.   [1] Garnier, ll. 3565-70.

[2] Stanley (p. 74) quotes no authority for this but Grandison, c. 5.

Church." But that he did not use the words " in the church "
to the Abbot of Pontigny is shewn by the early version of
the dream in Garnier, who says nothing about a church.
The assassination is "in the Consistory."

Such, then (in all probability), is the true account of the
words of the Archbishop to the Abbot, a *relation* of an ill-
omened dream concerning Cardinals and a *tradition* that he
was destined to die in the cause of the Church. Perhaps,
before the Martyrdom, when the Abbot reflected on his
reminiscences of St. Thomas, he would simply remember
how, at their last parting, the Saint revealed to him that he
had a dream of evil omen about the result of his contention
with the King, and had predicted his own death in the con-
flict. But, when the death had actually taken place "*for
the Church*," it was natural for the Abbot to make the death
part of the dream, and to adapt the details of the dream to
the facts of the Martyrdom. It was in this stage that
Garnier received the story. The murderers were not yet
" four," nor were they " knights," nor was the murder " in " a
church ; but the vision already included that vivid fact,
known all through Europe, the wound in "Becket's Crown."

§ 6. *The Vision at Pontigny*, (v.) *the growth of legend*

[803] The somewhat scandalous dream, as described (see
the last section) by Garnier — a little disrespectful to the
Pope, and absolutely hostile to the Cardinals—is retained by
the blunt Grim, alone of the Saint's biographers, in all its
force.[1] Grim also appears to have used, but erroneously,
some words of the poet, following the description of the
assassination. Speaking *in his own person*, Garnier says, "Well
did God promise that he should be slain in His cause for
Holy Church." But Grim and others appear to have taken

[1] Grim, ii. 413. "Tollir et desfuir" he renders "oculos illi effodere digitis
ac discerpere " ; "enrouir," "become hoarse," is "obmutescere."

this as referring to *an audible promise from God.* Grim con-
verts this into a separate revelation, not made at this time,
but after St. Thomas had left Pontigny : but Giraldus Cambrensis and the above-mentioned version of Fitzstephen place
it at Pontigny.

William conceals the word "cardinals" under the phrase
"the very assessors of the judge,"[2] in other respects
agreeing with Garnier ; but he goes a step further in assimi-
lating the prediction to fact by making the murderers " king's
attendants," and " four " in number. But neither he nor Grim
mentions any inculcation of secrecy on the Abbot from the
Archbishop. Herbert, retaining " the Cardinals," omits the
attempt to " gouge out the eyes " of the Archbishop, and the
description of the Pope's "hoarseness " : he also represents
the trial as taking place " in a church."

[804] But now the question would naturally arise among
readers of the Saint's life, How was it that so remarkable
a prophecy, tending to the glory of the Saint as a prophet,
had not been made known during his life ? None of the
three early writers meet this difficulty. But Herbert of
Bosham does, by saying that *the Abbot was pledged to secrecy.*
This is curious, in view of the fact that he adds that another
Abbot was a few days afterwards taken into the secret and
similarly pledged. Why did not Garnier mention this inculcation of secrecy ? Why was it reserved for the latest of
all the authoritative biographers to mention it ?

The probability is, that the predictive aspect is a later
importation. The Archbishop may very well have asked the
Abbot of Pontigny to say nothing about his ill-omened
dream concerning the Cardinals, as it would only discourage
his friends. Very likely, he may have said much the same
thing to the Abbot of Val-luisant. Then, after the Martyr's
death, when the inhabitants of every place that had been

---

[2] *Mat.* i. 51.

sanctified by his presence began to put in claims based on their connection with him, and when the Pontigny monks began to circulate the story of the vision and prophecy confided to their Abbot, those of Val-luisant would wish not to be left behind.

[805] The substantial element of fact, then, reduces itself to this, that the Archbishop, while at Pontigny, had a dream, in which he saw the Cardinals trying to tear out his eyes as he stood pleading his cause before the Pope. With this, the Saint's friends and biographers dealt in three ways. (1) Some, regarding it as predictive of his Martyrdom, assimilated its features to those of the murder, and minimized, or removed, the reference to the Cardinals : (2) others—but these fewer, and represented perhaps [3] only by Fitzstephen's later text—*substituted*, for this first vision, a second (derived from Garnier's comment on the first) in which the Saint received an oral communication from heaven that he was destined to glorify the Church by his blood : (3) others, such as Grim and the *Saga*, *made two visions*, instead of one.

CHAPTER II

LEGENDS RECORDED BY NON-AUTHORITATIVE WRITERS

§ 1. *Giraldus Cambrensis and Grandison*

[806] Giraldus, after describing the vision above-mentioned, says that on the second or third day after the murder, the knights went to a manor of the Archbishop's

---

[3] " Perhaps." If Giraldus Cambrensis was ignorant of the first vision, he belongs to this class. More probably, he knew and accepted it, but does not mention it here, because he is confining himself to stories that he "has not seen written." In that case, he belongs to class (3).

called Malling (Maulinges) for the sake of entertainment
after their successful exploit. There, the great table, at
which the Archbishops were wont to dine in public, suddenly
shook itself in such a way as to cast to the ground with a
great crash their " harness "[1] and other things placed thereon.
The servants approached with a light and examined the
table, but could find no reason for the marvel. A short time
afterwards, it was repeated : and now the knights came as
well to look. But no cause could be found. Then said one
of the knights, " Take hence these things, which even the very
table seems to think a shameful burden. Hereby we may
infer the nature of the deed we have perpetrated."

This story is briefly repeated by Grandison in the four-
teenth century, thus :[2] " And journeying all that night about
forty miles, they arrived in the morning at a manor of the
Archbishop's, called Southmallyng. There, entering the hall,
whereas (while dining) they had thrown their arms on a
great dining-table, the table, leaping back, threw them to a
great distance from itself, refusing to serve these sacrilegious
men."

[807] The earlier version is here in some respects the
more marvellous and less trustworthy. It may very well
have happened that the crash of the armour of the murderers,
falling from the table of the murdered Archbishop, may have
given rise to this legend : but that it should have happened
twice, is more in accordance with notions about the Fitness
of Things and "the mouth of two witnesses " than with probability ; and that one of the knights should have pronounced his own condemnation in consequence, is in the
highest degree improbable.

---

[1] " Hernesium," *Mat.* ii. 285. Giraldus adds, by way of explanation, "that
is to say their saddles and pack-saddles (sellas scilicet atque clitellas)." He appears
to misunderstand the word (O. F. "harnas"), which Grandison (ib. note) rightly
renders "armour (arma)."

[2] *Mat.* ii. 285 note.

The probable origin of this legend is exaggerated fact. There is no trace here, nor need, of linguistic misunderstanding. The "harness" was probably shaken from the table. But (against Giraldus) it was shaken only once ; and (against Grandison) the table did not "leap back and throw it to a great distance from itself (resiliens ea longius a se projecit)."

§ 2. Pseudo-Grim

[808] Just as the Apostle St. Peter, being the foremost of the Twelve, was naturally selected by many forgers as the patron of spurious Epistles, Apocalypses, and Gospels, so Grim—occupying in early popular estimation a more prominent place than any of St. Thomas's friends in connection with the Martyrdom—was chosen to be the fictitious author of several "Passions."

[809] (i.) One of these[1] relates—but with much more detail—the Pontigny healing of the dropsied monk described above (800-1). The writer professes to have derived it "from the faithful relation of a certain one of his companions and partners," who attested, on oath, that he had seen what he described. Since this "partner" is described as "sitting near" St. Thomas during the study of Scripture, and since Herbert of Bosham was St. Thomas's Scripture teacher at Pontigny, he is, doubtless, the "certain one" meant : so that the forger strengthens his position by claiming Herbert as the eye-witness and Grim as the recorder. Compared with Garnier's, this version shows a negative and a positive development. Garnier says that the Saint gave the patient something to drink, Pseudo-Grim omits this ; Garnier says that the man vomited poisonous matter ("venim et purreture"), Pseudo-Grim mentions "eleven little frogs."

[810] (ii.) "How could St. Thomas work miraculous

---

[1] *Mat.* ii. 287-8.

cures for sick and suffering folk all over the world and yet do nothing for the faithful Edward Grim, whose arm was almost severed in his defence?" This question was one that must have been asked at an early period; and the natural answer was, "Of course, as was fitting, the Saint healed him." But the prolongation of Grim's life prevented the early origination of such an affirmative legend. Doubtless, Grim's arm was not restored. If it had been, Christendom would soon have heard of it, and no biographer of St. Thomas would have failed to record it.

Pseudo-Grim, however, has the following: "So also to me—when a year had passed away and I had at last despaired of the uniting of [the bones of] my arm [2]—the venerable Martyr himself appeared one night, and, holding my arm, swathed it in a moistened strip of linen cloth, saying, 'Go, thou art healed.' But afterwards I swathed the arm in a cloth, dipped in holy water and in his blood, until, by the grace of God and the Martyr, the parts of the bone adhered to one another [3] by mutual consolidation. The right hand of that same arm affords this testimony to its consolidation, inasmuch as it has written this very story."

[811] If this legend had originated very late, it seems probable that it would have made the healing more rapid and complete. But it came too late, and was too manifestly contradicted by the silence of the best authorities, to survive as an authoritative miracle. It seems to have no basis at all except (1) an inference from the fact that Grim could afterwards write, and (2) the *Fitness of Things*.

(iii.) Of a different kind is the legend concerning the Saracenic origin of St. Thomas's mother, which was interpolated into Grim's narrative, and hence found its way into the *Late Quadrilogus*.[4]

[812] The writer says that he inserts this story "in

---

[2] *Mat.* ii. 288 "de brachii mei resolidatione."
[3] Ib. literally, "ossa ossibus."   [4] See 1a.

order that the wonderful predestination of the Saviour may
hence be perceived, so carefully and so mercifully bringing
together the parents *from the East and from the West*, and
from such diverse conditions of birth and circumstance." [5]
It has been pointed out (**587**) that similar motives induce
Benedict to terminate his Book on Miracles with one from
the extreme East and another from the extreme West : and
it is natural to conclude that this audacious myth must have
sprung from no other source than the *Fitness of Things*,
without any basis of linguistic error.   But it is possible that
the error may have been suggested, or favoured, by a mis-
taken rendering of some French tradition about St. Thomas
the Apostle, the namesake of the Martyr.   Garnier calls the
former " li pareins " [6] of the latter, and says that the Apostle
is the patron of the East and the Martyr is the patron of
the West.   If " pareins" were interpreted as " parent," this
might give rise to a story that a " parent " of St. Thomas
was connected with the East.   This would fall in with the
view of Pseudo-Grim, that the East and the West had equal
shares in bringing the Martyr into the world.

§ 3. *Poetic legends*

[**813**] The *Saga* relates (**192**) that the foot-prints of
the Martyr, in the place where he fought the good fight to
the end, were miraculously impressed on the pavement,
which melted like snow to receive the marks hereafter to be
kissed by pilgrims.   The same poem speaks of (**445**) a
stream of water miraculously springing up in the crypt,
where St. Thomas was buried, for the healing of the diseases
of mankind.   William of Canterbury [1] illustrates the manner

---

[5] *Mat.* ii. 453 " ut exinde videlicet facile advertatur quanta cura ac pietate, a
solis ortu et occasu, genere et conditione tam diversos, congregavit in unum
praedestinatio mirifica Salvatoris."

[6] " *Li pareins* fu ocis et gist en Orient," Garnier, l. 5766.

[1] *Mat.* i. 151.

in which such legends as these might spring up, when he describes a vision (even before the Saint's canonization) in which is heard an antiphon containing the words, "A wonderful deed did our Saviour in that He turned thy water into wine." Somewhat similar, perhaps, is the legend above-mentioned (81), undoubtedly very early, which relates how the dead body of the Archbishop, on the night of the Martyrdom, arose, and signed itself, and those who stood by, with the sign of the cross, and then fell again to earth. The miracle of turning water into wine is reported by a writer of the early part of the thirteenth century [2] as having occurred during the Saint's lifetime at the table of Pope Alexander : " One day when the Pope was sitting at table with the Bishop (sic), happening to be thirsty, he said to the boy waiting on him, ' Bring me some spring water to drink.' When it was brought, the Pope said to the Bishop, ' Bless and drink.' On his blessing the water, it was changed into wine, and he drank and gave thereof to the Pope. When the Pope perceived it was wine, he secretly called the servant and said to him, ' What did you bring to me ? ' He replied, ' Water.' ' Bring me some more,' said the Pope, ' from the same supply.' This was done a second time, and once more the Pope said to the Bishop, ' Brother, bless and drink.' The latter knew not that virtue had gone out from himself, but supposed that wine had been purposely brought. So he blessed, in the simplicity [of his heart], and again it was changed into wine ; and he drank and gave thereof to the Pope. But the Pope, still not believing, and supposing that it had happened through mistake, gave secret orders that water should be brought a third time ; and a third time it was changed into wine. Then the Pope trembled with fear, understanding that the man was a Saint, and that the mighty power (virtutem) of God had been celebrated in him."

---

[2] *Mat.* ii. 290, Arnold of Lubeck, who flourished about 1209 A.D.

§ 4. *Poetry and Romance*

[814] Some of the stories mentioned in the last section may have had some linguistic basis. The signing with the cross has been commented on above.[1] As regards the stream in the crypt, very soon after Easter 1171 it became the custom for pilgrims to take the Water of Canterbury from the tomb to all parts of Europe, for the removal of disease — sometimes by lotion, sometimes by drinking. Hence it would be quite natural, in Biblical metaphor, to speak of the "fountain for sin and uncleanness"—and for physical disease as well—opened by the Lord in the crypt of the Minster where the Martyr was buried. And whenever the Water was used successfully as a restorative, "making glad the heart" of some sick sufferer, by instilling new life into his veins, it might naturally be called a veritable "wine of life." The legend of the foot-prints is perhaps to be regarded as an instance of pure poetic hyperbole.

[815] Of a somewhat different kind are stories that have no linguistic basis but arise from the endeavour of a pious devotee to throw himself into the position of the Saint, so as to realise what was *fit* for St. Thomas *to do*— which soon is identified with what he actually *did*—in this or that contingency. For example, all devotees of St. Thomas were familiar with the proofs of his secret asceticism manifested on the night of his martyrdom by the discovery of his hair-drawers. The pious imagination, meditating on the minutiae of the routine of the Saint's life, seems to have asked itself what St. Thomas was to do when his drawers required mending. Was he to employ assistance? Then his secret would be divulged. That must not be. Hence,

---

[1] See 373.

early writers—as early, at least, as 1225 [2]—described how
the Saint, "ignorant and inexperienced in this work,"
attempted to mend his own drawers, and was "distressed
about what to do and did not even know how to begin "—
when "behold, the Queen of the world, not ignorant of such
tasks . . . saluted the Archbishop, bade him banish his
fears, comforted him that he might not fear, took the garment
from his hands, sat by his side, and repaired the rent with
perfect neatness."

Such stories as these correspond to the Hagada of Jewish
literature in which romances are clustered round Biblical
characters.

§ 5. *Oral tradition the source of early legend*

[816] One of the most instructive of the conclusions
above arrived at, is, that, in any outburst of religious enthusi-
asm based on historical fact, the earliest written accounts are
likely to include what Garnier calls "lying."

But there can hardly be a doubt that most of Garnier's
written "lies" were preceded by oral "lies." It is not likely
that in 1171-2 he would be able to draw largely on written
documents. Some of his evidence might be derived from
letters written in the heat of the occurrence, and, as we
have seen above, often teeming with inaccuracies ; but much
of it would come from word of mouth.

[817] When an inaccurate statement is committed to
writing in an early document, it can often be shewn to be
false by pointing out either the silence of contemporary
documents or some manifest misunderstanding. Thus, we
have seen that an early Passion (80) concluded with the
words, "Some one came in, when I had written the above,

---

[2] *Mat.* ii. 293-6 quotes the story from Thomas Cantimpratensis (*clar.* 1255),
but adds that it is also "told in various forms by Caesarius of Heisterbach," and
others. Caesarius is said (ib. 291) to have flourished about 1225.

asserting that one of the murderers of the Archbishop had turned mad and killed his own son." Here we see a legend coming into existence in its gossip-germ. Possibly it may have been a form of the common tradition that Tracy "turned against his own flesh."[1] In any case, it came into existence too early to survive. If it had originated fifty years afterwards, it could not have been so easily contradicted. Not having been contradicted, and being in accordance with the Fitness of Things, it would probably have grown, become prevalent, and we should believe it to this day. The same Passion that contains this story based on "some one's assertion," contains also the legend about the Archbishop's dead body blessing those by the bier; and the latter, like the former, is based on oral testimony, "the truth-telling relation of men."[2]

[818] This Passion, and the narrative of the Pontigny miracles by Garnier, shew that *within two or three years from a Martyr's death it is natural that legends should spring up about him*, and that *unless eye-witnesses commit to writing their reminiscences about him at a very early date, the legends are likely to prevail.*

§ 6. *Prevalence of legend inevitable unless contradicted by history*

[819] Suppose the *cultus* of St. Thomas had risen to the height of a religion, tinging with sanctity the biographies and Passions of the Martyr, and discrediting and suppressing any documents or statements in contemporary history that threw doubt upon the veracity of the sacred writings. The consequence would have been the absolute prevalence of legend, so far as concerns the fate of the four knights.

---

[1] Stanley, p. 105 "According to another, and, as we shall see, more correct version, he reached the coast of Calabria, and was then seized at Cosenza with a dreadful disorder, which caused him to *tear his flesh from his bones with his own hands*."   [2] *Mat.* ii. 289 "veridica hominum relatione."

[820] Herbert of Bosham asserts that they all died within three years (30) of the Martyrdom, and this is confirmed by "Matthew of Westminster" (30*a*). But Morville[1] did not die till after the first year of King John ; and Tracy, who was Justiciary of Normandy in 1174, was not succeeded in that office till 1176.[2] Baronius is quoted as authority for the statement that all but Tracy died, after three years of fighting, in Palestine, and were buried in front of the church of the Holy Sepulchre, or of the Templars at Jerusalem, or in front of the church of the Black Mountain.[3] Stanley[4] alleges Brompton and Hoveden for the fact that "dogs refused to eat the crumbs that fell from *their* table " :—which is probably an exaggerative induction derived from a saying of William of Canterbury that this *once* happened to Robert de Broc.[5]

Tracy, more particularly, has been made the subject of legends of disaster and a miserable end, in consequence of "the crime of having struck the first blow."[6] Departing to the Holy Land, he was prevented by adverse winds from reaching his destination. Having arrived at the ʹcoast of Calabria, he " was then seized at Cosenza with a dreadful disorder, which caused him to tear his flesh from his bones with his own hands, calling, ' Mercy, St. Thomas,' and there he died miserably, after having made his confession to the bishop of the place. His fate was long remembered among his descendants in Gloucestershire, and gave rise to the distich that—

> 'The Tracy's
> Have always the wind in their faces.' "[7]

---

[1] Stanley, p. 107, referring to Lysons' *Cumberland*, p. 127, Nichols' *Pilgrimage of Erasmus*, p. 220.

[2] Stanley, p. 108.

[3] Ib. p. 104, says that "the legend hardly aims at probabilities."

[4] Ib.   [5] *Mat.* i. 120.

[6] Stanley, p. 105, quoting Baronius, xix. p. 399 " primus percussor."

[7] Ib. p. 105.

This is all the more interesting because there is every reason to believe that Tracy was *not* the "striker of the first blow (primus percussor)." The eye-witness, Grim, says that it was Fitzurse. But conjectures, and hear-say reports about confessions, and oral traditions generally, asserted that it was Tracy. The latter assertion has been adopted by Stanley and Tennyson in this century and is likely to be believed far into the next—an excellent illustration of the protracted triumphs of falsehood over fact.

SECTION VII

INFERENCES FROM THE MIRACLES

CHAPTER I

THE GOOD AND EVIL OF THE MIRACLES

§ 1. *The evil*

THAT evil sometimes resulted from the belief in St. Thomas's miracles, and hence, indirectly, from the miracles themselves, is patent even in the pages of his eulogists.

[821] They soon encouraged both beggary and imposture. Well-to-do pilgrims, on their way to the Martyr's shrine, seem sometimes to have made it a part of their vow to give something to every one that asked alms in the name of St. Thomas. Often, no doubt, like the Chaplain to the Sheriff of Devon (560), they provided themselves with small change. But we have seen above that a girl who had been healed by the Martyr asked for silver (559): and she was probably not acting contrary to the precedents of the road. This recognition of the rights of glorified mendicancy led naturally to deceit of the worst kind. It was often profitable to beg one's way to Canterbury and back, even as an ordinary pilgrim : but if, besides, one could be cured of a disease, receipts might be greatly increased and a reputation might also be acquired at home for special sanctity. In order to obtain an immediate cure at the Martyr's tomb, no way was so certain as to pretend a disease that one could immediately lay aside there. That

these things were so, and were known to the monks, and
that the monks did their best to detect impostures, Benedict
proves, for the earliest years, and William for those later on.
But William seems, by degrees, to have given up the hope
of testing the truth of miracles alleged by the poor.   For
them, the temptations to deceit were too great.

[822] Nor were the clergy and monks themselves free
from similar temptations.   Not that they begged often for
themselves.   But they might advise the erection of a chapel
to St. Thomas in the neighbourhood, and to that chapel
would come offerings, and of these offerings the Priest would
partake.   Hence we find the Earl of Albemarle declining to
build such a chapel unless the " Man of God " who conveyed
to him the Martyr's precept would swear that he was not
influenced by any hope of private profit.[1]   Again, the *cultus*
of St. Thomas implied a most jealous observance, if not
exaggeration, of the secular rights of the clergy.   As John of
Salisbury observed,[2] this was one great reason for circulating
everywhere the Martyr's miracles.   The object was, not to
honour him merely, but to honour him by honouring his
cause, that cause for which he had given his life, " the rights
and liberties of the Church."   In the flesh, the Saint had
been very strict and hard indeed in demanding every
farthing of money and inch of land to which the Church was
entitled.   So he was still in the spirit—as at least the two
chroniclers of miracles (especially William) frequently state
or imply.   Over and over again, the slightest infraction of a
vow, or even delay to pay a vow, is represented as being
punished with great severity.

All this might enhance the worldly wealth of the Church,
but it did not tend to morality.   It was very well, for
example, that an oppressor, rejecting the widow's prayer for
her property wrested from her, should succumb to her curse

---

[1] See 613.   [2] See 661.

in the name of St. Thomas, crying out that he was " a dead
man " and falling at that instant dead from his horse:[3] but
it was not good that the farmer Helias should be deprived
by St. Thomas of a particularly fat bullock, because he had
declined to defer to a neighbour's casual suggestion that he
should give it to the Martyr.   The punishment might well
seem all the more severe because Helias had recently made
the Martyr a similar gift.[4]

[823] To these evils we must in fairness add the
intellectual degradation resulting from the neglect or contempt of physical remedies, a neglect inculcated by William
with evangelical fervour.   Nor must there be omitted the
mingled moral and intellectual deterioration arising from
the indiscriminate way in which the Saint seemed to bestow
his favours, refusing a cure to one, and (in precisely the same
circumstances, as it seemed) denying it to another—nay,
even punishing, in one child, conduct that he regarded as
disrespectful to his tomb, while not punishing it, perhaps
even rewarding it, in others who had not the excuse of
childhood.   On a combined view of all these evils, we might
be tempted to conclude that St. Thomas's miracles did more
harm than good.

§ 2.   *The good*

[824] Perhaps that conclusion would be true, if the
evils above-mentioned had not already existed.   If St.
Thomas for the first time had taught pilgrims to beg, and
sometimes to cheat ; if this Saint had been the first to
encourage the belief that Saints were better healers than
the regular physicians ; and if no other ecclesiastic, before
Becket, had unfairly and unwisely exaggerated the privileges
of the clergy, perhaps it might be maintained that the
Canterbury cures were not worth their price.   But it was

---

[3] See **595**.   [1] See **699**.

not so. Beggary and imposture, and superstition, and
narrow ecclesiasticism already existed. Grant that these
evils were indirectly increased by the emotional thrill that
ran through Europe, filling the minds of men with illusions,
and bringing thousands from all corners of the world to offer
prayers at the shrine of the new Martyr: yet was it nothing
that in those ages of brute force and cunning, a thrill of
sympathetic admiration for a brave monk, who had stood
up unarmed to contend against force for what he deemed
the cause of right and justice, should manifest itself by
wonderful dreams, and visions, and cures, and restorations,
and reanimations that sometimes seemed to amount to an
actual raising from the dead ?

[825] I should be disposed to think that almost all the
early miracles were facts, corresponding largely to the
descriptions of them—those, I mean, narrated in Benedict's
treatise as occurring in the days when the Martyr's fame
was not yet strong enough to suppress his enemies in the
flesh, when it was dangerous to be cured at his tomb, and
dangerous even to talk of being thus cured. But if these
early miraculous narratives were generally authentic or
historical, the "emotional shock" must have been strong
indeed. No other Saint canonized in the Christian Church
—so say St. Thomas's biographers, and probably with
correctness—could boast of so many acts of healing. Moreover, in the Lives of the Saints, the miracles related are
often very vaguely described and poorly attested : but, in
the books of St. Thomas's Miracles, several are so circum-
stantially detailed by chroniclers near the time, and so well
certified, that a scientific man, while denying their supernatural character, is forced to admit their extraordinary
nature, and to regard them as cures wrought through the
imagination, far exceeding in rapidity (and sometimes even
in completeness and permanence) anything that could be
effected by recognized medical means.

[826] Fully admitting that for every pilgrim cured at the tomb, and for every distant vow uttered and fulfilled, there were multitudes of pilgrims uncured and vows unfulfilled, we are, on the other hand, informed by the chroniclers that many others were cured, and many vows fulfilled, unknown to the monks of Canterbury. And even had that not been so, surely the list as it stands, after eliminating from it all doubtful cases, contains instances enough, not to be denied by any man of sense, sufficient to make it worth while for a hero to have died as the Martyr did, if only to produce them. Supposing that in the brief period under observation there were but forty or fifty cases of disease, agonizing, or loathsome, or both, given up by the physicians of those days as hopeless, but healed by the Physician of Canterbury: would they not, by themselves, constitute, for most men, a considerable life-work—much more, a considerable death-work?

§ 3. *Did the miracles result from the man or from the circumstances?*

[827] But it may be urged that these so-called miracles cannot fairly be attributed to Becket personally, but rather to the accidental place and manner of his death; that, historically, he was not a saint, but a man of hot and uncontrolled temper, finding vent in violence of act and word; and that, if he had died in the ordinary way, no virtue could have gone out from him to the sick and suffering. " Had Becket died in his bed," it may be urged, " people in England and France would still have been healed by miracles in the year 1171. The Saint, and the place, would have been different: that is all. Bury St. Edmund's would have been so much the more frequented, or so many more would have gone to St. James of Compostella. Canterbury would have been left alone, and Thomas—not Saint Thomas

but plain Thomas—would have rested, an unhelpful corpse, with other commonplace corpses of ordinary Archbishops in an unvisited grave."

[828] This is so far true that we must admit at once that Becket, dying an ordinary death, would probably not have cured a single spasm of rheumatism. But it by no means follows, either that other Saints would have made up for his deficiency, or that he is so far to be separated from his death that it is to be called an accident instead of an act. If Becket had died in his bed, pilgrims might still have gone to St. Edmund, St. James, the two Apostles in Rome, or the Tomb in Jerusalem ; but it would have been in the old slack and (comparatively) lifeless and formal way. There is no more reason to doubt that Becket caused a religious revival, than that Wesley and Whitfield did. The two chroniclers of miracles agree in asserting that the miracles brought with them an uprising of moral and religious fervour, and indirectly prove it by multitudinous details recorded without controversial purpose. It was brief indeed, but it was powerful while it lasted. The churches built by the Archbishop's former enemies as well as by his countless worshippers, are outward monuments of a strong inward protest against the violent and oppressive character often assumed by the secular forces of the time—or at all events of concessions from the strong to the strength of such a protest from the weak. It was not the Saxon against the Norman, it was the poor and weak oppressed against the rich and strong oppressor, that everywhere — alike in England and France and through the Latin-speaking world—rose up in the might of St. Thomas the Martyr, and decreed that he must be a Saint, even before the Papal edict had made him one. Most of those healed in the days of the earliest miracles have English names. But their passionate reverence and their wonder-working faith did not arise in their hearts from patriotic motives, because they were " English born." It was because

they were wronged, or liable to be wronged, that they took
up the cause for which the New Martyr of the English had
shed his blood.   The Church, though sometimes defective
and corrupt, was nevertheless felt by the poor to be often
their only protection against outrage, and the Martyr
typified her championing spirit.

§ 4. *St. Thomas a true Saint, though militant*

[829] And who shall say that Becket did not in large
measure combine with the cause of ecclesiasticism this
wider view of the rights and liberties of the Christian
Ecclesia, and that he did not deliberately prepare to lay
down his life for what seemed to him the cause of righteousness ?   In spite of an apparent mixture of motives, and
a possible alloy of personal antipathies and violent animosities,
he leaves the impression of a great and fearless soul regarding
itself as an instrument of a great and noble cause.   Had he
remained Henry's Chancellor, he might have been content to
abide in the feudal world, " the King's man."   But being led
—perhaps not forced, but led—into the Primate's chair, and
feeling himself thenceforth "Christ's man," he was moved
to look about him and to reduce things to order.

All great men of the permanently conquering type—
not nomad savage destroyers, but permanent conquerors—
have a craving for order ; and the "order" of Christ's
Church implied social development ; and social development
was incompatible with feudal brutality ; and against feudal
brutality the new Archbishop deemed, probably without
reason, that the only security in his days lay in a strict
and full maintenance, perhaps even in some enlargement, of
what may be called the secular rights of the clergy.   Being
what he was, and where he was, he was almost bound to
collide, as the champion of invisible powers, with the repre-
sentatives of visible and physical force : and his violent

death, far from being an accident, ought rather to surprise us because it did not happen earlier as the inevitable result of his life and character.

[830] Had St. Thomas been a St. Simeon Stylites, a cold-blooded ascetic, or a mere ecclesiastical machine, it is doubtful whether he would have appealed, as he did, to the imagination of the people of England, and, through them, to Europe. His biographies abound in testimony to his sympathetic and winning ways, and to his broad and almost worldly acceptance of the fashions of this world, combined with an inward purity of heart and a resolute determination not to conform to the world in his real self. A generous, passionate, and high-spirited " knight of the Holy Ghost," he moved among the knights of the world the flesh and the devil, with a non-ecclesiastical outward tolerance, learned perhaps when he was in business with his kinsman Osborn, and—on a larger scale and in higher life—in business as the King's Chancellor. Hence arose, perhaps, his habit of conciliating and outwardly conceding—sometimes even of appearing to compromise as to matters of principle—when it was ultimately certain that he would not recede a foot from the position defined for him by his inflexible will. It was this combination of the man of the world with the man of the Spirit that first induced him to assent verbally to the Constitutions of Clarendon and then to refuse to ratify his assent.

[831] His double nature shone forth clearly enough to strike the imagination of all England, when he "fought with wild beasts " in the hall of Northampton Castle. There sat the Saint, embracing the cross, deserted by his bishops, alone in championing the Church against the World : yet, when he passed through the hall to the castle gate, there walked the knight amidst the throng of his enemies, calling one a bastard, and another a scoundrel, and telling a third that he would have liked nothing better, had he been a layman,

than to compel him, at the sword's point, to withdraw the charge of "traitor." Meanwhile the English nation, represented by the mixed multitude outside the castle gate, awaited their Archbishop with loving and enthusiastic reverence, almost prepared to make a Saint of him already, and loving him perhaps the better when they heard that he had used as hard words about some of the King's knights as St. Paul and St. Peter about the enemies of Christ.

[832] Being what he was, St. Thomas provoked the knights to kill him, against their will, even in a church. Being also what he was, he took hold of the hearts of the English people, became to them a household word as well as a church word, and occasionally so far influenced their imaginations as to influence their bodies also. The miracles, then, like the Martyrdom, are a part of the man, and no student of facts should ignore them. If it is asserted that he so strengthened the Church as to prepare it to unite with the barons against King John, and that his real and permanent influence on posterity is to be looked for in such indirect contribution as he may have made towards the securing of the Great Charter of the liberties of the Nation and the Church—that is no answer to the question, "How did Becket strengthen the Church?" It is like Gibbon's attempt to explain the growth of Christianity by saying, among other things, that it deepened the belief in a future life, united its disciples in a close fellowship, and so on—the real question being, "*How* did Christianity—which was but one of many religions that inculcate the dogma of a future life—succeed better than other religions in 'deepening this belief,' and in stamping it on the lives, as well as on the creeds, of its early adherents? and *how* did it enable its members to 'love one another'?"

[833] These miraculous narratives, in spite of their large admixture of exaggeration, misunderstanding, and erroneous statement, distinctly help us to answer the question suggested

by Gibbon's imperfect explanation. They make us realize
how human nature—always weakly acted on by mere ideas,
and always craving for incarnations of those ideas—can
receive a great and simultaneous upheaval extending through
many churches and nations, from the noble death of a noble
man representing what seems to the masses a noble and
unselfish cause.   This is one of the many triumphs of mind
over matter.   Through ballads, sermons, pictures, and, above
all, through stories of pilgrims passing to and from the
Martyr's Memorial, there was gradually conveyed to the
minds of almost all the sick and suffering folk in England,
and to their sympathising households and friends, the image
of St. Thomas before the altar, clothed in white, with the
streak of blood across his face.   This vision, or this
thought, resulted in a multitude of mighty works of healing,
rescue from agony, restoration to peace and health.   What
wonder if these sank deep into the minds of the masses?
Wherever the church bells were set ringing for a restored
cripple, surely it cannot be surprising that in that village
St. Thomas should be a patron Saint—perhaps the Patron,
perhaps almost overshadowing Jesus Himself—for at least a
generation.   The wonder is, not that these marvels influenced
men so much, but that they did not influence them much more.

.

CHAPTER II

THE MARTYR AND THE SAVIOUR

§ 1. *The parallel between them*

[834] Some of the causes of decay in the *cultus* of St.
Thomas have been indicated above in the impostures, and
consequent suspicions of imposture, which soon connected

themselves with the miracles wrought in his name. But another reason lay in the Saint's own imperfections. Compared with that of St. Francis, St. Thomas's scope was indeed narrow. A strenuous champion of the poor and outraged, he had washed his robes in blood for the cause of righteous order, and was enabled to diffuse through the bodies as well as the souls of great multitudes that healthful shock and revivifying glow which it is sometimes a Martyr's privilege to bestow. But, as there is a distinction between "receiving a prophet" and "receiving a righteous man," so is there between "receiving a martyr" and "receiving a saint": "he that receiveth a martyr receiveth a martyr's reward, and he that receiveth a saint receiveth a saint's reward." To "receive" St. Thomas of Canterbury was one thing; to "receive" St. Francis was quite another. The former could help the body wonderfully and the soul indirectly; the latter could help the spirit of man with a continuous flow of help from which the thirsty can drink to this day, when the stream from Canterbury is almost dried up.

[835] Nevertheless the Martyr's work is not yet done. By this, I do not mean simply to assert the truism that we must continue to be the unconscious recipients of historical influence distantly derived from him through circuitous channels. As much as this might be said of any great Englishman. The peculiarity of St. Thomas's helpfulness for Christians at the present time is to be discerned in the old parallel, drawn by his contemporaries, between the Martyr and the Saviour. Protestants may be tempted to deny it, repelled by the fanciful exaggerations of Herbert of Bosham and the rest. Yet undoubtedly such a parallel exists, not indeed in respect of personality, but in the circumstances, and still more in the sequel, of their deaths.

§ 2. *The parallel in facts*

[836] Two men, put to death by the powers of this
world as disturbers of its peace ; two men who, after death,
immediately began to appear in visions, with the marks of
martyrdom upon them, and to utter words of help or warning,
and to work mighty works of healing, sometimes imparting
to those who believed in them the power of instantaneously
shaking off apparently incurable disease, sometimes imparting
the power of curing disease in others, through appeal to the
Saviour or the Martyr, sometimes reanimating the apparently
lifeless in such circumstances as to suggest a veritable raising
from the dead—here in itself is a parallel worth considering.
Again, what follows ?   By degrees, in both cases, the miracles,
after the first great outburst, diminish, fade away, come finally
to nothing.   In the Christian Church there remained for
many generations the class of professional exorcists : but
very soon they became little more than an empty name—
much like English shrines and relics of St. Thomas of
Canterbury in the early part of the sixteenth century, sacred
by traditions, and with many memorials of former wonder-
working efficacy, but themselves efficacious now no longer.

[837] Side by side with these acts of healing—marvellous,
indeed, but explicable from known natural causes—we find
attributed to both men, or to the Providence that worked for
them, acts inexplicable from any such causes, such as the
change of water to wine, the instantaneous withering of a
tree, the leaping or extraction of a fish out of the water in
order to provide for some special need, the stopping of a
mill-wheel by itself, the multiplication of money, or of food ;
and, in the case of both men, we find it possible to explain
these stories, when they occur in the earliest narratives, from
a confusion of the spiritual with the material, and from a
misunderstanding of metaphor as literal.

[838] It is often said concerning the Gospels, that, if some of them were written as early as thirty or forty years after Christ's death, there is not time enough to allow the growth of the legendary element from the misunderstanding of metaphor. How, it is asked, could the leaven so rapidly pervade the biographies of the Saviour that the legendary now appears almost inseparable from the historical? But here again we find a parallel and something more. Many of the accounts of the life and death of Becket were written *within five years of his martyrdom.* Many of the miracles—certainly those recorded by their earliest chronicler—were written down *at the very time of their occurrence.* Yet even in these early documents we find that writers, speaking from "veracious relation," record portentous falsehoods, or let us rather say *non-facts*, and that even writers depending upon the evidence of eye-witnesses, and sometimes (though much more rarely) on the witness of their own eyes, fall into astonishing errors, many of which take the direction of such amplification as to convert the wonderful but explicable into the miraculous and inexplicable.

§ 3. *The parallel in documents*

[839] Again, from the point of view of documentary criticism, there is much to be gained from a comparison of the Martyr literature with our Gospels. As there are four Gospels, so were there four Biographies of St. Thomas, recognized in very early times as especially authoritative. Tatian in the second century made a harmony of the four Gospels called Diatessaron : Elias of Evesham made a harmony of the four Biographies, and called it *Quadrilogus.* In blending the four, the Diatessaron sometimes alters, sometimes inserts, sometimes confuses one with the other : so does the *Quadrilogus.* Again, Tatian's Diatessaron was so freely remoulded in later times that the texts of the

Latin, the Arabic, and the Armenian versions hardly ever
agree together against the revised text of the orthodox
Gospels.   So, too, the *Quadrilogus* was recast ; and the
latest version, including extracts from Grim and Fitzstephen,
and adding legendary matter, was the first to be given
to the world in print, and still holds the usurped title of
The First Quadrilogus.   The fourth of our Gospels was
written long after the three : so was the fourth of the
authoritative lives.   The fourth Gospel professes to be
written by one who knew Jesus as a friend : the fourth
Biography was actually written by St. Thomas's intimate
friend and instructor in Scripture.   That Gospel makes
no mention of demoniacs and recounts few miracles : that
Biography expressly claims that it is written in order to
bring out the Man, and implies that its object is that the
Man should emerge from the miracles under which he was
in danger of being smothered.

[840] Besides our four Gospels, we know that there
were many others, and have reason to believe that in the
variations of our Gospel MSS. we find occasional traces of
earlier Gospels suppressed, or neglected, by the Church, and
now altogether lost.   As regards the Biographies we are
more fortunate in actually having many of those accounts of
the Saint's life and death that were discarded by the authors
of both the *Early* and the *Late Quadrilogus ;* and one of
these we find to be in many respects far more trustworthy,
and far richer in facts of interest, than some of the four
authoritative Biographies.   In the Gospels, there are traces
of different points of view in the writers : one regarding
matters as a Jew might, another as a Gentile ; one paying
attention to style, another thinking of nothing but fact ; one
omitting what another inserts, and *vice versa.*   There are
also here and there passages in which writers agree almost
verbatim, interspersed with others where they do not agree
at all, or only in the words uttered by Jesus and by those

with whom He is conversing. All these phenomena recur
in the Biographies, and still more frequently in the two
Books of Miracles.

[841] As our Greek Gospels shew signs of being derived
from a Hebrew or Aramaic original, which in some cases
may explain their divergences from each other, so our
Biographies shew traces of French influence in general, and
possibly of being derived in particular from a French poem
composed by an admirer of the Martyr, within five years of the
Martyrdom. Lastly, as we sometimes find aid in criticizing
our Greek text by reference to early Latin versions, so may
we be often helped in criticizing differences between our
Latin biographies by comparing them with an Icelandic
Saga on St. Thomas, which closely follows the best authorities
but sometimes adds traditions peculiar to itself, and which
was probably composed before, or soon after, the end of the
twelfth century, that is to say, little more than thirty years
after the Martyrdom.

§ 4. *Its bearing on New Testament criticism*

[842] From all these facts the inference is that students
of the four Gospels and collateral literature will do well to
study the four Biographies, the two Books of Miracles, and
the other early traditions, relating to St. Thomas of Canterbury. What may be the ultimate conclusions to which such
a study will lead, is not a question that ought greatly to
affect a real student and seeker after truth. Some, led by the
evidence to accept the miracles of the Martyr as supernatural,
may be confirmed in the belief that those of the Saviour are
also supernatural and that the evangelical accounts of them
may be accepted as exactly historical. Others, led by the
same evidence to deny the supernatural character of St.
Thomas's miracles, may be confirmed in their belief that the
Gospel miracles, being also natural, prove nothing as to the

divine claim of the Founder of the Christian religion. A third class—possibly, for some time, a small one—may agree with the present writer in some at least of the following conclusions :

[**843**] (1) In the two Books of St. Thomas's Miracles few or none of the early miracles, and in the Gospels none at all, can be explained by imposture.

[**844**] (2) In both cases, a clear distinction must be drawn between (*a*) miracles wrought on human nature, which are substantially to be accepted, and (*b*) miracles wrought on non-human nature, *e.g.* bread, wine, water, trees, swine, birds, etc. *The latter are not to be accepted as historical, but as legends explicable from poetry taken as prose (i.e. from metaphor regarded as literal) or from linguistic error, or from these two causes combined.*

[**845**] (3) The power of healing disease through the emotions extends not only to the paralysed, the deaf, dumb, and lame, but to the blind also, and to those afflicted with skin disease.

[**846**] (4) Death is sometimes preceded by several hours of apparent lifelessness, so that ordinary observation, and perhaps even average medical skill, may be unable to detect any trace of life. During this period, reanimation may follow from the passionate appeal of a nurse, father, or mother, if uttered under a strong faith in a Power that will raise up the [person alleged to be] dead. Sometimes, even without any such appeal as can be heard by the dead, the strength of the appellant's faith itself may produce the same effect.

[**846***a*] Hence it is quite easy to accept the story of the raising of Jairus's daughter. The raising of the Widow's son at Nain might also be easily accepted, so far as physiological considerations go. But the objections against it are, 1st, that Luke alone inserts it, 2nd, that it is omitted by the parallel narrative of Matthew *in the place where we might*

expect its insertion ; 3rd, that it shews traces of originating
from allegory misunderstood ; 4th, that its place in Luke's
Gospel—where it comes just before the Lord's words "the
dead *are raised*"—suggests that the writer may have been
predisposed to receive, as literal, some poetical tradition,
because the literal version agreed with *the Fitness of Things :*
"How could Jesus say, 'the dead *are raised*,' if he had not
raised at least *two* dead persons ? "

[**847**] The Raising of Lazarus is far more credible than
the Raising at Nain. If critics can hereafter explain the
omission of so striking an act by the Synoptists, there would
be no difficulty (regard being had to the personality of Jesus)
in accepting John's story as substantially historical, unless a
strong case could be made out for an allegorical origin.

[**848**] (5) Two or three accounts of the restoration by
St. Thomas of members that had been extracted or cut off,
are so extraordinary and well-attested that they deserve the
attention of experts. But probably there was no real restoration. So far as concerns the cases of blinding, the eye may
have been gashed, but not extracted, and there is evidence
to shew that, in days when such mutilation was a common
punishment for theft, it was recognized that some power of
sight might remain.

[**849**] In any case, even if St. Thomas's miracles of this
class could be accepted, the similar miracle assigned by
Luke's Gospel alone to Jesus (the restoration of the severed
ear to the high priest's servant) could not be accepted, and
for three reasons : 1st, it is omitted by the three evangelists
who describe the cutting off of the ear ; 2nd, one of these,
the author of the fourth Gospel, wrote long after Luke,
and must have known Luke's account. His omission of
it can best be explained on the ground that, he knew it to
be based on error ;[1] 3rd, its origin is easily explicable

---

[1] The theory that he omitted it as being superfluous, or well known already,
is too ridiculous to need refutation.

as a misunderstanding of an original tradition to the effect
that Jesus said " Let it be restored to its place." These
words were meant by Jesus to apply to *Peter's sword*,
which was to be put back into its sheath : but Luke, or the
tradition followed by Luke, took them to mean " Let *the ear*
be restored to its place."

[850] (6) The power of working extraordinary acts of
faith-healing does not necessarily imply the far higher power
of inspiring concord and mutual affection binding a com-
munity into one. The absence of any such power is con-
spicuous in the Martyr's case. The monks of Canterbury
were constant spectators of St. Thomas's miracles : yet there
are many signs that he had not bequeathed to them unity
among themselves. Repentance, confession of sins, personal
piety, and individual aspiration to holiness, were probably
stimulated for a time by his influence : but there are more
signs of it without, than within, the walls of the Canterbury
Minster. And even in the Church and people at large there
seems to have resulted from St. Thomas nothing of the
spiritual influence that came from St. Francis.[2]

[851] (7) The real use of these extraordinary acts is
that they break the monotony of palpable cause and palpable
effect in a fleshly, materialistic, and unimaginative generation.
Startled by the intrusion of a novel and impalpable cause,
the carnal mind is forced, first, to recognize the power of the
Spirit over the flesh in healing bodily disease, and then to
say to the Spirit, " Thou hast healed us : what wouldst thou
now have us to do ? "

Here it is that the spirit of the active, aggressive, militant,
and quasi-worldly Saint differs from that of the Saint pure
and simple — the Saint of peace and perfect insight, the
Saint of harmonious sympathy with the Powers of goodness.

---

[2] It must be admitted, however, that early and violent dissension arose among
the followers of St. Francis on the subject of the Franciscan Rule (see Sabatier's
Speculum Perfectionis, Introd. p. xix.).

And here it is also that even the highest in this chosen band of purest Saints seem to Christians to fall behind the Saint of Saints, the Man so wholly rapt into the divine Order that He is at one with the Father of all.

The spirit of St. Thomas had no power to pass into the hearts of men with a distinct and permanently vivifying message of its own, conveying to them peace, love, unity, and ultimate conformity of the human to the divine. But the Spirit of Him whom we worship has both that message, and that power. The time will come when His miracles will be rated at their true worth. Some will be read as mere emblematic stories exhibiting Him as the Bread of Life, the Controller of the Storm, the Promised First-born, the Son of the Blessed—the Song of the angels of heaven, and the Hope of men on earth. Others will be read as narratives of fact, shewing how, besides bearing the burdens of their sin, He sympathized with men's foulest diseases and sorest agonies of the flesh, and how virtue passed out from Him to banish physical as well as spiritual disorder. But not on account of either the one or the other will He be worshipped. He will be men's God for ever so far as He reigns in their hearts as the active representative of that Spirit of Life, Light, and Order, to which we are all aspiring, and in which we desire to live. The influence of the Martyr largely died with the decay of his miracles. The Spirit of the Saviour will then be most vitally present with mankind when they refuse, with the Fourth Gospel, to call His miracles by any other name than "signs," and when they recognize, as His "signs" of greatest might and wonder, not those which He worked once, but those which He is working now.

INDEX

"Agonotheta," for "athleta," **146, 176** (n. 16)

Alan, Prior of Canterbury, **22**; his high character, **540**; he supplements the biography written by John of Salisbury, **22**

Alms, miraculously provided or restored, **559, 560**

Altar, the, St. Thomas did not die before, **162** (comp. **133, 232, 276** (n. 26))

Anchors, recovered after vows to St. Thomas, **723**

Animals, miracles on: *see* Bird, Cow, Lamb, etc.

"Anon I." (indicates an anonymous writer commonly called, on no evidence, "Roger of Pontigny"), the character and date of his work, **25**; his relation to Garnier, **25a, 184a, 253, 401**; baselessness of evidence for calling him "Roger of Pontigny," **26b**; his accurate account of the first blow inflicted on the Archbishop, **254**; value of his evidence, **354**; his account of St. Thomas's rescue from drowning, **398**; question as to his name, **25, 422** (n. 1); is silent about St. Thomas's alleged miracles at Pontigny, **797-9**

Antiphon, in English, in honour of St. Thomas, sung in a vision, **594**

"Antiquity," declared "fatuous" by William, **643**

Arnold of Lubeck tells how St. Thomas changed water into wine, **595**

Ashes, dying on, **688** (n. 3)

Babe, a, sings Kyrie Eleison, **635**

Baldwin, Archbishop of Canterbury, **21**; Herbert dedicates his book to, **429**

Bath, waters of, **744**

Battle, trial by, **573**

Becket, Thomas: *see* Thomas, St.

Bedford, letter from the burgesses of, **711**

Beer is made miraculously to ferment, **579**

Benedict, date of his writings, **18**; supposed by some to have written a biography of St. Thomas, **50a, 107a**; his text probably given inaccurately in the *Quadrilogus*, **275a**; his trustworthiness, **404, 425a**; the singular value of his testimony, **449**; his candour in describing imperfect cures, **499-501**; is rebuked by a woman for scepticism, **514**; Benedict (or William) quotes Ovid, **536-7**; Benedict's style too simple for the monks of Canterbury, **538**; the style of his book alters when William "comes to his aid," **543**; silences dogs in the name of St. Thomas, **566**; chronological order is discarded toward the end of his book, **580**; the last part not in Benedict's style,

584 ; a miracle dated 1202 A.D., probably an error for 1192 A.D., 586 ; probably continued to collect miracles when Abbot of Peterborough, 588 ; contrast between Benedict and William in their narratives of leprosy, 768 ; two distinct styles in some of Benedict's narratives, 770

Bezant, a, preserved by St. Thomas, 663

Bird-miracles, 525, 642, 684, 692

" Bishop," for " Archbishop," 54

Bishops, rule as to number of, necessary for consecration, 697

Blasphemy against St. Thomas, forgiven, 667 ; punished, 595

Blinding, as a punishment for theft, 576 (see Mutilation) ; apparently sometimes imperfect, 577

Blindness, first alleged cure of, must be rejected, 433a ; other cures, 457, 499, 530, 534, 554, 677 ; a boy blind from birth, 500 ; a man blind from birth, his utterances on receiving sight, 522 ; a blind Cornishman cured, 523 ; a partial cure, 565 ; cured at the shrine of St. Laurence, 614

Blindness inflicted as a punishment, for imposture, 554 ; for contempt of the blind, 556 ; for filial disobedience, 557

Blood of St. Thomas, mixed with water, 424 : see Water of St. Thomas

Boetius, 643

Bolt, a, that "came off by itself," 87

Bone, extracted from a wound, deposited at the Martyr's tomb, 599 (n. 11)

Book, a, to be given for the chapel of a hospital, 694

Bosham, Herbert of : see Herbert

Bowels, diseases of the, 481-2, 453

Brito, or le Bret, Richard, 268, 289

Broc, Ranulf de, 440 ; called by St. Thomas "the son of perdition," 460

Broc, Robert de, 46-9, 422

Broc, William de, cured by St. Thomas, 510

Burial, speediness of, 732 (4) ; of persons killed by lightning, 649

Business, the evils of, 627

Cancer, 737

Candles, "measuring for," 474, 491, 495, 527, 719 (4) ; miracles relating to, 502-6, 536, 648

Canonization of St. Thomas, the, anticipated in a vision, 593

Canterbury : see Cathedral, Prior

Cap, the Archbishop's, struck off by Fitzurse, different accounts of this, 205 ; not mentioned by Garnier, 231, 252-4 ; Herbert's account, 276 (n. 24)

Captivity, deliverance from, 586

Cathedral, the, confused with the Palace, 108b, 208a

Cato, paralleled with St. Thomas, 592

Cecilia, St., sewing on festival of, punished, 535

Chains, loosed by St. Thomas, 619

" Chance," misuse of the word, 620

" Chapel," a word used by Garnier to mean the crown of the head, 292a, 362

Chapels are to be built to St. Thomas, 613 ; are built, 647, 695

Charms, employment of, 479, 490, 608 ; tried by a priest, 527

Cheese, miraculously revealed when lost, 528

Cherrystone in the nose, 496

Child (see Drowning, Miracles, etc.), sings Kyrie Eleison, 635

Childish terrors, 492

" Christ," i.e. anointed, a name given to St. Thomas, 709 (1)

Cilice, miraculously mended, 815

Clare, Earl and Countess of, 758

Clergy, the marriage of, 691

Clothing of St. Thomas, a patient wrapped in, 603 ; "a scrap" of it desired by the Bishop of Poitiers, 641

Coin, miraculously found, 531

Cologne, dialect of, 558

Colresand, 721

" Complodere," not " clasp " as Stanley translates it, 136 (n. 18), 272 (n. 18)

Compostella, pilgrimage to, 558

Confession, " to thirteen priests," 479 ; " eleven times a week," 495 ; offered by a father hoping for his daughter's recovery, 509

Confirmation, administration of, St. Thomas did not confirm on horseback, 533

Consumption, 507

Contortions, 485, 487

Contractions of limbs, 605, etc.

Convulsions at the Martyr's tomb preceding a cure, 468, 471, 483, 485

Cornishman, a, cured of blindness, 523

"Corona," meanings of, 224 (n. 12), 332 (n. 27)

Cow, a, restored to life, 700; killed by St. Thomas, 699

Cross, the, taken by a patient cured, 471

Cross, the Archbishop's, by whom carried, 70a

Crosses erected, 533

Crucifixion, visions of, 146, 162a, 426a

Crutches, thrown aside at the Martyr's tomb, 468, 470, 480

Crypt of Canterbury Cathedral opened after the murder, 469

Curbaran of Dover, "simple enough to pray for the Martyr," 531

Cures (see Imperfect Cures and Relapses), preceded by vomiting, 473; by sounds in the head, 474-5; by convulsions, 468, 471, 483, 485; by a feeling that the Cathedral was "too narrow," 483; gradual, 508

Cut thumb, healed, 552

Damascus, captivity at, 586

Date, of the Martyrdom, generally given wrongly, 318, 346; other confusions of, 347

Deafness healed, 475, 575

Death, often preceded by apparent lifelessness, 846; pious, after remedies had been vainly tried, 497-8

Death, Restoration from (see Drowning), 609; of a lamb, 630; of a bull by St. Silvester, 630; a doubtful case, 631; of a sucking-pig and a gander, 633-4; of an ox by the concubine of a clerk, 642; of a man struck by lightning, 649; a pilgrim restored to life in order to take the sacrament and die, 657; after seven days, related without attestation, 660; of two

children, 670; William declines to accept a case, without witnesses, 688; doubts another case, 690

"Decalvare," meaning of, 276a

Decline, 507

Deformity, 485, 535, etc.

Demon, apparition of a, 483

Demoniacs cured, 623; one talks various languages, 680

Denarius, St. Thomas bids a man offer a denarius, 526; miraculously restored, 559

Denial of cures, 476-7

Denis, St., 276, 623

Devizes, chapel at, 695

Diarrhœa, 482

Diocletian, coin of, 531

Disappointments for those expecting miracles, 476-7

Dishonesty detected, 491

Dislocation of arm, 529

"Dog, eating of," an error for "eating of flesh," 713 (n. 3)

Dogs silenced by Benedict in the name of St. Thomas, 566

Doors "open spontaneously," 88; the cloister door and the Cathedral door, 87-8, 93, 102 (n. 6)

Dreams, frightful, 459

Dress, vanity of, 666

Dropsy, 495, 565, 597

Drowning, deliverance from, 777, 783; restoration after, 567-8, 741

Duel, judicial, 573

Dumbness, cured, 466, 519, 578; William on the advantages of, 625

"Duplication," instances of, 347, 365-8, 726

Durham, bishop of: see Puiset, Hugh de

Dwarf, a demon in the form of a, 459

Dysentery, 481

Earth, fall of, 771

Edification, facts suppressed for, 379

Edith, St., 534

Edmund, St., seen in a vision with St. Thomas, 602; resorted to for a cure, 744 (6)

Edward I., his "wink," 363

Edwin, said by the French to mean "foolish," 687

Eels, a sign of water, **694**
Eggs, inscribed with the Martyr's name, **652**
Eilward (or Ailward) of Westoning, **710** : *see* Mutilation
Eleanor, queen, **747**
Elias, of Evesham, **22-3**
Elmo, St., his fire, attributed to St. Thomas, **668**
Elphege, St., **68, 255-7**
English, an antiphon in, **594**
Eparchius, St., **689**
Epilensy, or Epilepsy, three kinds of, defined, **598** ; cured, **598, 676**
Eucharist, administration of, deferred, but received after death, **667**
Evidence, internal, importance of, **385-92**
" Evovae," meaning of, **594** (n. 5)
Exaggerations, **425, 433**
Extremity, delivery in, **509, 608** (n. 5), etc.
Eyes, restoration of, **710** (11), possibly explicable, **718-20**
Eye-witnesses, evidence of, **358**

Face, tumour in, **470**
Falcon belonging to Henry II., **692**
Fall, recovery after a, **551**
Fall of earth, **771** ; of a wall, **755**
Fallacies : *see* Fitness of Things, and Duplication
Family differences healed, **574**
Fermin, physician of Canterbury, **426a** ; his vision, **592**
Festivals, working on, punished, **569, 605, 675**
Fevers, **453, 467**, etc.
Finding, miracles of, **620-2**
Fingers contracted and restored, **605**
Fire, preservation from, **548, 668** ; part of Canterbury Cathedral destroyed by, **671**
Fish, St. Thomas's, **790-4**
Fistula, **490** ; recurrence of, **667**
" Fitness of Things," instances of its influence, **296** (n. 66), **351, 375, 377-9, 447, 726, 811**
Fitznigel, **68a**
Fitzranulph, **116a**
Fitzstephen, William, date of his

biography, **15** ; the earliest edition of his work, **15a, 144** (n. 6), **317** (n. 3), **423** (n. 1), **795** ; contrast between him and Herbert of Bosham, **211** ; fond of allusions to Latin poetry, **267** (n. 7) ; differs from others in omitting the threats of outrage after the murder, **423** ; his account of the Water of St. Thomas, **424**
Fitzurse, Reginald, struck the first blow at the Martyr, **244-6** ; St. Thomas orders prayers for, **637**
Flood, deliverance from a, **703**
Flores Historiarum, **347, 367**
Foliot, Gilbert, Bishop of London, restored to health, **615-6** ; his steward (also called Foliot) convinced by a miracle, **522**
Foot, miraculously pierced, **681**
Footsteps, the last footsteps of St. Thomas, **162-5**
Foreign cures, **452, 552**
Forest laws, offences against, **573**
Francis, St., Legend about the baptism of, **192b**
French, a knight's son in England needs to be taught French, **632** ; Garnier praises his own French, **632** (n. 4) ; Benedict, in a vision, speaks French to the Martyr, who replies in Latin, **404a**
Fringe, a, of the Martyr's vesture, restores sanity, **650**
Froissart, textual variations in, **364**

Galen, quoted, **767** (1)
Gander, a, resuscitated, **634**
Garnier, date of his poem, **35-9** ; received information from St. Thomas's sister, **39a** ; praises the poor, **4** ; his relation to Anon. I., **25a, 184a, 253, 401** ; text seems corrupt, **112** (n. 22) ; his account of St. Thomas's rescue from drowning, **358** ; describes St. Thomas as working cures at Pontigny, **796**
Gervase, his account of the Martyrdom, **393-6**
Gibbon, his attempt to explain the success of Christianity, **832**
Giraldus Cambrensis, **796** (n. 9), **806-7**

Glasgow, Bishop of, **783** (16)

Glass, ancient vessel of, discovered, **677**

Glove, St. Thomas's, works a cure, **529**

Gospels, the, parallel between them and the biographies of St. Thomas, **839-40**

"Gradus," sing., a flight of steps, **143**; William substitutes "vestigia," **146**; various traditions about, **162-5**

Grandison, **340, 806-7**

Greek words, used and misused by William of Canterbury, **146** (n. 9), **611a**

Grim, Edward, date of his biography, **13**; did not bear the Archbishop's cross, **70a**; said by some to have been rebuked by the Archbishop, **226**; appears to have borrowed from John of Salisbury and an anonymous writer, **315a**; value of his evidence, **350**; inaccurate when he ceases to be an eye-witness, **357-8**; his account of St. Thomas's rescue from drowning, **397**; his account of the first miracle and the burial, **418-21**; declares that the Martyr was not at first appreciated by the majority of the monks, **418**; wounded while clasping the Archbishop, **218**; said by the *Saga* to have been miraculously cured the same night, **444, 810**; says that Benedict was disliked and insulted by King Henry, **541**; his name chosen to give authority to fictitious "Passions," **808**; details of his miraculous cure as given by Pseudo-Grim, **810**

Hair shirt, St. Thomas', a portion of, works a cure, **529, 758** (10)

Halter, a, preserved as a relic, **640**

Hameline, earl of Warrenne, **659**

Handkerchief, a, blessed by St. Thomas, effects a cure, **462**

Hanging, deliverances from, **638, 641**

Hawk, cured of a broken leg, **642**; restored to life, **642**; recovered when lost, **525, 642, 664**; story of one belonging to Henry II., **692**

Hawking, St. Thomas in his youth fond of, **397-401**

Head, pains in, **496, 575**

Hemorrhoids, **453**

Henry II., King, visited the tomb of St. Thomas, **17**; description of this in the *Flores Historiarum*, **347, 367**; his self-purgation at Avranches, **28, 416**; dreams that he is rescued by St. Thomas from falling into an abyss, **421** (n. 1); at first discouraged visitors to the Martyr's tomb, **431**; dislikes and insults Benedict, **541**; his public penitence, **592**; miracles for his sake, **618-9**; releases a prisoner whom St. Thomas has freed, **619**; hears a Templar's dream, **658**

Henry, the younger king, son of Henry II., makes war against his father, **416, 672**; his sorrow for the Martyr's death, **423**; the Archbishop of Rouen consecrates an altar to St. Thomas for, **615**

Henry of Houghton, the testimony of, **530**

Herbert of Bosham, instructed the Archbishop in Scripture, **19**; date and character of his biography, **20**; cannot be trusted as regards analogies between the Martyr and the Saviour, **108a, 327, 432** (n. 2); his prolixity, **223** (n. 8), **227** (n. 30), **326**; represents St. Thomas as falling before the Altar, **276** (n. 26); author of a letter ostensibly written by the Archbishop of Sens, **276a, 350** (n. 1); substitutes Robert de Broc for Hugh Mauclerc, **279**; his silence about the miracles, **429**

Herlwin, Prior of Canterbury, **540**

Hernia, **575, 758** (3)

Herring-fishers, delivered, **722**

Hingan, cured of fits, **581**

Holidays (on Saturday), custom of drinking on, **710** (1), see **777** (2)

Holland, preservation from flood in, **703**

Horse, falling through a bridge, **654**; recovered when lost or stolen, **620, 637**; eye of, cured, **517**

Hospital on Shooter's Hill, **694**

Hugh de Perac, a man of blood, **646**

Hugh de Puiset : see Puiset

Hugh of Horsea, also called Mauclerc, 280

Hugh of Morville : *see* Morville

Imagination, force of, 486
Imperfect cures, 486, 487, 499, 565
Imposture, the monks of Canterbury attempt to guard against, 455, 466; as to St. Thomas's Water, effects a cure, 563; fails to effect a cure, 563 (n. 5)
"Improvisum" (?) means "unprovided," 281
Influenza, 652
Ireland, Henry II.'s wars in, 17
Irish, spoken by St. Thomas in a vision to an Irishman, 612
Ithamar, St., of Rochester, a miracle claimed for, 521

James, St. : *see* Compostella
Jerusalem, pilgrimage to, 637
Jews, intercourse with, discouraged, 479
John of Salisbury, Bishop of Chartres, date of his biography, 16; specially mentioned by Fitzstephen as deserting the Archbishop, 126; writes for the Pope rather than for truth, 173; attributes to the knights the outrage on the Archbishop's body, 271; his inaccuracy unpardonable, 352; his literary reputation caused later writers to borrow from him, 383; his testimony to the number of the Martyr's miracles, 411; his letter to the bishop of Clermont attesting a cure of leprosy 661
John, St., a vision of, 673a
Justinian, on legacies, 645

Kings, visiting the Martyr's tomb, 441
Knife, wound from, 644, 681

Lamb, a, restored to life, 630
Lameness, cures of, 470, 485, 506, 535, etc.
Latin, miraculously written by a nun ignorant of Latin, 426; Satan compels a clerk to talk nothing but Latin,

653; a demon in a woman talks Latin, 680; St. Thomas, in a vision, replies in Latin to a question from Benedict in French, 404a
Laurence, St., cure in the shrine of, 614
Legend (*see Saga*), the legend of St. Thomas's fish, 790-4; the legend of St. Thomas miraculously rescued from drowning, 397-401; poetic legends, 813; legends may spring up within two or three years after a Martyr's death, 818; may have several contributory causes, 378a
Legs (*see* Lameness), waxen, offered to St. Thomas, 492
Leighton Buzzard, 710 (4)
Leper, employed to carry a message from St. Thomas, 732 (8)
Leprosy, the first cure of, 544; followed by a relapse, 544-5; a case attested by the Dean of Chesterton, 546; Gerard of Lille, 570; other cases, 810-2, 628, 661, 707, 744, 747, 767; various kinds of, 767 (8); no Saint has equalled St. Thomas in curing, 547
Letters of attestation (*see also* Puiset), attesting the cure of disease, 629; attesting deliverance from hanging, 641; from the burgesses of Bedford, attesting the restoration of eyesight, 711; from the Bishop of Norwich, attesting a cure of cancer, 738; from the Dean of Gloucester, attesting deliverance from a fall of earth, 772.
"Lictors," a name given to the Archbishop's murderers, 129 (n. 7), 277
Lightning, death by, 649
Liver, disease of, 461, 483, etc.
Losing and finding, miracles of, 620-2
Lucan, quoted by William, 721, 722, etc.
Luci, Richard de, converses with Henry of Houghton about St. Thomas, 532
"Lundrensis," for "Londoniensis," 25a
"Lying," Garnier on, 36; tendency to, 350-1

Madness, cured, 475, 486, 558, 653

Magic, the Canterbury cures imputed to, **488**

Magnusson, Eirikr, Mr., Preface, p. ix., on the date of Garnier's poem, **39***a* ; on the relation of Anon. L to Garnier, **25***a*

Mariners, miracles wrought for, **562**, **721-3**

Marlow bridge, **654**

Mary, the Blessed Virgin, mention of, inserted by Anon. X. in a narrative of Benedict's, **439** ; assists St. Thomas in mending his hair drawers, **815**

Matilda of Cologne, the madness of, **558**

" Matthew of Westminster," **30***a*, **347**

Matthew Paris, **347**

Mauclerc : *see* Hugh of Horsea

" Measuring for a candle " (*see* Candle), **778**

Medway river, drowning in the, **567**

Members, restoration of: *see* Mutilation

Memorial, the Martyr's tomb or Memorial, miracles worked near, **466**, **468**, **475**, **483**, **507**, etc. ; at first, the multitude were not admitted to it, **469** ; a boy punished by St. Thomas for lying on it, **476** ; the tomb surrounded with a wall, **486** ; a madman is cured after lying on it, **486**

Metaphor, treated as prose, **373-5** ; originates legends, **447**

" Milk," in a vision, meaning the Martyr's blood, **474**, **771** (6)

Millwheel, deliverance of St. Thomas from, **397** ; deliverance of a child from, **631**

Miracles of St. Thomas, the (*see also* Memorial, Cures), at first confined mainly to the poor, **403, 428** ; Benedict's account of the first miracle, **410** ; Fitzstephen's account, **424** ; Benedict's fifth miracle exaggerated by Anon. V., **425***a* ; attempts made by the Martyr's enemies to suppress the miracles, **427** ; Herbert's silence about, **429** ; throw light on the miracles wrought in the first century of the Church, **450** ; the first thirty, as given by Benedict and William re-

spectively, **453**; "mirthful miracles," **479** ; miracles of punishment (*see* Punishment); the moral effect of, **507-10** ; degeneration of, **617** ; a man of many miracles, **626** ; the use of, to preserve "the integrity of Divine law and the liberty of the inviolable Church," **661** ; "festive miracles," **662** ; miracles commemorated in the stained glass of Canterbury Cathedral, **736** ; the good and evil resulting from the miracles as a whole, **821-6** ; the fading away of miracles of St. Thomas and in the Christian Church in the first century, **836** ; false miracles and true, **837**, **843-9** ; the real use of, **851**

Money, miracles as to, **559-61**; why St. Thomas likes money, **627** ; offerings of money, **524, 544, 628** ; exacted by St. Thomas, **645**

Monks of Canterbury, the, their attempts to prevent imposture, **455**, **487, 509** (n. 5) ; dissensions among, **540**

Morville, Hugh of, **212-4**, **727** ; the date of his death, **820**

Murderers of St. Thomas, the, rumours about, **30** ; legends about, **820**

Musard (?) (Malae-Artes), pretends to be blind, and is visited with blindness, but cured, **554**

Mutilation, healed, **576, 710-20**; theft under the value of a *nummus* not punishable by, **710** (3) ; the cases of Eilward of Westoning and others, **710-20**; performed with cruelty, **714** ; these cases possibly, in part, explicable, **718-9**

Neck, broken, **660**

Newington, near Sittingbourne, miracles at, **533-5**

Nightmare, **459**

Northampton, the Archbishop at, **15**, **88**

Norway, pilgrims from, **664**

" Nummus," theft under the value of a, **710** (3)

Oblation of sinners refused, **622**

"Obols," miraculously provided, 560; restored, 621; refused by St. Thomas, 622

Obstruction, internal, 453, 472

Odo of Falaise, comes to the Martyr's tomb in disguise, 547

Odo, Prior of Canterbury, afterwards Abbot of Battle, 540, 652

"Offendere," means "come suddenly on," 155

Offerings to St. Thomas (*see* Candles), of waxen legs, 492; of waxen anchors, 723; of money, the first instances, 524; their efficacy, 642; of four silver pieces, 732 (7)

Ophthalmia, signs of prevalence of, 433*a*

Ordeals, 573; ordeal by water, 710 (4)

Oxen, recovered from thieves, 701

Palermo (?), 698

Pall of St. Thomas, miracle wrought by, 465

Paper, a paper of St. Thomas's miracles cures dropsy, 578

Paralysis, cured, 480, 508, 679; inflicted and cured, 727

Pardoner, a, 464

Participle, pres. act., used as past, 270*a*, 264, 268, 285 (n. 54) (comp. 328*a*)

Pater Nosters, to be said for the soul of St. Thomas's father, 562

"Patronus," the, of a church, 644 (n. 5)

Pebble, in the ear, a, 552

Perjury, punished miraculously, 487

Peter, St., a man punished for working on the day of the Festival of his Chair, 569

Phials for St. Thomas's Water, miracles respecting, 520

Physician, of Canterbury, the, 495, 598

Physicians, disparaged by William of Canterbury, 598, 599, 602, 603

Pictures of the Martyrdom, 249, 284 (n. 52)

Pig, restored to life, 633; preserved fresh after drowning, 662

Pilgrimage, a, on foot from Shropshire, 564; a vow of, changes a step-son's

hatred to affection, 574; cures take place during, 601; to be made on foot, not in a carriage, 603; a man punished for dissuading, 628; became profitable, 689; punishment for delaying, 732 (12); the prospective benefits of, 733 (5)

Pilgrims, kiss the footsteps of the Martyr, 163 (13); sang a hymn as they ascended the steps to his grave, 165 (n. 4); sometimes depart from Canterbury cured, unknown to the monks, 518; a pilgrim vows to give alms to everyone that asks in the name of St. Thomas, 560; a pilgrim, thrown overboard as dead, restored to his vessel, 636; a pilgrim restored to life that he may receive the sacrament and die, 657

Plagues, visit King Henry's army in Ireland, 600

Poetry and Romance, the origin of legends, 814-5

Poison, 653

Poitiers, Bishop of, 508, 641

Polypus, cured, 496

"Pomerium," for "pomarium," 52

Pontefract, 732 (1)

Pontigny, evidence from, to be regarded with suspicion, 800-1

"Pontigny, Roger of" : *see* Anon. I.

Poor, the, praised by Garnier, 4; the poor alone at first visited the Martyr's tomb, 428, 431

Pope, the, St. Thomas, in a vision, pleads before, 802; St. Thomas turns water into wine for, 813

Possession, demoniacal, 623, 680

Priests, large proportion of, in William's Book of Miracles, 452; a married priest, 691

Priors of Canterbury, 540

Prison, deliverance from, 619, 638

Procession, a, punishment for neglect to join, 681

"Proferri" for "praeferri," 70

Pseudo-Grim, 808-12

Puiset, Hugh de, Bishop of Durham, 656, 710 (13), 712

Punishment, miracles of, 488, 489, 595, 727 (*see also* Vows)

Pyx, a, holding the Water of St. Thomas, split, **479**

Quadrilogus, the two editions of, **1a** ; the Early *Quadrilogus*, by whom compiled, **21a**; errors of, **106** (n. 11); alters texts to harmonize them, **20a** ; duplicates the outrage on the Archbishop's body, **368** ; the Late *Quadrilogus*, **23** ; describes the miraculous withering of a tree, **378, 436** (n. 8)

Quinsy, **489**

Rain, averted from a nun, **550**

Redness in the sky, **33, 438**

Reginald Fitzurse, called "Reinaldus" by Grim, 170 (*see* **224a**) ; struck the first blow at the Archbishop, **244-6** : *see* Fitzurse

"Rejoice Jerusalem," the day of, **732** (8)

Relapses, **487** ; of a leper, **544** ; several instances related by Benedict, none by William, **545** (n. 2)

Relics, diseases cured by, **492** ; lost and miraculously restored, **585, 621**

Resurrection proved by miracles, **635**

Revelations, to Emma of Halberton, **606** ; to Godelief of Laleham, **607**

Revivification : *see* Death, restoration from

Richard I., false report of his return from captivity, **585**

Richard, Archbishop of Canterbury, **540**

Richard of Coventry, miracles accumulated for, **598**

Ring recovered, **621** ; rings used as charms, **608**

Robbers, delivery from, **637**

Robbery of money proved, **663**

Robert of Merton, **26, 126**

Rochester (*see* Ithamar, St.), pilgrims resort to, for cure, **521, 530** ; great fire at, **548**

Roesa, a name wrongly given to St. Thomas's mother, **27**

Roger, a "custodian of the sacred body," cures lameness in the name of the Martyr, **566**

Roger, Archbishop of York, an enemy of St. Thomas, **628** ; supplies Churchdown with water, **771**

Rohesia, the name of St. Thomas's sister, **27** (n. 8)

"Romance," the Romance language, "Romanum" distinguished from Latin, **653**

Rome, pilgrimage to, **558**

Rose, a name given by John Fox to St. Thomas's mother, **27** (n. 8)

Roxburgh, John of, delivered from drowning in the Tweed, **783**

Sacrament, "let earth or grass be your sacrament," **688** ; an Abbot scruples to give the sacrament, because he has partaken of "carnal food," **657**

Saga, the, date of, **40** : its regard for "the Fitness of Things," **98** ; relates a miracle about the Archbishop's footsteps, **163** ; substitutes "mitre" for "cap," **190** ; says that Grim bore the cross, **192** ; makes St. Thomas turn to the East towards the Altar, **232** ; substitutes the de Brocs for Hugh Mauclerc, **296**; describes St. Thomas's rescue from drowning, **400** ; says that the Holy Ghost descended on the blood of St. Thomas, **443** ; origin of its legends, **447** ; contrast between the *Saga* and a contemporary letter, **448**

Saints'-days, working on, is punished by disease, **535, 569, 675**

Saladin, **586**

Salerna, of Ifield, delivered from a well, **777**

Salisbury Plain, **511**

Saltwood, **287**

Samson of Oxfordshire, a dumb man, made drunk in order to detect imposture, **466**

Saracen, conversion of a, **698**

Saracens, captivity among, **586**

Satan, in the form of a maid-servant, **777** (3)

Saturday, holiday on, 710 (1), **777** (n. 2)

Saviour, the, accounts of the Martyr conformed to those of the Saviour, **108a, 201, 209, 226, 266** (n. 6), **378, 432** ; parallel between the Martyr and the Saviour, **834-8**

Scholar ("scholasticus"), a, cured of liver complaint, **483**

School-girl, a, in the twelfth century, **644**

Scotland, King of, the, defeated by King Henry's forces, **847, 672-3**

Sea (*see* Mariners), calmed for Prince Henry, **615**

Sefrid, a German monk, miracles reported by, **678-83**

Self-deception, or lying? **511**

Self-mutilation, **682**

Sens, the Archbishop of, letter from, **160*a***

Sepulchral vessel, punishment for ill-using, **677**

Sermons, narratives resembling, **599, 780**

Service-book provided for a chapel of St. Thomas, **694**

Severin, St., miracle imputed to, **508**

Ship (*see also* Mariners), a, comes back by herself, **721**

"Shipwrecked," how used, **777 (7), 783 (5)**

Shoes, finery in, punished, **666**

Shooter's Hill, **694**

Silvester, St., restored a bull to life, **630**

Sin before birth punished, **477**

Solomon of London, nearly a hundred years old, **493**

"Spiculatores," a form of "speculatores," **128 (n. 6)**

Spur, lost and found, **621**

Stanley, Dean, author of *Memorials of Canterbury*, unfair to "the monks," **65-6**; his representation of Hugh of Morville, **212-4, 303**; misplaces the Archbishop's "coarse" words, **217**; misled by Anon. II., **226, 237**; probably in error as to Tracy, **239**; misled by William of Canterbury, **258-63**; misled by Fitzstephen, **298-300**; misinterprets Fitzstephen's account about the desertion of the Archbishop's body, **337-40**

Starling delivered by invocation of St. Thomas, **693**

Stone, cure of, **581**

Stones, used as remedies, **490**

Storm, said to have followed the Martyrdom, **316**; probably without truth, **341-5**; a providential storm, **484**

Suicide, attempted, **690, 777**

"Super" and "sup-" confused, **787 (11), 793*a***

Swellings cured, **496, 529, 575**, etc.

Sylvester : *see* Silvester, St.

",Synanchy," **709 (2)**

"Taratantara,"danced by a boy restored to health, **583**

Templar, a, his dream, **658**

Tennyson, unfair to "monks," **65-6**; says that Grim bore the cross, **84**; his representation of Hugh of Morville, **212-4**; softens the Archbishop's last words, **216**; misled by Anon. II., **226**; misled by William of Canterbury, **258-63**

Theft detected, **626**

Thomas, St. (Water of: *see* Water); his parentage, **27**; his Martyrdom, **41-304**; represented as praying for his murderers, **180**; his wounds, traditions about, **264, 270 (n. 13), 284 (n. 50), 285, 331, 334**; his last words not those attributed to him by Fitzstephen and Stanley, **298, 312**; his Martyrdom misdated by most writers, **318, 346**; accounts of his Martyrdom conformed to those of the Saviour, **108*a*, 201, 209, 226, 266 (n. 6), 378, 432**; how saved from drowning, **397-401**; his asceticism, **408, 420, 422**; the appearance of his face, as seen in visions, **406**; his blood collected, **421-2**; his body hidden behind the altar of the Virgin Mary, **484**; his sanctity slandered, **489**; doubted, **492**; his "merry jests," **559**; his body remained in the crypt till 1220 A.D., **592**; he is blamed by patients whom he does not at once cure, **597**; because of relapse, **667**; speaks Irish to an Irishman in a vision, **612**; "offers his blood to enemies as well as to friends," **616**; why he is glad to accept money, **627**; orders prayers for Fitzurse, **637**; pushes a ship off a shoal, **722**; requites a former servant, 737 (16); his pilgrims are discouraged at first by the Abbot of Reading, 744 (2); appears to Salerna in a well, saying " Thou shalt not die," 775 (5); his alleged vision at Pontigny, 795-805; said by Garnier to have wrought cures at Pontigny, 796; explanation of the story of his mother's Saracenic origin, 812; turns water to wine for the Pope, 813; a true saint, though militant, 829-33; at Northampton, 831; the causes of his power over the English people, 829-33

Thomas, St., Apostle, associated with St. Thomas of Canterbury, 695

Throat, Satan constricting the, 751 (6)

Thumb, cut, cured, 552

" Thunder-clap, a," in a man's head, precedes a miraculous cure, 474

Tilting, 599 (n. 11)

Tracy, William de, probably not the striker of the first blow, 244-50; Garnier's account of, 288; legends about, 817

Tradition, oral, misleading, 433-4; the source of legend, 816-8

Traditions, about the Martyr's wounds, common to many writers, 382-4

Trance, a, 737 (7)

Translation, errors in, 362

Tree, a, miraculously withered, 378, 436 (n. 8)

Tumour (see Swelling), 478; " tumour of mind punished by tumour of body," 666

Tweed, the river, 783

Ulcers, 453, 737 (4), etc.

Variety, of diseases, 453; in the manner of cure, 513

Verbal corruptions, 32, 70 (n. 1), 71 (n. 4), 95 (n. 8), 324a, 324 (n. 16), 361, 459a, 532 (n. 4), 710 (10), 711 (12), 713 (n. 3), 793, 797 (n. 2)

Verses, English (see Antiphon); Latin, about the date of the Martyrdom, 318; about St. Thomas's Water, 608 (n. 5); about the Archbishop's

wanderings, 703 (n. 3); comic, 656, 706

Viaticum, the, a pilgrim restored to life to receive, 647

" Vicarius," the, of a " Patronus," 644 (n. 5)

Visionary terrors, 459

Visions, of Jesus, or the Martyr, crucified in the crypt of Canterbury Cathedral, 146, 162a, 426a; of St. John, 673a; of priests singing an antiphon to St. Thomas, 593-4; of the Martyr with the blood-streak, 727 (4), 406, 558, etc.; of " the angel of the English clothed in white," 646; of St. Thomas saying that he must cure one hundred and thirteen sick folk that night, 655; of St. Thomas clothed in red, 698, 712a; of St. Thomas clothed in white, with his pastoral staff, 710 (9); of St. Thomas barefoot, 607; of St. Thomas threatening with a staff, 645; of St. Thomas with St. Edmund, 602; St. Thomas's alleged vision at Pontigny, 795-805

Vomiting, caused by the Water of St. Thomas, 472-3, 510

Vows (see Pilgrimage), of a journey to Jerusalem, fasts, and denarii, 544; must be paid by a man for whom others have vowed without his knowledge, 598; punishment for delay in paying, 601; why St. Thomas heeds vows, 627; neglect to pay, terribly punished, 691; neglect to vow a bullock at a neighbour's suggestion, punished, 699

Wall, fall of a, 755

War, the Irish, censured by William, 600, 637; the civil, 485

Water, swallowed in drowning, described by William as miraculously returning to nothing, 637, 741 (8)

Water of St. Thomas, the, Fitzstephen's account of the composition of, 424: Garnier on, 442; used at first with diffidence, 458; miraculously multiplied and diminished, 463-4, 512; tin phials for, 464; slips miraculously away, 479; detects dishonesty, 491;

changed to milk, 682; to blood, 551; boils in a vessel, 512, 552; at first, not generally used, 751 (4); the non-mention of, sometimes proof of the early date of a miracle, 740; cures and revivifications wrought by, 483, 492, 741, 744, 758, etc.

Water, ordeal of, 573, 710 (5), 710 (7)

Water, ordinary, substituted for that of St. Thomas, effects a cure, 563; fails to effect a cure, 563 (n. 5)

Wax, legs imitated in, 492; a horse's eye, 865; anchors, 723; sold by the monks of Canterbury, 624

Web, a, stolen and recovered, 665

Well, a, deliverance from, 777

Well, St. Thomas's, the *Saga's* account of, 445

Welsh, the, their reverence for relics, 516; miracles on, 508-9, 565

Wharfe, the river, 662

Whitsun-eve, any one christened on, cannot be drowned or burned, 710 (4)

Whitsuntide, 1171, miracles during, 502-6; working on the Wednesday of, punished miraculously, 605

William of Canterbury, date of his writings, 17; confesses that he fled from the Archbishop's murderers, 142, 272; his fondness for Greek terms, 146 (n. 9), 611a; his appendix to his account of the Martyrdom, 320-4; his apparent allusions to Benedict, 414-5; his indifference to chronological order, 415-6; his principles in arranging miraculous narratives, 452; his attitude to Benedict, 538-42; conjectured by Mr. Magnusson to be a native of Ireland, 589; quotes Latin poetry, 592; traces of re-editing, 592; his fondness for technical terms, 612; quotes English, 594; quotes Irish, 612; says that the Martyr "does

greater works" than the Saviour, 616; his neglect of evidence, 625; blends Isaiah with Horace, 634; dramatizes, 644-5; quotes Boetius, 643; Virgil and Justinian, 648; Plautus, 656; reports an unattested wonder, 660; apparently Sub-Prior under Odo, 661a; his style degenerates still further, 674; oscillates between credulity and incredulity, 684-7; decides to accept the statements of rich people, 688-9; apostrophizes his own hand, 688; appears to have left a story incomplete, 705; seems to be correcting a narrative of Benedict's, 720; quotes Lucan, 721, 722; magnifies a miracle reported more accurately by Benedict, 721; Virgil's influence on, 723 (n. 3); quotes Galen on the cure of leprosy, 767 (1)

William of Monkton, followed by miracles during his travels in Italy, 626

"Windas," a, described by William, 723

Wine, St. Thomas's Water changed to, 594-5

Wink, a, attributed by Lingard to Edward I., origin of the error, 363

Wiscard, the King's falcon, miraculously healed by St. Thomas, 692

Witnesses, required to attest disease, 487, 509 (n. 5), 631

"Womb of the Mother," the Martyr is said to have been killed in, *i.e.* in the Cathedral, 228a, 294a

Woodcock, a, miraculously caught, 642

Worms, hung up in a church, 494; issue from patients, 478

Wound, a, received in tilting, healed, 599 (n. 11); other wounds healed, 453, 599, 646

Yngelrann, 727 (1): *see also* 727 (7)

York, Archbishop of: *see* Roger

Works by the late W. Robertson Smith, M.A., LL.D.

PROFESSOR OF ARABIC IN THE UNIVERSITY OF CAMBRIDGE

Demy 8vo.   Price 15s. net.

LECTURES ON
THE RELIGION OF THE SEMITES

THE FUNDAMENTAL INSTITUTIONS

New Edition.   Revised throughout by the Author.

Demy 8vo.   Price 10s. 6d.

THE OLD TESTAMENT IN THE
JEWISH CHURCH

A COURSE OF LECTURES ON BIBLICAL CRITICISM

Second Edition.   Revised and much Enlarged.

Post 8vo.   Price 10s. 6d.

THE PROPHETS OF ISRAEL

AND THEIR PLACE IN HISTORY

To the Close of the Eighth Century B.C.

Second Edition.

WITH INTRODUCTION AND ADDITIONAL NOTES

BY

The Rev. T. K. CHEYNE, M.A., D.D.,

ORIEL PROFESSOR OF THE INTERPRETATION OF HOLY SCRIPTURE AT OXFORD;
CANON OF ROCHESTER

A. & C. BLACK, SOHO SQUARE, LONDON.

THE APOCALYPSE OF BARUCH
Translated from the Syriac
By Rev. R. H. CHARLES, M.A.
TRINITY COLLEGE, DUBLIN, AND EXETER COLLEGE, OXFORD

Crown 8vo, cloth, price 7s. 6d. net.

"Mr. Charles's last work will have a hearty welcome from students of Syriac whose interest is linguistic, and from theological students who have learned the value of Jewish and Christian pseudepigraphy; and the educated general reader will find much of high interest in it, regard being had to its date and its theological standpoint."—*Record.*

"The learned footnotes which accompany the translation throughout will be found most helpful to the reader. Indeed, nothing seems to have been left undone which could make this ancient writing intelligible to the student."—*Scotsman.*

THE ASSUMPTION OF MOSES
Translated from the Latin Sixth Century MS., the unemended Text of which is published herewith, together with the Text in its restored and critically emended form.
EDITED, WITH INTRODUCTION, NOTES, AND INDICES
By Rev. R. H. CHARLES, M.A.

Crown 8vo, cloth, price 7s. 6d.

"In this admirable little book the Rev. R. H. Charles has added another to the excellent series of editions by which he has earned the gratitude of all students of early Christian literature."—*The Times.*

"Nothing has been left undone by the Author which could contribute to the settling of the text, the elucidation of the general purpose of the book, and the interpretation of particular passages. In short, it is worthy to rank with his edition of the 'Apocalypse of Baruch,' and higher praise than that could hardly be given."—*Primitive Methodist Quarterly Review.*

STUDIES IN HEBREW PROPER NAMES
By G. BUCHANAN GRAY, M.A.
LECTURER IN HEBREW AND OLD TESTAMENT THEOLOGY IN MANSFIELD COLLEGE; LATE SENIOR KENNICOTT SCHOLAR IN THE UNIVERSITY OF OXFORD

In crown 8vo, cloth, price 7s. 6d. net.

"The study of Hebrew proper names, then, with their meaning, their origin, and their classification, cannot be looked upon simply as a dry-as-dust branch of inquiry, but is one full of interest to the Biblical scholar who looks below the surface."—*Church Quarterly Review.*

"These 'Studies' may be warmly commended as a step in the right direction. They bring out into clear relief progress of religious ideas in Israel, and make an important contribution to the criticisms of Old Testament documents."—C. H. Toy, Harvard University.

"There is not a student of the Old Testament in Hebrew but will find it indispensable."—*Expository Times.*

A. & C. BLACK, SOHO SQUARE, LONDON.

www.ingramcontent.com/pod-product-compliance
Lightning Source LLC
Chambersburg PA
CBHW020937030726
47496CB00005B/1239